"Guess that old saying is true. Everything looks different in the light of day."

Shelby turned to fix her gaze on the tall figure at her side holding the baby carrier easily against his chest. That sight *was* different.

"I'm going to look around and see what I can find." Jax settled the baby carrier down on the wooden slats at her feet.

Clearly he expected her to stay put and watch over the foundling. Clearly the man did not understand that Shelby Grace was finished doing what other people expected. It took her only a moment to bend and unsnap the safety latches. She lifted the baby and cuddled her close, even as she headed to the steps to follow Jax.

"No one in Sunnyside would have been able to hide a pregnancy, much less a baby, for three months."

"You honestly think there are no secrets in this town?" He looked back over his shoulder at her. "Would you say everybody here knows all there is to know about you, Shelby Grace?"

Winner of a HOLT Medallion for Southern-themed fiction, and the Houston Chronicle's Best Christian Fiction Author of 1999, **Annie Jones** grew up in a family that loved to laugh, eat and talk—often all at the same time. They instilled in her the gift of sharing through words and humor, and the confidence to go after her heart's desire. A former social worker, she feels called to be a "voice for the voiceless" and has carried that calling into her writing. She lives in rural Kentucky with her husband and two children.

Kat Brookes is an award-winning author and past Romance Writers of America Golden Heart® Award finalist. She is married to her childhood sweetheart and has been blessed with two beautiful daughters. She loves writing stories that can both make you smile and touch your heart. Kat is represented by Michelle Grajkowski with 3 Seas Literary Agency. Read more about Kat and her upcoming releases at katbrookes.com. Email her at katbrookes@comcast.net, and find her on Facebook: Kat Brookes.

Bundle of Joy

Annie Jones

&

The Cowboy's Little Girl

Kat Brookes

LOVE INSPIRED
INSPIRATIONAL ROMANCE

LOVE INSPIRED®
INSPIRATIONAL ROMANCE

Recycling programs for this product may not exist in your area.

ISBN-13: 978-1-335-20195-9

Bundle of Joy & The Cowboy's Little Girl

Copyright © 2020 by Harlequin Books S.A.

Bundle of Joy
First published in 2013. This edition published in 2020.
Copyright © 2013 by Luanne Jones

The Cowboy's Little Girl
First published in 2018. This edition published in 2020.
Copyright © 2018 by Kimberly Duffy

This edition published by arrangement with Harlequin Books S.A.

For questions and comments about the quality of this book, please contact us at CustomerService@Harlequin.com.

Love Inspired
22 Adelaide St. West, 40th Floor
Toronto, Ontario M5H 4E3, Canada
www.Harlequin.com

Printed in U.S.A.

CONTENTS

BUNDLE OF JOY

Annie Jones

For my family, who give me the peace
when I need to write and plenty of space
if I can't get any writing done.

People were also bringing babies to Jesus
to have him touch them. When the disciples saw this,
they rebuked them. But Jesus called the children to
him and said, "Let the little children come to me,
and do not hinder them, for the kingdom of God
belongs to such as these."
—*Luke* 18:15–16

Chapter One

Nobody did anything without a reason, though reason was rarely behind the things that people did. Jackson Stroud didn't just believe that; he counted on it.

Guilt. Anger. Pain. Longing. The motivations were often so deep-seated that they were difficult to name. But Jackson—Jax, to people who thought they knew him well—knew what made people tick, or at least he figured it out more quickly than the average Joe.

That knack had served him well these past four years on the Dallas police force. Not as well in his so-called "personal life." Despite the best efforts of the older ladies at his church to set him up with perfectly lovely women, he'd never been able to turn off the drive to figure people out long enough to make a real connection. Certainly not long enough to settle down. He'd accepted ages ago that he was not the settling-down type.

"Okay by me," he muttered to himself in the darkness of his truck cab. That just meant there were no broken hearts in his wake when he moved on. Jackson Stroud always moved on.

So when he veered off the brightly lit highway down

a darkened ramp in the middle of the night, he did not do so lightly. Bone tired, he needed to stretch his legs, get some coffee and maybe…

From nowhere, the headlights of a silver SUV speeding precariously close to the centerline slashed across Jax's line of vision. He hit the brakes and swerved toward the shoulder. His own lights came to rest on a dark sign by the road: Y'all Come Back to Sunnyside, Texas.

He grumbled under his breath, then guided his truck back onto the road and drove on until he pulled into the well-lit parking lot, under the signs Delta's Shoppers' Emporium and Truck Stop Inn and The Crosspoint Café. Framed by huge glass windows, a lone clerk stood at a counter. He was intently texting at his post.

Jax's boots hit the ground with a thud. He rubbed his eyes, then his jaw. He needed a shave. He knew he looked rough—but felt only hungry.

He put his hand over his stomach, but it was his conscience that made him admit that hunger had not led him to take the off-ramp tonight. Somewhere in the darkness of this warm spring night, it had dawned on him that without the familiar trappings of his work around him, he suddenly felt cast adrift.

He turned toward the Crosspoint Café. A hot meal, maybe a conversation with a waitress who would call him "honey" and make him feel, at least for a few minutes, like he wasn't all alone in the big, wide world—that was all he needed. He reached into his truck to grab his steel-gray Stetson, slammed the door shut, then took a step in that direction. The lights inside went out.

"Hey, if you want something, you'd better hurry." The clerk stood in the mini-mart's open door a few yards away. He shouted, "Whole place shuts down in twenty minutes!"

"Café already looks closed." Jax gave a nod and started toward the mini-mart.

"Yeah?" The lanky young clerk frowned, then shrugged it off. "Maybe Miz Shelby has something to do."

"Miz Shelby?" Jax chuckled softly, instantly picturing a sassy red-haired Southern belle in a pink waitress uniform and white apron, smacking gum and pouring out advice about life as freely as she did rich black coffee while she flirted with her transient clientele. "Maybe Miz Shelby met a handsome stranger and—"

"Hey! Don't you say stuff like that about Miz Shelby! She taught Sunday school to almost every kid in Sunnyside at some time or another, and for your information, she don't even know any strangers."

Jax fought the urge to argue that not knowing someone was what made them a stranger. "Sorry, kid. I didn't mean anything by it. I'm sure Miz Shelby is a fine lady."

In his imagination, the unseen Miz Shelby's hair was now white, her face lined and her life full but still missing something.

"You bet she is. Even if she wasn't, ain't been no one around to run off with, anyways." The young man with the name tag reading Tyler on his blue-and-white-striped shirt leaned back against the open door and checked his phone again. "You showing up and a jerk who tried to steal some gas are the only action I've seen around all night."

Not that the kid could see much of anything beyond the small screen in his hand, Jax thought. Then his mind went to the speeding SUV. Like any good cop, he wondered if there was a connection, if something more was going on.

Before he could ask the kid about the incident, the sound of a cat mewing caught his attention. Maybe not a mew—definitely the cry of a small animal, though, probably rooting for food out there in the lonely night.

"Anyways," the kid said, heading back inside, "I don't know what's up with Miz Shelby, but I'm locking the doors at eleven."

Jax nodded. No gas stolen. Not his jurisdiction—or his business. He decided to let it go and followed the kid inside.

The sound demanded his attention again. Close to the café, maybe on the wide, rough-hewn wooden deck? Jax turned to pinpoint it and caught a movement briefly blocking the dim light from inside the café. Someone was moving around inside.

A screech of a wooden table leg on concrete. The clank of metal, followed by a crash of dishes. A shuffling sound. Then a soft whimper of that small animal in the darkness. Was something up in the café, which had closed uncharacteristically early? Was there an injured animal nearby that needed help?

The sound was none of his business, either, but he wouldn't be able to walk away not knowing if there was something he should have done and didn't. The boards of the café steps creaked under Jax's boots. He wished he had a flashlight. A shape filled the glass window in the café door. He started to call out for whoever had closed the café to stay put until he could check things out, but the subtle mewing drew his attention again.

He glanced down to find a square plastic laundry basket covered with small blue-and-white blankets.

Something moved slightly without revealing anything beneath the blankets. He thought of the sound and drew a quick conclusion. Someone, probably knowing good ol' lonely, grandmotherly type Miz Shelby worked the late shift at the Crosspoint, had left a basket of kittens on the doorstep.

The doorknob of the café rattled, and Jax bent down to snag the basket. "Hold it, there's a—"

The sickening *thwock* of the door whacking his head rang out in the night. The door had knocked his hat clean off, but thanks to a gentle nudge from him, the basket had been spared.

"Ow." He squeezed his eyes shut for a split second. When he straightened up and opened them again, he found himself gazing into the biggest, bluest, most startled eyes he'd ever seen. Eyes that were wet with tears.

"What hap… Why…?" The young woman staggered back a step, clutching a folded piece of paper and an overstuffed backpack covered with multicolored embroidered flowers.

She was just a little bit of a thing. The brief glimpse of her outline through the window had told him that much. It hadn't told him that she was maybe in her late twenties. Or that when he looked into her face, his heart would race, just a little.

"Don't tell me. *You're* Miz—"

"I'm sorry…I was just… We're closed." Still standing in the threshold, with the main door open slightly behind her and the screen door open just a sliver in front of her, she set the colorfully decorated backpack down. She glanced around behind her, then set her jaw and reached inside to flip on an outside light. "I know the sign says our hours go later, but tonight we're closed. Goodbye."

Her tone had started out steady, had faded and then had ended firmly again.

He bent slowly to snatch up his hat. His banged-up temple began to throb. "I could see that you were closed. That's why I came over here."

"You came here *because* you saw that we were closed?" She stiffened, then leaned out enough to steal a peek outside, her gaze lingering on the lights of the store, where Tyler was texting away, paying them no notice.

That afforded Jax a moment to take in the sight of her. And what a sight. Her hair was neither blond nor brown, with streaks that beauticians might work hours to try to produce but only time in the sun could create.

When she caught him studying her, she blushed from the quivering tip of her chin to the freckled bridge of her nose. Her lips trembled. He thought for a moment she'd burst out crying, as the telltale tears proved she had been doing. She was obviously in a highly emotional state. Scared, maybe. Vulnerable, definitely.

He put one hand out to try to soothe her. He wasn't sure what he would say, but he would speak in a soft, re-assuring tone. He'd help her because…well, that's what Jax did. He helped. Whenever and wherever he could. "It's all right. I just—"

"Didn't you hear me? We're closed, cowboy." Her posture relayed a confidence her voice did not. "Go."

She blinked a few times, fast, but tears did not well up in her eyes. In fact, Jax got the feeling that if she could have made it happen, fire would have shot from them. And that fire would singe his hide considerably.

That thought made him grin. "Actually, I'm not a cowboy so much as I'm here to—"

"I don't care who you are or what you want. You need

to leave here and be whoever you are elsewhere." She gripped the edge of the door as if it were the railing on a sinking ship.

The sight of her small hand white-knuckled against the rough wood stirred something protective in his gut, even as her insistence that he leave tweaked his suspicions about what was going on here. Was there a message in her behavior? Was his instant attraction to the lady throwing off his finely honed ability to sense danger and motivation?

"I'm Jax." The name that no one had called him for so long came out quickly and naturally in her presence. "That is, *you* can call me Jax."

"Jax?" Her lips formed the name slowly. She shook her head, as if she didn't understand why he was still standing there, whatever he asked to be called.

"That is, I'm Jackson Stroud." He steadied the small basket at his feet, then stood tall, settled his hat on his head, lowered his chin slightly and added with what he hoped was a disarming smile, "Kitten rescuer."

"Kitten…?" She glanced downward at the basket, which she might have knocked over with the door if she hadn't beaned Jax instead. Yet she didn't seem the least bit concerned about the injury to his head.

The screen door creaked loudly as she came outside at last. She knelt down, peeked under the blankets, then turned her face to look at him. The fire in her now had an ominous quality, as if the first sparks of suspicion had become a bed of banked embers that had the potential to smolder on for a very long time. "What is the matter with you?"

"Well, I did recently take a rather nasty blow to the head." He rubbed his temple and gave her a grin.

The clerk stuck his head out the door again. "Everything okay over there, Shelby Grace?"

"Shelby Grace," Jax murmured. He liked that better than Miz Shelby. It felt good to say, all Southern charm with a touch of faith. She sounded like a woman he could reason with, maybe even win over if she'd just listen and—

"Call Sheriff Denby, Tyler." She bent over the basket and fussed with the blankets for a moment.

"He ain't gonna like being woke up this time of night," the thin young man called back.

"Sheriff? There's no call for that." Jax took a step back as he dipped his hand into his pocket to withdraw his badge. Wait. He didn't have it on him anymore, and even if he did, it wouldn't mean anything here and now. He stepped back again and held his hands up. "I was just trying to do the right thing, ma'am."

"The right thing? You have the gall to talk to me about…" She gathered the blankets back up again, reached into the basket, lifted the contents out all at once and stood. "Call Denby, Tyler. Tell him it's an emergency. We have a no-account lowlife here who just tried to abandon a baby on my doorstep!"

Chapter Two

"Baby!" The ruggedly handsome cowboy standing inches away from the doorway of the Crosspoint Café looked genuinely shocked at that news. "Lady, I don't have a baby, but if I did, nothing in the world would make me drop it off somewhere and walk away."

She wanted to believe him. But then, Shelby tended to want to believe everyone—her dreamer of a dad, her liar of an ex-boyfriend, all her friends and coworkers who told her that things weren't as bad as they seemed. And she had paid the price for that.

Shelby drew in a deep breath and went over the three promises she had made to herself last night. She had felt so strongly about them, she had included them in the note still clutched in her hand.

1. Never forget that with God all things are possible.

2. Never let anyone else tell her what she "should" feel.

3. *Never, ever* trust a cowboy.

"I'd like to say I believe you, but..."

She skimmed her gaze over the man before her. Tall, lean, dark-haired, with steely eyes burning into her from the shadow of a gray Stetson. He was the picture of cool, calm and all-cowboy. The culmination of years of disappointment in men like this made it impossible for her to simply trust whatever this one had to say.

"But I did come out and find you bent over this basket. How do I know you didn't leave it and weren't just about to take off?"

"Sheriff Denby says to stay put. He'll get here as soon as he can," called Tyler Sprague, the teenage clerk, whom Shelby had known since she'd watched him in the church nursery.

"Okay." Shelby clutched the basket close, relieved to have a chance to look away from the stranger. "Let's get her inside."

The cowboy cocked his head. *"Her?"*

She stopped mid-turn, her foot raised above the threshold. "What?"

He leaned in close. Closer than she'd normally have allowed a man to get to her, especially one she didn't know. "You called the baby her."

She could hear her own heart beating. Heat surged up from her neck to her cheeks, then all the way to the tops of her ears. She raised her chin to try to look beyond the man who had just challenged her—in more ways than one—to the kid standing behind him. "We're taking *him or her* inside, Tyler."

The young man gave the thumbs-up even as he began heading for the mini-mart entrance. "I'll close up and come over."

The man held the door open for her and the baby in the basket, waiting until she passed so close that the blankets brushed against the sleeve of his denim jacket. Then he murmured, "You said *her.*"

Shelby went sailing across the threshold, which she thought she would never cross again, her head held high. "I didn't want to say *it*. Babies are human beings, not its."

Once inside, he whisked his hat off his head like a true Texas gentleman. "That much I agree with, but still…"

"Just what are you accusing me of?" She set the basket down on the tabletop. She could see the man's eyes much better now. That wasn't making it any easier for her to talk to him. She bent her head and gazed down at the infant's small, sweet face instead. "That is what you're doing, right? Accusing me of something?"

"I was just asking a question." He stood there for a moment, with expectation hanging in the air between them.

Shelby had never been grilled by the police in her life, but she kind of got the feeling this was how it would be. She pressed her lips closed, getting the sense that anything she said could and would be used against her. And yet she didn't feel threatened so much as…

His gaze sank into hers.

She took a quick, sharp breath and didn't let it out until he looked into the basket. His eyes narrowed. After a moment, he shook his head. "What kind of person would not only forsake their child, but also leave it alone in the night outside a closed café?"

"We weren't supposed to be closed," Shelby said softly, unable to take her eyes off the small pink child in the basket. A baby whose appearance here tonight had foiled her big plans.

The baby stretched and squirmed. Long lashes stirred, then lifted. The baby looked right at Shelby, then at the road-weary, bleary-eyed cowboy.

"She's so… I just don't see how anyone could…" The word strangled in Shelby's throat. Tears burned in her eyes—again. She would have thought after the past few days, since she had made up her mind what she had to do, that she'd cried all the tears she'd been allotted for a lifetime. But nope, here they were again. "I'm sorry. It's just been a long day and…"

"Her eyes are blue," he murmured.

"Lots of babies have blue eyes at first," she assured him, swiping away what she resolved would be her last tear with the back of her hand.

"*Your* eyes are blue." He jerked his head up to nail her with a discerning stare.

Really? This total stranger, this cowboy kitten rescuer, was testing her like that? Any other time in her life, she would have stumbled all over herself to assure him she was above reproach…because, well, she was in this instance. But tonight, with her new resolve to take charge of her life, she decided to give as good as she got.

She gave one last sniffle, then moved around the suspicious, questioning cowboy slowly, her gaze fixed on his face. "You just called the baby *her.*"

He glowered at her—for about two seconds. His smile broke over his face slowly, not at all like the bold grin he had flashed at her earlier that had thrown her completely off-kilter. This smile, and the way his broad shoulders relaxed as he rubbed the back of his neck and shook his head as a concession to her standing up to him, warmed Shelby to the very pit of her clenched stomach.

"Maybe we should look for a note or something." He started to reach into the tangle of flannel blankets.

"Wait." She stuck her hand out to stop him. The instant her fingertips brushed his jacket, her breath went still. She curled her fist against her chest and managed to sound a little less flustered than she felt as she asked, "Won't the police want to look for fingerprints?"

"Not likely. First of all, you won't get prints off flannel. Besides that, unless whoever left this baby has a criminal record in a database easily accessed by the local cops, it really won't be an issue." He reached in, cradled the whole body of the small infant in his large, strong hands, then lifted the baby up.

Despite her clashing emotions, Shelby couldn't keep herself from smiling at the sight of the cowboy and child framed by the window of the silent café. "You seem pretty sure of what you're doing."

"Spent a lot of time in foster care. I learned a lot about looking after little ones." He shifted to get the baby situated right against his broad shoulder.

"No, I meant…"

The baby let out a soft sound, then snuggled in close, drawing its legs up. A tiny milk bubble formed on the sweet little lips, which made those chubby pink cheeks almost unbearably pinchable.

The stranger leaned back to check out what was going on with the baby. Then he smiled—just a little and only for a half a second at most.

Shelby sighed.

"Around here, everybody knows how to tend to babies and children and old folks and…whatever needs tending to." Except the one guy she had hitched her heart to, she couldn't help noting to herself. Mitch Warner hadn't known how to take care of anyone but himself, and he'd even done that poorly. "What I meant was that you seem to know a lot about police work."

"*That* I picked up *after* foster care." He began to pat the child's back.

She stood there, probably looking like a deer in the headlights, waiting for him to elaborate. How did he pick up his knowledge of police procedures? Was he the type to associate with lawmen...or lawbreakers?

"Why don't you check for a note?" He jiggled the baby slightly and nodded toward the basket.

She rifled through the tangle of pastel-colored flannel blankets. "Here are a few disposable diapers and a full bottle. Nothing else. No note. No personal items."

"I figured as much."

She looked up to find him staring at her. Or, more accurately, straight into her—as though he were searching for something she wanted to keep covered up.

He settled the still sleeping child back into the basket. Shelby reached out to pull the top blanket up over the baby. He did the same.

Their hands brushed. The warmth of his calused palm eased through her chilled fingers.

This time she did not yank away, but let her hand flit from the blanket to the baby's soft curls and on to its soft, plump cheek. "If you don't mind, I was just going to tuck the baby in and say a little prayer for...the baby... and for whoever left the baby here."

He nodded. "That's kind of you. I'm more than a little ashamed that I didn't think to offer that myself."

That caught her off guard. "You want to join me in a prayer?"

"For the child, yes, ma'am, I would. I don't know if I can be so gracious toward the one who walked off and left her...." He bowed his head and shut his eyes, then opened them once again to nail Shelby with a look as he added, "Or him."

Shelby took a deep breath, acknowledged both the remark and the reservations they both still held for one another with a curt nod. "All right, then…"

"Jackson Stroud." He held his hand out.

"Shelby Grace Lockhart." She gave his hand a quick, firm shake and, just before she let her hand slip from his, added in a soft whisper, "Jax."

The use of the name he had first given her seemed to hit home with him. It appeared to set him off his game for a split second before he nodded to her and bowed his head.

She bowed her head, too, but she did not close her eyes. Instead she focused her gaze on the compelling face of this innocent, seemingly unwanted child as she prayed.

"Every creature matters to you, Lord. Everyone is loved. Sometimes it's hard to remember that none of us is ever truly alone when we feel lost. Sometimes it's hard to know what to do and who to trust. Please, Lord, help me…help us…to show your love to this newcomer. And through it all, let us not forget your mercy for whoever found themselves in a place where they thought it best to leave this precious one here tonight. We place them and ourselves in your loving hands. Amen."

"Amen," he murmured.

"Amen? Y'all holding a revival in here or something?" Tyler came striding in with his phone in one hand and earbuds swinging in his other with every step. "The store is all locked up tight. Sheriff Denby just pulled up outside."

Shelby spun around to face Tyler, her heart pounding.

A mix of panic and embarrassment swirled through her at the idea of being seen praying with this man, whom she had met only moments ago and clearly had no reason to fully trust.

"Just another hard luck case for Shelby Grace," she could imagine folks saying. Someone else who would fill her head with promises and her heart with hope, when anyone else with any sense would know it was all a lie or a dream. Shelby had had her fill of that. That was why she had been headed out of town tonight. Slipping away after her last shift, leaving nothing but a note to explain that it was time she started over in a place where she wasn't known as softhearted Shelby. That was the best way to make an exit from the Crosspoint Café once and for all.

Of course, now that exit would have to wait. She tucked the note into the old backpack she'd had since she was a teen, and looked for something to keep her busy. "I'll make coffee."

"You think this will take long?" Jax called out as she hurried off. "I have plans."

"I hope those plans include watching the baby for the next few minutes, while I do this." Shelby dove into the task, grabbing a bright red plastic container from a shelf above the coffeemaker.

"Trust her, man. If anyone knows how to get around the old guys in town, it's Shelby Grace." Tyler took a seat at the long service counter and began swiveling back and forth on a stool.

"That so?" Jackson Stroud studied her through those piercing, narrowed eyes once again. He might have looked menacing if not for the fact that the whole time he kept one hand protectively on the side of the basket, making sure the baby didn't wriggle it off the tabletop.

"You want to get this done quickly? Then coffee is the only way to go." Shelby pulled out the carafe and held it up like she was filming a commercial for it.

The mysterious cowboy just scoffed.

She set the carafe down hard.

He tipped his head to her, as if to say he would bow to her expertise.

That small triumph buoyed her movements as she got out the filter and opened the container. With the rich aroma of coffee filling her nose, she tipped out a spoonful of grounds and said, "Sheriff Denby is not a young man. It's late. The least we can do for him is have some coffee waiting so he can tackle this case with a clear head."

"Clear head? That may be hoping for a bit much," Tyler joked.

"I was supposed to retire over a year ago." The familiar booming voice of Sheriff Andrew Denby—Sheriff Andy to the locals—echoed in the café as he appeared in the doorway. "But they can't find a replacement willing to work my hours for the amount the county budget can afford to pay. Nights like this, I don't wonder if I'll ever retire. Who are you?"

Jax held his hand out to the man, but his expression remained reserved. "Jackson Stroud. I found the basket."

"I'm sorry, Sheriff Andy, but this couldn't be helped." Shelby poured water in the machine, flipped it on, then turned to find the older man peering down into the basket on the table.

"It's not just a do-nothing job, you know." The sheriff spoke directly to Jackson Stroud, who nodded politely.

"We get our share of excitement coming in off the highway. Anyone they hire needs to be a diplomat to work with the town council, a stickler to meet state and county regs, a detective and apparently—" he reached in, lifted the baby up and gave a sniff "—a diaper changer."

"Oh, Sheriff, let me take care of that." Shelby rushed forward.

"You pour the coffee. This ol' grandpa knows which end is which." The sheriff gathered baby and clean diaper and headed for the restroom, calling over his shoulder, "So no idea who the parents are? No clues? No note?"

"Nothing." Shelby set the coffee down.

"*She* had a note." Jax eyed her. "And a backpack full of stuff on her way out the door after closing up early. If you look at her face, you'll find she's been crying."

The sheriff reentered the room. He, Tyler and Jax all locked their gazes on her at once.

Shelby felt as if she'd been slapped. "What? You can't possibly have seen all that."

Sheriff Denby slipped into the restroom without any further response.

"I don't know how you do police work around here, but some people might call that a clue." Jax raised his voice to make sure the sheriff heard.

"Yeah? Well, around here, it's what we call besmirching a good woman's reputation!" Shelby came around the counter, her pace underscoring the quick clip of her irritation at what this total stranger seemed determined to pin on her. "I may be a soft touch. I may have wasted most of my life waiting for my father's dreams of raising quarter horses to pay off so he could buy us this café like he promised. I may even have thrown away three of my twenty-eight years thinking Mitch Warner would stop running around with other girls and settle down with me, but…" Her voice broke. Her heart pounded. She had never admitted all of that out loud to anyone. Pouring it out to Jackson Stroud left her feeling vulnerable but justified when she jerked her head high and concluded, "I am not the kind of girl who would have a child without being married and if I were a mother. Let me assure you, I'd never leave him or her. I'd do anything in my power to protect my baby…"

"It's a girl." Round-faced Sheriff Denby appeared with the freshly diapered infant and handed her to Shelby.

"Surprise, surprise." Jax cocked his head and crossed his arms. "No chance you knew that already?"

Shelby sighed and shook her head at the implication in his question.

"And her name is Amanda," the sheriff went on. "At least that's what it says in fancy stitching on the corner of this blanket she was wrapped up in."

"Hand-stitched, huh?" Jax looked at the corner of the blanket, then at Shelby's decorated backpack. "Any flowers on it?"

"You have got to be kidding." Shelby couldn't help but laugh as she spoke to baby Amanda to get her point across to everyone. "This guy thinks I'm your mother, sweet pea."

"Shelby Grace? A mama?" Sheriff Denby snorted out a laugh that someone else might have taken as an insult. "No way could she have had a baby and kept it a secret around here. Maybe somebody could have, but not her. We all know her story."

"I don't," Jax said in a soft tone that bordered on dangerous—but also carried interest.

"This ain't about you." Sheriff Denby moved to the counter, picked up the coffee carafe and flipped over a cup on the counter. But he didn't pour. "This is about Shelby Grace."

"Right. We agree on that, at least." Jax adjusted his hat, and the movement came off as a kind of sly tip of congrats to the sheriff for being on his side.

"What do you mean? About me how?" Shelby cradled the baby higher in her arms, but that did nothing to temper the sinking feeling in the pit of her stomach.

"Everybody in town knows your story, Shelby Grace. We all know about your daddy, about that Mitch. Some of us even know that you broke your lease and packed up all your belongings today."

"Huh?" Tyler glanced up and blinked. "You moving, Miz Shelby?"

"I don't know your story, Miss Lockhart, but I do know that *that's* an interesting development."

People were not supposed to find out this way, not by hearing it couched in supposition and gossip, and certainly not before her father. "It doesn't matter, Tyler. None of this has anything to do with me and—"

"Hold that thought right there, young lady." Sheriff Denby flipped a waiting coffee mug over on the counter and helped himself to a steaming hot cup. "There is a more than passing fair chance that whoever left that baby on the doorstep, when you were here closing up all by your lonesome, left her here for *you* to find."

"Makes sense to me." Jax turned toward the door, then looked at Tyler. "You said someone tried to steal gas from the station tonight. Did they happen to be driving a silver SUV?"

"Uh, no. Actually, when I looked up and saw a faded red Mustang slide up to the pump, I thought it was Mitch come to see Miz Shelby. So I stopped paying attention until they took off fast. That's when I thought maybe they'd filled up and run off without paying, but turns out their credit card had been denied and they didn't get a drop."

"Mitch?" Jax leaned one elbow on the counter, gave Shelby a hard look, then glanced at the baby. "Any particular reason this Mitch might have come by tonight and not hung around to talk to you face-to-face? He a *friend* of yours?"

"An *ex*...friend," Shelby said, oddly defensive in this man's presence. Still, she searched the baby's face for any similarity to Mitch, who she had forgiven more than once for cheating on her.

The man stared her down with an expression that made her feel he knew all about Mitch and his cheating ways, though that would be impossible. Wouldn't it?

"This Mitch wouldn't be the kind of *ex-friend* who might think you'd be a good person to raise his child, would he?" Jax asked, sounding far too matter-of-fact for that kind of question.

"The last thing Mitch Warner would have wanted was to be a daddy," Sheriff Denby snorted.

Shelby tucked the baby in closer, as if that might conceal how strongly her heart was beating at the very idea that Mitch might have done something like this. "Of course, we are conveniently overlooking the possibility that the baby was left by someone who doesn't even *know* me. Someone *we* don't know, for that matter."

"Like me?" The man with the cool eyes and the quick smile cocked his head at her.

"I'm just saying that we all know one another around here. You just showed up." At the worst time. Or maybe the best, if he had no connection to tiny Amanda. "Tonight, of all nights."

"You want to know who I am, Miss Shelby Grace Lockhart? I'm a man who served four years with the Greater Dallas police force." He reached into his back pocket and withdrew his wallet, glanced down at it, grimaced slightly and put it back. "At least I used to. Now I'm, for all intents and purposes, homeless and unemployed for the next couple of weeks."

He gave her a wistful smile that hinted he expected her to find that notion so preposterous, she would have to laugh. She didn't know whether to smile or shake her head at that.

He nodded at her nonresponse. "You got me. I'm pretty much the most likely suspect in your child abandonment scenario."

"Yup." Andy Denby set the coffee cup down on the counter without a drop ever going in his mouth. "Not trying to be punitive. Got to consider what's right and best for little Amanda. My wife is the town's only physician, so it makes sense we get the child to my house to be checked over."

"So that means…" Jax narrowed his eyes and held out his hands like a man waiting to carry out an order.

"That makes it official. This is a case. I'll call in what details we have tonight, see if there are missing children reports that might be connected. Whatever else needs to be done can wait till morning." The sheriff turned to grab a to-go cup and poured his untouched coffee into it as he half spoke, half yawned. "C'mon, Shelby Grace. The old doc will be tickled pink to have you and that little one stay with us for the night."

"Stay? In Sunnyside?" Her mind raced. She had planned to be long gone by morning, to have begun a whole new life. "Can't you just take the baby and…"

"And what?" Sheriff Denby took the emptied ceramic cup around behind the counter and disappeared long enough to bend down and drop it in the dirty dishpan. He motioned to her, then to her backpack. "Allow you to leave town before we get statements and figure out what's best for little Amanda?"

Shelby held her breath. How had the sheriff known she was fleeing town tonight? Had she been that obvious? She turned to Jackson Stroud, as if she actually hoped that somehow he would spring to her rescue. That was his style, right? If he was telling the truth, that he had come over to save a basket he thought held kittens, then why wouldn't he save her?

The man in the Stetson stepped forward. "So that's it? I can get back on my way, then?"

Cowboys. Shelby let out a huff. You couldn't trust them, at least not to do anything but think of their own hides.

"Absolutely…*not*." The sheriff put the lid on his to-go cup with a soft click. "It's late. I can't call around to find somebody to put you up, so I'm asking nice. Will you just bunk at the Truck Stop Inn for the night so we can sort this out with clear heads tomorrow morning?"

"I can let you in." Tyler started toward the back of the building, motioning. "It ain't fancy, but there's a couple rooms with cots and a shower that we rent out to truckers by the night."

"Tell Miss Delta to bill the department for it." Sheriff Denby clapped his hands together, then motioned for Shelby to hurry up and get her things together. "As of now, this is an official investigation. I'll thank you not to leave town, Stroud, until after we speak again."

"I was only joking about being homeless and unemployed. I have a job waiting for me in Miami. I was on my way there tonight to find a place to live and get the lay of the land before I start work." Jax followed behind Tyler. "I can't stay here indefinitely. I have—"

Denby gave the stranger a hard look that cut him right off. But when the man got even with the sheriff, it did not escape Shelby's keen eye that the older man added something to the conversation that made the wandering cowboy's wide shoulders stiffen. He glanced back at Shelby and the baby.

The world seemed to stand still for a moment.

Then Jax nodded to no one in particular and said, "I guess I can spare some time. But as soon as I have nothing more to offer this case, I need to get on my way."

Chapter Three

Jax rolled onto his side. The whole framework of the old cot creaked. When he'd climbed between the scratchy, bleached brilliant white sheets last night, he hadn't expected to get much sleep. He thought he would never get comfortable or be able to quiet his mind after the day's events. But the minute his head had hit the pillow, the prayer he had shared with Shelby had come echoing back to him, and a sweet peace had washed over him. The next thing he knew, the dim light of the new day was creeping through the crack where the shade did not quite meet the windowsill.

He checked his cell phone for the time and swung his legs over the side of the bed. Head bowed, he rubbed his fists into his eyes. Tyler had said that both the café and the convenience mart opened at six in the morning. That meant, he calculated, he had twenty-five minutes to get ready for…

For what? A few hours ago, his course had been set. If you'd asked him then, he'd have told you without hesitation that he'd be in Miami this morning. He'd be scouting out apartments, looking over the exclusive gated community where, on the first of next month, he'd start his job as head of security. Now he didn't even know what to expect beyond getting up and getting dressed.

That his lack of control in this new situation didn't have him on edge was not like him at all. Jax was a man always one step ahead of everyone else. He pressed his eyes shut tightly. For a moment he considered praying for guidance, but in the end he decided what he really needed was determination. He set his own way, and his way was toward Miami before the end of the day.

He sighed as the peace of last night turned into a weight pressing down on his shoulders. That weight did not lift as he cleaned up with the toiletries Tyler had gathered for him last night. He'd feel better if he could put on clean clothes, but that would have to wait until he reached Florida tonight.

He walked into the Shoppers' Emporium part of the building in time to see the spectacular sunrise over the wide-open Texas landscape, framed by a large plate-glass window. It was the loveliest thing he'd seen in a long time.

"Make that the second-loveliest thing," he murmured to himself as Shelby Grace Lockhart suddenly stepped into view from around the corner in the parking lot. Her hair was windswept, her expression determined, and both her hands gripped the handle of a baby carrier.

"Miss Delta?" Shelby peered in with her cute little nose all but smashed against the glass. "You in there yet?"

"I'm coming. Just hold on to your—" A woman who looked to be a few years shy of sixty, with hair the color and consistency of sunburnt hay, bustled past him, then slowed. She gave him a quick once-over and cocked one penciled eyebrow. She paused long enough to plunk her fist on her bony hip and ask him, "Cowboy or trucker?"

"Cop," he said, then corrected himself. "*Ex*-cop, that is."

Shelby knocked on the door. "Miss Delta? I'm kind of in a hurry. You'll never believe what happened last night."

"And I can't wait to hear all about it," Delta murmured in Jax's direction even as she pivoted and went to unlock the front door. "Shelby Grace, where did you get that sweet little fellow?"

"It's a girl," Shelby corrected at the exact same time the words left Jax's lips. Their perfect timing didn't take the edge off her pointed tone as she added, "*Someone* left her outside the café last night."

Shelby gave Jax an unyielding stare. In return, Jax gave Shelby…the biggest grin he'd ever grinned. Which wasn't saying much, since he never grinned. Or he never used to. But there he was, unable to stop himself.

"How is she doing?" he asked, his eyes on Shelby's face.

"Doc Lovey checked her out. She's in good shape, but a little underweight for what Doc thinks is a four-month-old." Shelby shifted the weight of the carrier and, in doing so, got a bit off balance.

"Doc Lovely?" Jax asked as he rushed forward and scooped the carrier up out of her hands. It felt light to him. No, it wasn't the carrier that felt light. It was him. Like that weight he had felt since plotting his getaway from here had lifted.

"Lovey. Sheriff Denby's wife. It's a nickname, but everyone around here calls her that." Miss Delta tipped her head back a bit so she could give Jax another once-over, then fixed her attention on the baby in the carrier. "Lovely is what *this* sweet thing is. What a cutie. Who could have ever left something this precious?"

"Someone who knew they were placing their baby in good hands," Jax said, almost under his breath. He met Shelby's hesitant gaze and held it until she took a deep breath and smiled.

"That's a sweet idea, I guess," Shelby whispered.

But? She did not say it, or even hint that there was more to say, but Jax felt it. Something else was going on with Shelby Grace Lockhart. Anyone else might have prodded, peppering her with questions to find out more, but Jax knew that people's true motivations showed in their actions, not their words. So he held his tongue and waited.

Shelby glanced over her shoulder toward the café, then down at baby Amanda in the carrier, which Jax held easily by the handle. "But I can't…I don't have it in me anymore to take on one more person's broken promises."

"Promises?" he asked softly.

"A baby left on her own in the dark of night?" Her eyes met his. Her hair swept over her shoulder as she shook her head. "If that doesn't say someone somewhere broke a promise and now wants someone else—"

"You," he interrupted.

"Me." She nodded in agreement. "Now someone wants me to do what everyone knows Shelby Grace does so well. Pick up the slack. Put the pieces back together. Always be there. I just don't think I can do it anymore."

He wanted to speak to her of faith. Of knowing where to find strength. Of what it felt like to be a child caught in the middle of a world with no Shelby Graces in it. Instead, he swallowed his opinion and supported her with a quiet "yeah" and a nod of his head.

She shuffled her feet, then squinted toward the large window, where the sun had begun to shine in and create shadows around them.

Clearly she wanted to get moving. But where? And why? None of his business, of course. Under other circumstances, he would have let it go. He studied her profile, the curve of her cheek. The shadows under her eyes told of a sleepless night. He couldn't let it go—not with the simple question Sheriff Denby had asked him echoing in his mind. *Why Shelby Grace Lockhart?*

"I can't believe there's nothing this little sweetheart needs," Delta cooed as she gave the baby's head a pat. "I'm going to go see what I can find."

"Don't trouble yourself, Miss Delta." Shelby raised her hand in a halfhearted attempt to slow the juggernaut that was Miss Delta of Delta's Truck Stop Inn. "Doc Lovey got us diapers and formula from the county health department. After I help the sheriff look for any signs of who might have left the baby, I volunteered to take her to social services over in West…more…land." Shelby's shoulders sagged as the older woman hurried away, rattling off a list of things she wanted to gather for the baby.

"Here kind of early, aren't you?" he finally asked. "I don't see the sheriff anywhere around."

"There's something I have to do at the café before then."

"Oh?" He narrowed his eyes. It was a simple technique to speak little and act like you expected an answer. Oftentimes people complied without even knowing why. Other times they hesitated, then felt compelled to fill the silence, usually with the very information Jax needed.

Shelby did neither. She took the carrier and settled it on the counter. In doing so, she put her back to Jax. "Delta, will you watch the baby for a few minutes? I'll come back for her just as soon as I—"

Jax clamped his hand down on the woman's shoulder, partly in reassurance, partly to tell her he would not be so easily dismissed. "Don't bother. I'll bring her over."

Shelby whipped her head around. Her shoulder went from strained and tense under his touch to stiff but confident. It was a small shift, but one that let him know she would not be intimidated by him, that she had the grit to hold her own ground.

"You?" Miss Delta poked her head out from behind a round display of candy a few feet away. She gave Jax a once-over, then a twice-over. "Pardon my saying so, but you hardly look like the babysitting type."

"Foster care," Shelby said before Jax could come to his own defense. She pressed the handle of a baby carrier, labeled Property of the Sunnyside, Texas, Police Dept., into his hand. "Meet me in the café in a few minutes."

Somewhere in the shop, something fell off the shelf. As soon as Shelby left, Miss Delta tiptoed from behind that shelf and whispered, "You gonna let her do that? Take that baby to Westmoreland?"

The question, and the implication that Jax had any say over what Shelby did with the child, caught him off guard. "Is Westmoreland really that bad?"

"You know what I mean. Take her to…" Delta hurried over to cover the baby's ears, and even then she spoke in a whisper. "Social services."

Baby Amanda gurgled.

Jax's heart clenched. He had been eight when his

mom died and he'd been taken to social services. It was a moment he hadn't thought of in years, and yet he was not foolish enough to think it hadn't affected him every day of his life.

"What choice do I have?" He wasn't asking rhetorically. He really hoped she had another suggestion.

"I asked you first," she said, in a way that left the impression that if she did have some ideas, she wasn't going to just blurt them out to him. He got that. He was not only an outsider, but he was a total stranger, too. Yet her choice to keep her thoughts to herself actually made his opinion of her go up a couple more notches.

Jax didn't say a word to that effect. But he did turn to stand next to Miss Delta, looking down at the innocent in the carrier. After a moment, he looked the older woman in the eyes and said softly, "I know I'm a stranger here, but I don't think for one moment that Shelby Grace or Sheriff Denby would let this child go anywhere that wasn't the right place for her to be."

"I know that, young man. I just hope you do, as well." Miss Delta nodded, then looked down at the baby. She touched the child's head and bent to give her a kiss on the forehead, which left a bright pink smudge. "You said you were an *ex*-cop?"

"Yes, ma'am. On my way from four years of service in the Dallas area to a dream job doing private security for the ultrarich in Florida."

"Dream job?" She stood back, squinted one eye shut and pressed her lips together to make sure he knew she had sized him up good. "For a man like you? Doing the bidding of the 'ultrarich' sounds more like a nightmare."

"It's helping people without the complications of… the people." That was as best as he could describe it on the spot. He had to admit, the overly simplified explanation didn't make him proud of his choice.

Miss Delta homed in on that right away. She shook her head, causing the necklaces she wore to jangle softly. "*That's* what you have your heart set on? Spending your days as a hired *helper?*"

He repositioned his grip on the baby carrier and his boots on the concrete floor and assured her, "It is."

"In Miami, Florida?"

"Got a contract that says that's where I'm supposed to be."

"Yet here you stand, at the door of the Shoppers' Emporium in Sunnyside, Texas." She narrowed her eyes and tapped the toe of her shoe, which was much too fancy for standing on your feet all day.

"What?" Jax demanded, knowing the woman wanted to say more.

"Nothing." She gave an exaggerated sigh and shook her head. "Only, I wonder if you ever considered that you might just be where you are supposed to be already."

Jax froze for a moment to try to piece together what she meant by that. He was just a guy who had happened by, right? He didn't have any reason to get involved. And yet...

He leaned down to wipe the lipstick off Amanda's head. "I'll take that under consideration, ma'am."

"I believe you will." Miss Delta reached out, grabbed his chin and drew his face close enough to plant a big ol' kiss on his whiskered cheek. "I really do believe you will."

That was how he came to walk through the door of the café, swiping at his cheek with the sleeve of his jacket, carrying a foundling baby, grinning and looking for Shelby. Questions about and reactions to the little one in the carrier began flying at him the second he walked into the café from the few patrons who had begun to shuffle in and settle down for their morning meal.

"What a sweetie."

"How old…?"

"Just precious!"

Questions and reactions to the little one in the carrier began flying at him the second he walked into the café from the few patrons who had begun to shuffle in and settle down for their morning meal. Jax knew they all meant well, but being the center of all this attention was not his style. He was more a stand back and observe kind of guy. Yet with each new set of eyes trained on him, he wanted more and more to retreat.

Retreat? When had that *ever* been his reaction to anything?

Since he had someone to protect, was his instinctive response.

Jax raised the baby up, forced a wincing smile as he moved away from the prying gazes and began looking around for Shelby to help him out. She wasn't at a table. Or behind the counter.

"You cannot do this, Shelby Grace. Not now!" The tense, stressed twang of a man's voice made Jax turn. He spotted Shelby through the opening to the kitchen, arguing with a man with faded blond hair pulled back in a ponytail.

He couldn't help thinking of Denby's concern that whoever had left the baby had basically targeted Shelby Grace Lockhart for a reason. Old beliefs twisted in Jax's gut. Emotion and agendas based on selfishness sometimes made people do desperate things.

He thought of Delta's cryptic advice that he was where he needed to be. Suddenly being here, with this baby and Shelby, felt all wrong.

Without hesitation, Jax headed for the swinging kitchen door.

"I can't do it anymore," Shelby argued, her own voice pitched high with a mix of pleading and anxiety. "You're going to have to find a way to make the payment or start riding a horse to work."

"Shelby, hon, talk sense." The man reached out for her.

Jax found his hand, the one not holding the handle of the baby carrier, doing the same.

Shelby evaded the man's grasp with a quick duck of her shoulder, and in doing so, she also put herself out of Jax's reach.

"I am talking sense. For the first time since I realized, deep down, that you were never going to make a go of the ranch, and I was never going to own this café." Shelby turned to look back, raised her hand, then brushed away a stray curl that had caught on her eyelashes. "I can't tell you how much I wanted to believe, to go on dreaming that some day…but last night I looked around and realized that someday isn't coming. We've given it all we've got, and we have to face the fact that we can't do it, Dad."

"Dad?"

Shelby turned to look at Jax.

Before she could tear into him for listening in on a private—if intriguing—conversation, Jax said, "I was actually thinking it might be smart to start looking around for any clues now, before too many people disturb things."

She sighed, then gave him a single nod. For just a moment, he thought she might cave in to her father's wishes and stay. She certainly wasn't quick to rush off, and her tone carried the heaviness of resignation as she finally agreed, "You're right. Let's go out the back way and walk around to the front. The sooner we get this behind us, the sooner I can get on with what's ahead of me."

Chapter Four

With one hand firmly wrapped around Amanda's carrier handle, Jax hustled them outside, where the aroma of pancakes and bacon followed them. The damp warmth of the café kitchen met the fresh morning air, and Shelby took a deep breath.

"Guess that old saying is true," he said with a quiet intensity. "Everything looks different in the light of day."

Shelby scanned the view behind the café. It all looked familiar to her. Too familiar. Sunnyside, Texas, from any vantage point, was not the view she'd expected to greet her this morning. She turned to fix her gaze on the tall figure at her side, now holding the baby easily against his chest. That sight *was* different.

He glanced her way and shook his head, a smile playing over his lips.

Her heart fluttered. "I…I don't know…what you mean."

"This changes everything." He motioned toward the back parking lot.

Shelby frowned. "It does?"

"It was so late when I got here last night that most of

these houses already had their lights out." He narrowed his eyes, his gaze fixed on the row of neat little homes across the small lot and a strip of grassy ground beyond it. "I didn't realize all these houses were so close back here."

"Oh. Well, it's a small town. Everyone practically lives on top of everyone else. At least it feels like that some days." Shelby's shoulders ached, and her head began to throb. "You said it changes everything?"

"Sure. Last night I was thinking that whoever left the baby came by car, so they made quite a trip in order to reach you. But with people living this close? Maybe it wasn't you but the café that was the draw for the baby. They left her someplace they could watch to make sure she was okay."

A cloud passed over the rising sun. Shelby shivered.

"I'm going to look around and see what I can find." He settled the baby carrier down on the wooden slats at her feet and gave her a nod before heading out.

He expected her to stay put and watch over the foundling. Clearly the man did not understand that Shelby was done doing what other people expected. It took her only a moment to bend down and unsnap the safety latches holding Amanda in place. She lifted the baby up and cuddled her close, even as she headed to the steps to follow Jax onto the gravel that served as an employee parking lot.

"No one in Sunnyside would have been able to hide a pregnancy, much less a baby, for three months, let me assure you."

"You honestly think there are no secrets in this town?" He looked back over his shoulder at her. "Would you say everybody here knows all there is to know about you, Shelby Grace?"

She pulled up short. Her stomach clenched. It was like he was looking right through her. She thought of the note she had written last night, of her deepest fear, which she was sure no other living soul knew or would understand.

"You know who owns all three of these vehicles?" Jax motioned toward the dust-covered blue pickup truck, the ten-year-old minivan and the lime-green convertible parked side by side in the lot.

Shelby forced her mind back to the task at hand—gathering information to find whoever had left Amanda. "Um, the convertible is Miss Delta's, the minivan is mine and the truck—"

"Is also yours," he said, finishing for her, sounding somewhere between speculative and show-offy at having come to that conclusion. "That's the payment you need your dad to take on, I'm guessing."

"I bought the van so I could cater some local events once I saved up enough to… Well, it doesn't matter now. My dad's truck bit the dust, and he couldn't get a loan for a new one. So good ol' Shelby got one for him."

"Good ol' Shelby," he muttered as he strode on from the back parking lot to the side of the building. He kicked the toe of his boot at a clump of grass, then lifted his head and studied where the paved customer lot ended just by the edge of the deck.

The baby squirmed in her arms and made a soft, fussy sound, pushing at the blanket flap swept over her head and wadded against her now-warm pink cheek.

"Do you really think we might find something helpful out here?" Shelby rearranged the blanket and baby so that Amanda could wave her arms freely. That allowed the sun to shine on her sweet, round face.

"It's not so much about thinking at this point." He raised his hand to his temple, his expression a mask of concentration. He was completely immersed in the moment. Cool. Focused. Intense. "Trying to outthink the situation is how people jump to conclusions. That can tempt them to try to prove themselves right instead of trying to find the truth."

Shelby glanced over her shoulder, back at the café, where she had thought through her own situation hour after hour. She had felt trapped in a role not of her own making, unable to spread her wings. She had obsessed over the fear that she would never own her own business. That no man would ever love her enough to be faithful to her. That Mitch Warner was the best she would ever do and that she would end up like her father, always chasing a dream forever out of her reach. As she stood here now in the daylight, Jax's words went straight to her heart. Had she been trying to prove her conclusions about life in Sunnyside, or had she been seeking the truth? "Man, you're good at this. Anyone ever tell you that?"

He glanced up and met her eyes. A smile tugged at one corner of his mouth. "I haven't even done anything yet."

"But you're going to." Shelby had no idea how she knew that, but she knew it beyond the shadow of a doubt. After a lifetime spent around men who didn't seem able to do anything, she *knew*. "So just what is it that you're going to do?"

"Right now?" He lifted one shoulder, then let it down. "I'm gonna look around."

"Oh." That should not have disappointed her as much as it did. "So you don't have any hunches?"

Before he could answer, Amanda sneezed.

"Oh! God bless you, sweetheart," Shelby whispered.

Jax turned, and his expression warmed as he, too, mouthed "God bless you" to their tiny charge. No sooner had the words left his lips than his shoulders stiffened and his voice went hard. "No. No hunches. Other than that whoever left that little cutie did it in a hurry."

"In a hurry like someone committing a crime?" She settled the baby on her hip and made a quick swipe to wipe the tiny pink-tipped nose. Once she had thought of it, the theory came quickly to her lips. "Like somebody kidnapping a baby and then panicking and deciding to ditch it somewhere?"

He frowned.

"Or in a hurry like someone ripping off a Band- Aid?" she asked, feeling a bit like she should have led with that. "You know it's going to hurt, so you do it as quickly as possible. Get it over with."

"Yeah. Yeah, like that Band-Aid thing," he muttered as he scanned the tall grass, his eyes narrowed to slits. "I don't think it's a kidnapping case. I'm sure Denby checked to see if there are any alerts for a missing infant and acted on that right away."

"Sheriff Andy did go back to the office last night." She watched Jax a moment, not sure what to do. Just twenty-four hours ago, she had resolved to take charge of her life and had thought she might actually pull it off. She might really leave Sunnyside. Now? Now she needed to ask Jax a question she realized she probably should have asked herself yesterday, when she had packed up her few personal belongings and had told her landlord to keep the cleaning deposit. "What are you looking for, exactly?"

"I don't know, *exactly*." He reached up in a gesture Shelby recognized as a man adjusting his cowboy hat to shade his eyes. But there was no hat, so at the last second the man rubbed his palm lightly through his dark hair. "When people get in a big hurry, they don't think straight. They come up with a half-baked plan and carry it through before they get cold feet."

Shelby shifted her feet nervously back and forth.

"That's when they make mistakes."

"Then again, something this monumental surely had a lot of thought behind it." Shelby pulled her shoulders up. His comment was not aimed at her or her emotionally charged decision to turn her back on everything she knew. Still, it put her on the defensive. "It wasn't necessarily an impulse."

"No." He shook his head. "A woman abandoning a baby in the night, even with the most trustworthy person in the whole town, isn't something she's going to plot out."

The most trustworthy person in the whole town. On one hand, hearing him describe her that way sent a shimmer of pride and happiness through her. On the other hand, it seemed a pretty improbable expectation to live up to. Shelby looked at baby Amanda, then at Jax, and in doing so, she knew. She *wanted* to live up to it. She wanted to be worthy of the trust placed in her. "You're so sure it was a woman? Her mother?"

"Maybe someone else was with her, but there is the footprint of a woman's shoe in the mud." He knelt down and touched the ground, then stood again with something small and pink in his hand. "And I believe with all my being she was the mom. A kidnapper wouldn't have brought this."

"She had to be so desperate," Shelby whispered, her heart aching at the sight of the floppy home-sewn bunny in his hand.

"Had to be," he said in a way that sounded like he had some kind of personal stake in that conclusion. He stood and walked over to where Shelby stood holding Amanda. "To do this, she clearly didn't think she had anyone in her life she could turn to…except you."

He held out his hand with the humble handmade toy in it for Shelby to take.

Shelby hesitated, then reached out, her hand almost trembling.

Her fingers brushed his.

For less than a second, he held on to the toy. Shelby couldn't explain how, but much like when they had prayed together over Amanda last night, she felt a connection to this cowboy who had walked into her life when she had needed it the least—and Amanda had needed it most.

Without warning, Jax loosened his grip. The rabbit slid through his large, rough hands, the long ears dragging through his blunt, calloused fingers.

It felt like a passing of the responsibility to Shelby. Jax had found the baby. He had stayed long enough to help Sheriff Denby. He had found what clues he could. The rest was up to her.

Shelby turned the crudely sewn animal over in her hand and shook her head. "You're right. There's no one else to take this on here. No one except good ol' soft-hearted Shelby Grace Lockhart."

* * *

They had waited another twenty minutes for Denby to show up at the café before Shelby's father remembered to tell them the sheriff had called right after the pair had gone out to the back parking lot. The town's deputy on duty had had to go out to oversee a dispute between two neighbors, and Denby needed to stay close to the office. He wanted them to bring Amanda there to give their statements.

"A desperate mother who thought of Shelby as her only resource?" Sheriff Denby came around to the front of the large wooden desk in his cluttered office to peer into the face of the baby in Shelby's arms before he leaned back to make a seat of the edge of the desk. "I pretty much came to that conclusion last night."

With Shelby settled into the only chair in the room, aside from the one behind the desk, Jax leaned one shoulder against the wall. He crossed his arms. "Then why didn't you share your theory last night, instead of asking me—"

"Because I was hoping you'd come at this with a fresh set of eyes, Mr. Stroud. Or should I call you Officer?"

"Just Jax is enough." Jax held up his hand. "I'm a civilian now."

"No such thing. Once a lawman, always a lawman." The older man groaned a bit as he rose from his perch on the corner of the desk. He winced and straightened slowly. "Of all people, I know how hard it is to walk away from the calling."

"The *calling?*" Jax swept his gaze over the walls of the office, which were covered with plaques, framed photos and citations that recounted a history of service. Just standing here humbled and touched him. His few short years on the force paled in comparison to this kind of work, and his new job? Well, it didn't compare at all.

He tried to tell himself he'd still be helping others in Miami. But he couldn't stay convinced of that when he turned his head and found himself looking at Shelby cradling Amanda. How could patrolling the playground of those who could afford anything in the world compare to standing up for and protecting those who had nowhere else to turn?

"I don't know." Jax shook his head. "Maybe you're right. Maybe it's hard for some people to leave the life of a lawman behind. A calling, like you say. But me?"

"You?" Shelby made a big show of rolling her eyes and laughing at Jax's weak protest.

Amanda fussed at the sudden, albeit soft, outburst.

Shelby didn't miss a beat. She curled the baby close and rose deftly from her chair. Her feet did a *scuff, scuff, shuffle* over the old floor, lulling the baby into woozy contentment, and with hushed words she still managed to knock Jax off his guard and send him reeling with her insight. "You mean the would-be kitten rescuer just rolling through town who let himself get waylaid into a situation with a lost baby? Or the guy who got up at dawn to help with an investigation and make sure everything was okay?"

"Okay, okay. You got me pegged, Shelby Grace." Jax held both hands up and laughed. He turned around to face her.

She pulled up short in her pacing, stopping just inches away from him, with baby Amanda in between them.

"You got me," Jax repeated barely above a whisper.

She blinked her clear blue eyes in an expression that

seemed half startled, half flustered. She started to step to the side.

Jax did the same. "I…here…let me…"

Neither seemed able to complete a thought, much less an action or a sentence.

Sheriff Denby did not have that problem. "Good. We're all clear on that. Then everything's settled, right?"

"Settled?" Jax repeated the word hardly above a murmur. Never in his whole life had he felt settled—nor did he want to feel that way. But standing here, looking at Shelby holding Amanda…

Denby clapped his hands. "Let's make it official."

"Official?" Jax said.

"Yes, sir." Denby went around the desk and whipped open one of the drawers. As he fished around inside it, he said, "I'm going to deputize you, son. So you can escort Shelby and this baby over to Westmoreland."

"You're going to what?" Jax stepped back without thinking. He smashed into a row of awards, which slid sideways and fell forward. He had to act fast to save them from crashing to the floor. "Why?"

"Why?" Sheriff Denby chuckled as he pulled out a badge. "Think a hotshot lawman from… Where did you say you were from, son?"

"I'm not from anywhere. Until yesterday, I lived in Dallas. As soon as I leave Sunnyside, I'm going to live in Miami for a while."

"Dallas," Denby said as he pulled out a file and slapped it on the desk. "That's the one I called to check you out."

"You what?"

"Ran your license plate last night, after I left here. Made some calls." The white-haired sheriff met Jax's eyes, almost in a challenge at first. A pause, then a slow, kindly smile followed. "Didn't think I'd trust you with our Shelby without checking you out first, did you?"

Jax looked at the woman standing at his side with her mouth hanging open, those fire-spitting eyes fixed on the man behind the desk. He laughed. "Blame you? I'd have done the same things myself."

"I know you would have, son. That's why I'm asking you to step up now and help us all out." Denby opened the file and pointed at the paper. "Sign here, and I'll swear you in."

"What do you mean, trust him with me?" Shelby came forward. If she hadn't been holding Amanda, Jax got the sense she would have pushed her way around the desk and met Denby nose to nose, or as close to his nose as she could get beyond his rounded stomach. "I can take care of myself, Sheriff Andy."

"I'm sure you can, but for now your job is to take care of Amanda, so just for today I think you need someone else to look after you. I can't leave the office, so…" Denby snatched up a pen and offered it to Jax. "Just for one day. For Shelby."

She shook her head. "I don't need—"

For Shelby.

Jax took the pen and signed his name, even knowing that somewhere along the line he was going to pay for letting himself get involved like this.

Chapter Five

Shelby fidgeted with the seat belt, when she really wanted to stretch back and check the straps holding Amanda's car seat in place. Why she thought she would know how to buckle in the carrier better than Jax, she didn't know. In fact, as far as babies went, the man seemed to have a lot more experience than she did. Slyly, she glanced over at him from under a spiral of hair that had fallen over her forehead and cheek.

"Ready?" he asked in that deep, resonant Texas drawl of his.

"For what?" she almost whispered. She would have *had* to have whispered it, because meeting his gaze in these close quarters had all but taken her breath away.

The minivan lurched forward. "Let's do this."

He had not made up some reason to make her drive, as her dad would have. He did not whine about the one-hundred-twenty-mile round trip or mutter about how long it might take with the social services department. Her ex, Mitch, would do that every time they spent more than a few minutes doing something that didn't interest him. No, Jackson Stroud just did what needed to be done.

Shelby marveled not just at that, but also at how impressed she was. She wanted to tell him so but couldn't help thinking that "Thanks for doing what you do" was an odd compliment. So as they passed the sign reading Buffalo Betty's Chuck Wagon Ranch House, 19 Miles, she blurted out the first thing that came to her lips. "You look good behind the wheel of a minivan."

"I what?" He gave her a sideways glance, then fixed his cool dark eyes on the road ahead and gave a deep-throated chuckle. "Shelby Grace, are you… Was that your way of flirting with me? Because if it was, I've heard better."

"I wasn't…that is… I didn't…" Shelby gulped in the big breath she had been about to take.

His chuckle opened into a warm, soft laugh. "Relax. No man wants to hear he looks good driving a minivan. I'm just having some fun with you for saying it."

"Fun. That must be why I misunderstood." She took a deep breath and slouched back against the gray upholstered seat. "It's been so long since I've done anything truly fun, I'm afraid I don't even recognize it when I see it anymore."

"Maybe that explains it."

"Explains what?"

"The sadness on your face last night, when I first looked into your eyes."

"Oh, that. Actually, I…" She didn't owe him an explanation. Her whole life had built up to that moment when she had finally decided she needed to get out of Sunnyside, to start fresh somewhere else. Somewhere where nobody thought of her as softhearted Shelby and did things like leave their infants in her care. She thought of the note she had written detailing her feelings. A swirl of emotions followed and carried with it the memory of that first instant that she'd laid eyes on Jax. Then of praying over Amanda with him. How had all of that led to this?

She turned her head to watch the familiar landscape slide by for a moment before she decided the best course was to change the subject. "What happened to your cowboy hat?"

"Left it back at the Truck Stop Inn. Won't be wearing it where I'm going, so I thought…" He left that thought unfinished. "What happened to you last night that had you crying?"

Shelby looked out the passenger-door window, not wanting him to see how much the directness of the question had thrown her. "I thought cowboys never went anywhere without their hats. Where would you be going that you wouldn't need it?"

"I don't wear my hat all the time, because I'm not that kind of cowboy. Like Sheriff Denby rightly observed, I'm the Dallas lawman type of cowboy. Or I was. I've got a job waiting for me in Miami. Head of security for a community of elite homes." He rattled the answers off in an emotionless drone. But his tone did lighten as he added, "There. Does that answer all your questions?"

Not by a long shot. Where this man was concerned, it seemed like each new thing she learned only raised *more* questions. She got the feeling that pushing for more answers would only irritate him. Shelby resigned herself to the idea that she would probably never know much about the man beside her. She nodded. "Yes. Thanks for humoring me."

A second sign, this one much bigger and painted in garish hues, loomed ahead on the side of the road. *Break-*

fast All Day Long at Buffalo Betty's Chuck Wagon Ranch House! 5 Miles, Endless Smiles Ahead.

"You're welcome," Jax said. "Now maybe you can return the favor and humor me. Because I've got a burning question I've got to ask."

Shelby tensed. She didn't think she could take another question about what had led her to that point in the café last night. One more, and she might just spill her guts and start sobbing over the things she felt she'd never have: love, a home, a family of her own and control over her future. Just thinking about it all made her eyes moist with unshed tears. "Oh, Jax, I don't know—"

"What in the world is a Buffalo Betty, and what about her chuck wagon and ranch house is going to make me smile?" He jerked his thumb over his shoulder in the direction of the sign they had just passed. "Endlessly, no less!"

That was not the question he had intended to ask her, and she knew it. A wave of relief washed over Shelby at his willingness to let her off the hook. How many times had other people used her vulnerability to press their advantage, to get her to go along with their wishes? The fact that Jax saw her turmoil and gave her a way out made her words practically tumble out over each other as she explained, "It's a local attraction. No, I take that back. It's *the* local attraction. A theme restaurant that serves bison, among other things, with a general store, play park and a handful of friendlyish buffalo on the grounds—fenced off away from the visitors, of course. But there is one big moth-eaten old thing that you can pet and feed."

"I don't know whether to ask you just how many buffalo you think you can scoop into a handful, or to make sure I heard right. You can both eat and feed buffalo there?"

"I guess I never thought of it that way." Shelby laughed. "I haven't been there since I was a kid."

"Then we should go now." He had already veered off into the lane to exit as he said it.

They pulled into the parking lot, found a spot and shut the engine off.

"Now? Shouldn't we be getting Amanda to the authorities?" Shelby's protest might have seemed more urgent if she hadn't said it while gathering the baby's things so they could hop out of the minivan the second the engine stopped.

"Technically, since Sheriff Denby deputized me, Amanda *is* with the authorities. And I have it on good authority that it will be in everyone's best interest to stop." He slammed the door shut firmly, as if emphasizing that no further discussion was needed.

Shelby smiled.

That's what he'd done it for, Jax thought as they took the more scenic of the walkways leading from the parking lot to the restaurant proper. He'd disrupted the whole trip just in the hopes that he could make Shelby smile.

"Oh, look, there's the old buffalo. I'm going to get something to feed it. Can you hold Amanda a sec?" She handed the child off to him like they had done the exchange a thousand times.

She trusted him. So much so that she didn't even hesitate. This, in turn, made Jax smile.

Shelby rushed off toward a huge woolly beast standing stock-still behind a wooden fence.

Amanda kicked and wriggled in his arms, and Jax looked down at her. "What?"

Another kick.

"I saw tears in her eyes. My brain said 'Fix it.' That's all. And by the way, I do not have to justify myself to someone whose side of the conversation consists of cooing and milk bubbles." He reached into his pocket to pull out a tissue from the wad he'd tucked away for just this situation, and cleaned off a fresh glob of spit from Amanda's chin.

"Here, let me have that." Shelby was at his side in a heartbeat.

"I am perfectly capable of cleaning up a baby's—"

"For the buffalo." Shelby whisked the tissue paper from his fingers and motioned for him to follow.

"It's a mechanical buffalo." Jax laughed when he got close enough to see it. "I had thought it was a bad idea to let people hand-feed a real one."

"Watch! It vacuums the trash right out of your hand." Shelby placed the tissue in her flattened palm, and with a whoosh, it disappeared.

Shelby laughed.

Which made Jax laugh.

Which made Amanda gurgle.

"She laughed!" Shelby pointed at the baby. "It was an itty-bitty baby laugh, but she did it."

"She's too young."

"She's advanced for her age."

"Everybody thinks their baby is a genius, don't they?" A kindly older woman leaned in to peer at Amanda, then raised her wrinkle-framed eyes to Jax and said, "Of course, in your case, I am absolutely certain it's true. Such a bright baby."

"She looks like you," the woman's slightly younger companion said to Jax as she peered at Amanda.

"Do you think?" The first woman leaned back and shifted her scrutiny from Jax to Amanda, then to Shelby. "I'd say she looks more like her mother."

"She has his dark hair," her companion countered, then, as a seeming afterthought, smiled kindly at Shelby and added, "But she does have your beautiful blue eyes."

Shelby shook her head and held up one hand. "She's not—"

"She's not wearing a hat." Jax shaded the baby's eyes with his hand. "We really should get her out of the sun."

"What a blessed baby to have such a loving daddy," the younger woman said with a sigh.

"And mommy, of course," the older of the two hurried to add. Then she reached toward Amanda, paused to get a nod of approval from Jax, stroked the child's tiny hand and said with genuine warmth, "Life is short. It goes so fast. Trust me on this." She put her hand on the younger woman's shoulder. "You think I'm just looking at your baby, but I know that you're looking at *my* baby here, too. It seems no time at all since she was a baby. Enjoy every minute while you can."

Jax called out a thank-you. Why go into the whole story here and now? It would all be over and behind him soon. "Maybe we should get one of those old-timey photos taken before we hit the road."

"We? The three of us?"

"Or the two of you, if you'd rather."

"Jax, we don't know this baby…or each other, for that matter. Why would we—"

"Because life *is* short, Shelby. Amanda is blessed with us now, but that's going to be over and done with when we get to Westmoreland. It's just my way of…I don't know…"

She cocked her head. "Buying a littlè time?"

"If you're accusing me of something, Shelby Grace, you need to make it clear."

She didn't push it. But then, he could tell by the look on her face that she wanted to; she just wasn't sure how he'd take it. Or maybe she wasn't sure how she'd deal with it if he didn't take it well.

So they went on into the restaurant in silence only broken up by small talk with the hostess who seated them promptly.

"I am starving." Jax settled the baby carrier, which he'd retrieved from the minivan, into the special chair the hostess had brought for them. "Hadn't even realized how hungry I was until I saw what I was missing."

"Missing?" Shelby fussed over Amanda before situating herself at the table.

"Dinner. Midnight snack. Breakfast." He counted off on his fingers. But when he finished that list, his heart kept ticking things off—a family, a life. "I think I'll order everything on the menu."

"I believe you." She pulled her chair out, then leaned in over the table to address him in a rushed whisper. "Not because you're that hungry, but because I think you're stalling."

He waited until Shelby had taken her seat before he asked, "Stalling?"

He wasn't denying it. He just wanted to hear why she thought he'd do it.

She paused a moment, then folded her hands on top of the table. "You don't really want to give Amanda over to the authorities, do you, Jax?"

He sank into his seat, unfurling the cloth napkin to place it in his lap. "I told you, for now I am the—"

"I know. You're 'the authority.'" Shelby spanned her hands in the air, as if reading a banner stretched across the wall. She grinned and shook her hair back from her sun-blushed cheeks. "But an authority who is reluctant to give this baby over to the non-temporary, Denby-appointed, deputy-type authorities."

He dropped the napkin into his lap, leaning forward over the table to challenge her. "I bet you couldn't say that again in a hundred tries."

She leaned in to meet that challenge. "See? More stalling. I'm right, aren't I?"

She was, and he liked it. He usually didn't like it when someone saw through him this easily, but with Shelby? He shook his head. That was one of the reasons he didn't want to rush through this one day they'd have together.

He chose to tell Shelby the other reason. "Even another hour for the mom to come back and keep this kid out of the system is worth it."

That got her interest. She tipped her head to one side. "You think the mom will come back?"

He looked at the helpless child in the seat beside her. He knew what it was like to get lost in the system, to have no one looking out for you. "That's what I'm praying for."

"And then what?"

"Then what?" He ran his hand back through his hair. He hadn't really given it that much thought. His whole time in the foster system, he'd dreamt of a day when someone would show up and give him a family. "Then she gives this baby a chance for a real family. We help her get counseling and support. We help her choose a solid adoption solution, not leaving the baby hanging in the system as they work it out piece by piece. We do whatever we can to see that she finds it in her to put Amanda's needs first."

Shelby reached across the table, her fingertips brushing his. "You don't think the state social services can do that?"

"I think they want to. They mean to. They will try, but in the end, not even the best intentions can make up for being in a home with people who love you and want you to be a part of their family forever." It was more revealing than he had meant it to be. He had a lot of respect for all the people who tried to help improve the lives of children, but respect was not the same as coming to terms with his past. Admitting that to himself made him suddenly question his own motives for...well, everything.

"Sorry for your wait, folks. But I'm here now to take care of y'all." A dead ringer for the imaginary waitress Jax had first expected to find at the Crosspoint Café appeared at the table, order pad in hand. "Just tell me what your little heart desires."

"Something I know I'll never be able to have," Jax whispered as he looked at Shelby and the baby.

"What's that you say, honey?" The redheaded waitress crinkled up her nose at him.

"He's been joking that he wants everything on the menu," Shelby chimed in, shaking her head as she looked over the specials clipped to the laminated page in her hands.

The waitress laughed. "Well, all righty then. How about I go get a couple of cups of coffee and give you more time?"

More time. That was what his heart desired. More

time for Amanda and whoever had left her. *That* was what was needed. The waitress couldn't get it for Jax. But maybe he could find a way to get it for himself.

Chapter Six

It was just after 10:00 a.m. when Jax pulled the minivan into the lot next to the decades-old social services building just behind the county courthouse in Westmoreland. He had to cruise through the lot twice to find a spot, and when he did, it was in a far corner. He pulled into the spot, but his hand hovered over the key before the finality of shutting the engine off. It was only a slight hesitation, but it was all he would allow himself.

He looked at Shelby as if to ask, "Are you sure we don't just want to take her back to Sunnyside?"

Shelby heaved a resigned sigh.

The brake creaked as he set it just before he tugged out the key. Jax moved swiftly from that point on, getting Amanda out and carrying her up the outside steps and through the halls cluttered with people in various stages of getting or giving assistance.

"So much need," Shelby whispered. "Doesn't it make you wish you could do something to help?"

"I do…" Jax cut his words short. He had meant to say, *I do what I can,* but that was no longer true. In the police force, he had served others each and every day, no matter what their circumstances were. If he took a job doing security for a wealthy community in Miami, would he still feel that same sense of service?

Before he could concoct an answer he could live with, they crossed the threshold into a waiting room outside an office. In a flash, Jax felt nine years old again. It was as if his mom had just died weeks ago, and no family member could take him in. He was just an unwanted kid with nowhere else to go.

A knot twisted low in his gut. He clenched his teeth to force himself not to go there. He tightened his grip on the handle of the baby carrier. Amanda's situation was not the same as his. Her fate would be so much better.

Please, he prayed silently as he looked at the face of the child who had come so unexpectedly into his life. *Please give Amanda a life full of love and hope.*

"Jax?" Shelby put her hand on his arm.

It surprised him, and he roused from the intensity of the moment to find those blue eyes riveted on him. Even with his heart in turmoil, Shelby's presence made him smile.

"I was saying a prayer for Amanda's future," he confessed quietly.

Her hand closed on his forearm. She smiled, but her eyes remained somber. "I've been doing that all morning."

Always a man of action, Jax used that shared concern to act as an advocate on Amanda's behalf. "Shelby, it sounds like we both aren't sure this is the right thing for Amanda. Maybe we should—"

"Right this way." A silver-haired woman wearing a comfy suit and a ready smile appeared in the doorway and motioned for them to follow her.

She looked kind, motherly even. Jax tried to focus on that as the social worker asked Shelby questions and took notes in an open file, entering data into a computer. But all he could think about was how it felt to be that little boy sitting in a big chair, hearing secondhand the hard reality that his family wasn't ever coming back for him.

His focus shifted to Amanda, sleeping soundly in her carrier. She would have no memory of this day, but one day she would have to come to grips with the reality of it. Or she would wrestle with it for the rest of her life.

Amanda kicked. Her tiny fist opened and closed, and Jax could practically feel those tiny fingers closing around his heart. He couldn't help all those people in the hallways. He no longer served the people as a police officer. But he could do something for this little baby.

That was what was in his head when the social worker began talking to Shelby about the overload of cases, the cutbacks they had all had to make. He couldn't help making quick assessments as the state worker explained about the dearth of foster homes able to take in infants.

"I've never handled a child abandonment case myself," Jax heard himself interjecting into the middle of the conversation, one where he had no business offering anything but support. "But I do know from the other side of things that a lot of times, the state looks for a relative or a trusted person in the community to step up and care for the baby until something more can be resolved."

The social worker cocked her head and looked Jax over slowly, nodding. He didn't know if she was mulling over his conclusion or sizing him up as a former foster kid.

Shelby didn't look at him at all.

But Jax had no doubt as to her opinion of his not-so-subtle observation an hour later, when the two of them were headed out the door of the government building with a file full of paperwork in one hand and Amanda in her carrier in the other.

"Don't be mad, Shelby. It's not permanent."

"You just don't get it." Shelby stormed ahead, her feet hitting the pavement like they were in a pounding competition with her heart.

"Was I wrong? The social worker agreed it would be ideal for Amanda to remain in Sunnyside, where she was left, just in case the mother comes looking for her." He reached for the handle of the carrier to lift it from her.

"I didn't say you were wrong." Shelby deftly evaded his grasp, her gaze fixed on the minivan at the far end of the still crowded lot. "I wouldn't have agreed to it if I thought you were wrong."

"What then?" His long stride overtook her quick steps easily. This time, when he wrapped his hand around the carrier handle, Shelby had no choice but to stop in her tracks. He pulled the carrier gently toward him. "Tell me, Shelby. I can't fix this unless I know what it's about."

"Fix it?" She wound her fingers around the handle, feeling her resistance to letting go work all the way up from the small of her back to her shoulder and down to her white knuckles. She had no idea what to think of this man. First, he had all but volunteered her to put all her plans, even if they were non-plans, and all her life, which in the big picture was also more of a non-life, on hold and to take on the care of a whole tiny other person indefinitely. But when he realized that might create a problem for her, was he actually willing to do something about it? "What do you mean? You want to fix the situation, or you want to fix me so I won't mind the situation?"

"Fix you?" He laughed and shook his head. "There ain't nothing wrong with you, Shelby Grace."

Heat flashed through her cheeks at his bold yet sweet remark.

"You said I didn't 'get' why doing what's right for Amanda has you so worked up," he went on, gentleman enough not to mention her girlish blush. "I want to fix that. I want to do what's right, not just for Amanda, but for you, too."

Shelby studied his face for a moment. She had no reason to believe him, not given her track record with trusting men who only told her what she wanted to hear. But she did believe him. She believed him with all her heart.

"I wish you'd have thought of that before you volunteered me to be Amanda's foster mom." The weight that she felt had settled onto her shoulders rolled off as she finally expressed what had been troubling her since… well, ever since she could remember. "It's not that I don't want to do the right thing, that I wouldn't sacrifice whatever I had to for someone I love or someone in need. I'd just like to be the one to offer, not to just find it all laid on my doorstep with the expectation that softhearted Shelby will take up the slack. Does that make sense?"

His cheek twitched. He looked at the baby between them, then out toward the minivan. At last his gaze returned to her, and he nodded slowly. "You want your life to be your own."

Shelby smiled. "Actually, I'd like to think my life is the Lord's. But that doesn't mean that I don't have dreams, Jax. They may be small ones, not like you and your big job in Miami, but they're mine and I'd like the chance to follow them."

"I said I'd stick around long enough to find a temporary foster home for Amanda," he reminded her, his hand still clasping the handle, the toes of his cowboy boots just inches away from the cross-trainers she considered her best choice for travel shoes. "I never once said it would be with you."

"In Sunnyside?" Shelby used both hands to keep Amanda and the carrier in her possession. She did not whine. She did not scold. She simply stated what everyone who had ever known her knew. "Who else would it be with? Any other place you might find would just be a stop on the way to my doorstep."

"Is it so bad, really? As I recall, an hour ago you were the girl who wanted to help all these people." He motioned to the scads of cars around them. He paused long enough for his calling her to task to sink in, then gently took the carrier, put one hand on Shelby's back and escorted her toward the minivan. "You can't help them, but then, isn't the saying that charity begins at home?"

"Home!" She stopped and put her hand to her head. The dull ache between her shoulder blades from handling the baby in her carrier crept upward to her neck and the base of her head. "I don't even have one of those."

"What do you mean?"

"Only that I have...*had* the cutest apartment over a garage in my rent bracket in all of Sunnyside." She dragged her feet the rest of the way to the minivan as the reality sank in. "Maybe the only apartment, garage or otherwise, in my rent bracket in Sunnyside. And I broke my lease on it yesterday."

"Then unbreak it." He opened the side door and began to get Amanda settled in the car seat.

"Right. Unbreak it." She looked at the minivan she had bought with such big expectations. She'd ended up saddled with it and a truck payment. Last night she had thought she had finally gotten up the courage to walk away from responsibilities that others had chosen for her. Today she had not only all those, but a whole raft of new ones, too.

Unfortunately, once something is broken—be it a heart or trust or promises—it was not easy to return it to the way it was.

The drive back was quiet. Jax drove. Amanda slept. Shelby plotted.

At least that was what he thought she was doing over in the passenger seat with her phone in her hands, her fingers flying over the screen. More than once she called up the calculator function, tapped in some numbers and then raised her head and stared off into the distance.

He wanted to offer a penny for her thoughts, but it seemed grossly undervalued given the circumstances.

"You know, Shelby, I've been thinking," he ventured as they pulled into the parking lot of the Truck Stop Inn and the Crosspoint Café, and she finally closed the calculator screen. "What if we set up a fund to help take care of Amanda? I'd be happy to pitch in what I can now, and once I'm in Miami—"

He cut his thought short as he slowed the minivan to a crawl in the lot. He had to do both to avoid running over the toes of half the town of Sunnyside.

"I think that's a great idea." Shelby waved to a group of high school girls holding up signs advertising a car wash. "Apparently you aren't the first to think of it!"

He guided the minivan through the crowd, and when they glided past the gas pumps, he rolled down his window to greet Miss Delta, who was shaking a jar full of money like a set of maracas.

"Sneak out of town for a few hours and lookie what happens!" she said with a smile.

Shelby laughed and leaned over to talk to her through Jax's window. "Did you organize all this after Tyler got my text saying I was going to foster Amanda for a while?"

"Now, you know better than that, darlin'. Nobody in this town would have to wait to lend a hand if a hand needed lending!" She shook her head. "Nope. Soon as word got out about the baby, your daddy got out his biggest tip jar, set it smack down on the counter and told everyone who had ever skipped out on giving him or you a gratuity they had better pay up, because every cent was going to help that sweet little baby."

Shelby shut her eyes for a moment.

Jax gripped the steering wheel as he replayed Shelby's dismay at having others always assume what she would do and charging ahead to do it in her stead. He shifted in the seat and opened his mouth, not quite sure what he was going to say.

Before he made a sound, Shelby chuckled. A smile broke over her face. She shook her head. "And that, right there, is why my daddy will never save enough money to buy the Crosspoint Café, much less buy a truck or get his dream horse ranch running. Bless his big ol' heart."

Jax relaxed. "So you're okay with this?"

"I'm okay," she said, so softly that he more saw her lips form the words than heard her.

He reached out to put his hand on her shoulder in a show of support.

Outside the minivan, people cheered their return to

town. Money jangled in Miss Delta's hand. Shelby practically glowed with pride over her father's gesture.

Jax marveled at the love and generosity surrounding them. He'd never known anything like it. And in his new line of work, private security for the ultrarich, he would not likely see it again.

He dropped his hand away from Shelby's shoulder. Moments later, after they parked, he took the carrier holding Amanda.

"Is that her? Let us see, Shelby. Can I hold her?" people called as they pushed toward the minivan to get a peek at the baby.

Shelby turned to him. "I…uh…"

"Amanda has already had a lot of excitement today." Jax stepped up with his hand up to keep people at bay. Shelby might not need him for support, but she still needed someone to help her stand up for herself, and for Amanda. "I know most of you don't know me, but Sheriff Denby deputized me to help out with this case. That makes this baby my charge until further notice."

Shelby rushed to help him get Amanda out of her carrier. Their hands practically tangled as they unbuckled the child and removed her from the blanket. Finally, she lifted the baby out and placed her carefully with Jax. For just that instant, he, Shelby and Amanda seemed like the only people on the face of the earth.

They appeared to have a special bond that nobody could breach. It felt like a promise fulfilled. Was this what it was like to have a family?

The fact that he even asked himself that question startled Jax. He looked deeply into Shelby's blue eyes, hoping to find an answer there.

She smiled up at him tentatively before the crowd

started to close in around them, cooing and laughing, oohing and aahing over the helpless human being cradled in his arms. The feeling dissipated—or maybe it expanded.

"So if y'all don't mind," he went on as he curled the baby close to his chest, "*I'll* be holding Amanda, and you can all come around and introduce yourselves—to both of us."

For the first time in his life, Jax went from being part of a family to part of a community. And he *liked* it.

Talk about sending up a red flag. Those were not emotions that he could afford. Contrary to what Miss Delta thought, Jax did not belong here. At least not for more than another day or so—however long it took to get Shelby and Amanda settled in a new place and the case on the right track.

"And if anyone has any information that might help us figure out who left this little sweetheart here last night, I'd appreciate you sharing it with me in the next twenty-four hours," he said good and loud, to be heard over all the chatter.

"Why the next twenty-four hours?" Shelby asked, standing on tiptoe and leaning against him as she reached in to slip a pacifier into Amanda's pudgy mouth.

"Because as soon as I gather as much info as I can and make sure you two have a safe place to stay, my work here will be done."

Chapter Seven

Frantic fund-raising, topped off with a chili supper at the café and countless recountings of the session with the social worker, had filled the rest of the day and evening. After inhaling a meal, Shelby had whisked the baby back to the Denby household. Everybody understood that she had definitely earned and needed a chance to rest and regroup. Jax had intended to follow, making the excuse that he wanted to discuss the case further with the sheriff, but Doc Lovey had put her foot down. No visitors.

"Our girls have had enough for one day, don't you think, Deputy?" she had asked in a drawl as big as Texas itself. It was fitting coming from a rawboned redhead who looked more suited to the role of cowgirl veterinarian than town physician.

"*Our* girls?" Jax had asked as he watched Shelby load the baby into the minivan amid a circle of friends and well-wishers.

Doc Lovey had pressed her hand to his back and had given him a pat, explaining, "The whole town has fallen in love with that baby girl now, sweet thing. And we all laid claim to Shelby Grace when she wasn't much older than little Amanda is today. They're in our hearts now and for always, right where they belong."

"But I reckon that's a sentiment you understand, isn't it?" Miss Delta had appeared at his side and had looped her arm through his like they were good ol' pals from way back.

Jax had been gazing into the distance, trying to decide how he wanted to answer that, when something caught his eye. A Mustang with faded red paint, like the one Tyler had described as having been at the gas pumps the night Amanda was abandoned. His first instinct was to push through the crowd and try to chase it down on foot, but even as the energy to do so coiled tightly in his body, the car eased its way along and reached the exit onto the main road. He had to give up on the idea. He'd never reach the car in time, and his actions would tip off the driver that someone was watching them.

After all, this person could be the key to securing Amanda's future. At the very least, it could be this Mitch guy, someone who had hurt Shelby in the past. Either way, they seemed comfortable coming and going in the community for now, and Jax wanted to keep it that way until he got the chance to talk to them.

"Yes, ma'am," Jax said, finally answering Miss Delta's question, and with much more conviction than he had felt a few minutes earlier. "I believe I do understand, a little."

He wasn't just saying that. That small change haunted Jax through the rest of the evening spending time with the locals.

That night he dreamt of palm trees and ocean breezes and giant babies with gold-plated pacifiers. He dreamt of chasing red cars in a minivan that couldn't quite keep up.

And Shelby. Wherever his dreams took him that night, Shelby was there, Amanda in her arms.

So it seemed the most natural thing in the world for his whole mood to lighten when he spotted them in the back of Miss Delta's store, in front of the community bulletin board, bright and early the next morning.

"Good morning, beautiful!" He raised his hand in greeting as he came up to them.

"Jax! Shhhh." Shelby ripped off a phone number from an Apartment for Rent flyer, glancing around them. "It's not that I'm not flattered, but you've seen how fast gossip spreads in this town. I do not need anyone thinking there is anything between us but—"

"Amanda," he said, finishing for her, then squatting down to stroke the head of the baby happily gurgling in her carrier on the floor near Shelby's feet. "I was talking to Amanda."

"Oh." She blushed from the collar of her Texas Longhorns T-shirt to the tips of her adorable ears. Pushing her hair back from her eyes, she acted as if she suddenly found the phone number and info on the one-bedroom apartment fascinating.

"Though you are pretty easy on the eyes yourself." He stood and grinned at her. "And I don't care who knows I think so."

"Thank you, but I think you're being generous. Maybe you didn't see the dark circles under my eyes." She scanned the flyer again, running her finger along the line that included the monthly cost. Without comment, she shook her head and crumpled up the phone number. "Turns out one of *Amanda's* beauty secrets involves getting plenty of exercise, mostly by screaming, kicking and crying all night long."

"Is she okay?" Jax went down to peer into the carrier again. He placed the back of his hand to the baby's forehead, not actually sure what he would feel if she had a temperature, or what he would do about it.

"Doc Lovey looked her over and said she seems fine." Shelby knelt down beside Jax. She fussed with the small quilt cushioning the now sleeping baby. "Maybe it's because of a change in formula or all the travel or just being overly tired from her big day. Doc's advice was to note how often it happens, keep a journal of feedings and so on…and to find an apartment with very thick walls."

Jax chuckled at that.

"Right now I'd settle for an apartment I can afford."

"Well, I don't know how thick the walls are." Miss Delta poked her head around the corner of the wall where the notices were posted. "But I do have a place where I think you'd be happy—and the price is right."

"Miss Delta, are you sure?" Shelby strolled through the hallway of Miss Delta's rambling Victorian home. "You've always been so protective of your privacy, which is no small feat here in Sunnyside. Renting a room to us when Amanda has sort of been adopted by the whole town is kind of like throwing the doors open to everyone, isn't it?"

"Are you kidding, honey? I'd love for folks to think they can come over for a visit whenever they please." Miss Delta ushered them into the large kitchen. She directed Shelby to settle Amanda on the table and take a seat. "Ever since I inherited this place from my late aunt and uncle, I dreamed of filling it with a big family. But since Mr. Right never came to Sunnyside, I missed out on that for myself."

"If Mr. Right didn't show up here, why didn't you go looking for him?" Shelby got Amanda situated, then sat and took a good look around at the bright, roomy old-fashioned eat-in kitchen, which already felt like home to her. "Or for whatever it was you wanted in life?"

"Because I had what I wanted in life—people who love me, work I enjoy, a home. Fetch me some tall glasses from up there, won't you, Jax honey?" She pointed to an upper cabinet, then reached into the refrigerator and pulled out a big pitcher of iced tea. "I wanted a Mr. Right to add to my life, not to make it from me."

Was that meant as a message to Shelby? What did Miss Delta know about the plans Amanda's arrival had disrupted? Shelby shifted restlessly in her seat.

"Besides, even if Mr. Right did show up here, I suppose there was always a chance he wouldn't stick around." Miss Delta took the glasses from Jax and clunked them down on the counter. "Not everyone finds the sense of belonging in Sunnyside that I do. Wouldn't you agree, Jax?"

Jax cocked his head.

Another message. No denying it. Shelby crossed her arms. "Miss Delta, much as I appreciate this offer, I'm afraid my moving in here with a baby for an indefinite amount of time will be too disruptive for you."

"Don't you see, Shelby? That's why you *should* move in here. I could use a little disruption in my routine." She waved her hands to shoo the man toward the refreshments on the table as she smiled impishly at him and said, "Everybody can, don't you think, Jax honey?"

If he planned on answering that, they'd never know, as Miss Delta directed him wordlessly to the large pitcher of tea and went on talking to Shelby.

"For years this quiet old house has been my sanctuary." She raised her head for a moment, as if listening for something, but only silence answered her. "A place where the woman every single person in town feels they can order around gives the orders."

"Order around? *You?*" Jax scoffed, setting the pitcher on the table next to the glasses without having poured a drop.

"When you run a business like mine in Sunnyside, you become like a mama to everyone who walks through the doors, young man." She grabbed the pitcher by the handle and raised it, as if offering him a toast, before she tipped it and began pouring out the icy amber liquid. "And they have expectations that like a mama, I will always be there to do what they need doing."

"And like a mama, you don't hesitate to tell them what you think about how they are running their lives," Jax observed, sidling up next to her to relieve her of the heavy pitcher and take over tea pouring duties.

"And like most kids, even full-grown ones, they do not always listen to my wise advice." She scowled at his intrusion but did not fight his assistance.

"Oh, all right, all right. I'll take a room with you." Shelby got it. The whole stubbornness about accepting help, the hidden messages about how her life might end up like Miss Delta's—not one bit of the subtext had missed her attention. That didn't mean she couldn't still make her own decisions concerning what she did about it. "But I *am* paying rent."

"You don't have to pay me anything." Miss Delta picked up the glass of tea that Jax had just finished pouring and set it down decisively in front of Shelby. "In fact,

I think you should quit the café and take care of Amanda full-time while she's with us."

"Miss Delta, as the town mama, I'm shocked you didn't hear that I already quit the café." She lifted the glass and took a sip, giving that time to sink in.

Miss Delta took a seat at the table even as she raised her finely plucked eyebrows in surprise. "I had heard a rumor, but you know that as a good Christian woman, I don't take stock in town gossip."

"You know it's not gossip when I tell you that I have been saving money since I was a teenager. I have enough to…" *To get me out of Sunnyside and into a whole new life.* Shelby thought of her savings tucked away, half in the local bank, half in her suitcase. Now that that plan had fallen by the wayside, Shelby decided she didn't want anyone in town knowing about it. It would only make for another story about how Shelby's big heart always got in the way of her big dreams. "Enough to allow me not to work and to take care of Amanda for a while *and* pay you some rent. And she is a ward of the state, so her needs will be taken care of financially. So I *have* to pay rent."

"All right." Miss Delta threw up her hands, then pushed back her chair. "If y'all will excuse me a minute, I want to go upstairs and make sure your room is ready before I show you to it."

Miss Delta's magnolia-scented perfume had not faded from the air when Jax braced both palms flat on the table and leaned in close over Shelby to say, "She's going to take whatever money you give her and hold it back for you, you know."

"I know." She searched his face and got lost for a second in the warmth of his brown eyes, in the way his mouth seemed just about to break into a grin. Her pulse thudded in her ears fast, then faster. Suddenly the fact that he was so close she could notice all these things made her panic. She shot up from her chair, trying to put herself on a more equal footing with him. "I'm surprised you figured that out about Miss Delta, though. You've only been in town a few days, but already you seem to know folks."

He did not step back, as she had expected he would. "There are some folks I'd like to know better."

"Some folks take time to know—to really know them." With anyone else, she would have retreated a step, maybe all the way across the room. But with this man, she didn't feel the need to back down, to try to do as everyone expected and give in to the image of soft-hearted Shelby. Her newfound confidence rushed out in her voice as she added, "Even then, I bet they could surprise you."

"Yeah? People don't usually surprise me at all. The idea of someone I could never completely figure out is…" He inched close, until his face was over hers. Not quite as if about to kiss her, but as if making the promise of a kiss to come.

Shelby took in a deep breath.

The doorbell rang. Shelby jumped and pulled away from Jax so quickly, she bumped the table.

Amanda roused and began to fuss quietly.

"I know that sound. If I don't calm her down right now, she's going to work herself up into a wail." Shelby practically dove for the baby.

Jax headed down the hallway toward the front door. His footsteps stopped as the door creaked open and Sheriff Denby's voice bellowed, "So here's where everyone got to! Came into the café and Truck Stop Inn to catch up on the case with my newest deputy and ended up talking to myself!"

"About the case," Jax said, sounding not the least bit distracted by what had just happened. "Maybe you and I could have a word alone?"

"Alone? In Sunnyside?" The sheriff laughed softly over the sound of his keys jingling. "'Less you plan to accuse one Shelby of leaving that baby herself—again—or call Miss Delta a conspirator…"

Miss Delta came hurrying down the stairway to the foyer and stood with her hands on both hips right where Jax could see her. Shelby hoisted Amanda onto her shoulder and, patting the baby's back, took up a position right behind Miss Delta.

Jax shot a look straight past the older woman, targeting Shelby. His cheek twitched, and then he sighed and shook his head. "I just think not enough's been done to find that red car, the one Tyler thought belonged to Shelby's ex-boyfriend."

"You don't know what I've been up to while you were…" The older man gave the younger man a slap on the back and concluded pointedly, "Taking care of the girls here, son. I've known Mitch Warner since I had to give him his first talking to for rowdyism while he was still in middle school. I've made it known that I want a word with him. It may take him a while, but he'll give me a shout."

Jax looked at the sheriff, then at Miss Delta, then at Shelby and the baby. He clenched his jaw, then exhaled. "Okay then. Looks to me like everything that *can* be done has been done."

"The social worker said that statistically, mothers are

usually reported or turn themselves in, in cases like this," Shelby offered. "So from here on out, it's just a matter of waiting, right?"

"Yup." Sheriff Andy's thinning white hair shone almost ghostly in the bright sunlight streaming in from the window of the front door. "No idea how long it might take. If you want to stick around and wait it out, Stroud, I could use an experienced deputy around here. Been looking for one I could train to run for sheriff one day, finally let me retire."

Jax shook his head. "Much as I'd like to see how all this turns out, I have a job waiting for me in Florida."

"Dream job," Shelby reminded him softly.

"What?" He homed in on her as if it were just the two of them standing there.

"When you talked about it before, you said it was your dream job," she reminded him.

"Oh, did I? Yeah. I guess." He ducked his head slightly and ran his hand through his dark hair like a cowboy who suddenly wished he had a nice wide hat brim to hide under to get out of the directness of her gaze. "Except, after the dream I had about it last night, I'm hoping I'm wrong about that."

"Well, if you're going to be hitting the road, son, I'm going to need your badge." Sheriff Andy seemed oblivious to the quiet intensity of the exchange between Jax and Shelby. He held out one beefy hand to the man.

"It was only temporary." Jax handed the badge back. "I don't even know why I pulled off at your exit that night, anyway."

"Probably because you realized there was something in Sunnyside you needed," Miss Delta offered, reaching out to give the man's arms a squeeze.

Jax frowned. Not an angry frown, but the kind a man made when he wasn't quite sure what was being said to him, or how to respond.

"She means you were hungry or tired or thirsty," Shelby explained, giving Miss Delta a warning glare not to try to make more of this than it warranted, especially on Shelby's behalf.

"Yeah, that's what I said. There was something that you knew you couldn't get on that long, dark highway." The squeeze turned into a pat. "Something that you knew wasn't waiting for you at the end of your trip."

Jax studied Miss Delta for a moment. He did not contradict her. Or laugh at her conclusions.

Amanda drew her knees up and waved her fists, gurgling red faced against Shelby's tensed shoulder.

"Maybe you're right, Miss Delta," was all Jax said before he leaned over and gave the wriggling baby a kiss on the head. As he did, his eyes met Shelby's.

It seemed like the whole house fell silent for far too long before Sheriff Andy stepped up, lifted Amanda from Shelby's hold and said, "Didn't you get all that cantankerousness out of you last night, little one? Let Uncle Andy take you for a walk and see if we can't improve your mood."

"Hang on. I'm coming with you. We'll take her upstairs and pick out which room will be her nursery." Miss Delta swept her hand out, directing the sheriff along ahead of her. She put one foot on the bottom step, then turned to Jax. "I'd say goodbye, but I have a feeling I'm going to see *you* again. Whatever led you here? This truck stop mama does not believe you found it yet."

Jax opened his mouth to reply, but Miss Delta had whipped around and hurried up the stairs, calling out to Sheriff Andy to go to the room all the way at the end of the hall and see if he didn't think it was meant for Shelby and Amanda.

That left the pair of them standing alone in the foyer.

"I guess this is the part where I thank you for everything you've done to help me with Amanda." Shelby started to hold her hand out for a firm goodbye handshake. When he kept his hands stuffed in his pockets, she quickly pretended she needed to tuck a strand of hair behind her ear.

"I didn't do anything, really, except some really fancy minivan driving." He held his hands up, as if steering the van, grinned and gave her a wink.

"You looked good doing it." She laughed.

"Naw…" He feigned humility.

"You did. You *know* you did," she teased. "And you gave me a few hours of fun at Buffalo Betty's, which I hadn't had in forever. I'll always be grateful for that."

"You say it like you don't expect to have any fun again for a long time."

"Well, I do have some responsibilities," she said softly. "So I…uh…just want to say…"

Only she couldn't say it.

Jax nodded. "Me too."

"I didn't say anything," she protested.

"You didn't have to. Remember, I know what folks are thinking." He smiled, tapping his temple. He turned his back and reached for the doorknob.

Selby paused for a moment, not sure what to do next. She'd been stalling, just hoping that somehow she'd suddenly find a way to tell Jax how much his brief time in her life had meant to her. She wanted the nerve to let him know she wished they had met at a different time, under different circumstances.

If Shelby needed to tell him anything—and she wasn't exactly sure what she wanted to tell him—she had to do it now. "Or maybe you just *think* you know what people are thinking, because that means you can keep thinking instead of feeling what you don't want to be feeling."

He froze in his tracks. "I don't know how I feel about what I think you just said."

Shelby didn't even know what she'd said, and when she realized that, she broke into laughter. Jax joined in. It was the kind of laugh that people share to break the tension, sweet and a little bit silly. It created one last special moment just between them. Just what they needed to bring things to an amicable end.

"It's really been good getting to know you, Shelby Grace."

Know her? Jackson Stroud was never going to really know her. He was going to drive away and take his dream job in Miami, believing she was nothing more than what the town saw—softhearted Shelby. He'd never see the woman she so desperately longed to become. He'd never know that she had bigger dreams than being a waitress and that she had had, if only for a brief moment on a dark, momentous night, the courage to follow them. He'd never know that unless…

"Goodbye, Jackson Stroud. I'll be praying for you. Have a safe trip, and don't forget us." She went up on tiptoe and, with every ounce of her fleeting confidence, kissed him once on the lips.

And, unbeknownst to him, she slipped the note she had meant to leave on the door of the Crosspoint Café that night they met into his pocket.

"Goodbye, Shelby."

Chapter Eight

He was two full tanks of gas and an empty stomach down the road before Jax had any reason to reach into his pocket to pull out some spare change to pay for a snack at the gas station.

"Hey, Mister! You dropped something." The kid in line behind him stopped to retrieve a wrinkled piece of paper folded in quarters.

"That can't be mine. It's…" He looked closer. He recognized that paper. It was the note Shelby had had in her hand when she came to the café door, crying, on the night they found Amanda. He took it from the kid's hand. "It's not supposed to be in my pocket. Thanks for spotting that."

He glanced back at the soft drink and bag of chips in the young man's hands and told the clerk he wanted to pay for those as well as his own.

"You don't have to do that," the kid said. "It was just a piece of paper."

"You didn't have to say anything when you saw I dropped this. And to me, it's more than just a piece of paper." Jax had no idea how much more until he got back

into his truck, settled in with his snack and opened the
folded page right there in the gas station parking lot.

*To whom it may concern—plus a whole lot of people
it doesn't concern but who will want to know about it,
anyway.*

Jax couldn't help but smile at Shelby's unmistakable
style.

I love you all.

Jax paused and just let his eyes rest on the phrase a
moment. It was so simple and yet so all-encompassing.
And he did not doubt for one second that Shelby meant
it. She really did love whoever she thought would end
up reading this letter.

Of course she hadn't even met Jax when she wrote
those words.

*I love this town. But it's pretty clear that if I ever hope
to make a life for myself, I can't stay here any longer. I
think it's time I followed my own dreams. Don't worry
about me. I've got all your love and all you've taught me
coming with me, starting with these three rules:*

1. Never forget that with God all things are possible.

2. Never let anyone else tell me what I "should" feel.

3. Never, ever trust a cowboy.

Jax scowled. He could actually see the brim of his
cowboy hat lying on the seat beside him from the corner of his eye. His stomach clenched.

She had all but told him the first two, but the man who
thought he knew everybody's motivations had missed
the third.

I mean it. No cowboys. I don't need the heartache.

"Heartache," he murmured. It was not a term he ever
wanted to associate with Shelby Grace.

See, good old softhearted Shelby has learned a thing

or two over the years. So don't worry about me. I'll be in touch when I find someplace to start again where I can be the person I am meant to be.

For now, I leave you with my love and prayers.

Shelby Grace Lockhart

Jax ran his fingertips over the round, careful penmanship of Shelby's name. He remembered the tears in her eyes the night she had intended to leave this for her father and friends to find. These words had cost her dearly, and she had given them to him and him alone.

It was a humbling responsibility she had given him. A gift of insight and a secret that so few people would ever have trusted with a stranger. He folded the note in half, then in half again. He reached over and pushed the button to open the truck's glove compartment, but even before the thing could spring completely open, he flicked it shut again.

Not just any stranger, he thought as he looked beyond the note to the Stetson on the seat. Jax never thought of himself as a cowboy, but he sure did look like one that night outside the café. And Shelby had found a way to trust him, eventually, in a way she trusted no one else.

Jax's actions had curtailed her attempt to leave town, to make that fresh start, but more importantly, he'd left her sleepless and emotionally vulnerable in that town, with the cowboy who had broken Shelby's heart still out there.

He tucked the note in his shirt pocket and started the truck's engine. In minutes he was heading back in the direction he had just come from, unfazed by the long hours of driving ahead. He knew his responsibility in Sunnyside was not done, and prayed that he wasn't too late to be worthy of Shelby's trust.

* * *

It had taken hours for Shelby to fall asleep, but when she had, she had slept so soundly that she didn't hear her cell phone ring in the middle of the night. She glanced at the "unavailable" number the next morning as she fed Amanda a bottle.

She stifled a yawn and dismissed it out loud to Miss Delta as the older woman headed off to work. "Usually when I get a call with a hidden ID, it's someone trying to sell me something. I'm not going to worry about it."

"That's smart, honey. You can't do anything about it if you don't know who it was. They'll call again if it's important. Especially if it was whoever left Amanda." Miss Delta stopped to do one more check of her blond hair and peachy lipstick in the mirror before she snatched up her huge pink faux alligator purse, slung it over her shoulder and hurried out the door.

A chill swept over Shelby's exhausted body. Could it be? She hoisted the baby onto her shoulder. After only three days, Amanda had already become part of Shelby's life and had taken a piece of her heart, and maybe a bit of her memory, as Shelby had all but stopped thinking about a birth mother out there possibly wanting to make contact.

"I had sort of gotten used to the idea that you'd be with me awhile, Amanda sweetie. I want what's best for you, of course, but…I guess I was hoping *I* was what was best for you."

No sleep. No Jax. No job. And the idea taking seed in her head that Amanda's mother had her number and had used it. It was no wonder that Shelby decided she'd let somebody else make her breakfast that morning.

"If you came to get your job back, you're too late,"

her dad called out through the service window between the counter and the kitchen the minute Shelby walked through the doors of the Crosspoint Café.

"That fast?" Shelby hustled in and settled the baby carrier down in the first empty booth, then slid in with her back to the morning mayhem of the only breakfast joint in town. "I know it's hard times out there, but I can't believe anyone in Sunnyside would be *that* quick to grab my old job."

"Who said I hired someone from Sunnyside?" her dad shot back over the clunk of a couple of heavy plates being set down. "Order up!"

"I got it. I got it," came a familiar male voice that made Shelby sit up and twist around in the seat.

"Jax!"

Jackson Stroud lifted two plates piled high with eggs, bacon and hash browns in both hands. "Got hungry people waiting. I'll be over to take orders from you—that is, to take your order—in a minute, Miss Shelby Grace."

He was dressed in a long white bib apron, which covered his blue shirt and jeans, and his hair was a jumble of waves. The dark stubble on his face provided a contrast to the whiteness of his teeth as he flashed a broad grin at her.

Shelby's heart melted then and there. She honestly could not have imagined a single person she would have rather seen this morning than the one man who could help her figure out who had called last night and what to do about it. And he looked so adorable, too.

Once he'd set the plates down at a nearby table and asked how everything looked, he made his way to her side. Crouching beside her seat, he withdrew a pad and pencil from the pocket of his apron and finally looked right into her eyes. "What would you like, Shelby?"

To know everything is going to be all right. Then, gazing into the eyes of this man who was still here when *here* was not where his own dreams led him, Shelby sighed. Maybe everything wouldn't be all right, but this moment was right. Maybe that would be enough. "I'd like to know what you are doing here."

He chuckled softly and dropped his gaze to the floor, shaking his head. "I read your note."

"Oh." Her stomach clenched.

"And I just couldn't be another cowboy that let you down."

She whispered a thank-you, knowing that was not big enough to cover the depth of her gratitude.

He smiled, just a little, and acknowledged her thanks with a nod.

She wanted to say it again, and then again. She wanted him to know just how much it meant to have someone know the real her and still have come back to—

The reality of it all hit her just then. Jax had read her note. He was the only person who knew her secret—that she thought she would never have the life of her dreams if she stayed in the place where everyone cared about her so much. She pressed her lips together for a moment to muster her courage, then said, too quietly for anyone else to hear, "I gave that to you only because I thought I'd never see you again, and that you'd never see anyone here again. I just wanted one person to know how I felt, not how I was supposed to feel."

"I'm honored to be the first person to know that. Though *you* know how you feel, Shelby. That's some-thing some folks never really figure out. But you?" He shook his head. His smile came slowly. He didn't just look at her; he met her gaze and they connected there. "You know who you are, girl. So I'm technically the second person who knows."

It wasn't particularly eloquently put, but it said it all. She knew who she was. "No one in my life has ever gotten that, Jax."

"Don't worry. I won't tell anyone what was in the note. I know it was a big deal that you picked me."

Shelby had picked him. Out of all the people she could have told who would have understood, she had chosen Jax.

"I'm sorry if I made a mess of your plans," he said.

"No! You didn't. You *couldn't*."

"I think I did." He shook his head. Even through the aroma of thick-cut bacon in the air, his motion brought with it the scent of fresh soap and men's aftershave. "First, by sticking my nose in the meeting with the social worker so that you ended up having to stay here to take care of Amanda, and then by leaving you before that situation was really resolved."

"No, don't feel bad about that. It was the right thing to do. Look at her." She reached into the carrier and lifted out her precious charge. "I was only fooling myself to think I could have left her in Westmoreland with strangers and taken off to follow my own bliss."

"Hi, cutie." Jax brushed his knuckle over the baby's plump cheek. "Miss me?"

Amanda's smile lit her whole small face.

Jax did not just reflect its light, but joined it with a grin that made Shelby actually laugh softly.

Amanda reached up and wrapped her hand around Jax's bent finger.

"I think she did." Jax laughed. "I think she did miss me."

She wasn't the only one, Shelby wished she had the courage to say.

Still smiling, he tugged free from Amanda's hold and stood at last. "You can tell me what you want anytime, Shelby."

"Really?" Her whole life, she had longed to have someone who actually cared what she wanted. Who would invite her to speak her mind, instead of assuming they knew what she would do or what was best for her. The idea of someone—of Jax—asking made her heartbeat skip a little.

She took a deep breath and looked up.

Jax pressed the pencil to the pad. "*Anytime* meaning hopefully real soon. I have other tables to wait on, so…"

"Oh. Yes. I…" She became so flustered, she actually picked up a menu to get some idea what to order. She stared at the laminated page and blinked, willing herself not to blush at having let herself get so sidetracked by this man who had come to mean so much to her so quickly. "I…don't…"

Jax slid the menu from between her fingers. "Why don't I surprise you?"

"Surprise?" In other words, trust him. "Okay. Sounds like fun."

"Then, fun it is." He gave her a wink and turned away.

She sighed, relieved to have a moment to regroup and refocus, get her mind off how she had gotten so far off track once again.

"Shelby?" Jax looked back at her. "I meant that."

"Oh, I know." She shifted in the bench, wondering who was watching them. "You take your fun pretty seriously."

He laughed, then leaned in. "You can always tell me what you want. I promise to listen and not decide I know what's best for you."

"Thanks, Jax."

He nodded, then straightened up and headed to the kitchen. He called out to the other patrons as he made his way through the café. "Be back with a refill as soon as I get this order in. Decaf, right? Got enough syrup there? Everything tasting okay?"

People responded with friendly ease.

Shelby shook her head at how seamlessly he fit into the fabric of the small community. Yet she couldn't help reminding herself that he had come back to finish what he'd begun, not to start a new stage in his life.

She reached over to make Amanda comfortable, saying, "He's not bad, is he? Wish I had more time to get to know him, but we both know he's going to be out of here as soon as—"

"Any guy who would walk away from you, Shelby Grace, isn't a man worth you wasting your time on."

Her whole body tensed at the intrusion of another familiar male voice. This one definitely *not* so welcome. Her mouth formed the name that she didn't have breath enough to say out loud. *Mitch Warner.*

"You should know. You walked out on her time and time again yourself, Mitch Warner." Sheriff Andy's voice carried over the sound of the café door swinging open and shut again.

Shelby didn't need anyone coming to her rescue, not even the man pledged to serve and protect the whole town. She tucked the blanket with the embroidered name protectively around Amanda, then raised her head, angling her chin up. She focused her mind on the promise that God would give her strength.

"I can handle this, Sheriff Andy." She threw back her shoulders and aimed a cool look at the man with the reddish-brown hair in the beat-up straw cowboy hat. "What are you doing here, Mitch?"

"I don't know what you think you *have,* Shelby Grace, but Mitch is here because I asked him to come round." The sheriff slid into the booth across from Shelby and Amanda. "Seeing as we have an eyewitness putting his car here on the night of the baby being abandoned, I thought he and I needed to have a little chat."

"Eyewitness to *what?* What night are you talking about? You didn't say anything about—" Mitch had started to make himself cozy by settling in beside Shelby, but now he stood again. "Wait! Did you say baby?"

"Mitch Warner, meet Amanda." Shelby scooted away from the carrier, to make it easier to see the baby and harder for Mitch to share the seat with her.

"Shelby? Denby? Who's this?" Jax set a platter down on the table in front of Shelby.

"Shelby says her name is Amanda," Mitch said with a shrug. "Who are you?"

Jax started to say something, which Shelby suspected was a little more abrupt than introducing himself and giving Mitch a warm "How d'y'do?" but she beat him to it. "Mitch, this is Jackson Stroud. Jax, this is Mitchell Warner."

The two stared each other down, neither offering a hand to shake or an inch of ground.

"Now that those introductions are behind us, what I want to know is—who is *this?*" Shelby indicated the stack of pancakes with blueberries for the eyes, a straw-berry for the nose, raisins for the smile and a cowboy hat with a lengthwise slice of banana for the brim and whipped cream for the top.

"I thought I'd give you a cowboy to make you smile for a change." Jax grinned at her, then gave Mitch a cold-eyed glare. "You're in charge. Go on. Take a bite out of him."

Shelby couldn't help but laugh. "Thanks."

"For a change? What's that supposed to mean?" Mitch tipped his beat-up straw hat back on his head.

"It means we've got some questions for you…cow-boy." Jax stepped toward Mitch, crossing his arms over his broad chest. "Starting with why someone spotted your car around here the night the baby was left here."

Mitch did not back down. "First off, I don't owe any explanations to a waiter. Second, I ain't been around the Crosspoint since Shelby and I decided to not see so much of each other."

"Not to see *so much* of each other? You were sneak-ing around with two other women! The last six months of our so-called relationship, I barely saw you at all." Shelby looked down at the pancake cowboy Jax had concocted to remind her that she didn't have to settle for heartache from anyone.

You know who you are. You know what you feel.

Jax's conclusions, mixed with her own outrage, spurred Shelby to speak her mind to Mitch at last. "Mitch Warner, you are a cheater and a liar. Somebody left this precious, precious baby on my doorstep a few nights ago, and someone else reported seeing your flashy red car out by the—"

"Hold on there. Red car? Did you say *red* car?" Mitch snorted, shook his head and slapped his grubby jeans.

"Flashy? Did you call that sun-faded, rusted, bumpered Mustang flashy?" Jax asked.

Shelby whipped her head around to respond to the man who loved jumping to conclusions about people and thinking he knew all about them. Clearly this was his way of saying he thought her feelings for Mitch had blinded her to the truth about him, and his junker of a car.

"I don't even *have* that car anymore, Shelby Grace." Mitch tipped his hat back down, casual as could be, and laughed. "Couldn't have been me over here that night."

"So you deny you own the car but not that you're a cheat and a liar." Jax folded his arms over his broad chest. "Interesting."

Shelby, who had just settled the baby back down in her carrier, inched toward the outer edge of the booth. "Jax, this isn't your—"

"Ain't you got tables to wait on?" Mitch sneered, tugging his hat even farther down over his eyes.

"Take a look around, pal." Jax stepped closer still. "They are all way more into what's going on at *this* table than at their own."

"Nicely observed." Sheriff Andy slipped from the seat and stood, clearly ready to intervene. "But I think you both need to consider Shelby's feelings and keep this to a low roar."

Both Jax and Mitch turned to the sheriff and started to speak.

"Stop it. Stop it, all of you. I don't need anyone to consider how I feel, because nobody here has ever stopped to *ask* me how I feel." Shelby bolted up from her own seat so fast that she bumped the table, the platter and the silverware, all of which clanked and clattered.

Amanda started in her carrier.

Shelby held her breath.

Mitch scowled.

Sheriff Andy and the whole café seemed to take a collective breath and hold it.

Jax leaned over to take a look.

A fraction of a second of quiet greeted them; then Amanda let loose with a wail.

"I'll take her, if you want." Jax held out his hands for the crying child. "You can handle this."

With his encouragement barely out of his mouth, Shelby reached for the baby and handed her over to the man in the busboy's apron. She *could* handle Mitch. And Amanda. And the prying eyes of everyone in Sunnyside. But knowing she didn't have to, at least not today, felt so very nice.

Jax curled the baby into the protection of his strong arms, and the infant immediately started to quiet down. Bouncing the baby gently, he turned to walk away with her, then looked back at Shelby. "I think you have a cowboy to take a bite out of."

Shelby decided not to answer that.

"Bring me a coffee, will ya?" Mitch called out.

"Not until you settle up what you owe from the last time you were in here and the time before that." Shelby's father, Harmon, marched up to the table and slapped a bundle of receipts down.

"I, uh, I'd have to run to the bank first." Mitch felt around his pockets, as if that proved he had every intention of paying. "I loaned a friend my last twenty last night and, uh…"

"Why don't I pay those in exchange for a few answers from you, Mitch?" Shelby pulled her wallet out of her purse and handed her debit card to her father.

Her father protested the idea, as did Sheriff Andy, until she reasoned with them. "Did you ever think if Mitch paid off his bill here and told us everything he knows, then you can ban him from coming back? He'll have no excuse to come around anymore."

A few minutes later Shelby had signed the receipts where her dad had run the tabs as a credit card. Mitch tucked the receipts in his pocket as proof he didn't owe anything, and explained that his red car had been in the shop for two weeks, and he had been borrowing friends' cars until he could get his Mustang back.

The car story satisfied Sheriff Andy, who headed off to his office, grumbling about being too old for all this.

Shelby couldn't shake her reservations about the whole situation.

"Thanks for paying off my debt, Shelby Grace." Mitch stood at the door of the café and patted the receipts in his pocket. "Let's get together sometime soon. I know I disappointed you, but maybe we can still be friends?"

From the kitchen she heard the sound of her father and Jax cooing over Amanda.

"You said it yourself, he ain't going to hang around Sunnyside forever. When he's gone, you'll wish you had someone to count on." Mitch waited until she turned back to him again to add, "I've changed, Shelby. I honestly think I could be a one-woman man, with the right woman."

"Thanks, Mitch," she said softly. "I hope that's true, but that one woman isn't going to be me."

She doubted that Mitch could have changed as much

as he claimed, but wasn't that the nature of her own faith? Wasn't trusting people part of who she was?

She watched the man she had once hoped would help her build a real life saunter out the door.

"You okay?" Jax put his hand on her shoulder.

She turned with her arms open, wanting more than anything to get a great big cuddle. "Oh! Where's Amanda?"

"Harmon's got her."

"Harmon? You mean…my dad?" They'd met twice, and Jax was already on a first-name basis with her father? Her father, who absolutely *hated* his first name and made almost everyone but Miss Delta call him Lockhart.

"Don't worry. He knows a thing or two about baby girls," Jax assured her. "Why don't you sit down and eat your breakfast?"

She glanced back at the pancake. The fruit had slipped; the whipped cream had gone all watery. Shelby sighed. "Actually, I'm not hungry anymore."

"Then what are you going to do today?"

"Maybe I'll go back to Westmoreland. I'd like to do some shopping for Amanda." She fought the urge to yawn and lost. "Or maybe I'll see if I can't sneak in a nap."

"You shouldn't drive that tired. If you wait until my shift is over at two, I'll take you."

"I don't want you to go to any trouble." As soon as she said it, she realized she didn't mean it. After watching Jax leave last night and encountering Mitch today, and knowing Jax would leave again in time, she wanted him to go to as much trouble as he was willing to. She wanted to have this little space of time when this one person who "got" her would go to great lengths to show her that she was worth his time and effort.

"It's not imposing." He scooped up the platter with the sad, droopy cowboy breakfast on it and guided her around in a circle so that she faced the door between the café and Miss Delta's. "The breakfast rush is winding down. Go ask Miss Delta if you can crash in one of the rooms at the Truck Stop Inn."

"But Amanda…"

"Has about half a dozen babysitters right here." He motioned with the platter toward the customers, who didn't even pretend not to be listening in. A couple even waved at her as if to volunteer for duty. "Let someone else be the soft touch for a few hours, Shelby."

She laughed. "I think you are anything but a soft touch, Jackson Stroud."

"Then you know how much I really want to do this for you." He urged her forward, set the platter on the counter, put his hands on her shoulders. "Let me. Please?"

He wasn't asking her to let him be a soft touch. He was asking her to show she trusted him.

She pressed her lips together. Before she could say anything, Amanda began to cry in the kitchen.

Her father tried to calm the child, to no avail.

"It's not right to leave her here with you guys. You have work to do." She started for the kitchen.

Jax snagged her by the arm. "Shelby, we're big boys. We can—"

"I know I don't have to be the one to care for her right now, but I want to." Shelby moved his hands away, giving a gentle squeeze as she slid her fingers along his. "Jax, I may not have a lot of time with her. You, of all people, should appreciate how that makes me feel."

"I do," he whispered, then cleared his throat and stepped back. "But we're still on for that shopping trip this afternoon, right?"

"Count on it," she called as she went to collect Amanda and try to figure out how to get some rest and keep that promise.

Chapter Nine

Shelby came bursting through the swinging doors of the Crosspoint Café with a bounce in her step and a swing in her ponytail. "Doc Lovey has been watching Amanda for a few hours while I caught up on sleep, and she says she won't mind doing it a few hours more. In fact, she and Sheriff Andy said they'd be insulted if I came back before supper time."

Jax set the gray plastic tub in his hands on the table crowded with dishes next to him. He glanced at the clock to find that his shift had ended fifteen minutes earlier. Except for a time when he couldn't get a debit card to go through the system and the customer had gotten agitated with him, his day had gone quickly and smoothly.

He stole a peek into the kitchen through the server's window to find Shelby's father joking it up with the waitress who was supposed to be on duty now. Harmon Lockhart didn't seem the least bit inclined to remind Jax his work was done, and Jax couldn't help wondering how many times the man had allowed Shelby to keep on working while he whiled away his time visiting or carrying on with his own shift.

Jax tugged at the wet tie of his big apron, ready to slip it off and dive into whatever he could do to help Shelby.

Shelby turned Jax's way again, her face bright. "That gives us plenty of time to drive to—"

The rough, wet fabric of the apron string wrapped around Jax's thumb. It dug in and pulled. Normally he wouldn't even have flinched. But after a shift taking orders, cleaning tables and clearing away other people's food when he hadn't had time for a bite himself, his defenses were down. Jax winced and muttered under his breath.

Shelby frowned.

Jax managed a smile. "I finally figured out why they call the person who usually does this a busboy." He slumped into a seat, tilted his head back and shut his eyes. "Because at the end of the day, you feel like you've been hit by a bus."

Shelby's footsteps sounded soft and swift toward him.

"Poor thing," she said, with the lilt of laughter coloring her words.

Jax opened his eyes to chide her for her lack of sympathy and found her bending over him, her face inches above his.

When their eyes met, she gasped and pulled away.

"Why, Miz Shelby, what were you doing?" Not only did he not move away, but he leaned toward her, closing the distance between them again. "You were going to kiss me on the forehead to make it all better, weren't you?"

"No. No. I was just going to..." She stepped back. She tilted her head to one side, openly considering what he'd said. When she spoke, there was a soft mix of humility, humor and awe in her hushed tone. "Yes. I was going to kiss you on the forehead and make it all better."

The emotion in her voice touched Jax. And, like most interactions in life, made him wonder at the motivation behind it. Embarrassment at having been caught and called out? Confusion over the level of trust and connection the gesture implied toward him? Or concern that after only twenty-four hours as a child's caregiver, her maternal impulses had already taken such a strong hold?

Her expression did not give her away. This woman, with trust issues and a need to please so strong that she had to write a note to say goodbye rather than confront her own father, certainly wasn't going to admit out loud what was going on in her head.

So Jax let it be. Which was not like him, either. He and Shelby had already begun to change their own patterns for one another. The realization gave him a twinge between his shoulder blades, but he didn't have time to chew on the bit of insight. He stretched his aching legs and threw out his arms to try to work loose that tightening in his back. "Okay. Let me get a cup of coffee— correction, make that let me get my fourth cup of coffee today—and we'll go shopping for baby goods."

"Four cups? Of coffee from the Crosspoint Café? I think that's above the legal limit." She laughed. "Please, don't do that to yourself on my account."

He narrowed his eyes at her.

"I mean, on *Amanda's* account," she added, rushing to correct herself. "That is, people have been stopping by all day to bring things. A loaner crib, some clothes, a stroller. We can easily get by a day or so or until…"

"Until we find her mother?" he asked.

"I was going to say, 'Until you can go with me,' you

being the closest thing I have to a baby whisperer and all," she teased.

"Me? Baby whisperer?" A few days ago he would have railed against the term. So maybe it was the exhaustion talking when he said, "I like it."

"Whether we find who abandoned Amanda or not, I still need to get some things for her. First, she's with me legally until the authorities say otherwise. Finding the person who left her won't change that."

"The person who left her?" He finally got the apron off and tossed it over the end of the counter. "You can't bring yourself to say 'mother'?"

"Just being precise," she argued.

"I know. With anyone else, I'd wonder if you had a sneaking suspicion you know who left her." He rolled his sleeves down, never taking his eyes off Shelby's face. "Like maybe that Mitch character."

"He has been driving a different car." Shelby didn't mean to sound like she was defending her ex, but she had to admit it came out that way.

Jax must have heard the hesitation in her voice. He held firm by the kitchen door and prompted, "But?"

Shelby sighed and confessed the thought whirling around in her brain all afternoon. "If there were any person on the planet I'd think would seek me out to leave his responsibilities on my doorstep, I'd pick Mitch first."

And her own dad second—not to leave a child but to dump his responsibilities on her.

Jax put his hand on her shoulder, partly to support her emotionally, partly to support himself physically, and called out, "Hey, y'all. My shift is over. I am out of here."

Before Shelby's father or the middle-aged mom picking up a few shifts as the café's afternoon waitress could reply, Jax draped his arm around Shelby's shoulders and guided her to the door. "So, a couple hours without the baby? What is there to do in this town with my feet up and my guard down?"

"Guard down?" she asked, shading her eyes with one hand as they stepped into the afternoon sun.

"After a day listening for clues, observing every detail of everyone who came into the place, I'd like to go someplace where no one could possibly be Amanda's, um, the person who left Amanda."

Shelby sank her teeth into her lower lip as she eyed her dad's pickup truck. "How are you at ranching?"

"I may be a city kid, but even I know you can't do much ranch work with your feet up," Jax said as the minivan went bumping along a pitted old road. He had offered to take his truck, but Shelby had insisted he rest and relax.

"You can if those feet are in the stirrups of a saddle." Shelby guided the minivan down a long, dusty driveway and through an iron fence with the gate hanging open.

"Saddle?" He braced one arm against the dash as he scanned the property that spilled out before them. *Spilled* was the best way to describe it. An old trailer, some faded lawn furniture and a simple barn with a tin roof lay in front of them, looking like a child had left a handful of broken toys strewn under a cluster of small trees. He searched for any signs of life. "Like on a horse?"

"Yes. On a horse." She got out of the minivan and met him in front of it. "I thought you were a cowboy, cowboy. Don't tell me you don't know how to ride."

"I grew up in foster care in Dallas." He followed her to the barn, which looked better-kept than the trailer bearing the name Harmon Lockhart on the mailbox. "I wear a cowboy hat because I got used to wearing a hat as part of my uniform."

"In other words, you can't ride." She shook her head and motioned for him to follow her inside the barn.

"I *can* ride." He eyed the three horses in their stalls. One of them snorted and stamped its foot. "I just don't, usually."

"Well, consider this a most unusual day," she said with a laugh in her voice and a playful smile on her pretty face.

He hung back to get the best view of her moving through the barn. Sunlight streamed through gaps in the wood, creating shafts of golden light. As she moved along and disturbed the straw beneath her feet, tiny flecks of dust rose up and sparkled around her. Jax liked the effect. He liked it very much.

"Would it be rude of me to note that you are a lot sweeter when you've caught up on your sleep?"

She didn't answer, probably because she had fixed all her strength and concentration on wrestling a large black leather saddle from its resting place and onto the complacent roan standing in its stall, munching on hay.

Jax rushed to her aid.

"I've done this thousands of times before, Jax." She tried to wrench the heavy saddle from his grasp. "I can handle it."

"I know you can, Shelby." He could have easily lifted her burden, but he knew she would resent having it taken from her. He needed to help her surrender it instead. So he leaned in close, so close he could see every lash framing those expressive blue eyes, and said softly, "You can do anything you put your mind to, including letting me help you now. Because in a few days I'll be gone and wondering if there was anything more I could have done to make your life easier. Even if only for a few minutes."

"Okay," she whispered. "Help all you want."

He tried to take the saddle.

Shelby's hands clung to it, drawing her in his direction right along with it.

"Shelby…"

She was so close now, her hair fell across her shoulder and onto his sleeve. "Hmm?"

"If you want me to help, you have to let go."

"Oh!" She released the saddle and stepped back. "You put the saddles on. I'll cinch."

He did as he was told, and she dove into her end of the deal. Jax watched her fingers practically fly through the process of securing the cinch. She was something. Feisty, but not so much that she ran roughshod over others' feelings. Serious about whatever she put her mind to, but with a heart full of fun and hope.

Jax just couldn't…

The horse stamped its foot, and Shelby dodged out of the way. Jax came back to the moment. What he *couldn't* do was stand here and think about Shelby. There was no future in that. So he decided to ask about the past— the immediate past.

"So, what did you do on your first day of leisure?"

"Leisure? Taking care of a baby is not for sissies, buddy."

"I meant your first day not working at the café." Jax laughed. "Besides, I thought you were an old hand with kids."

"Old?" She made the final tug on the cinch. The horse

shifted its weight. She patted its side to calm it then put on the horse's bridle.

"Experienced," he corrected, running his hand along the horse's rippling neck muscles.

"Where'd you get that idea?"

"Before I even laid eyes on you, Tyler told me that you taught Sunday school to every kid in town. It seemed like everyone I waited on today either had you as a teacher or their child does now."

She conceded his point with a shrug and a shake of her head. "They can't get anyone else to do it."

"That's not why you do it any more than that's why the sheriff stays on year after year." He followed her to the next stall, watched her arrange the saddle blanket then lifted the saddle and settled it on the back of a brown gelding. "You do it because you love it."

She caught the cinch between her fingers, placed one hand on the flank of the waiting animal, paused, then said, "No, I do it because I love *them*."

Once again he'd missed her motivation, seeing only his own. "Helping people has always been *my* goal."

She tightened the cinch. "How is that different from what I just said?"

"I didn't give much thought to caring about the people I helped." He brushed his hand along the horse's neck, not sure if it was the serenity of the darkened barn, the comfort of the calmly waiting animals or just the nearness of Shelby that got the truth out of him so easily. He shifted his boots in the straw but did not stop himself from admitting, "I did it because it made me feel important, because I thought no one else would, because—"

"Because no one helped you when you needed it." She straightened up and put her hand on his. "We often do things to heal the hurts we feel in life by trying to put them right in other relationships."

"Really? You're going to try to sell that idea to *me?* The guy who prides himself on knowing why people do what they do?" He chuckled, not because he felt insulted, but because he found her attempt to figure him out endearing.

"Oh, Jax."

"What?" He realized she had not moved her hand from his.

She didn't say another word. She didn't have to.

"You got me. I'm justifying my actions to myself." He didn't move his hand away from her, but fixed his attention on the paleness of her small fingers against his tanned skin. "Time and time again, people at the café told me if they were going to leave a baby with anyone, it would be you."

She slipped her hand away from his and went to work putting on the horse's bridle. "I know, because I'm a big pushover."

"Because you were the one who taught them about trust and devotion and putting the needs of those you love ahead of your own needs."

"Like I said, pushover. The kids I taught in Sunday school know that better than anyone." She held her hand up to keep him from contradicting her, guided her horse out of the stall then moved to mount it. When she got up in the saddle, she tipped her head to one side. "Wait a minute. The kids I taught in Sunday school!"

"What about them?" he asked over his shoulder as he went to mount the other horse.

"We're pretty confident it's not someone currently in town, but I taught for years and years. Some of those kids don't live in Sunnyside anymore. Jax, do you think it could be one of them?"

"Good place to start." He swung himself up into his saddle. "Do you have records of your classes or photographs that might jar your memory?"

She nodded her head. "I'm sure I have some. Not every year, and the ones with kids old enough to have a baby probably wouldn't be digital. They'd be in photo albums, all packed up."

"You should go through your moving boxes and see if you can find them. I can help, if you want." He settled into the saddle and tested the reins to get a feel for them. "And before you tell me I'm willing to help in trying to reunite Amanda and her mom because I lost my own mom, that's not why I'm offering."

"Oh?"

She was using the "Don't say too much, and just let the other guy do the talking" technique, which Jax favored in interrogations. Smart girl. It worked. "This time I want to help because I care about the people involved."

"Is that so?" She gave him a sly smile, then clicked to her horse to get moving. "I think the people involved might feel the same way about you."

"What's that supposed to mean?"

"It's pretty simple, if you ask me." She turned her horse. Walking out the barn door, she clicked again, this time with a gentle kick, and called out behind her, "See if you can keep up."

The brown gelding took off at a fast trot, which didn't compare to the racing beat of her heart. Somewhere in her neatly boxed-up belongings, she might find the face of Amanda's mother. And a not quite cowboy who had come back to her aid once already—and might or might not care about her—was going to help her look for it. She didn't know how she felt about any of that.

Shelby looked over her shoulder to see Jax maneuver his horse around and follow after her like a real pro.

He didn't so much as lose his cool once as he rode after her, and in a minute overtook her.

She pulled gently on the reins to slow her horse to a walk. "I thought you said you couldn't ride."

"I didn't say I couldn't. I said I *didn't*." He brought his horse around and slowed it to match the pace of hers.

"You know that's not how I took it. I thought you were a man who says what he means."

"I am, but that doesn't mean I say any more than I need to."

"That's one of those kinds of things that seems like sound advice, but then you think about it a minute…" She gave him what she thought was a serious, probing look.

He laughed out loud, reaching down to stroke the mane of his mount. "So, you grew up out here?"

"We lived in a little house in town until I got through high school. My mom died the summer after I graduated, and I went off to college that fall. The end of that school year, I came back to Sunnyside to find Daddy had sold the house and spent all the proceeds to buy this place." She raised her face and let the sun warm her cheeks and the wind ruffle her hair back. "There was no more money for me to continue with my schooling."

"So you dropped out of college?" Jax asked over the steady clop-clop of hooves on heat-hardened Texas clay.

"I took a break. Or that's what I told myself I was doing." She gripped the horn of the saddle, her face still raised into the breeze. "I got a little apartment and a job at the café."

"And you found out you liked it and thought maybe it could become your life's work," Jax said, finishing for her.

"Well…" She dragged the word out, unwilling to go so far as to agree with Jax's version of things. "I like the people, old friends and new ones coming in off the highway. I like hearing their stories, and I like the consistency of seeing them day after day. It's kind of like having a great big family."

"Family, huh? So is that how your dad got involved working there? You wanted to make it a family business?"

"Daddy? *He* had big plans for this place. He was going to rent stalls and give riding lessons. He even built a little arena for junior rodeos, the whole deal."

Jax looked around. She could practically hear him counting down the things that *weren't* there.

"Then the economy went belly-up," she explained. "And I got him a job at the café to bring in some extra cash to tide him over, saying he'd put any extra in a fund to help me buy the place. Only there never was any extra, and…"

"And he was the first cowboy to break your heart?"

The question took her breath away. When she recovered, she didn't answer directly. "You're actually a very good horseman."

"I'm a better lawman."

She knew that was his way of saying he had done some fine detective work and had seen through her evasion. But he was not the only one capable of that. "If

that's what you do best, then why are you going to Florida to be a neighborhood night watchman?"

He didn't have an answer.

Gotcha, Shelby thought. "Ready to let these ponies
stretch their legs? If you think you can handle it, that is."

"I can handle it," he assured her. "And if you thought
I couldn't ride, why'd you take off like that right out of
the barn? Trying to ditch me?"

"Not on purpose," she said before she kicked her
horse lightly in the flanks to take off. "But then, it seems
like not a lot of things in my life get done on purpose,
so maybe you'd better hang on and be ready for wherever we end up."

Chapter Ten

They rode for an hour or so, then brushed down the horses, fed them and headed back to town.

After that, and on top of a shift at the café, Jax was bone tired. Shelby had known he would be. Had she done it so he'd go back to his bunk and rest, instead of pushing her to go through her old photos to see if any faces sparked an idea of who might have left Amanda?

She wasn't trying to throw things off course. Not on purpose. But if they didn't get around to it, well, she wasn't going out of her way to make it happen.

Over the next two days, she found herself doing just about anything to keep the two of them—the *three* of them, since Amanda was always with them—busy. Too busy to get around to unpacking old photo albums, much less combing over them for faces.

The young woman who had been so certain a week ago about what she wanted to do now couldn't seem to make herself do anything, except care for Amanda and spend time with Jax.

Nothing else seemed to matter. The clock was ticking. Jax had to leave for Florida in two days, max. That made him work all the harder to try to make some progress on the case.

Shelby just wanted to make the most of whatever time they had together. She hadn't been the one to abandon Amanda. Whoever had done that knew what they had done, where they had left the baby and, according to Jax and Sheriff Andy, who they had left her with.

The story of the baby left at the Crosspoint Café had made the local papers, been covered by TV news in both Texas and Louisiana. They had taken the basic information to the Internet, and word had spread through social media. Sometimes it all made Shelby flinch.

Jax had concluded that whoever left Amanda had been desperate. For some reason they had done it without leaving a single clue as to their identity. What if pursuing them so aggressively was only fueling that desperation? What if it made things worse?

"I think you should make a plea." Jax had met her in the parking lot behind the café shortly after seven that morning.

"But I didn't do anything," she protested as she worked Amanda out of her car seat. "Isn't that something a criminal does?"

"Not a plea bargain. A plea." He gestured with both hands folded together. Like *that* made it any clearer. "We do a video. If we're right that whoever left Amanda wanted you to have her, that means they feel a special connection to you. They trust you."

"I guess so." She pulled Amanda close, holding the baby's cheek against her own. Amanda snuggled in tight, winding her fingers through Shelby's hair. Shelby sighed. "I mean, I *know*."

Shelby did know. She had been fooling herself to

think she'd ever be able to move forward in her life without having done every last thing possible to find that person. "What exactly are you suggesting?"

A few yards away, the café door swung open and Mitch Warner stepped outside. Shelby tensed. She made a quick search of the lot and spotted the familiar red car that Mitch had driven for years.

"So you make a pitch, this plea." Jax kept right on speaking, moving closer to Shelby and Amanda as if sheltering them. "You assure the person who left the baby that they are not in trouble. They need to come forward. It's what's best for Amanda."

"I don't know if I can do that, Jax," she said softly, crossing the lot until they reached the steps.

"Speak from your heart, Shelby." Jax stepped in front of her and put his hands on her shoulders. "It will be on every TV in the area by the late-night news."

"*What* will be on every TV in the area?" Mitch asked in a hard tone as he came down the front steps of the café toward them.

"I know you're right, Jax. I know I should jump at the idea, but I'm not sure it's the right thing to do. Let me think about it." Shelby stepped around him to find her ex-boyfriend standing before her. She wound her way around him, as well. "I thought you said you didn't drive that red car anymore, Mitch."

"I don't. That's not my car."

Shelby spun around and looked at Jax.

He nodded. "You take the baby inside and ask around to see if anyone knows who owns that car. I'll go get the license number."

"Let me help, Shelby. I'm not that same guy you couldn't count on." Mitch wrapped his arm around Shelby's shoulder, his hand patting the baby's head. "I can help you and Miranda."

"Her name is Amanda." Jax brushed the other man's arm away. "And we don't need your help."

Shelby sighed. "Jax, he's only trying to—"

"Hey! Hey! Don't you get in that red car and drive away from this town for parts unknown!" Mitch's arm swung from Shelby's shoulder to wave wildly as he hurried down the step toward the lot. "People here want to talk to you about you-know-what!"

Jax and Shelby twisted around in time to see the brake lights of the red car flash and the vehicle tear out of the lot, headed toward the highway.

"Why did you do that?" Jax bunched Mitch's T-shirt in one hand as he pulled the other man nose to nose with him. Actually, given how much taller Jax was, nose to chin.

"I was trying to help. I told you I've changed, Shelby." Mitch held out his hand to her. "While this guy was ordering you around, I heard that car engine start up and had to help."

"*That's* what you call helping?" Jax asked.

"Jax! Back off." The stress of thinking that someone who might have their only clue to who had left Amanda was skulking around Sunnyside, popping up right at the Crosspoint, put an edge in Shelby's tone. "He was doing his best."

"You're taking his side?" Jax gestured toward Mitch. "You believe his story that he's changed?"

"I don't know what I believe anymore." She cradled Amanda in one arm and pressed her fingertips to her temple, trying to make herself focus.

Was she angry that they'd lost the witness, or that

the witness could appear at any time and threaten her growing relationship with Amanda? She didn't want to believe the worst, but she couldn't help questioning her own heart in all this. She took a deep breath, knowing she needed to spend some time in prayer over it all.

In the meantime, she put her hand up to try to get things under control again. "Getting angry with someone who is trying to help isn't, well, helpful."

Before Jax could say more, which Shelby knew would make Mitch say more, which Shelby felt sure would only confuse her more, the door of the café swung open.

"My day off, Harmon." Jax stepped back and raised his hands the way a kid might as he said, "Not it."

"It's cool, Jax man." Harmon Lockhart mirrored Jax's gesture. Laughing, he turned to her. "I thought I saw your van in the lot. Then you didn't make it inside. There's my girl!"

Shelby's tension eased at the sight of her dad's broad smile and open arms. She stepped toward him.

He reached out and lifted the baby from her arms, instantly going into full-on baby delighting mode, making silly noises and faces.

Amanda cooed and laughed and tangled her tiny hand in his faded blond ponytail.

They might have fought and fussed over the years over everything from his lack of financial responsibility to how fast he expected her to get the orders out at the café, but Shelby loved her dad. Loved him so much that when she had wanted to leave, she could not tell him to his face, because she knew it would break both their hearts. Amanda's arrival had been the push she needed to stand up to him, quit her job and tell him he had to pay his own bills. Things between them had improved remarkably since then.

"Funny, I thought *I* was your girl, Daddy." Shelby went up on tiptoe to give her dad a kiss on his tanned cheek.

"You will *always* be my girl, Shelby Grace." He gave Shelby a kiss on the cheek in return, then made a goofy face for Amanda's enjoyment. "I may not have always proved it to you. I may not have always been the best dad in the world, but who knew how much I'd take to being a grandpa?"

"Foster grandpa," she said pointedly. She needed to remind herself as much as her father of their precarious status.

"Grandpa is grandpa," Harmon shot back. "Y'all come to spend the day with me? Breakfast rush is over. My shift'll be done before you know it."

"I'm just here because I saw Shelby pull in while I was standing near the window in Miss Delta's, trying to get a good cell signal." Jax narrowed his eyes and fixed them on Shelby, saying softly, "Playing phone tag with my new boss for a couple days. I get the feeling he's getting restless."

Why Shelby found that news unsettling, she didn't want to think about. Instead she turned to her father. "I guess we've spoiled you by coming by for breakfast every morning."

"Gotten to be a pattern, all right." Her dad's face lit as if he had suddenly remembered something. He reached into his pocket and pulled out a gleaming blue plastic card. "Fact, so much I guess you left this here one of them times."

"My debit card?" Shelby couldn't remember when she

had used it at the café. Or when she had used it at all. She'd been relying on the stash of cash she'd taken out of savings when she expected to leave town. People all over town had donated the things she needed for Amanda's care. "Wow. I don't think I've used it since…Did I use it the day you were here, Mitch?" she said, turning around to look at her ex. "Mitch?"

"He took off toward Miss Delta's after your dad came out," Jax told her.

Shelby sighed. She wanted to believe Mitch had changed. She really did think he was trying. But it was so typical of that man to have headed off the minute the conversation wasn't centered on him or something of interest to him.

"I've got to get back to work." Shelby's father gave her another kiss, this time on her temple. "I'm taking my girl inside to show her off some. You ought to be more careful with your bank card, Shelby Grace."

"Did your dad just try to school you on money matters?" Jax grinned at her.

"Mitch trying to be helpful. Dad being smarter about finances than I obviously have been. It's a world turned upside down, I tell ya." She met his gaze, and her heart leapt.

"I don't know whether to help you set it right again or to tell you to hang on and enjoy the ride."

He had said exactly the right thing. Exactly what she had been feeling. Shelby smiled. She wondered if, after the arrival of Amanda and the impending departure of Jackson Stroud, her world would ever be the way it once was. "I vote for enjoy the ride…while it lasts."

"Okay then." He gave her a nod. "Where shall we start?"

She looked at the card in her hand, then at the doorway through which her father had taken Amanda into a world of kindness and love like the baby had probably never known. They had found the baby with absolutely nothing and had given her everything when they gave her a home and love. But they couldn't promise her those things forever.

"Start?" Shelby shook her head, then laughed. "I have a great idea. Let's go shopping!"

Jax stood at the end of the long hallway in the mall in Westmoreland, waiting for Shelby to return from changing Amanda's diaper. His fingers brushed the edge of the slim phone in his pocket. He could probably get a full signal here if he wanted to call his future boss and check in.

"If," he muttered to himself, staring at his inverted image in the curved chrome top of a nearby trash can. He couldn't help thinking of Shelby, marveling at how her world seemed turned upside down. He knew exactly how she felt.

And he didn't like it. The night he pulled off the highway to grab a bite to eat at the Crosspoint Café, his life had been set. He had had plans. He had had a direction. He had...

"Everything is taken care of!" Shelby came striding down the hall, Amanda grinning in her arms.

He'd had nothing. And he had *liked* that. Nothing to hold him back or weigh him down. Nothing to stand in his way. Nothing to set his world on its head, so no reason to care if it ever got set right.

Shelby and Amanda reached his side, and his gaze lifted from his own image to the reflection of the three of them in the large plate-glass shop window across from them. In an instant, the world looked righted again.

"Let's start at the baby shop over there." Shelby pointed, and Jax put his hand on her back to allow her to step in front of him and lead the way. To everyone around them, he knew, they seemed a happy family. Shelby the perfect mom and wife, he the loving husband and doting daddy.

Those were not terms he ever thought anyone would ever apply to him, even mistakenly. The baby held her arms out to him, and he took her without a moment's hesitation.

"Okay, you kept the conversation on all the things you wanted to look at for Amanda the whole drive here." "And off the topic of making that plea or going over your old photographs," he chose not to add. "But can you tell me *why* you feel you need all that stuff? I mean, you've had tons of donations from people all over town."

"I know, and it's been amazing, the outpouring of support." She stepped inside the store filled with cribs and furniture and clothing and took a deep breath, as if inhaling the scent of the pastel candy colors everywhere—yellow, green, purple and, of course, pink and blue. "But most of those things were hand-me-downs. Bought with someone else in mind and easily cast off."

"Some people would call that recycling. Good stewardship, you know."

"You're right. I get that. A waitress at the Crosspoint doesn't save enough to give herself a fresh start in life without knowing a thing or two about good stewardship." She stopped to look over a display of the tiniest shoes Jax had ever seen. She plucked up a pair that looked like satin ballet slippers and showed them to him, her eyes practically sparkling. "What do you think?"

"Personally, I prefer a good pair of boots."

"I don't mean for you."

"I don't, either." He spun the display around half a turn and picked up a pair of pink and silver cowgirl boots no bigger than the tiny slippers in Shelby's hands.

"Maybe we'll get both." She laughed. "Who knows, maybe her grandpa, um, *foster* grandpa, will finally get to work on that dream ranch and have her riding before she can walk."

"Shelby…"

"But they are both precious and just perfect for you, Amanda." She gave the child a kiss on her chubby hand. "No matter what, right?"

"Shelby, you know it might not work out that you have her long enough to see her ride a horse, much less take her first step."

"I know, Jax." She fidgeted with the baby's hand-me-down outfit, getting it just so before she looked up into his eyes. "Why do you think I wanted to come shopping for her today?"

He had no idea. That's right—Jackson Stroud, who prided himself on knowing the reason behind every person's actions, had no clue about this blue-eyed waitress with a heart bigger than the state of Texas. "I asked you that question first."

"So Amanda will have some things that are hers. Not secondhand. Not bought with love for another child." Shelby's voice cracked. She clenched her jaw so tightly that when she tipped her head back to try to stay the wash of tears in her eyes, Jax could see her swallow as if to push down a lump in her throat.

He wanted to take her in his arms, kiss her head and tell her it was a good thing she was doing and not to cry.

Before he could reach for her, she moved away, touching things in the store as if they were precious treasures as she went along. "Most people have that, you know? A stuffed animal, a pair of booties, a photo, some keepsake from when they were a baby. Something that tells them, 'From the very first day God placed you in my heart, you were loved.'"

Now Jax had a lump in his throat. He thought of the blanket he had carried in his luggage from foster home to foster home and had tucked under his pillow for years, until it was nothing more than a rag. He had eventually retired it to a trunk that was now sitting in storage in Florida, waiting for him to come claim it. His mom had wrapped him in that blanket when he was a newborn, and it was all he had left of her. Even he, jaded and seemingly forsaken as he was by his later childhood, had what Shelby wanted to give Amanda.

"Okay then, let's get them both." He put the cowgirl boots on top of the ballet slippers, then glanced around. "I think we're going to need a shopping cart."

They filled up two baskets the shop provided before they moved to the checkout.

"When we're through here, I'll take this stuff to the van and we'll see what else we can find for her," Jax offered.

"Oh, what a darlin', darlin' little girl. How old is she?" the clerk asked as she began ringing up the purchases one by one.

"Almost four months," Shelby said, touching her finger to the baby's nub of a nose.

"Only *four months?* And look at you! You've already got your figure back! She's your first, I'll wager."

"Well, she's—"

"I have three. All boys. What I wouldn't give for a reason to buy one of these." The clerk peered closely at the tag on a bright pink tutu, never even noticing the discomfort in Shelby's expression as she shifted her weight and tried to explain the situation. "I tell you, I have yet to lose those last ten pounds of baby fat after my youngest was born."

"Really, I never—"

"How old is your youngest?" Jax stepped in to protect Shelby from getting emotional over having to tell Amanda's story again. If Shelby knew that was why he had done it, she'd probably have a fit, he realized. So, he decided on the spot, if the diversion didn't work, he'd try something new. Anything to keep the tears out of those blue eyes.

"My youngest? Oh, he's nine."

"Months?" Jax asked, even as Shelby glowered at him for butting in.

"Years!" The clerk laughed and hit the total button. She announced the price, accepted Shelby's debit card and swiped it through the slot in the front of the machine. "Just put your pin number in there."

Shelby obeyed, then held out her hand to take the card back.

The clerk started to hand it over, eyes on the digital screen in front of her, then froze. "Oh, dear."

"What?" Selby leaned in to try to get a peek at what had the clerk obviously unsettled.

"Your card was denied."

"It must be a mistake. I know for a fact I have plenty of money in that account. Can we try it again?"

They did, with the same result.

"I don't understand."

"Well, it's not giving me any information on this end." The clerk frowned. "Do you think you could have reached the one-day limit on your account?"

"This is the first time I've used it in days."

"Because it was out of your hands for days." Jax hated to sound like a cop bringing up an ugly and uncomfortable possibility. "I think we better make a call to the bank."

Chapter Eleven

"A thousand dollars is a lot of money to me." The printout of her bank account's activity rattled in Shelby's hand. She scanned the numbers again, then again, before she finally laid it down on Sheriff Andy's desk for him to look over. Then, before he could actually do that, she began pointing out where the money had gone. "Five hundred of it since midnight last night, buying things online. That was my limit for the day."

Sheriff Andy adjusted his reading glasses, pursed his lips and finally had to snatch away the page to give it a good long look. "Looks like the thief played it smart at first. Spent a little bit here, a little there, so you wouldn't notice. Just like the others."

"Others?" Jax folded his arms.

When he first followed them into the office, lined with file cabinets and an American flag, a big metal desk and chairs, Shelby worried she'd feel overwhelmed by his nearness. Now she realized Jax would ask the questions the situation had her too frazzled to ask.

"Had three other cases of local folks reporting money missing from their accounts." Sheriff Andy flipped open a file on his desk and laid Shelby's bank statement on top of the pile of papers inside. "May be some more belonging to people just passing through that we don't even know about, and some folks may not have caught on yet."

"It's my fault. I should have known my card had gone missing." She wasn't sure whether to be angry or burst into tears.

"You've had a lot on your plate, Shelby." Sheriff Andy gave her a fatherly pat on the hand. "What with caring for Amanda and doing all you can to figure out who might have left her."

Shelby pressed her lips together. Her heart grew even heavier with the knowledge that she had tried harder to find Amanda's mother.

"Any progress on that from your end?" Jax stepped in to ask the sheriff.

"Doc Lovey has kept her ears open." He absently bent the shell of his ear forward as he studied the file before him and kept speaking. "Which, speaking strictly as her darlin' husband of thirty-six years, is an accomplishment, because she'd rather keep her mouth open, asking questions and getting to the heart of matters."

"I bet she'd say the same of you," Shelby teased.

"Me? No. I've found, like our friend Jax here, a good lawman learns as much or more from what doesn't get said as what does." The sheriff closed the file, peeled off his reading glasses and rubbed his eyes. "Pays to keep your mouth shut sometimes."

"You speaking as a husband or lawman?" Jax asked.

The sheriff laughed. "Anyway, we haven't got any credible tips or clues. You get anywhere trying to jog your memory, Shelby?"

"I just… I haven't…" She felt embarrassed at her inability to make progress. "Can we talk about this stolen money thing right now?"

"I don't know what to tell you." Sheriff Andy held his hands out to his sides. "This is our first case of something like this targeting locals, to be honest."

"We saw a lot of this kind of identity theft in Dallas." Jax moved forward and put his hand on the closed file. With a look, he seemed to ask permission to check it out.

The sheriff hesitated, then gave a gesture of consent. "If you can offer any advice, then, I'd appreciate your consult on it."

"The online purchases may be your key to tracking down the thief." Jax flipped through the pages, back and forth, then back again. "Check where the orders came from, where they were sent…"

"We did a few, much as time and manpower allowed, but in the end, whoever is doing this is using the cards all over the area and using a different computer every day. A few at libraries, one at a hospital, using Wi-Fi or no-contract cell phones in coffee shops, hotels, fast-food places."

Jax shook his head. "It may take these people months to get it all sorted out and to feel confident they won't get hit with a problem over it again."

"Worse than that." Shelby put her head in her hands. "It makes me wonder who I can trust, even in Sunnyside."

"What do you mean?" Jax tossed the file down.

"The card was lost in the café. Doesn't that mean someone in Sunnyside must have been using it?"

"Maybe, maybe not." Jax moved around to the same side of the desk as Sheriff Andy. "You ever run a check on Mitch Warner?"

"Mitch? Jax, the man might have been a liar and a cheat, but he would never have stolen money from me." Even Shelby couldn't believe she'd used that as her best defense for the man she had been so infatuated with for far too long.

"I didn't see any reason to check on Mitch." Sheriff Andy scooted over. He clicked the mouse, and the computer screen flickered on. "You got a hunch?"

"Just see if he still has that red car registered in his name."

Jax hated leaving the sheriff's office without any solid information about Mitch Warner, but a call from the dispatcher about multiple small but urgent issues had taken precedence. So over Denby's complaints about reduced staff and aching knee joints, Jax had shuffled Shelby into the minivan and returned her to Miss Delta's house, where they'd left Harmon Lockhart watching Amanda.

"That ol' cowboy cook dad of yours does look like a natural as a grandpa," Jax said as he and Shelby sat in the parked minivan outside the house. Mostly he wanted to get Shelby's mind off her money woes. Also, he had grown to like that ol' cowboy cook, and since Jax's time in Sunnyside would soon come to a close, he wanted Shelby to understand that he was leaving her in good hands. "Kind of makes you want to rethink that third life rule of yours, the one about never trusting cowboys."

"Oh, I've been rethinking it all afternoon long." She pressed the button on her seat belt, and it retracted into place.

"And?" He undid his safety belt, as well.

Shelby put her hand to her forehead and winced. "I

think I may have to revise it to read 'Never, ever trust anyone.'"

He reached over and took her raised wrist in his hand. "Shelby, you can't live like that."

"Why not?" She jerked her arm free. "You do."

"What?"

She let out an exasperated sigh. "Why else are you constantly trying to figure out people's motivations and why they do what they do? So you can get ahead of what they may do next."

"That's good police work," he protested.

"You're not a policeman anymore, Jax," she said softly, running her hand down his arm as if offering him comfort.

Jax had nothing to say to that. Or maybe he had so many things to say to it that no single thought rose to prominence. Shelby was right. On all counts. And worse, she had beaten him at his own game when she revealed it by uncovering the motivation behind the way he chose to live his life. He didn't trust anyone.

Or he hadn't trusted anyone. Until Shelby. That was why he couldn't let her embrace this new attitude. He knew the lonely and bitter life it could lead to.

"Shelby Grace, I've just got to say—" The electronic notes of his ringtone cut him off. He glanced at the phone on the dash to see the Florida area code and number below the photo of the community clubhouse where his new office would be located. It was his new boss. He reached out and slid his thumb over the button to send the caller to voice mail. Eventually he was going to have to talk to the man, give him an update and a firm date of his arrival. But not just now.

"You know, I think you should be reevaluating those

life rules of yours, Shelby." He reached out and took her hand. "Starting with asking yourself why you put that 'With God all things are possible' as number one."

"God I trust. It's people who are giving me a problem right now, Jax."

"Nope. Sorry. Doesn't work that way."

"You're the one who thinks Mitch is involved."

"I did not say that. I also didn't say there aren't some people out there who don't deserve your trust. But, Shelby, you've got to trust that there are plenty of good people out there." Jax fixed his gaze on the porch, where Miss Delta had settled on the arm of Harmon's rocking chair, and the pair of them were cooing to Amanda. "You are looking at two who certainly earned it, your dad and Miss Delta."

"Three," she said softly. "I see three people who have earned my trust."

"Amanda is kind of young but—"

"I'm looking at you, Jax." She leaned in and placed a kiss on his lips.

With that kiss, Jax felt his ties to Sunnyside, Texas, and Shelby beginning to slip away. He reached out to her. He touched her hair, her face, and leaned back in, unwilling to let go yet. Just one more kiss, a real kiss, a goodbye kiss before he—

A loud banging from the back of the minivan made them both jump.

Shelby gasped. She pulled away and looked around.

Jax gritted his teeth, determined not to let loose on Harmon for his idea of a joke in scaring them, only to look up and find Harmon and Miss Delta still on the porch—and Sheriff Denby's grinning face at the driver's side window.

A few minutes later, they were all sitting on the porch with ice-cold lemonade in tall tumblers in their hands.

"So, Mitch did still own that red car?" Jax asked

"He reported it stolen this morning," Denby confirmed.

"Before or after we saw him at the café?" Jax pressed the issue.

"Right after, it would seem. Got the info on it in that flurry of calls that came in while you were in my office, since the car was registered in this county."

"One cowboy. That's one cowboy who can't be trusted," Jax rushed to remind Shelby.

"Mitch Warner? A cowboy?" Harmon scoffed. "What's the saying? A cat can have kittens in the oven, but that don't make them biscuits. That boy ain't no more cowboy than…" He looked at Denby, then at Jax, and shrugged. "Than a kitten is a biscuit."

"You all think Mitch stole from me and made this up to cover for it, don't you?" Shelby shook her head.

"It's wrong to jump to conclusions." Miss Delta rushed to play the diplomat, but not a single face on the porch reflected that attitude.

"I'd sure like to ask him some hard questions." Denby took a long sip of lemonade.

Jax sat forward on the porch swing. "*Like* to? You mean you aren't going to?"

"Not 'less I can get him to come to the office, son. I don't have time to run him down. I'm operating on a skeleton staff as it is."

"I've seen your staff, Andy, honey." Miss Delta got up and gave him a brisk rub across the shoulders. "They are some of the best-fed skeletons I've ever seen."

Denby chuckled. "I would personally like the time

to take up jogging and some of that exercise dancing to take the pounds off, if I could ever get my name off the ballot for sheriff."

Again Jax's phone went off. He knew better, but somehow the ring seemed more insistent this time, almost aggressive. He took a peek at the caller ID.

Shelby leaned her head next to his to ask, "A building is calling you?"

He glanced up and into those eyes. The eyes that had first touched his conscience with teary defiance now held a sadness that he could not bear. He sent the call to voice mail once again.

"I can't help you with that dancing thing. I don't even know if I can get the image of you trying it out of my head anytime soon." Jax stuffed his phone in his pocket. "But I think I can help you with Warner."

"You want your badge back?" Sheriff Denby pinched the lemon slice from the side of his glass and gave it a squeeze, sending lemon juice squirting into his drink and onto his uniform. "That's a temporary fix. No pay. If, on the other hand, you wanted me to talk to the mayor, I could arrange a political appointment to a higher office." He raised his tanned, beefy hand to brush a droplet of lemon juice off the boldly etched Sheriff on his shiny gold-and-silver star.

"Just deputize me. I'll find Warner and see what he knows before I have to head to Florida."

Chapter Twelve

"What are you doing here?" Mitch met them in the driveway of a small frame house in a neighborhood a couple of miles outside Sunnyside.

His shirtsleeves were unbuttoned, his hair a mess, and he was hopping on one booted foot while trying to pull his second boot on. He looked like he'd been sleeping or, at the very least, lying on the couch, watching TV in the middle of the day.

Shelby slipped out of the passenger side of the new temporary deputy's sleek black pickup. He'd said he didn't want to tip Mitch off that they were looking for him by being seen around town in Shelby's minivan. That rang true enough to her, but she also noted that the tall, broad-shouldered man in the low-fitting Stetson climbing out of that big black truck made an impressive—to some people, maybe even intimidating—sight.

Mitch glanced her way, then back at Jax, then back at her again. "Hey, Shelby. How'd you know where I was living now?"

Shelby winced. Mitch seemed to change his living arrangements every six to ten months, always saying he was moving up to the next good thing. Why hadn't Shelby realized he might really have just been moving away from the last bad thing?

"You filed a police report today. Gave this address." Jax strode right up to Mitch, close enough that if the shorter man lost his balance while struggling to put his boot on, he'd go face-first into Jax's chest.

"I don't know what you're here for, Stroud, but I…" Mitch forced his foot into the boot, then stomped it on the cement drive a few times to get it all the way on. When he straightened up, he squinted at Jax and spoke through clenched teeth, like a bad guy in a Western hoping to call the hero's bluff. "I reckon you're sticking your nose where it don't belong."

"Got the authority of the great state of Texas, or at least this county's sheriff's department, which says I *do* belong here." At this point, on a TV show, the deputy would flash his shiny badge to add some clout to his words. Jackson Stroud didn't need that kind of clout. "I just came to ask you a few questions."

"I didn't do nothing." Mitch turned to Shelby. He stabbed his fingers through his reddish-brown hair a few times, squashing it into place as he asked her, "You believe me, right, Shelby?"

"I want to believe you, Mitch." That summed up their relationship and probably explained why other people thought they could predict her responses and sometimes needed to push her toward the best action. She wanted so badly to think everyone was really trying to do the right thing. "You just make it hard to do."

"Because of this place?" He motioned to the house behind them. "I don't live here. I mean, my name's not on the lease. I've just been crashing with some friends until I can get on my feet."

"What friends?" Jax asked, eyeing the house.

"Uh, people." Mitch shrugged. "They come and go. It's not a formal deal, you know. They're good people, and they help each other out."

"By loaning each other cars?" Jax asked. He stepped to one side and craned his neck to check the side of the house.

"Yeah, exactly." Mitch folded his arms and anchored his boots in the middle of the drive.

The two of them gave Shelby the feeling of a storm brewing, and it made her stomach tighten.

"Then what did you do with your car, Mitch?" Jax crossed his arms, as well, fixed his eyes on the other man and narrowed them to slits. "Loan it to someone, then report it stolen to cover up for…something?"

"Yeah."

Jax shot a quick glance in Shelby's direction.

"No!" Mitch threw his hands out.

"What is it, yes or no?" Jax pressed.

"Yes, I did loan my car out but, no, that ain't the whole story. I got my car back, and this girl, Courtney, who I'd let use my car before, disappeared with it."

"So you're sticking with that story?" Jax spoke softly, without even a hint of a threat.

In fact, if Shelby had her eyes closed, she might have thought Jax was actually accepting Mitch's story. Yet the immovability of his stance, even the hint of a smile on his otherwise calm face, gave the feeling that Mitch was about to learn firsthand why you don't mess with Texas's lawmen.

"It's true," Mitch protested.

"So you have no idea where the red car is?" Jax nodded, recounting the details. "The car that was in the parking lot this morning, when you tipped off the driver of said car to hit the road?"

"Oh, Mitch." Shelby had had as much of the man's lies as she could stand. "What have you done?"

"Listen to me, Mitch. I'm trying to help you, give you a shot at doing the right thing. Take it. Tell me what's really going on."

"Nothing, man." He held his hands up and took a step back from Jax, then turned to Shelby. "I mean it, Shelby. I'm innocent."

"Mitch Warner, I can think of a lot of words to describe you, but *innocent* is not one of them." Her head was swimming with all this information. "Stolen or not, Mitch, you knew who was driving your red car all along, even way back when Sheriff Andy first asked you about it, didn't you?"

Mitch grimaced.

Shelby's heart sank. "You wanted me to believe you had changed!"

Mitch squirmed.

"Look, I don't know you, and I don't know if you've changed or if you've always been the man I see standing here right now," Jax said, leaving no doubt that the man he saw before him did not impress him much. "I do know that there is someone out there who left a baby on a doorstep. That is an act of desperation, which tells me that person needs help. By refusing to tell us what you know, you may be keeping them from getting that help."

"I…I didn't think of it that way." Mitch peered over his shoulder, then cleared his throat.

"You have a full name to give us?" Jax maneuvered

his way between Mitch and the house. "A whereabouts would be even better."

"She's got so many names, I can't remember them, and if I knew her whereabouts, then I wouldn't have reported my car stolen, would I?" Mitch took a couple of shuffling steps toward the house.

Jax shifted just enough to block Mitch from having a clear path inside. "You'd tell me, would you?"

Mitch seethed silently for a moment, then took a deep breath and let it out in a big huff, looking more like an exasperated teenager dealing with a tough teacher than a grown man facing an officer of the law. He motioned toward the front steps of the house, as if asking them to pull up a chair and get comfy. He sat down on the left side of the bottom step.

Shelby took the second step from the top, on the right side.

Jax remained standing, but with one boot on the bottom step, not far from Mitch. He looked ready for anything Mitch might say or do.

Shelby was grateful for that and for all he was trying to do for her here. She shaded her eyes to look up at him, standing so tall against the bright Texas sky, and before she knew it, she found herself smiling.

Jax nodded her way. The smile he gave her seemed to tell her not to worry, he had everything under control.

"Now, where were we?" Mitch asked, clapping his hands together, then rubbing them and grinning. "You were here to get the lowdown on finding my stolen car?"

"If that's what you have to tell yourself in order to finally give up some useful information, then sure, that's why we're here." Jax stretched his arm out and rested one hand on the iron handrail. "We needed the lowdown, so naturally we thought of you."

"I told you what I know. My buddy who owns this house met Courtney at a bar a few weeks ago." Mitch jerked his thumb over his shoulder to the small but neatly kept home. "Since then she's been around, comes and goes, borrows cars but always brings them back with gas in them, so nobody minds. That's all I know."

"She borrow your car the night Tyler said he saw it at the gas station?"

"She could have. I mean, without me knowing it. Sometimes if there are a lot of people, a person just grabs the keys and takes the last car in the drive."

"Friendly place," Jax said to Shelby, sounding far more congenial than she'd have expected him to be. He even dropped his hand, as if just about to accept Mitch's explanation. Only, he clearly had not accepted it, which made it all the more pointed when his expression went flinty, and he homed in on Mitch. "But didn't you tell Sheriff Denby your car had been in the shop at that time?"

Mitch opened his mouth, then shut it. He made a sort of halfhearted gesture with both hands. He started to speak again but stopped. Then he sighed and turned to look up the stairs. "Here's the thing, Shelby."

"Oh, no!" Shelby stood right up. "Not the old 'Here's the thing,' Mitch. When you start in with that, you might as well say, 'Let's draw a big red circle around what I'm about to tell you, because *this* is the part I want you to believe, in spite of all evidence to the contrary.'"

Jax laughed. "I'm getting a feeling that nobody is going to buy what you're peddling with that line anymore, Mitch."

If someone else had said that, they would have meant Shelby was not going to buy what Mitch had to say. They would have been letting Mitch know what they thought Shelby felt and what she was going to do. But when Jax said it, because of the way he said it and because of who he was, what Shelby heard was "Shelby's made herself crystal clear, and I agree with her."

She pulled her shoulders up. "Just tell us what you know about this Courtney, Mitch. No excuses. No long stories."

"All right! All right!" Mitch stood up, looked up the steps, then out at the driveway. "My car *was* in the shop, because Courtney took it that night, put over a hundred miles on it and somehow knocked the muffler loose. This time, she really did steal my car."

"Warner, man, your story just does not hold together." Jax shook his head. "How could she have stolen your car when you told her to drive off in it this morning?"

"What do you mean?" Mitch looked sincerely confused, maybe a little hurt, by the line of questioning. "Didn't you hear me yellin' at her *not* to take it to parts unknown?"

Jax clearly wanted to respond to that, but the look on his face said he had no idea how.

"I believe him, Jax. He may be a practiced liar, but he clearly needs that practice. Take him by surprise, and he's not so…" She looked over the disheveled man standing there, scratching behind his ear and shifting from foot to foot. "Smooth."

Jax chuckled, not laughing *at* Mitch but *with* Shelby. It was a subtle kindness and cool control that marked him as a thorough professional and a good man. It was the kindness-and-good-man part of that equation that had Shelby weak in the knees.

Jax took a deep breath and pushed his hat back on his head. He exhaled, shaking his head. "Okay, then, Mr. Smooth Guy, I'm guessing you also don't know anything about Shelby's debit card situation."

"Just what they're talking about in the café," Mitch said, tucking his hands in his back pockets.

"You mean the café this morning?" Jax asked, seeking clarification.

"Yeah. Sorry, Shelby. Tough break, huh? But the bank covers that kind of thing, right?"

"This morning, when we saw you?" Jax asked, pressing on.

"Yeah, that's what I said," Mitch snapped.

"Jax, why are you being so…"

Jax started speaking the same time she did, and when she let her words trail off, he kept talking. "In the café this morning, when we saw you, hours before Shelby even found out about what happened with her account?"

"Yeah." Mitch did not miss a beat. "People were talking about who all had their accounts hacked around town, so when you said Shelby had a problem…I'm not stupid. I did the math."

"You know, Mitch, I believe you." Jax gave the other man a buddy boy–style smack on the back. "You have done the math."

Shelby knew that Jax had no interest in being Mitch's buddy. "What's that supposed to mean, Jax? Are you accusing Mitch of something?"

"You asking me if I'm suspicious of the guy, the answer is yes." He looked right at Mitch and did not back down. "But I'm just doing the job Sheriff Denby expected of me. Asking questions, looking for motivation."

"You want to know my motivation? It's taking care of Shelby. That ain't no lie. Look me in the eye, Stroud. You'll see it. That ain't no lie."

Jax did look Mitch in the eye, and to Shelby's surprise, her ex held that look and did not back down.

"Okay, Mitch. You want to do right by Shelby, then if you see this Courtney or if you hear from her—"

Mitch held up his hands to let Jax know he was miles ahead of him. "I'll let her know you're looking for her."

"Please don't. In fact, maybe it would be best if you didn't *do* anything. Just ask her if she was there the night Amanda was left, and if she was, if she saw anything—a car, a person, a note flying off in the wind. Even something that doesn't seem important but got her attention. Just find that out and let us know. Got it?"

"*That* I will do." Mitch nodded at Jax, then faced Shelby, and his expression softened. "I won't let you down, Shelby."

"I believe you, Mitch." She smiled as she came down the stairs past Mitch, then past Jax, who lingered behind for just a moment.

"I believe you, too." Again Jax played the buddy card, putting his arm about Mitch's shoulder and giving a shake. Then he leaned in close and spoke low in a tone that sounded anything but friendly. "I also believe I wouldn't want to be you if you do anything that hurts Shelby or Amanda and keeps them from getting this resolved."

"What did you ever see in a mess like that Mitch?" Miss Delta didn't even let Shelby finish recounting the story of their exchange with her ex-boyfriend before she started shaking her head and tsk-tsking.

Shelby had insisted on coming straight home to Miss Delta's after that. She had missed Amanda and hadn't wanted Miss Delta to feel taken advantage of by being asked to watch her for any longer. Jax had intended to drop Shelby off and circle back to watch the house for a while, thinking this mysterious Courtney and the red Mustang might show up again once she felt the coast was clear.

However, just dropping someone off was not an option in Sunnyside. Miss Delta and the baby had been waiting on the porch for their return, and the minute he'd pulled into the drive, she had rushed up and had started asking questions. Then the offer of pie and coffee. And before he knew what hit him, Jax was seated in the bright, welcoming kitchen with a fork in his hand and the whole story on his lips.

"Mitch?" Shelby acted almost offended by the suggestion of her bad taste in men. Though the twinkle in her eye when she looked at him gave her away. "Weren't you listening? Jax was the one making the veiled threat."

"Veil? Me?" It was his turn to overplay the outrage. "I never once wore one of those in my life."

Miss Delta let out a peal of laughter.

Shelby smiled and shook her head, murmuring something to the baby in her arms about Jax's silliness. The room went quiet for a moment before Shelby seemed compelled to add, "Go ahead. Make a joke out of it all, but I'm telling you, Mitch was not lying."

"No argument from me." He took a bite of pie.

"Really?" Shelby jerked her head up from fussing over Amanda.

"Sure. Especially if you were listening." Jax lifted his coffee cup and peered into the dark, rich liquid swishing against the delicate white china. "He practically told us he would warn this so-called car thief we were on her trail."

"He's not a cop, Jax. He didn't know what he was supposed to do."

"*That* I will do." Jax poked the air with his fork, as if underlining every word for emphasis. "That's how he put it when I told him all he had to do was get us some more information."

Jax couldn't help feeling he was losing ground to a guy who had broken her heart over and over already. People who cared for Shelby didn't care for Mitch—and he had probably played a hand in the theft, or at least protected the person who had stolen a chunk of her life savings. It should have aggravated him, or at least annoyed him. Instead he found himself grinning at her and thinking, *That's my Shelby.*

His Shelby? No, Shelby was her own woman. And if he could just get her to the point where she didn't bring this Mitch character back into her life and where she had done all she could for Amanda, Jax could move on with a clear conscience. A heavy heart, but a clear conscience.

"Hey, since I'm here, why don't we go through those photo albums?" He set the fork down on the empty plate and wiped a paper napkin across his mouth.

"After this day?" She stroked the baby's head. "Jax, I just don't think I'm up to it."

"Not to worry, sweetie. I spied that box marked Books and Photos in your stuff stacked in the hallway." Miss Delta gave a wave of her hand that made it clear that the petite powerhouse didn't mind doing a task one bit and wouldn't be deterred from it. "I'll bring it down to the kitchen, where the light is good, and we can all help you out."

"Miss Delta, you don't have to—"

In a flash of blond hair and bargain-store baubles, Miss Delta was gone.

"Why are you resisting this?" Jax picked up his plate and Shelby's and took them to the sink. "Don't you want to find Amanda's mom?"

"Yes. I do. Of course I do."

Even with his back to her and the rush of water pouring from the faucet into the sink as he rinsed the dishes, he could practically hear her squirming in her chair. When he shut the water off, he twisted his head to catch sight of her over his shoulder. "But?"

"But…" Shelby ran the back of her hand over Amanda's cheek, then along the baby's arm. She touched the tiny ballet slippers Jax had insisted on buying after Shelby's card had been turned down. "Maybe Amanda's birth mother doesn't want to be found."

He shook the dishwater off his hands, then dried them on a towel hanging from the handle of the stove. "Okay. Interesting thought. Want to tell me more?"

Not only did Shelby seem to want to tell him more, but suddenly it was as if she couldn't help herself. She got up from the table so quickly that the legs of her chair screeched over the old floor.

"What if by seeking her out, I break the trust she placed in me by leaving Amanda on my doorstep?" With Amanda in her arms, she came close to Jax, her eyes filled with concern. "What if her circumstances are such that she needs no one to know about the baby, and then

I show up and ruin everything? We don't know, Jax, and if…if…"

"And if you never find Amanda's mom, you never have to give her back?" He asked it with a heart full of concern, and not an ounce of accusation.

Tears filled her eyes.

Jax went to her, putting one hand on her shoulder and one on Amanda's head. He waited until she met his gaze. "Shelby, you know that's not how this is going to go, right?"

"No, I don't know anything right now, Jax," she whispered, laying her cheek against his shoulder.

"This from the girl who stood right there telling me that when Mitch was smooth, he was lying. You heard him smooth talk his way around, knowing too much about your missing debit card, and you still wanted to believe the best of him?" He stroked her hair back from her face, kissed the top of her head and laughed softly. "How can you not believe the best of this situation?"

"With God all things are possible." She raised her head. She swiped away a tear and sniffled. "You reminded me of that when I said I wanted to change my third rule of living."

"Maybe I *should* have told you to change that third rule from 'Never trust a cowboy' to 'Quit trusting Mitch Warner.'" He pinched her chin between his thumb and forefinger, paused to soak in the warmth and beauty of her eyes, then leaned in to plant a kiss on the baby's head before he moved to the table to finish his coffee. "You're Amanda's foster parent until the state makes other arrangements. Unless you find the mother and she resigns her parental rights to the state or agrees to a private adoption."

"Is that what you want, honey?" Miss Delta appeared in the doorway with a cardboard box in her hands. "Are you honestly thinking of adopting Amanda?"

Shelby's cell phone kept her from answering. "Well, will you look at that? It's the guy who you said I should give up on." She pressed the talk button. "Hey, Mitch. What's up?"

"What does he want?" Jax took the box from Miss Delta and set it down on the table with a thud.

"He texted Courtney after we left, and he just heard back," Shelby whispered.

"He has her cell number? That would have been nice to know. Sheriff Denby might be able to—"

"Shhh." Shelby put her finger to her lips, even as she scrunched her whole face up to concentrate on the voice on the other end.

Miss Delta rushed in to take the baby and give Shelby the freedom to stick her finger in her ear and cut out the sound around her.

"Say that again, Mitch." She gasped. "That's what she said? The blackest hair she'd ever seen? Oh, Mitch, I know who that is. Thank you. Goodbye."

"You know who Amanda's mother is?" Miss Delta dropped into a kitchen chair, baby and all.

"We're looking for someone who knows me, who is old enough to have had a baby, who doesn't live in town or have anyone in town who would have known she had a baby, and has the blackest hair you've ever seen. Yeah, I know." Shelby tore open the box on the table and pulled a bright blue photo album free.

Jax moved in to look over her shoulder. Miss Delta hopped up and did the same, Amanda and all.

The pages flipped back and forth before she suddenly

put her finger down just below a young girl's face. "It's Amanda."

"It *is* Amanda. She looks just like her!" Miss Delta's earrings went swinging as she shifted from looking at the photo to looking at the baby.

"If Amanda wasn't bald and chubby and a baby." Jax squinted at the photo, but he just couldn't see it.

"No. The name on the blanket. I think it wasn't meant to tell me what to call the baby. It was telling me who left her. Amanda Holden. Everyone called her Mandie." Shelby took off out of the room, calling out over the sound of her footsteps, "Amanda lived with her grandmother from summer through Christmas the year her parents split."

Jax slid the photo out from the plastic covering and checked the back for any more information. When he saw nothing, his attention drifted to another photo, this one of a fresh-faced Shelby standing by her dad and a painted sign with two hearts on it and the words The Lockhart Ranch.

Miss Delta stole a peek at it. "Look at how young Harmon looks. Shelby fell in love with that place the second she saw it."

"Loved it? I didn't think she ever lived there."

"Maybe I misspoke. She loved the *promise* of the place. After her mama died, Harmon sort of came unmoored in life, and I think she believed that ranch would give him, and her, the thing they had lost. A home."

"The promise of a home," Jax echoed. He brushed his finger over the image, feeling privileged for the glimpse into what made Shelby who she was.

"See?" Shelby came into the kitchen, holding up her backpack and the embroidered blanket they had found

Amanda in. "I taught Amanda how to do embroidery just like this."

"You were wondering if she wanted you to find her or not." Jax smiled. He had noticed the similarities in stitching style that first night. He couldn't help wondering if the girl Shelby had taught had ever considered that it wouldn't be obvious to Shelby. "I think you have your answer."

Shelby took the baby they had been calling Amanda into her arms and pressed a kiss to her cheek.

Jax slid the photo of young Shelby hoping for a real home back into the album, then looked at the woman standing before him, hoping to become a real mom. "Now you have to decide what to do about it."

Chapter Thirteen

Jax left her to let it all sink in, reminding her that as an acting deputy, he had a duty to report what he had learned. He couldn't promise what that would bring. His actions might bring a swift conclusion. Or the report might get lost in the shuffle of bureaucracy and prolong things indefinitely. Identifying Amanda's birth mother would, by his estimation and personal experience with having been a ward of the state of Texas, wrest control of Amanda's situation from Shelby in favor of the state system. Even if she was allowed to keep Amanda, it would be as a foster caregiver, not as an adoptive mom.

That was worst case, of course, but still.

"Hey, it's almost supper time. We all know how happy Sheriff Denby would be to get a call asking him to come to the office so I can file a report about something Mitch Warner claimed to have been told," he had concluded. "Why don't I go pick up some things for dinner, we invite Harmon over and you think about it all?"

In other words, she needed to come to terms with the situation and decide how she would handle it—soon.

Gathering up the photo album with Mandie Holden's

picture in it, she retreated to the sanctuary of her rented room and cuddled up in a large old rocking chair with baby Amanda in her arms. She hummed a lullaby, but the child did not seem one bit sleepy.

So, rocking gently, she pulled out the photo of Mandie.

"You know who this is?" She showed the old photo to the baby. "We think that's your mama. Your birth mama. Yes, we do."

Baby Amanda clapped her hands over the picture, then tried to chew on one corner.

"Well, Miss Delta does. She says you look just like Mandie." Shelby wriggled the photo free and studied the image of a young girl with long black hair, big brown eyes and olive skin. "Jax says he doesn't see it at all. I don't know. I mean, if it's not her, it would be such a coincidence, wouldn't it?"

She set the picture aside and then realized a second photo had been taken from inside the album and lay loose in the pages. She slipped it out and found herself staring into the face of her father and her younger self.

"And these people here?" She twisted her wrist around to put the photo in Amanda's sight but out of her reach. "These are the people who already love you like you are their very own flesh and blood. At least, these are *two* of the people who already love you like…" The words snagged in her throat. "You want to know who else loves you? Miss Delta, that's who. And Doc and Sheriff Andy and…Jackson Stroud."

She tucked the photo back in the album, shut it and sighed. "He may not admit it, but I can tell that man is just crazy about you, kiddo, and when he goes away, you won't ever even remember he was here."

A tear rolled down her cheek. It all seemed so very much to carry by herself. A baby. A desperate mother who put her highest trust in Shelby. A guy she had trusted, and who had broken his word countless times, would still stick around, while the one man she trusted and who had never let her down would be leaving. How did she make sense of it all?

Shelby thought of her three rules for her new life and bowed her head. Holding the baby she had come to love close to her heart, she prayed for the wisdom to know what was right and the strength to do it, to do what was best for Amanda, no matter what.

She must have drifted off to sleep after that, because the next thing she knew, the doorbell rang downstairs and it had started to get dark outside. She got up and changed the baby's diaper and put her in a sweet pink outfit, then straightened herself up and took the back stairs into the kitchen, where she found Miss Delta and Jax unloading grocery sacks.

"There she is," Harmon called with his arms spread wide. "There's my girl!"

"I'm not falling for that again, Dad." Shelby lifted the baby away from her dad and, without meaning to, placed the child right in Jax's waiting hands.

The tall man with the penetrating eyes took the child like he'd been doing it forever, and met her gaze. "So, did you come to any conclusions while I was gone?"

"Yes," she said firmly. Clinging to the baby's tiny hand, she followed along behind Jax until he stopped, and the three of them became their own little quiet island in the big, bright kitchen. "I want somebody to tell me what to do."

"I thought you *didn't* want people doing that." Shelby's dad kicked his booted foot up to rest on his knee and tilted his chair up on two legs.

Miss Delta's mouth set in a firm line. She narrowed one eye and crossed her arms, but instead of getting after Harmon about sitting at her kitchen table properly, the woman aimed her discerning gaze at Shelby.

Jax lifted Amanda onto his shoulder, and even the baby seemed to home in on Shelby.

"I didn't want people thinking they knew what I was feeling, or volunteering me to do what they thought I should do," she corrected. "And then expecting me to do it and feel happy about it."

Harmon dropped the feet of his chair to the floor with a clunk.

Miss Delta tipped her head to the left, then to the right, sending her dangly earrings swaying.

Jax held Amanda before him, a perplexed look on his face. "Did *you* understand that, sweet thing? Because I have no idea what your foster mom just said."

Hearing Jax call her Amanda's mom touched Shelby in ways she had no idea how to defend against. That was what it had all come down to, hadn't it? She was conflicted about finding Mandie because only one of them could be Amanda's mom. "Just tell me what to do, Jax."

"I can't, Shelby Grace. Nobody can, or at least nobody should." He leaned back against the counter to touch her face lightly. "You are the one who has to live with the consequences, so you have to make this decision. What do you want?"

"What do I *want?*" To keep Amanda. To help Mandie. To know that Mitch and her father and Miss Delta were all going to be the people they truly seemed to want to be, to have the lives that God wanted them to have. She wanted Jackson Stroud to stay in Sunnyside. She wanted…a home. But none of those things were certainties. In fact, some of them were most likely never going to happen.

She shook her head. "I don't know that what I want even matters, Jax."

"It matters because until you know what you want, you aren't going to do what you need to do to make it happen." He stroked her cheek. "And all of us who love you won't be able to resist rushing in and trying to do what we think is best for you."

Shelby could feel her father's and Miss Delta's eyes on her, but she couldn't get Jax's words out of her mind. *All of us who love you.* For one fleeting moment, she thought that maybe at least some of the things she wanted could be hers. "Jax, I—"

"So you need to decide. We can take the information Mitch gave us—which amounts to a secondhand tip from an unreliable source—and turn it in to the system, and you can wait and see what happens. Or—"

"I know what I want." The instant he had said "You can wait and see," not "We," it all became clear to her. Even as she claimed to be an independent-minded woman who trusted the Lord, her whole life she had relied on other people to define her. She couldn't do both those things. She was choosing independence and trusting God. "I want to be Amanda's—the baby's—mom."

"All right! I'm gonna be a real grandpa!" Harmon sprang to his feet, took the baby from Jax's arms and began whirling her around the room.

"Oh, sweetie, that's a wonderful idea. I wish I'd had that kind of gumption when I was your age." Miss Delta rushed forward and gave Shelby a kiss on the forehead.

Shelby rolled her head just enough to look past the fringe of stiff hair-sprayed blond curls brushing her cheek and temple and find Jax, his unwavering gaze fixed on her. This was it. She was in charge. "And I want you to help me do it."

Jax called Sheriff Denby first. "I say we work backward from what we know now, and forward from what anyone in town might have known about Mandie and her grandmother years ago."

"Makes sense to me. I'll get the word out," the sheriff said in a matter-of-fact tone.

Jax covered one ear to make sure he had heard right in the clatter and chatter building around him at Miss Delta's. He raised his voice to improve the odds of being heard. "You're not coming over?"

"Sounds like you've got a handle on things there." Sheriff Denby also spoke louder than he needed to. "I've got more than enough to do here now that we know we're looking for this Courtney girl in connection with Mitch Warner's stolen car."

"Courtney, Mitch, the car he now says was stolen showing up here on the night the baby was left, the identity thefts of customers of Miss Delta's place and the Crosspoint?" Jax shook his head. "I can't help thinking there's a connection."

"Yes, and her name is Shelby Grace Lockhart." Sheriff Denby paused to let that sink in before adding, "So you take extra care of our girl and call me if you find out anything more."

They hung up with that thought in Jax's mind. Shelby was the point where all this intersected. He had worried initially that this put her at risk of physical danger. Now, having come to know her, he knew she had put herself in danger—not of physical harm but of having her heart broken. He would do anything to protect her from enduring that again. That meant he had to find this Amanda and convince the young woman to make her wishes for Shelby to raise the baby a reality.

Jax took the lead from that point. He spoke to everyone personally, no "Someone told me" or "I heard this or that" allowed. Between that and whatever Sheriff Denby did on his end, it didn't take long before people were simply showing up at Miss Delta's house to volunteer information. This relegated Jax to the front porch, where he could make sure he didn't miss anyone but could avoid the chaos and the crowd shuffling through the rooms and hallways inside.

"Hey, Tyler." Jax stuck out his hand to the kid who worked part-time at Miss Delta's.

Tyler, who had been standing at the foot of the front steps, fixated on his phone for at least a minute, raised his head. "Hey, man!"

Jax waited for the kid to come up the steps and shake his outstretched hand.

A car pulled up and parked on the street. Headlights flicked off. Car doors slammed. People got out and called greetings.

Tyler didn't move. Jax went down the steps and forced the issue. Taking the kid's hand, he shook it, as if to say, "Be a part of the world, kid. This is how it's done."

The man he was almost two weeks ago, when he left Dallas, would never have made that concession. That man would not have cared that some kid wasn't participating in the goodness of small town life.

"Oh." Tyler caught on and actually responded to Jax's

overture with a solid grip. He even made eye contact and smiled. "My mom told me to come over and see if you needed anything from me."

Jax put his hand on the young man's shoulder, feeling like he'd accomplished a small victory. "Not sure what you could do. Unless you've recalled some details from that night you thought you saw Mitch Warner at the pump?"

The kid held up his phone, as if to say that was where his attention had been focused.

Jax nodded, mulling over whether he should say more about life going on all around them and not missing it. Around them, fireflies had begun to flicker and flit, and Jax had to strain to make out faces in the dimming light. A pang of guilt hit him. Who was he to tell someone to be more engaged in life? Up until he'd come to Sunnyside, the only reason he'd paid attention to people and his surroundings was to try to figure them out, to make his case or to keep them from getting close.

He tapped the edge of his own phone. Then had a thought. "Hey, Tyler. You were texting when I drove up to the Crosspoint the night we found Amanda. Any chance you mentioned seeing Mitch to whomever you were texting with?"

"Uh." He looked down at his phone and hit the contact icon. "Yeah. I think I did."

Jax stepped in closer, a bit stunned to see the number of contacts scrolling past under the boy's skimming thumb.

"I think I said I hoped he didn't fill up and take off," Tyler said. "Because I knew how much it would embarrass Miss Shelby for her old boyfriend to be caught stealing from Miss Delta."

"Can you check back through your old texts and find out what time that happened?"

"It'll take a couple minutes, but sure." Tyler nodded.

"Come inside and join the party while you do that." Jax gave a jerk of his head and headed up the steps.

It pleased him more than he could ever have anticipated when Tyler followed his lead, came into the foyer and actually interacted with people even as he searched through his old texts.

Shelby came up behind the young man and gave him a friendly shake. "Hi, Tyler. The light for that's better in the kitchen. And there's food."

"Cool." Tyler didn't have to be told twice.

As he disappeared into a cluster of folks laughing and talking, Shelby sidled up to Jax, who chose to stay close to the screen door. As they stood side by side, she folded her arms and said, "You know, I worried when you started asking people to come here to talk to you directly that Miss Delta would resent the intrusion."

"Are you kidding?" Jax took the whole scene in, in a long, sweeping glance. "She's like a queen holding court. And with Harmon in the kitchen? They're putting everyone at ease, making my job easier."

Shelby looked up at him. Her face, lit by moonlight on one side and the mellow glow of the old crystal chandelier above them, took on a kind but wistful expression. "Well, if nothing else comes out of this, I will always consider it a blessing that I got to see Miss Delta get at least a taste of her lifelong dream."

Jax opened his mouth to ask something that had nothing to do with the task ahead of them. Nothing to do with figuring out anyone's motivations. Nothing to do with anything but listening to Shelby, sharing a moment with Shelby. "What do you mean?"

Shelby's eyes met his, and for a moment he thought she might just shrug it off, but when she spoke softly, almost achingly, about Miss Delta's dream, he understood why.

"You know that Miss Delta said she always wanted to have a home filled with love and family here in Sunnyside."

She might as well have been talking about herself. Jax had no doubt about that. It touched his heart, but it also set off an alarm in his head. He might have made that dream come true for one night for Miss Delta, but he couldn't do the same for Shelby. His future lay down a different path.

So he did his best to redirect the conversation. "I was asking what you meant by 'if nothing else comes out of this'?"

"I mean…" She blinked. Tears washed over those beautiful blue eyes. Her lower lip quivered. She tipped her chin up, and in an instant her composure returned and she spoke with grace and acceptance. "I mean that even if we find Mandie, Jax, there is no way of knowing how it will all turn out."

He should have been relieved. He had thought the same things again and again, but hearing it from Shelby, it got to him. He took her in his arms and held her close, hoping to provide some comfort as he said, "I know. But, Shelby Grace, I have to believe it will be okay. Clearly Mandie wanted you to have Amanda. We just have to make that happen through the proper channels."

For a moment she just stood there in his arms.

Jax wondered if he had crossed a line. If he should let go, back away and make a joke or—

Shelby wound her arms around him, tentatively at first, then tightly. She buried her face in his chest. She did not cry, but sighed the way someone does when they finally surrender their burdens, if only for a little while.

Jax closed his arms around her and laid his cheek against the soft waves of her hair. He inhaled the scent of her and the night and the aroma of home cooking, and felt the loneliness of his past melt away. He might not carry that feeling for the rest of his life, but he would have this memory.

"Uh, sorry to break this up, y'all." Tyler stood beside them, his phone in one hand, a grilled cheese sandwich in the other. "But I got that text time for you, Jax."

Jax reluctantly pulled away from Shelby.

She let her hand drag across his arm as she moved back. With each step, her smile grew from weak to reassuring.

Jax smiled, too, then checked the phone. "Okay, I wasn't expecting this."

"Everything okay?" Tyler asked.

"Yeah, that was a lot of help. Thanks, Tyler." He patted the kid on the back to send him on his way. When the young man slid the phone into his pocket and joined a group talking in the parlor, Jax shook his head and scowled. "Something's off here, Shelby. And it goes back to Mitch and his story about this mysterious Courtney. According to the time of Tyler's text, he saw that red car at nine thirty-nine. The silver SUV ran me off the road around ten thirty-five. There is almost no chance that Mandie sat in a big silver SUV at the café for at least an hour with nobody noticing."

"I admit I was distracted that night, but it doesn't seem likely, does it?" Shelby pivoted just enough to stare out the screen door at all the vehicles parked outside, as if confirming she would have noticed the SUV in that amount of time. "Wait! *I* missed a call in the middle of the night from an unknown number. Is there some way to trace it and see if it was Mandie?"

"Let's see." He held his hand out. "Give me your phone."

Even after handing over her phone, Shelby's fingers flitted around the edge of the small device resting in Jax's palm.

"Even though it showed up unknown, the police can find out the number, right?" she asked.

Jax saw the time and date. "They can, but they won't have to."

"Why?"

He pulled his own phone out and flicked the screen on. "Because I'm the one who called you that night."

"You?"

"Yeah, I'd just found your note and…" The memory of reading her words and knowing he had to come back to her twisted in his gut. "And I called to tell you I was coming back."

"I see," she whispered.

"Maybe I should add my number to your contact list to keep that from happening again." He wasn't asking to do it; he was telling her that they needed to have each other's information because it wouldn't be long before he'd be gone again.

"Thanks." The tremor in her voice told him she understood the implications of his offer. "I'd hate to feel like every time I got a call from an unknown number, I might think it's you, telling me you're coming back."

Jax froze. He stared at her phone in his hands because he couldn't look at her. He wanted to say something, but what?

"The lady told me to speak to the deputy?" A middle-aged woman came marching down the hall, aimed directly at them. Just before she got to Jax, she stopped and gave him a puzzled look. "But you're the busboy at the café, aren't you?"

"I'm both," he admitted, a little glad for the interruption. "And, honestly, I'm neither."

She frowned.

"If you find that confusing, imagine how *I* feel." Jax laughed.

Shelby laughed, too, and hers sounded as strained and hollow as his had.

The woman shook her head and jumped in with what she had to say. "I bought Louella Holden's old house. I have contact information for her son. Would that be any help?"

"Everything new that we learn is helpful." Jax put his hand on her shoulder. "This might just be the information that brings this whole case together."

Miss Delta came waltzing by to offer a glass of tea as he slipped into a quiet room to make a quick call to Louella's son. It was a brief conversation, and filled with tension, but he did find out where Mandie was living now—and one other thing, which shook his whole system of looking for motivations in people to the core.

Chapter Fourteen

He motioned for Shelby to follow him to the back porch. They stepped into the serenity of the late spring night, and the chaos filling the old house seemed a million miles away. So did her fears and anxieties. She inhaled the smell of wonderful food, night-blooming flowers and Jax's aftershave. Years from now, when someone asked her what she remembered about the stranger who had come to town and had found the baby she hoped would then be her daughter, she would think of this moment. She knew it.

Jax leaned against the railing and held up his phone. "I spoke to Mandie's father."

Shelby closed her eyes to say a quick prayer for peace and good judgment, no matter what followed from this moment on. She opened her eyes and squared her shoulders. "Did you get her number?"

"I certainly hope not." He shook his head. "Shelby, Mandie's father hasn't spoken to her in years."

"Years?" She tried to comprehend that. "I can't tell you how many times that summer someone would say to me that Mandie came from a broken home. I guess I had no idea how broken."

"He knew nothing about any baby, though the idea seemed far-fetched to him."

Shelby chewed her lower lip for a moment before admitting, "You know, it does to me, too. Nothing about leaving a baby in the night fits with the girl I knew."

"Her father had no phone number for her, but he could tell me that when he and his second wife split three years ago, she stayed in Westmoreland to finish her senior year of high school. He believed Mandie could still live there." Jax curved his hand around her shoulder and lowered his head, putting them eye to eye. "Because last he heard, she'd been living with her stepsister, Courtney. Oh, got a last name on her, too, finally. Collier."

Shelby's breath stopped. Just stopped, as if the wind had been knocked out of her.

"Mandie and Courtney…" She tried to make the pieces fit together. "You think Mandie was part of it all, of stealing from my bank account?"

Jax didn't say a word.

That told Shelby more than she wanted to know, so she decided to tell him a thing or two. "I don't believe that. I can't. Not for one minute, and I think we need to find her and get this all sorted out as soon as possible. How do we do that?"

"We could find a place to set up a laptop around here and do some searching online and see what we come up with. Or…" He held up a scrap of paper. "We could sneak out of here, get in my truck, drive out to this address and see what we find."

"Let's do it."

Of course, they couldn't really sneak away. As an

acting deputy, Jax had to let the sheriff in on their plan, such as it was. And Shelby had to get Miss Delta to agree to take care of baby Amanda. Still, they managed to do that without telling her, or anyone else at the house, why they needed to dash off.

"You know, some people will jump to conclusions about why we left," Jax told her as he opened the door to his truck and offered his hand to help her climb in.

She hesitated, stole a look back at Miss Delta's bustling Victorian, then slid her hand into his. "Let them talk. People will do what they do. You can't stop them. You can only love them and live so that no matter what they say, you know God is pleased with your choices."

She stepped up into the cab. When she settled in, she found Jax still standing in the open door, inches away.

"What?" she asked.

He leaned in from the shoulders up, close enough now that she could see the muscles in his cheek twitch, as if he were holding back a grin. "Just a week caring for Amanda has changed you, Shelby."

"For better or worse?" she whispered.

"I honestly didn't think you could get any better," he said in a voice almost as still and quiet as hers. "But you have."

She broke away from the intensity of his searching gaze. "Everyone can always grow for the better, Jax."

"See? There you go again, better and better." He chuckled deeply in that engaging way he had. Pushing away from the truck, he slammed the door shut.

Shelby took advantage of his absence to fan her cheeks, which she hoped hadn't gone positively scarlet over the man's nearness.

Seconds later, Jax got behind the wheel and shut his

own door. His presence seemed to fill the cab of the truck, and when he started the engine and looked her way, his gaze homed in on her as keenly as his observation. "'Everyone can always grow for the better' is not the sentiment of a girl who wrote about never trusting again, who decided to give up on her dad and friends and hometown rather than believe she could find her dream right here with them."

Shelby mulled that over as they drove in tense silence through the darkness toward both Amanda and Courtney's last known address. It wasn't until they turned onto the street and Shelby noticed Sheriff Andy's official car parked a few houses away that she finally spoke up again. "I wish Sheriff Denby didn't have to be in on this. Won't it send the message she's in trouble?"

"She *is* in trouble, Shelby." Jax pulled into the center of the driveway. "If she left the baby or did any of this, or knew about it and did not turn her stepsister in, there are plenty of ways she could be very much in trouble."

Suddenly Shelby realized that Jax, and even Sheriff Andy, saw this so differently from how she did. The sheriff had parked out of sight to avoid tipping anyone off. Jax had parked in a way that would keep anyone from getting a car out of the garage and taking off.

"I get that Mandie is also a very troubled girl." He pressed a button to lower the truck's window as Sheriff Andy came up the walk. Clearly he planned to talk with the man without the telltale sound of the truck doors closing to signal their arrival. "That doesn't change the fact that she abandoned a baby, or that there's some connection to Courtney, who at the very least is accused of stealing a car."

What she had told Jax about loving people and doing

what the Lord expected weighed heavily on her heart. "If I could just talk to her…"

"The law is not devoid of mercy, Shelby, especially in Andy Denby's hands," he reminded her.

"I know."

"By seeing this through the proper way, Mandie can get what she needs—counseling, medical aid, legal advice," Sheriff Andy chimed in as he reached down and quietly opened her door. "Keep that in mind when you talk to her."

"Shelby? You want to send Shelby in first? Alone?" Jax shifted in the seat with enough pent-up energy to rock the whole truck gently.

Sheriff Andy stepped back to swing the door open. "Shelby is with us because Shelby *needs* to be with us, not just for her own interests, son."

Jax gripped the steering wheel. He didn't offer further objections, but he didn't have to—his concern about her involvement created a palpable prickle in the air around them.

"It will be okay." Shelby reached out and gave his arm a squeeze. "You're going to be right here if I need you."

The strain in his posture eased. He leaned over in the seat to put his mouth near her ear, saying with conviction, "Count on it."

"I want to," she murmured.

For just that moment in the darkened closeness of the truck's cab, Shelby wanted him to know that even though she understood it couldn't last, she believed with all her heart she could count on him.

He leaned closer still, close enough for a sweet stolen kiss.

Shelby shut her eyes in anticipation.

"Aren't you two getting a bit ahead of yourselves?" Sheriff Andy barked from the drive.

They moved apart.

"I guess I'd better…"

"Yeah. Go." Jax cleared his throat and squared his shoulders. "I'll watch for trouble from here."

Sheriff Andy made a sweeping motion, like a footman escorting Cinderella from her coach. "We don't even know if either of the girls still lives here, or if either is home, you know."

Shelby nodded. She took a deep breath.

Jax opened his door and stepped out of the truck. She didn't even hear his boot steps on the driveway. Then he was simply at her side, his hand on her back. "I know you're scared, Shelby. Not of Mandie, but of what might happen once you confront this whole tangled-up mess of a situation."

"I can do this. I know what I want, Jax." She kept her attention fixed on the door, and on the most important thing in all of this. "I want whatever is best for baby Amanda, no matter what the cost to me."

Jax folded her into an impulsive hug. "Mandie made a good choice when she decided to leave her baby in your care."

Buoyed by his confidence and closeness, Shelby went up on tiptoe, placed a kiss on the man's cheek, then turned and hurried up the drive and onto the porch. She flexed her hand, shook out the stiffness in her reluctant fingers and rang the bell.

It felt like minutes before she heard the shuffling of feet and a woman's voice call out, "This had better not be who I think it is, because I meant it when I said I'd call the cops if I ever saw—"

The door swung open. A young woman with the blackest hair Shelby had ever seen stood in the doorway. Shelby thought she whispered the woman's name, but in the intensity of the moment, she wasn't sure she even remembered her own name. From this second forward, nothing in her life could ever be as it was before baby Amanda came into her life. Even if Mandie had no connection to the child, which seemed wildly unlikely, Shelby knew she would never rest until she had found the child's mother and set things right.

In the measure of a heartbeat, the young woman's expression went from dark as thunder to bright excitement. "Miss Shelby? I can't believe it! I'm so happy to see you."

Mandie Holden threw herself at Shelby with so much force that it carried Shelby staggering backward a step or two before she found her footing and returned the joyous embrace. "Mandie! It *is* you. You do still live here, and you look…" Shelby wriggled away to take a good long study. "You look so grown-up!"

"Twenty-one last month!" The young woman beamed.

"Twenty-one? How is that possible?" Shelby counted back all those years and realized that seven years was a bigger gap when Mandie was twelve and Shelby was nineteen. Now, instead of thinking of Amanda's birth mom as a child, she viewed her more as a contemporary. That thought empowered her more than she expected.

"We need to talk, Mandie." She was not dealing with a young girl in trouble, with no life experience, who had made a hasty emotional choice, but with someone old enough to have made better choices. Someone old enough to have asked about the baby she'd left. Those would have been the first words out of Shelby's mouth. "Can we come in?"

"We?" Mandie flipped her long black hair over her shoulder and peered out into the yard.

Shelby motioned to Sheriff Andy and Jax.

The men came forward.

"A sheriff? Oh, no, what now?" Mandie put her hand to her forehead, as if suddenly hit with a pounding headache. "Is Courtney in trouble again?"

Sheriff Andy and Jax slowed the pace of their approach as they exchanged a look that Shelby could only think meant they didn't quite buy Mandie's surprise.

"So, you still have contact with your stepsister, Courtney?" Shelby took Mandie by the arm to turn her away from the scrutiny of the two lawmen. Yes, it was a protective gesture that had good ol' softhearted Shelby written all over it. Shelby didn't care what it looked like. She cared only about Mandie and Amanda and getting all this sorted out. "Does Courtney live here with you? When did you last see her?"

"Yes. That is, she did live here until about a week ago, when she took off." She moved ahead of them into the small house.

The furniture was a bit on the shabby side, but no more so than most people her age just starting out would have. Shelby saw no sign of extravagance that might have been bought with other people's money. She also saw no sign of a baby having lived in the home. Not even a photograph.

It tugged at her heart. "Mandie, I—"

"I don't know where Courtney is, y'all." She whirled around to face them, meeting Sheriff Andy, then Jax, then Shelby squarely in the eye as she said, "But you could probably find her if you could find that guy she's been hanging around with—"

"You know *that guy's* name?" Jax stepped forward to ask.

Mandie shook her head. "She said he *gave* her a car, and the next thing I know, the cops showed up saying he reported it stolen."

"Mitch," Shelby muttered, closing her eyes to keep from having to face Jax and from feeling like a foolhardy girl for having taken Mitch back into her life time and time again. Shelby sighed. "Look, Mandie, we didn't come here about that."

"Not *just* about that," Sheriff Andy corrected.

Shelby opened her mouth, trusting somehow that she would find the right words for what she had to ask, but no sound came.

Jax moved in behind her, taking her tense shoulders in his big, gentle hands. He literally and figuratively had her back. "Mandie, Miss Shelby brought us all the way over from Sunnyside tonight because she needs to know… Why did you leave the baby, and what can we do to help you deal with all this?"

"The baby?" A crease formed between Mandie's dark eyebrows, even as she let out a perplexed sort of laugh at Jax's phrasing. "You mean Amanda?"

"I thought *you* were Amanda." Sheriff Andy shifted his weight. The silence of the small room amplified the creak of his black uniform shoes and gun holster.

"I am. But so is the baby Shelby is adopting. That is, that's what Courtney named her. I made her a blanket with her name on it. I kind of hoped you'd keep it—the name, not the blanket—well, also the blanket, but if you wanted to call her something else…"

"Whoa, whoa, slow down here." Jax threw his hands up in a gesture so calming and sure that everyone seemed to pause and take a breath.

"*Courtney* named her?" Jax tipped his head, leaning one ear in Mandie's direction, as if to say he wasn't sure he'd heard right. "Aren't *you* the baby's mother?"

"Me?" Mandie put both hands to her chest and stepped backward so quickly, she knocked over a plant stand with a withered cactus on it. She didn't even care when the whole thing toppled to the floor with a dull thud. She just rallied and put her fists on her hips as she asked, "Did Courtney tell you that?"

"None of us have ever even met Courtney." Shelby bent down, scooped up the poor undernourished plant, set the stand upright and put the pot back where it belonged. "All we've had to go on is a blanket with the name Amanda on it and a secondhand report of someone with the blackest hair she'd ever seen at the Crosspoint Café the night we found an abandoned baby there."

"Oh, no! Abandoned?" The younger woman looked genuinely pained at that news. She put her hand over her mouth. Her face went pale. She shook her head and sank into a nearby chair. "I should have known something was wrong. She lies about everything, you know. Of course she'd lie about this."

This time when Shelby did a visual check of the sheriff's and Jax's expressions, she saw concern.

"Abandon Amanda?" Mandie looked up at Shelby, her eyes imploring. "I just don't get why she would do that."

"We can't help you figure it out until we hear the whole story." Jax moved closer.

"Start with Courtney and the baby." The sheriff got out a pad and pen to take notes.

Mandie nodded to acknowledge their request, waited for everyone to take a seat in the small room and then began to unfurl a vivid story about her younger stepsister's many struggles after Mandie's father and Courtney's mother split. For years the family and those who wanted to help had dealt with Courtney skipping school, shoplifting, staying out late. When Courtney's mother had moved to get a fresh start, she had even allowed Mandie and Courtney to rent the family home from her in hopes it would give them some stability.

Just a couple of years out of high school, Courtney had become pregnant. At first it seemed like just the thing to get the girl on the right path. She took care of her health, stopped drinking and smoking and went to church with Mandie a few times. The baby's father had promised they'd marry as soon as he got a job and had some money saved up.

"The baby's father? Mitch?" Jax asked.

"No. A boy she went to school with. He hung around as long as his folks paid the rent and Courtney's bills, but then after they had the baby, neither of them seemed able to take care of Amanda. Or really wanted to." Mandie looked down at the floor, her shoulders slumped. "I'd have done it, but look around here. I'm not ready for that kind of responsibility. I couldn't give the baby what she needed."

"But you thought of someone who could," Jax prompted, stealing a glance at Shelby.

Shelby pressed her lips together, fighting the urge to burst into tears at the whole story.

"I remembered how good you were with kids, Miss Shelby. How much your daddy loved you, how much everyone in town loved you. And I told Courtney about you." Mandie gave Shelby a big smile. "Courtney didn't meet this Mitch until a few weeks ago, when she started going over to Sunnyside every few days—which she told me was to meet with you about adopting Amanda."

Jax leaned forward in his chair. "Let me guess. She also told you that Shelby was giving her money to help out with her expenses."

"Yes." She nodded, paused, then fiddled with her hair and added, "Don't tell me *that* wasn't true, either."

"She got my bank information and stole about a thousand dollars before I even knew it, Mandie," Shelby said.

"Oh, Miss Shelby!" Mandie shot up from her chair and came over to where Shelby was sitting on the couch. She knelt on the floor and folded her arms over Shelby's knees. "I must have asked her a million times if I could talk to you on her behalf or join your meetings, and she told me she wanted to do it herself, to stand on her own. It seemed like such a positive step, taking responsibility, that I... Can you ever forgive me?"

Shelby reached out and took the younger woman's hand in hers. "Forgive *you?* You did nothing wrong."

Mandie's inky black hair shimmied from side to side as she shook her head vehemently. "I feel so guilty that I couldn't get Courtney to straighten up, the way you did for me."

"I didn't do anything but spend time with you, Mandie."

"I know. You spent time on me when nobody else seemed to have any to spare for me. Now I work full-time. I'm taking some college courses. And I teach Sunday school—preschool, but it's a start."

"It's a wonderful start, Mandie!" Shelby stood and gave the young woman a hug.

"All thanks to you, Miss Shelby." Mandie hugged her right back, and it seemed clear the meeting was winding down.

"Do you have a way to contact your stepsister?" Sheriff Andy asked, pen poised over paper. "Any idea when you might see her again?"

"Well, since this guy reported her stealing his car, and she knows people are onto her for hacking their debit and credit card accounts, it's a pretty safe bet she'll show up here before too long."

Sheriff Andy asked for a photograph of Courtney, and when Mandie found one, Shelby captured the image on her phone. Then Sheriff Andy wrapped up his part in it all and left to go coordinate what he had learned with the Westmoreland Police Department.

"Night, Miss Mandie." Sheriff Andy tipped his head to the young woman seated at Shelby's side. "Thank you for your cooperation."

He placed his hat on his head, gave Jax a look that Shelby couldn't quite decipher and let himself out.

Jax, sitting on the edge of the chair across from the couch, looking ready to spring into action at any moment, turned toward them. For the first time since he'd rushed to the aid of what he had thought were kittens in a basket on the Crosspoint's deck, he seemed uncertain about what to do next.

He slapped his hands against his denim-clad legs. He started to speak, then refrained. He appeared genuinely pleased when his phone chimed out his no-nonsense ringtone, and he tugged it from his pocket. "I should probably see who this is."

As the picture of the building in Miami spread across the small screen, he frowned. His forehead creased and his eyes went almost squinty, as if he thought he could intimidate the object into silence.

"It's okay. We're pretty much done here. Answer it if you need to." *Need* to. Not *want* to. Shelby had chosen her words purposefully. If Jax wanted to get back to his real life, the life he was on the path to creating when he took the detour into Sunnyside almost two weeks ago, Shelby did not want to know. But doing what a person needed to do—that she understood, and she would do nothing to interfere.

His hesitation did that job for him as the call went to voice mail, indicated by a buzz and a different kind of chime.

Jax let the phone rest on the arm of the chair for a moment. He sat back in the seat, kicked his right boot up to rest on his left knee, then adjusted his position and did the opposite. Finally, his large hand hovering just above the cluster of icons on the screen, he picked up the phone.

"Ladies, if you'll excuse me?" He stood. "I've got something to take care of before we get back on the road, Shelby."

Shelby watched until he completely disappeared out the front door before she turned to Mandie again. So many things she longed to say, so many messages she wanted to give to both this young woman and to baby Amanda's birth mother. She just didn't know where to start. "I want you to know that I have loved every second of having baby Amanda in my life, and I don't know what I will do if—"

"Oh, Miss Shelby, don't even imagine that Amanda will be taken from you. The baby's father gave up his rights, and his parents were happy to have Amanda go to you."

"So Courtney has everyone believing she went through the proper channels?" The whole story saddened Shelby, but this news gave her a ray of hope. If Courtney had made her intentions to choose Shelby to raise Amanda clear, and the father and paternal grandparents had agreed to that, then in all likelihood the adoption would go through smoothly.

"They may want to see Amanda from time to time, but they're not interested in raising a baby. They told Courtney that firsthand when she would take off for days and leave Amanda with them."

"I can do that." For the first time in days, when she said she could do something, she felt sure she actually could, not just hopeful that she'd try her best.

"I'll do whatever I can with Courtney, or with the legal people, to make sure they know the baby belongs with you."

"Thank you, Mandie. That means a lot." She took the young woman's hand and gave it a squeeze. "And it would also mean a lot if you'd just call me Shelby. I don't even remember how that Miss Shelby stuff got started, but I never have liked it. It makes me sound a million years old, especially when half the town, some of them only three or four years younger than me, calls me that. Nobody asked me if I wanted to be called that. They just thought I'd like it."

"Oh, Miss Shelby, I don't know if I could."

"You *have* to," Shelby insisted, speaking up for herself at long last. "We're friends now, and it's what I want."

"Okay then…Shelby. Everything will work out. You'll see. That sheriff will see to it that Courtney doesn't pull anything funny, and that Jax guy?" Mandie's dark eyes grew big. She let out a long low whistle and shook her head. "I don't think he'd let anybody do anything to hurt you, *ever.*"

Not on purpose, she thought, but because of Jax, Shelby knew she would be hurt. And yet she knew now that she could handle it.

"With him on your side, you and Amanda have nothing to worry about."

Shelby almost blurted out that the Jax guy wasn't in this for the long haul. That, in fact, the call he had just gotten was most likely a summons for him to hit the road. One he had no reason not to answer, now that there wasn't anything more for him to do about finding out who left Amanda.

Instead, she gave Mandie a hug, reminded her to do as Sheriff Andy asked to cooperate with his investigation and thanked her. Then she headed out to join Jax, knowing that she had another goodbye in her near future.

Chapter Fifteen

Though Shelby had smiled all the way through the five-minute-long hug fest filled with thank-yous, encouragements and promises to keep in touch, as soon as the truck hit the highway headed back to Sunnyside, she began to cry softly. The tears flowed the whole way back, and Jax didn't say or do anything to try to stop them. Shelby deserved to have this time to just let go, to not have to fear the repercussions of showing her emotions.

He couldn't change the situation with Courtney or Mitch or Amanda. He could, however, protect her from the assumptions and expectations of practically everyone in Sunnyside.

He stole a glance her way.

She twisted around in the seat, keeping her face to the side window, but the shiver in her shoulders and a slight sniffle gave away that she hadn't worked through things yet. He'd seen this time and again in people of strong character, strong determination and even strong faith. They kept moving forward, allowing nothing to deter them from their goal, then often lost control when it all came to a conclusion—even a happy conclusion.

The truck's headlights slashed across a sign advertising Buffalo Betty's Chuck Wagon Ranch House.

"Hey, maybe when all this is settled, you and Mandie can take Amanda back to the restaurant and—"

"I don't think so," she said quietly.

"I know it's a lot to process. But you're on the downhill side now." He believed that, and it gave his words renewed energy as he assured her, "Once Sheriff Andy files official charges of child abandonment against Courtney, things should be on track for you to start the process of becoming Amanda's mom, right?"

"I know. I'm relieved about all that." The heaviness of her sigh belied that claim. "Mandie said over and over that Courtney has no interest in keeping the baby, that the time she had Amanda made her see she wasn't ready for parenthood."

"I hope that's true, but…" Jax wished he could tell her there wouldn't be bumps along the way, but he had dealt with people like Courtney over and over in his experiences in the foster care system and as a cop. There were so many unknowns at play, so many possible outcomes. He believed with all his heart that Shelby would fight for what was best for Amanda and that it would work out, but he couldn't pretend she wasn't in for a struggle. "When this all catches up with her, you realize that Courtney could use severing Amanda's parental rights as a bargaining chip."

"I don't care. I still want to work things out for Amanda." She sat up straight in the seat and shook her hair back like a woman filled with new resolve as she added, "And for Courtney."

"For Courtney?"

"Yes. For Courtney." She shifted in the seat just

enough to angle her upper body toward him. Her whole face took on that fierceness he had seen in her that first night, when she thought she was standing up to the kind of man who would leave a baby on a doorstep. "This is Amanda's birth mother, Mandie's stepsister. I know she's made a lot of mistakes, but it sounds like she's had a lot of people let her down in life, Jax."

It took everything in him not to bust out in a big old grin as she spoke.

"I just hope she gets a chance at redemption, at making up for those mistakes," she went on. As she looked out the side window again, her voice grew softer. "That's all. I want everyone in this to know God's love and mercy and to have a better life."

"Of course you do."

Shelby whirled her head about so fast, Jax half expected to hear the sound of a whip cracking. Her eyes all but shot fire. He'd seen *that* look before, and it made his heart sing.

"Are you making fun of me, Jackson Stroud?"

"That's the furthest thing from my mind," he said with quiet conviction. He had always looked for people's worst motivations as part of his work, and as an excuse not to get close to them, he now understood. Shelby didn't look for shortcomings in anyone, and even when presented with them, she considered how to help those people overcome their issues. Jax was better for just having known her.

"No. In fact, I was just thinking how much I admire you, Shelby Grace. How much I've learned from you in this short time we've known each other."

She opened her mouth to say something sassy—he could just read it in her posture and the flush in her cheeks. Then the moment passed, and as his confession seemed to sink in, she went a bit gushy, pulling her shoulders up and tilting her head to one side. "Really?"

"Really," he said, not hesitating to confirm his statement. He did hesitate before he said what he knew needed to be said next, and when he spoke, he kept his eyes to the front, not even stealing a glimpse to see how she took his words. "And because of that, I know it's going to be okay for me to leave now."

She didn't argue or ask anything more about his plans. She turned her head again, and they drove on until the truck went gliding into Sunnyside.

"Wait, this isn't the way to Miss Delta's house," she said, pointing toward the street he had just passed.

"I know. That's the phone call I made. I asked Harmon to bring Amanda and meet us at the café." Jax guided the truck around to the back lot that the Crosspoint Café shared with Miss Delta's Shoppers' Emporium and the Truck Stop Inn, as if he'd done that very thing day after day for years. "I wanted to give you a minute to compose yourself and not have to do that in front of everyone."

She managed a nod and whispered, "Thank you for that."

"And I wanted to tell her goodbye."

Jax pulled his truck into a spot that allowed him to see the street and know when Harmon arrived with the baby. He knew it would not be long, and he wanted to make the most of this last little time he had alone with Shelby.

She sniffled and tugged a tissue out of her purse. "I grabbed a wad of these from Miss Delta's house because I thought I'd need them for Mandie."

Always thinking of others first, Jax thought. He decided not to say it, in case it might make her feel defensive. In his book, this woman needed no defense of her emotions or actions. "Shelby Grace, in case I haven't made it clear already, meeting you, spending time with you, well, you...*you* have changed me for the better."

"Oh, Jax, that's..." She gave him the shiest of smiles, then opened her door and gave a not quite convincing laugh. "That's a pretty big responsibility to lay on my shoulders."

He opened his door and climbed out of the truck. Over the solid clunk of both doors falling shut, he called out to her, "I thought it was a compliment."

"Oh, it is." She rummaged in her purse for a minute, then retrieved her cluttered key ring. It jangled in her hand as she started toward the darkened café. "I am so humbled that you think that, but you know what I think?"

He didn't follow her. "What?"

She turned and put her hands on her hips. "That maybe I was just an instrument of the Lord in whatever has affected you this week."

"That's fair." He nodded.

She gave a little bow, like a diva accepting an ovation, then turned and headed toward the café, her steps crunching in the gravel of the small lot.

Jax watched her retreating. There, with only the bright moon to light their way, Jax could not see any telltale signs as to her mood or mind-set. But he didn't have to. In just this short time, he had come to understand Shelby Grace Lockhart in ways he had never understood another person alive.

He planted his own feet in the gravel and, even as they settled in slowly, unevenly, called out after her, "But I hope you recognize that by being you, by having the kind of heart that's open to so much love, you gave the Lord a lot to work with."

Her steps slowed, then stopped. She cast a look at him over her shoulder.

He went to her, brushed her hair back with one hand and said, "I will never forget you, Miss Shelby Grace Lockhart."

"Oh, Jax. That's the sweetest thing anyone has ever said to me." She looked up at him, a smile on her lips but the threat of tears in her eyes. She laid her palm on his cheek, then let her hand fall to the side of his neck, his shoulder. Then she lifted it away and smacked him hard once on the upper arm. "I can't believe you waited until you had to go to say it."

"Hey, I thought I was being nice!" He rubbed his arm, even though he had barely felt the blow.

"Being nice just before you say goodbye is…is… It's just crummy, that's what it is. Now every time I think of this time and your part in it, this is what I'll think of. Not all the good, just the goodbye! It's a rotten thing to do to a girl, Jax, to leave her with that kind of—"

Before she could get another breath to press on with her rant, Jax stepped in, wound his arms around her and kissed her. Not the quick, tender kisses they had shared along the way, but a real kiss. A goodbye kiss.

The seconds went by, counted out by their beating hearts, and the kiss ended.

Shelby tried to push away from him, but he held her just a moment longer. "Whenever I think about my time in Sunnyside, that's what *I'll* remember."

Stay. If she just said that one word, Jax might actually…might actually have to tell her no. He had a contract. People counting on him. Shelby had a lot to work out here, and trying to fit in a relationship on top of it all wasn't fair to her.

Shelby had had enough of other people using her good nature to get what they wanted. Jax couldn't be another one. He had to leave Sunnyside, for Shelby's own good.

The glow of headlights turning into the lot from the road made Jax let go and move away.

Shelby bowed her head and did the same.

Less than a minute later they were in the café, Miss Delta, Harmon, baby Amanda, Shelby and Jax.

"Hey, beautiful," Jax whispered as he took the baby in his arms one last time. "I know you won't remember me, but I hope you know that I'll be praying for you every day, just like I did the night we found you. Praying that you will find your way. Praying that you will be happy."

Any further words caught in Jax's throat. He clenched his teeth tight and settled for just giving the child a kiss on the head. When he saw Sheriff Denby slip in through the unlocked back door, he handed the baby back to Shelby, lingered a moment with the two of them, then headed over to resign.

"Not going to stay and see this to the finish, then?" Denby asked before he would take the silver badge glinting in the overhead lights of the café.

"I made a promise to be in Miami. This is one cowboy who always keeps his promises," he said.

"I guess I was wrong about you." Miss Delta shook her head.

"How so?" Jax asked as he fit his Stetson on, preparing to get back on the road, to get on with the life he had planned before this detour.

"I thought you were where you needed to be. Seems like it was only where you ended up on your way to where you needed to be." She gave him a sad smile, then stretched up to give him a kiss on the cheek. "I hope you find what you're looking for at your next stop."

Jax hoped so, too, though he sincerely doubted he would.

"So, you're really going to go. I guess you got your answer, then?" Denby flipped the badge over in his open palm.

"Why Shelby Grace? Yes, because everybody trusts her and she deserves that trust." The answer came quickly to Jax's lips.

"I wasn't asking that question literally, son." The older man shoved the badge into his shirt pocket, then gestured toward Shelby at the counter, talking to her father. "I was asking if it wasn't worth finding out why, out of all the people in the whole wide world, someone, anyone, would leave a baby with Shelby Grace Lockhart."

Shelby moved the baby to her other shoulder, her cheek brushing the baby's cheek, her eyes glittering with delight and maybe the beginning of tears.

Jax nodded. He didn't know if he smiled or if his eyes reflected the emotions of the moment. He took a deep breath and answered Denby's question simply. "I think I know why."

"And you're still gonna leave, anyways?" The older man shook his head.

The question hit Jax like a sucker punch to the gut. Rather than let anyone, even someone who had been as close to a father figure as Jax had ever had, see how much it cost him to leave Shelby, he made a joke. "You just want me to stay so you can groom me to take over your job so you can retire."

"That your fancy big-city police-procedure detective

training talking, son, or that gut feeling about why people do what they do that you claim to have?"

"Little bit of both." Jax adjusted his hat and shifted his boots in line with the shortest way to the door.

"Hmm." The sheriff studied him with his lips pursed; then he lifted his shoulders and gave a shrug that somehow conveyed more disappointment than disinterest. "You'd think between the two of them, you'd have done a better job figuring out what was going on."

Jax met the sheriff's eyes. He couldn't tell if the man was joking or not.

"What I want, son, what *any* man who serves and cares about people wants, is what's best for *them,* not himself." He put his hand on Jax's back. "Count it as a blessing if they work out to be the same thing."

Jax nodded. "I will."

"Got no reason to believe that, son." His expression said he wished he could believe it. "You haven't so far."

Jax wanted to argue with the man, but the tough-as-leather sheriff gave a snort, shook his head, turned and walked away, leaving Jax standing there, all alone among people he had known only a few days, but whom he cared about more than he could express.

So he left it at that, left anything else he felt or hoped unsaid. He raised his hand and told them that if he left right away, he could be in Miami by tomorrow afternoon.

Shelby moved toward him, but he held up his hand to hold her off. They had said their goodbyes. He didn't think he could go through another one and still get in that truck and leave.

And he had to leave. For Shelby's sake.

Chapter Sixteen

By Friday of his first full week on the new job, Jax had already begun to count out his days in terms of "How long until lunch?" "How long until my next break?" "How long until quitting time?" Except with this new job, there was no quitting time. More than once, that had made him think of Sheriff Denby's halfhearted complaints about working in a small town. Jax knew the man had loved his years of service, and was loved and respected in return for all he gave.

Here there was no respect to speak of, and certainly no love. No respect for boundaries. No consideration of him as a person, deserving of personal time or basic personal pleasantries, like learning his name.

Before his time in Sunnyside—before Shelby Grace Lockhart—that would have been just fine with him. Now when most people who bothered to speak to him, usually to demand something, called him Jack, or worse, Jackie, he cringed. To be fair, he hadn't learned the names of many of the people in the gated community, either. He tended to think of them by descriptions of their houses—the yellow villa on Bradford Street. Or by their cars—Mr. Leave a Space between That Truck and My Jag. He had never once tried to figure any of them out. Why they did what they did just did not interest him.

In fact, he had spent more time in these past few days trying to figure out why he had done what he had than ever before in his whole life. He thought it was for Shelby, but now with the gift of time and distance, he had to wonder. Had he really put her first—or used that as an excuse?

It must have been the right thing to do, he argued. If it hadn't been, wouldn't Shelby have called and asked him to come back?

"Why?" he heard himself whisper in the silence of his truck cab, where he'd gone to sit during his afternoon break to check his phone messages.

The answer to his question did not come, so he settled for who, what, where and when as told in texts and missed calls from Denby, Miss Delta, even Tyler.

"Courtney Collier turned herself in yesterday. She said she had a change of heart and wanted to do the right thing. I suspect that Mandie got Shelby Courtney's phone number, and our girl's been doing what she does so well. She may just love that lost lamb right back into the fold yet. If anyone can do it…" Denby had paused, as if he wanted to make sure Jax took a minute to let that sink in. Then the older man had cleared his throat and added, "Just thought you'd like to know."

Next came a call from an attorney who would be working on Shelby's petition to adopt Amanda, with a request to speak to him to get a statement about the night they found the baby. It made him smile to know things had begun to get resolved, and Shelby was making progress toward becoming Amanda's mom.

Tyler sent a quick text: Can I ask Mandie Holden out even if I have to testify against her stepsister, or is that against some law?

"Yeah, against the law of probability that she'll say yes." Jax chuckled, then felt badly that the kid might get shot down. He tapped in the only answer that he could think of, then let his thumb linger a moment over the send icon before he touched it and sent the message: Okay to ask but maybe you should talk to Miss Shelby first. She'll have your answers.

Miss Delta had called to say that it seemed wrong to charge him for that last night because he didn't actually use his room at the Truck Stop Inn. She wanted to send him a refund if he'd give her his new address. "Oh, and by the way, that Mitch Warner wanted to move into your room in the inn. Harmon was all set to run him off, but Shelby beat him to it. Said he was one cowboy she had learned could not be trusted."

"That's my girl," he whispered with a small laugh. "That's my Shelby Grace. *My* Shelby Grace," he repeated, this time not finding even the hint of amusement in the term.

He took a deep breath and leaned his head back, his eyes shut. When he had first heard of this job and decided it was the thing he needed to get away from Dallas, where people had begun to actually care about him, he hadn't even heard of Shelby Grace Lockhart. Now it seemed everything, even his misery in this place, this job, came back to her.

If only he could hear her voice again. If she would just call…

"Hey! Jack! What're you doing out here?" A sharp rapping on the window inches from his face gave Jax a start. He turned to find the president of the neighborhood association red-faced and beady-eyed, with his nose almost pressed against the window as he blustered, "Have you forgotten why you came here?"

Jax pressed a button, and the window rolled down with a steady whir. "What did you ask me? *Why?*"

That was the big question that had dominated Jax's life. Why did he take this job? Why did he take the turn-off to Sunnyside that night? Why was he here?

Why Shelby Grace Lockhart? Sheriff Denby's question. The question that had compelled him to stay in Sunnyside when it was not a part of his plans came ringing back in his mind.

That question was easy to answer. People came to Shelby because she had a servant's heart. She didn't just say it, but she believed that with God all things were possible. And despite what she said about trusting cowboys, she trusted God more than her fears.

If Jax's heart was changed by knowing her, why was he on the same path he'd started down before they'd ever met?

"I came here because I thought living in a place where I got a big check to always stay a stranger was the way to keep from ever losing anyone again. The way I lost my mom or all the foster families I lived with." Jax swung the truck door open, more to encourage the other man to back off physically than because he intended to get out. "I thought this place sounded like a dream come true."

"If you want to go on drawing those big checks, you'd do well to do your job." The man pulled his shoulders up with enough force to make his thinning hair waft out of place, revealing his receding hairline. "Not sit in your vehicle, wasting time on the phone."

Jax looked at the device in his hand and realized there was one more call in the voice-mail queue. "My Shelby Grace."

"What? Did you hear me?" the man barked.

But Jax couldn't hear anyone or anything but the voice on the other end of the line saying, "What are you doing? You know better than…Jax? Jax, I'm sorry. Amanda must have dialed your number. I, uh, I don't know if I ever told you thank you, but in case I didn't… thanks for helping me figure out what I want in life and telling me not to be afraid to go for it. I hope you're doing the same."

Shelby had stood up to Mitch; she had worked to help Courtney no matter what others might have thought of that. She didn't need him to leave to do those things. They were in her all along. It wasn't her needs that had caused him to leave Sunnyside, but his. What had motivated him? Fear? Grief?

He had to ask himself, what was in him? Was he a man of faith and service? Was he a family man or…

"This time is coming out of that big paycheck you say you came here to get." The man tapped his gleaming gold watch, then turned to storm off.

"Yeah, well, what if I don't care about those checks anymore?" Jax climbed out of the truck and took a good long look at his surroundings. They had every luxury, every convenience, and not one single thing that mattered to him. "What if my dreams have changed?"

The man blustered a moment, then stabbed his finger in Jax's direction. "You just don't forget your place, you hear me?"

"Yes, actually, I do. I hear you loud and clear, and I think that's very sound advice."

* * *

Shelby finished filling the last of the ketchup bottles in the café and twisted the cap on tight. With the expenses of the adoption process looming ahead of her, she was happy to pitch in whenever Harmon needed a hand, especially at night, when Miss Delta was all too happy to watch over the baby. They had almost finished closing up when a flash of headlights drew her attention. She checked the clock. "It's almost eleven. Should I lock the door?"

"Do it," Harmon called back. "Tyler's still got some customers. If somebody's hungry, they can grab a snack over there. I'm bushed."

"Not too bushed to go over and visit the baby, like you do every night, I bet," she joked as she headed to the door to turn the lock.

"I love my granddaughter," he called back as he hung up his apron and reached for his beat-up old straw cowboy hat hanging on the wall.

"And it doesn't hurt that when you visit her, you get to spend time with Miss Delta, does it?" After all these years, for her father and Miss Delta to have realized their happiness might just be right here in Sunnyside with each other warmed Shelby's heart. It also made her wonder about her own future.

She stole a peek through the blinds on the café door, looking past the lot with a cluster of vehicles still in it to the road that led to the highway and beyond. "After all the papers are signed, Amanda and I can live anywhere, can't we?"

"You thinking of running off somewhere, sweetheart?" Harmon snapped off the lights, and the café went dark except for a faint glow from the light kept constantly burning in the kitchen.

For one fleeting moment, that thought took Shelby back to the night she had thought her only chance to make a life for herself lay in running away. She closed the blinds and shook her head. "No. I belong here. Amanda belongs here. That doesn't mean there won't ever be times that I won't look in the direction of, say, Florida and wonder—"

A scuffing noise outside the door cut her off. She acted quickly and swung the door open.

"Sorry, we're…" A dull *thunk* and a gray cowboy hat tumbling backward on the café's front deck made her gasp. She raised her eyes, and her heart stopped. "Closed."

"I can see you're closed." Jackson Stroud didn't even bother to scoop up his cowboy hat. "That's why I came here. I was hoping to catch you alone before the whole town heard I had come back and started deciding how you should feel about it and what you should—"

Shelby threw her arms around his neck and kissed him.

"Do," he said, finishing his thought when he got the chance to take a breath.

"Nobody tells me what to feel or how to act anymore, cowboy," she said, unable to keep from smiling as she looked into Jax's face.

"Good. Because I know some people might say we haven't known each other long enough for me to say this, but Shelby Grace Lockhart, I love you and I came all the way from Florida to tell you so."

"Florida," she said in a wistful, faraway voice. "I

was just thinking Amanda and I might want to go there someday."

"Yeah? I hear it's a great place to take kids on a vacation."

"Or to live."

"I guess so, if that's where you belong." He wrapped his arms around her and lifted her feet off the ground. "Me? I'm kind of thinking of settling down somewhere else. Got any thoughts on a place called Sunnyside, Texas?"

"Now, what would ever motivate a man like you to do that?" She touched his cheek.

He put his nose to hers. "Did you not hear me say that I love you, woman?"

"Yeah." She smiled a smile that seemed to shine from her eyes all the way down to her toes. "I thought I did hear that."

"Funny, I didn't hear the same from you."

"Maybe if you said it aga—"

"I love you, Shelby Grace Lockhart." He set her down and kissed her. Then he kissed her again. Then he laughed and said, "I love Amanda. I love this nosy little town and the people who are, even as we speak, peering out the café and emporium windows and taking videos with their cell phones...." He glared at Tyler, standing only a few feet away. "And I have come all this way to tell you this is where I need to be, this is where I want to be and you are who I want to be here with."

"A simple 'I love you' would have been enough." She sighed. "Because I love you right back, Jackson. I love this town, too, and I want to raise Amanda here... with you."

"Shelby Grace, are you proposing to me?"

"Oh, I… That's not… I just meant…" She stepped back. "Jax, I'd never…"

"Well, I would." He got down on his knee, started to reach into his pocket, then turned back to Tyler, who was still standing nearby. "This I don't mind if you record on your cell phone."

"Yes, sir," the kid said, holding the object out.

Jax fished a small box out of his pocket and opened it as he said, "I know we haven't known each other long, but I have never felt so at home as I feel when I'm with you. Will you marry me?"

Shelby's eyes filled with tears, and her heart filled with joy. The word turned to dust in the tightness of her throat, but that did not stop her from nodding her yes.

In a heartbeat Jax swept her up in an embrace. Jax kissed her, and the people around them cheered.

"Yes," she said, louder this time. "I can't wait to start a life with you, Jax."

"You may have to write some new rules for living, you know," he teased as he slid the ring on her finger.

"Let's talk about that later." She looked at her ring, glittering in the moonlight, and laughed. "Right now, let's kiss again!"

Another cheer went up from the onlookers.

They did kiss again, then hurried off to tell Miss Delta, Sheriff Andy and Doc Lovey and, of course, to hug Amanda.

Epilogue

Six Months Later

"Who do you think should walk her down the aisle?"

"If you want my vote, I say her daddy. It's what all the cool girls are doing today." Harmon adjusted his bow tie and held his arm out properly crooked for his daughter to slip her hand through.

"Her daddy," Shelby murmured, her heart so filled with love and joy she wondered if people would see it beating through the intricate white lace of her gown. "I like that."

"Imagine how *he* feels." Harmon chuckled.

Shelby didn't have to imagine. One look at Jax's face as he stood waiting at the altar with Amanda in his arms, and she knew. The man loved her. And he loved the little girl who had toddled down the aisle, clinging to his strong, sure hand moments earlier. The little girl they had found one night when they both felt lost and alone, who would officially become their daughter right after Shelby and Jax returned from their honeymoon.

They took their vows before the Lord and everyone

they loved, then headed to the Crosspoint Café for their reception. When it came time to leave and for Shelby to throw the bridal bouquet, she lifted it high, gave a wink to Mandie, her maid of honor, then picked her target out in the crowd.

"Oh!" Suddenly she froze with the bouquet over her head.

"What?" Jax asked.

She brought the bundle of roses and jasmine down and slipped a folded piece of paper out from inside the satin binding.

"There." She handed the single page to him, cocked her arm, aimed and let the bouquet fly.

Miss Delta didn't even bother pretending she thought Shelby ever planned to toss the flowers to anyone else. She caught them single-handedly, then hoisted them up like Lady Liberty with her torch. "You know what this means, Harmon Lockhart. I'm the next one to get married, and if it ain't you, then I may have to snag the next cowboy cop who happens by in the night for my own self!"

The wedding party cheered, and the party went on. Jax and Shelby slipped away, and as they got into the truck with the just-hitched sign on the tailgate, Jax unfolded the paper and read it aloud.

"To whom it may concern, and the only one it does concern, my loving husband, Jax.

I'm not going anywhere. No matter what. Because I love you and I know now there is only one rule I need to make a life with you."

"With God all things are possible," he said without having to even read it.

"With God all things are possible," she echoed.

And with one more kiss, they left the café behind them, though only for a five-day honeymoon, and started their new life as husband and wife.

* * * * *

THE COWBOY'S LITTLE GIRL

Kat Brookes

I'd like to dedicate this book
to my wonderful agent, Michelle Grajkowski,
with 3 Seas Literary Agency. She has been
so incredibly supportive with my writing
endeavors, always believing in me. She's also a
dear friend. I feel so blessed to have her in my life,
both professionally and in friendship.

I would like to extend my deepest thanks
to Ryan Sankey from Sankey Pro Rodeo, who
offered me a wealth of information when I was
researching this rodeo-cowboy series. She was
always willing to answer any questions I might
have had without hesitation. Sankey Pro Rodeo has
four Saddle Bronc of the Year PRCA awards, twelve
PRCA Stock Contractor of the Year nominations, as
well as many PRCA and Montana Circuit awards.
They've been featured on ESPN, *USA TODAY*,
Western Horseman and CMT. More information
on Sankey Pro Rodeo can be found at
www.sankeyprorodeo.com.

Thanks be unto God for his unspeakable gift.
—*2 Corinthians* 9:15

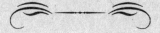

Chapter One

A persistent knocking at the front door of his ranch house had Tucker Wade setting the half-eaten grilled cheese he'd made himself for dinner back onto the plate beside him. Dropping his booted feet from the rough pine coffee table to the wood-planked floor, he stood to answer the door.

His first thought was that it was his oldest brother, Garrett, stopping by to shoot the breeze after returning from tending to Wilbur Davies's sick cow. Garrett, the town's only vet, had gotten called away, leaving Tucker and his other brother Jackson—older by just one year— to see to it the horses were fed and settled in for the evening. But his brothers rarely knocked. And if they did it was a loud, firm rap on the door, not the tentative tapping that had him moving into the front entryway. Not to mention it was near dark and they all followed an early-to-bed-and-early-to-rise routine.

Very little surprised Tucker, but nothing could have prepared him for the shock of opening the door to find his long-lost wife looking up at him. A woman he'd come to accept he would never see again. Didn't care to see again, truth be told. But there she stood, in the fiery red-orange light of the setting sun, looking every bit as pretty as he remembered and yet so very different.

The wispy blonde ponytail Summer had always worn had been replaced by a short, smooth haircut that hung longer in front than in the back. A formfitting navy skirt and matching jacket replaced her well-worn jeans and usual T-shirt. And... Tucker's gaze dropped lower, a dark brown brow lifting. *Heels?* The Summer he'd known would never have worn high heels, no matter how good they looked on her. Even her cowgirl boots had low heels. But then again, he'd only *thought* he'd known the girl he'd exchanged vows with six years before.

All the hurt, anger and confusion he had worked so hard to suppress after Summer took off without a word threatened to surface once again. Thickly lashed ice-blue eyes—eyes that had once held only warmth, now stared back at him with something akin to...mistrust? *Him.* The man *she'd* run out on.

"Tucker Wade?" his long-lost wife asked as if she wasn't quite sure it was him.

A frown tightened the line of his mouth. While he'd admittedly filled out a good bit in terms of muscle, no longer the lanky, bull-riding twenty-four-year-old she'd exchanged vows with at the Laramie County Courthouse, he was pretty certain she knew it was him. What sort of game was his wife playing now?

"I'm sorry to show up unannounced this way," she continued. "And this late in the day. But I had to meet with clients before setting out for Bent Creek."

There it was, that same Texas twang that had drawn him to his wife in the first place. "Why are you here?" he demanded.

Undaunted by the glower he was sending her way, she met his gaze head-on. "I thought it would be best if you heard what I have to say in person, instead of over the phone."

"*Now* you want to talk?" he said, anger writhing though him. "Well, this might come as a surprise to you, but I no longer have any interest in anything you have to say."

"I can't blame you for feeling the way you do," she said softly, "but if you'll just give me a chance to explain…"

"What are you doing here, Summer?" he cut in gruffly, not bothering to suppress the ire he felt toward her. He didn't want explanations. It was far too late for that. In fact, he wanted nothing at all from his wife.

"I'm not Summer." She looked away for a second as her voice filled with emotion. Then, looking up at him with those same silver-blue eyes he'd worked so hard to forget, she said, "I'm her sister Autumn."

What? Tucker blinked back his surprise. First, his wife shows up out of the blue, with no warning whatsoever of her impending arrival, and then she starts spouting nonsense? Who was Summer going to pretend to be next? A sister named Spring, or maybe Fall since it was mid-October? If his wife had a sister, he surely would have known about it.

Dear Lord, give me strength, he prayed.

"I know it's been a few years since we've crossed paths," Tucker grumbled in irritation, "but I'm pretty sure I haven't forgotten what my own wife looks like. Even with all that fancy polishing you've done to change your appearance." Which he begrudgingly had to admit looked really good on her.

She stiffened. "It's not polish. This is who I am."

He gave a derisive snort. "You forget who it is you're talking to. *This*," he said, waving a hand from her designer heels to her pretty little head, "is who you are until you decide the life you're living right now isn't really what you want. Then you'll just up and leave whoever it is who's fool enough to care about you at that time, without so much as a goodbye, and start a whole new life for yourself somewhere else." The jagged edge of the memory of what she'd done to him leaving the way she had all those years ago still cut deep.

She shifted uneasily. "She said you could be stubborn, but if you'll just hear me out…"

He had no idea why his wife had to be told by someone else, whoever "she" was, about his stubbornness. Especially when she used to tease him about it when they were dating. Or had she blocked everything about him and their marriage from her mind?

"I don't want your explanations," he said through tightly gritted teeth. It was five years too late for that. "Go back to wherever it is you came from, Summer. You don't have a place in my life anymore."

To his surprise, his clipped words brought a swell of tears to his wife's eyes. Her emotional response had him shifting uncomfortably where he stood. Maybe he had spoken a little harsher than he ought to have, but she'd done far worse to him all those years ago.

"I'm not Summer," she insisted once more. "And *she* won't be starting her life over," she added, her lower lip quivering slightly with that announcement. "At least not here on earth. My sister's gone."

Had his wife suffered a head injury of some sort? Was that why she was claiming to be someone else? "Sweetheart," he said, trying not to let the flood of emotions he felt at seeing her again show in his voice, "you're standing right here."

"Summer never told you about me, did she?" she asked as if she'd somehow been wronged. Then she shook her head and cast her gaze out across the yard. "No," she said sadly, "of course she didn't." Turning her attention back to him, she said, "I'm Autumn Myers. Summer's twin."

He raised a skeptical brow. "Her twin?"

She gave a slight nod. "Yes."

Tucker's gaze zeroed in on her slender perfectly arched brows, to where they disappeared just beneath the much shorter strands of hair that now framed his wife's heart-shaped face. "You have a scar," he heard himself saying.

"What?"

"The scar above your brow," he prompted with impatience.

"No," she said, "I don't." Reaching up, she pushed the hair away from her face.

"Other side," he muttered with a deepening frown. What kind of fool did she take him for? He'd been there when she'd gotten stitched up after her fall during one of her barrel races.

Without another word, she showed him her other brow. Even in the fading light of day, there was no denying the smooth expanse of skin where the scar had been.

Tucker struggled to drag in even the slightest of breaths. This woman standing before him was not his long-lost wife, no matter how much she resembled her. "Summer's dead?" he said, the words soft and gritty as he tried to process that something like that could even be true. She was so young. And while he had harbored a ton of resentment toward his wife after she'd walked away from the life they'd started together, to the point where he never ever wanted to see her again, this was not the way he'd wanted that to happen. Tucker's heart squeezed.

"Yes," Summer's twin replied. Never had one word been so filled with emotion.

"What happened?" he rasped out, finally accepting the truth for what it was. The woman that he'd once fancied himself in love with was dead. May she rest in peace.

"Summer took her horse out for a ride near our home in Cheyenne," she began, tears shimmering in her eyes.

"Summer was living in Cheyenne?" he muttered in disbelief. That was where his wife had chosen to put down roots? Not back home in Texas, in whatever town it was she had grown up in, but in Cheyenne. In the very place they had exchanged their wedding vows. How had they never crossed paths? Not that he'd stuck around very long once things ended.

"Yes," she began, the words catching as she looked up at him. "And if I had known about you…" She paused, shaking her head. "I'm afraid my sister didn't always think things out the way she ought to."

That was the Summer he remembered. But then that was another thing that had drawn him to her back then. They'd met at a rodeo, him a tough-as-grit bareback rider and her, a highly competitive barrel racer. They'd been young and reckless, looking to grab life by the horns and then hold on for wherever the ride might take them.

"I'm sorry," he said. "I didn't mean to interrupt. Knowing she'd lived so close just took me by surprise."

She nodded in understanding. "Summer was on her way back to the house when a rattlesnake spooked her horse and she was thrown." A sob caught in her throat with the last of her explanation.

"You don't have to say anything more," he told her, regretting the pain his question had caused her. While he no longer felt what he once had for his wife, Autumn Myers was still dealing with the grief brought about by the loss of her sister. He couldn't even begin to imagine how he would feel if he lost one of his brothers.

"It's all right," she assured him as she swiped a hand over her tear-dampened cheek. "As her husband, you have a right to know. My sister ruptured her spleen when she fell. They did emergency surgery to repair it, and she managed to hold on for a couple of days, but then infection set in and her body began shutting down."

Tucker closed his eyes, saying a quick prayer for the woman he'd married.

"That's when Summer opened up about the secrets she'd been keeping. *You* being one of them," she told him with a sorrowful frown. "I forgave her. I only pray the Lord did, as well."

Tucker dragged a splayed hand back through his thick chestnut hair, trying to digest everything she was telling him. It was hard to believe that the high-spirited, head-strong girl he'd once loved was gone.

"I'm sorry," he managed, the words coming out strained. He stood there, a part of him longing to close the door and shut reality out, pretend this moment had never happened.

"No," she mumbled despondently as her gaze shifted to the car she'd driven up in, which was parked a short distance from his house, "I'm sorry. You deserved to

know the whole truth a long time ago. I pray that someday you'll be able to forgive my sister for the choices
she made, as well."

"The whole truth?"

"There is something my sister should have told you
about before walking away from your marriage," she
answered.

"I'm not so sure it matters anymore," he told her. He
was over any feelings he once had for his wife. There
was nothing Autumn Myers could say to him that would
change anything.

"You still should have the right to decide if it does
one way or another," she said, her face a mask of determination.

It was clear she wasn't about to let things go, not until
he'd heard her out. Tucker nodded. "If it will take some
of the burden off your heart, then I'm willing to hear you
out. Would you like to come inside and talk? I could fix
you a glass of ice water or lemonade."

She nodded, her gaze drifting back toward her car
once more. "But there's something I need to do first."
With that, she turned and walked away.

Tucker stepped out onto the porch as he watched Autumn make her way to her car. It was clear her sister's
death still weighed heavily on her, driving all the way
across the bottom of Wyoming from Cheyenne to Bent
Creek just to inform him in person of Summer's passing.
Oddly enough, he found himself wishing he could say
something that might set her mind at ease about what
her sister had done. Something to let her know that it
wasn't her burden to bear.

Her sister's passing. Nausea stirred in Tucker's gut at
the very thought of it. Time and distance from the situa-

tion had made him realize how hastily he and Summer had gone into their marriage. They'd been too young and far too impulsive to place the proper amount of thought into what they were doing as they stood before the judge at the Laramie County Courthouse that day. And, yes, he'd been hurt, and more than a little confused, when she'd taken off the way she had. Anger had followed. It had taken a fair amount of praying and suffering months of inner turmoil trying to pinpoint exactly what it was that he'd done wrong to send Summer running before he'd finally come to accept that she'd made the right decision in ending their hasty marriage. Whatever her reason may have been.

Not that it had ended completely. Legally, they were still husband and wife, something he'd made no attempt to rectify. One failed marriage was enough for him. As long as he and Summer were still legally wed, he could never make the same mistake again. Giving his heart away to a woman and risking the possibility of it being trampled all over again was something he was determined to avoid at all cost. *Only now Summer is gone*, he thought with a pang of sorrow. And that made him a widower.

His attention shifted back to Autumn Myers's retreating form, noting with some confusion that instead of settling herself behind the wheel of her bright yellow Mustang GT she circled around to the rear passenger side. A soft, somewhat sad smile moved across her face as she reached out to open the back door.

He lost sight of her for a moment as she leaned into the back of the brightly colored sports car. A second later, she took a step back from the vehicle and motioned to someone in the back seat. A tiny head with a mass of long curls hopped out to join her.

With the little girl's hand tucked securely in her own, a now unsmiling Autumn held his gaze as she walked back to the porch. *She has a daughter*, he thought to himself. One she must have brought along to meet her uncle by marriage.

The fading rays of the afternoon sun glinted off the mass of curls that hung over the child's downturned face as they crossed the yard. Chestnut curls. An unsettling sensation moved through him. Why that was, he had no idea. He looked questioningly to Autumn as she guided her young daughter up onto the porch.

"Tucker Wade," she said before looking down at the little girl who now had her tiny face pressed into her mother's skirt, "this is my niece, Blue Belle Wade. That's Bell with an *e*," she clarified.

Tucker's thoughts scrambled to process the words she'd just spoken. *Her niece.*

"Blue," she continued, "this is—"

"My daddy?" the little girl mumbled as she dared an inquisitive peek up at him through the protective barricade of her reddish-brown curls that served to hide most of her face.

"Her what?" he gasped as her name filtered through his mind. Blue Belle. Summer's favorite flower. The same ones he'd given her a bouquet of when he'd asked her to marry him.

"Yes, sweetie," she answered, her tone tender. "This is your daddy." Autumn's gaze lifted to meet his. "Tucker Wade, meet your daughter."

His daughter. How was that possible? But her hair was the same reddish-brown shade as his own.

"Blue," Autumn said, gently nudging her niece, "say hello to your daddy."

His daughter's little face turned slightly as she peeked up at him. "Hello," she said timidly, burying her face once again in the soft fabric of her aunt's skirt.

Autumn ran a soothing hand down over her niece's curls. "Sweetie, we came all this way to meet your daddy. I think he deserves a chance to see that pretty smile of yours."

His little girl pulled away ever so slightly and tipped her chin upward. And then she smiled. The long spiraling strands of her hair fell away to reveal a heart-shaped face very similar to Summer's and Autumn's. But it was Blue's wide green eyes and the lone dimple that appeared when she smiled that caused his heart to lurch. Those were *his* eyes. And that was undeniably the Wade family dimple that dipped into one side of his daughter's baby-soft cheeks.

His daughter. A barrage of emotions swept over Tucker as he stood looking down at her. He was a father. That revelation had his world tilting. He struggled to steady himself as spots danced around in his vision.

"Tucker?" he heard Autumn say, concern lacing her voice. "Are you all right? You look mighty pale."

He gave a forced laughed. "I'm better than all right. I'm a daddy." Yet, even as he spoke his words of reassurance, darkness began to fringe his vision.

"How's come he's swaying like a tree in the wind?" he heard his daughter ask.

"Tucker?" Autumn said, the concern-filled utterance bringing him back to full awareness.

He blinked hard and then cleared his throat. "Sorry," he said. "This is a lot to take in."

"Would you like to call someone?" she suggested, looking as if she expected him to drop into a dead faint any minute. "One of your brothers perhaps?"

The only time he'd ever come close to passing out had been when he'd gotten bucked off Little Cyclone during the Pioneer Days Rodeo up in Lander several years back. Landing on your head in a rodeo was cause for a little head spinning, yet he hadn't gone down. He was made of sturdier stock than that. However, the little bombshell Autumn Myers had dropped on him just moments before had nearly managed to do what Little Cyclone hadn't been able to—bring this Montana-bred cowboy to his knees. *Nearly.*

Tucker shook his head. "No need."

"You're really tall," Blue announced, craning her neck as she stood peering up at him.

He chuckled at Blue's observation, thankful that some of her shyness seemed to be easing up around him. "Not as tall as my brothers. Your uncles," he clarified. "They both top six foot. I'm only five foot eleven."

"I have uncles?" his daughter said excitedly.

It was hard not to let the injustice of what his wife had done, shutting him out of their child's life, seep into his tone. Summer had denied his parents the chance to get to know their only grandchild, and his brothers the opportunity to spoil their niece. "Two of them," he said with surprising calm, as the anger he'd once felt toward Summer after she'd walked out on their marriage returned to simmer just below the surface of his light-hearted demeanor.

"Do they live here, too?" asked Blue, looking around.

"No," he said. "This is my place. Your uncles have homes of their own that they live in on the ranch."

His daughter looked out over the land surrounding them. "I don't see them."

"That's because they're spread out across our family's nine-thousand-plus-acre ranch."

"What's an acre?"

"It's a measurement of land," Autumn explained.

"Do we have acres?"

"We do," she answered, glancing around. "But your daddy's property is a whole lot bigger than ours back in Cheyenne. We only have forty acres there and far fewer trees."

Blue swung her curious gaze back in his direction. "Do you have a swing set behind your house?"

"I'm afraid not," he said. "Never had the need for one."

She turned to her aunt. "Can I bring mine here if my daddy wants me to live with him?"

Autumn's eyes shot up to lock with his, a frown pulling at her glossy pink lips. "My sister's last request," she explained. "One I'm struggling to honor."

He hadn't even given that any thought. Tucker knelt in front of his daughter and took her tiny hand in his. "Of course, I want you to come live with me. I would've brought you here to live with me sooner if I had known about you." He looked to Autumn. "Thank you for bringing her home."

"Home is yet to be decided," she said stiffly. "I'm only here because my sister asked me to let you know about Blue. I'm not about to leave my niece in anyone else's care, not even yours, until I know in my heart that you're capable of doing right by her."

And he wasn't about to lose his daughter after only just finding her. "Understood," he answered with a nod, appreciating the protective stance she'd taken when it came to Blue. "But you should understand, too, that I intend to do whatever it takes to have my daughter in my life." Autumn Myers was about to learn that her niece's daddy was a man of his word. One worthy of the daughter the good Lord had blessed him with.

Autumn drew the quilt atop Tucker's guest bed up over her niece and then tucked it in snugly around her tiny form.

Blue gave a sleepy smile. "'Night, Aunt Autumn."

"Sleep tight, sweetie," she said, leaning in to kiss the top of Blue's head. Then she walked over to the suitcase she'd packed Blue's clothes in for their trip there. She'd chosen to bring a good week's worth of outfits, not knowing if they would be staying but deciding it was best to be prepared just in case. It seemed tonight, at least, they would be staying.

When Tucker had invited them into his home, even going so far as to fix them grilled cheese sandwiches because Blue had told him they hadn't eaten dinner yet, her niece had barely been able to keep her eyes open. Autumn had decided it best to call it a night and set up a time to meet with Tucker the following day. She'd had every intention of taking Blue to one of the nearby hotels she'd called before coming to Bent Creek to check on room availability, but Tucker had insisted they take one of his guest rooms.

When she'd politely refused Tucker's offer, not wanting to impose, he'd told her that his house was Blue's as well, and it was long past time she had a chance to stay there. He topped that statement off with a heartfelt *please* before adding that he intended to take himself out to the barn to sleep on the cot he'd set up a few weeks prior when he'd wanted to watch over one of his horses that had been under the weather at the time.

Not quite the actions of a selfish, responsibility-shirking cowboy, which she had believed him to be for the past five-plus years. He appeared to be quite the opposite. At least, when it came to first impressions. Tucker had accepted Blue into his life without a moment's hesitation, seemed more than willing to prove himself and had even offered to sleep in the barn to give them some privacy. All of that and a soft spot for animals. Throw in that rugged cowboy look that both she and Summer had always been drawn to, something Autumn had learned was best to avoid. What was there not to like? Other than the fact that Tucker Wade's very existence could mean a lifetime of heartache for her if Blue ended up being raised by her daddy.

Autumn busied herself with getting Blue's clothes ready for the next day, hoping to take her mind off the handsome cowboy who had managed to steal at least a piece of her sister's well-guarded heart.

"Does my daddy have horses?" Blue asked sleepily.

Her daddy. How odd those words sounded coming from her niece, Autumn thought, struggling not to frown. "I thought you were sleeping."

"I am," her niece replied. "Almost. Does he?"

"He does," she answered. "In fact, your daddy has a ranch filled with them." From what she'd learned, Tucker Wade and his brothers were stock contractors for rodeos, dealing specifically in the horses used for events like saddle bronc and bareback bronc riding. Apparently, Summer had been keeping tabs on her husband from afar, collecting news clippings, and even a detailed report from the private investigator her sister had hired the year before, unbeknownst to Autumn. They all showed a man who was hardworking, always willing to lend a hand to help those in need and a man of unbending faith. He'd retired from the rodeo circuit to run stock horses with his two brothers.

"But I didn't see any."

"Maybe because you were fast asleep when we pulled in. Besides, they were probably off running through the hills."

"I don't like horses."

While Autumn had never been as at ease around horses as Summer had, she didn't fear them like Blue did now. Her niece had always displayed the same passion for animals as her mother had. At least, until Summer's accident. Blue would spend hours on end out in the barn with her momma while Summer tended to Alamo, the eight-year-old quarter horse her sister had purchased that past year.

Having a horse of her own again had given Summer back some of that spark that had been missing since she'd had to sell her beloved Cinnamon, the horse she'd ridden during her barrel-racing days, to help pay for the cost of formula and diapers for Blue. Her daughter's needs had always come first with Summer. Unlike it had been with their own mother.

Autumn settled herself onto the edge of the mattress with a sad smile. "Your momma wouldn't want you to blame Alamo or any other horses for what happened. Snakes are very scary creatures, even to big, strong horses. Alamo just wanted to get away from it."

"I don't like snakes, either," Blue said with a yawn.

Autumn managed the semblance of a smile. "That makes two of us, sweetheart."

"I miss Momma."

Just shy of five years old, her niece should still have her mother in her life. The sadness in Blue's eyes whenever she spoke about missing her momma never failed to make Autumn's heart break.

"I know you do, sweetie," Autumn replied past the lump that had risen in her throat, still trying to come to terms with the recent loss of her sister herself. Summer had been gone for nearly six months and it still didn't seem real. Her twin, older than Autumn by mere minutes, had been called home to the Lord a week after being thrown from her horse.

"Are you gonna leave me, too?" her precious little Blue asked fearfully.

Autumn fought back an onslaught of tears. How was she supposed to answer that? Because if her sister's last wishes were carried out, she would be leaving Blue in the care of a man who hadn't even known his daughter existed.

"Not a chance," she heard herself reply. If this life-changing drive to Bent Creek, Wyoming, two counties away from Cheyenne, and the only home her niece had ever known, turned out the way Autumn hoped it would, her niece would be coming home with her for good. Despite the fact that she had been struggling since Summer's passing to place her complete faith in the Lord, Autumn sent up a silent prayer that she would be able to keep her promise to her sister if Tucker managed to prove himself worthy. In that case, she would make sure she stayed in her niece's life. Still, she couldn't even begin to imagine her life without Blue in it. Her niece was a living, breathing piece of Summer. All Autumn had left of her sister. And it was the love she had for her twin, as well as her not-quite-three-year-old niece—because that was all the older Blue was at the time—that had motivated Autumn to sell her real estate business in Braxton, Texas, where she and Summer had grown up, and move to Wyoming to be with them.

Blue turned onto her side, snuggling deeper under the blue-and-green-floral quilt. "Do you think my daddy liked our surprise?"

She had told Blue they were going to surprise her daddy with a visit and not to feel bad if he didn't seem happy about it, that some people didn't know how to handle surprises. Truth was she was preparing her niece in the kindest way she knew how for Tucker's possible rejection. If that had happened, Blue wouldn't feel the least bit unlovable. An emotion Autumn had experienced firsthand. But Tucker, though thoroughly shocked, had seemed to be overjoyed to learn that he had a daughter.

"How could he not when you're the surprise?" Autumn said, reaching out to stroke her niece's long curls.

With a sleepy smile, Blue closed her eyes and gave in to the exhaustion she'd been fighting.

Autumn closed her eyes as well, only not in sleep, but in one final prayer that night. *Dear Lord, please have a care with my niece's tender heart when Your will, whatever that may be, is done.*

Chapter Two

Autumn, cup of freshly brewed coffee in hand, moved to stand at the edge of the porch, her gaze skimming over the vast land around her. She loved all the warm colors that came with the fall season. The brilliant golds and vibrant reds with bold splashes of burgundy. The same colorful palette that now dotted the towering trees that surrounded Tucker Wade's ranch and filled the distant hills. Earthy shades of green and brown carpeted the ground below, making the colors in the trees above stand out even more.

Closing her eyes, she breathed in the cool, crisp air that filled the mornings at that time of year. Much to her surprise, a feeling of peacefulness settled over her as she stood in the faint chill of the early morning, listening to the faint sounds of nature stirring to life around her. It was a peacefulness she hadn't known for a very long while.

The unexpected calm that filled her at that moment took Autumn by surprise. Especially when one considered her reason for being there. Maybe it was a sign from God that everything was going to be all right. She'd certainly prayed hard enough. And there was no doubt in her mind that Blue was better off with her than with a man whose entire life centered around horses, whether it was riding them or getting them rodeo ready. Tucker Wade would have a very hard time convincing her otherwise.

Then again, what if this was the Lord's way of telling her that Bent Creek was the right place for her niece? That Blue would find contentment in this vast, horse-filled land hours from the only home she'd ever known.

No, Autumn thought in a panic, *the right place for Blue is back in Cheyenne with the one person who loves her more than anyone else ever could.* She had to believe that. Surely, the Lord knew that, as well. He'd seen the sacrifices Autumn had made for those she loved. For Blue.

That precious child filled her heart to overflowing. She didn't need a husband or even children of her own to make her happy. Not as long as she had Blue.

Not as long as she had Blue.

No sooner had that thought gone through her mind than the feeling of serenity that had come over her only moments before began to slip. In its place, the very real fear of losing her cherished little Blue Belle. A fear she'd been struggling with ever since Summer let loose the secrets she'd been keeping for so long. Secrets Autumn found herself wishing her sister would have taken with her to the grave.

Guilt filled her instantly at even harboring such a thought. Blue deserved to know her daddy, just as Tucker Wade deserved to know his little girl. They had both been denied the opportunity for far too long. Autumn couldn't let her own selfish needs and wants stop her from doing what was right. Doing what the Lord would want her to do.

"Morning."

Autumn jumped, her eyes flying open at the deep, baritone sound. Hot coffee sloshed over the rim of the cup she held clutched in her hand, causing her to wince.

Tucker Wade was there in an instant, standing on the other side of the porch's railing as he reached out to ease the cup from her stinging hand. "I didn't mean to startle you," he said apologetically as he set the coffee cup onto the railing a safe distance away. Then he pulled a red-and-white-print handkerchief from the back pocket of his jeans and handed it to her, asking worriedly, "You okay?"

She took the offered square of colorful cotton and dabbed at her hand. "I'm fine," she said with a half-hearted smile.

His gaze dropped to the red spots on her hand, and his frown deepened. "You need to run that hand under some cold water." Without waiting for a reply, he turned and made his way around to the side of the house, returning a moment later with a garden hose in hand. The water was coming out in a slow, gentle trickle. "Hold out that hand," he said.

"I really don't…" she began to protest, then seeing the determination on the cowboy's face had her saving her breath. Holding her hand out over the railing, she watched as Tucker Wade ran the cool water over the reddened patches of skin the spilled coffee had left behind.

"Better?" he asked, glancing up at her with a warm smile.

But the smile wasn't what drew and held her attention. It was his eyes. Slightly more brilliant than Blue's, she decided. A vivid shade of bright green. Like the heart-shaped leaves found on lemon clover. And those thick lashes...

"Autumn?"

She snapped out of her thoughts, her cheeks warming at having been so distracted by this man. So what if Tucker Wade had striking eyes and a kind smile? A handsome face had nothing to do with the man's ability to care for his daughter. She gave a quick nod. "Yes. Thank you."

"Glad to help." His smile widened into a teasing grin as he worked to shut off the hose's nozzle. "Maybe I should have suggested you help yourself to the orange juice in the fridge instead."

Her gaze touched briefly on the coffee cup atop the porch railing and then back to Tucker Wade. "I didn't sleep very well last night, so waking up to the aroma of freshly brewed coffee was a most welcomed thing." Not only had Tucker insisted she and Blue spend the night there instead of driving into town, he'd set the timer on his coffee maker so it would be ready for her when she awoke.

"That makes two of us," he admitted with a sigh.

"You should have slept in the house last night," she said with a frown.

"It had nothing to do with that," he assured her. "We cowboys are used to camping outdoors, so a cot in a barn isn't so bad. I just had a lot on my mind."

"Understandable." She glanced toward the sun that was slowly rising up from the distant horizon and then back to him. "At least Blue slept well last night," she said. "Not a single nightmare."

"You expected her to have bad dreams here?"

"I didn't know," she said honestly. "They happen on occasion. Ever since her momma died."

"Maybe the distraction of being in a new place will help to ease her nightmares."

"I pray it does." She glanced toward the rising sun and then back to Tucker. "So are you always up this early?"

"Earlier, usually," he replied. "I'm a bit off my game today."

She nodded in understanding. "The coffee's still hot if you'd like a cup," she offered. Despite his reassurances, she knew he couldn't have been very comfortable doing so with the nights getting so cold, but she appreciated his willingness.

"Coffee sounds good," he replied.

"Blue should be getting up soon. She's an early riser, but I expect her to be up even earlier this morning, considering this is her first breakfast with her daddy."

He glanced toward the front door, his expression one of nervous apprehension.

Autumn laughed softly. "It's not as if you're about to face a den of lions as Daniel once had to. Blue's a very sweet, loving little girl."

His gaze shifted back to her. "My little girl," he said as if in awe of the words that he'd just spoken, his voice choked with emotion. "And I don't have the slightest idea where to begin."

That admission couldn't be easy for a man like Tucker Wade. Cowboys were a proud lot. She should have been encouraged by his honesty, a sign that maybe he wasn't mentally prepared to raise a child. But she found herself offering him a reassuring smile. "I'd start with a 'good morning' once she wakes up and then prepare to answer a lot of questions. Everything from 'Are clouds made up of cotton balls?' to 'Why can't chickens fly?'"

Tucker chuckled.

"Laugh now," she warned playfully. "But don't say I didn't warn you once the questions begin. Your daughter can be very inquisitive."

"Duly noted."

"You cook?" she asked in surprise.

The corners of his mouth lifted, revealing a lone dimple. The same dimple her niece displayed with every smile. "A man's gotta eat." That said, he started off around the house, dragging the garden hose behind him. "Plain to see where Blue got her 'inquisitiveness' from," he called back over a broad shoulder before disappearing from sight.

The moment Autumn realized she was still smiling, she forced her mouth into a tight line. She would not, could not, like Tucker Wade. He was the enemy. The one person who could take away the only family she had left. Not waiting for Tucker, she grabbed for her cup of coffee and marched determinedly back into the house.

Hearing the front door to his ranch house close, Tucker took a moment to calm his racing thoughts. There were times as he'd stood talking to Autumn that he found himself thinking of Summer. How could he not? Autumn was the spitting image of his wife, except for having shorter hair and more of a businesslike style of dress. And she was every bit as pretty. Not at all surprising, considering they were identical twins. Yet, Autumn seemed different. Where his wife had always lived her life being her true self, her sister seemed more reserved; guarded, almost. Not that the situation they found themselves in didn't give her reason to be, but Tucker found himself wondering what she would be like with all those protective layers peeled away.

When Autumn had let down her guard for those brief moments that morning, allowing her more playful side to come out, she reminded him even more of her sister. But she wasn't Summer, the woman who had run out on him, taking with her a very huge part of him—his daughter.

His daughter. A lump formed in Tucker's throat, causing him to swallow hard. He was somebody's daddy. Blue's daddy. She was the most precious responsibility he'd ever been given. He knew nothing about raising children. She knew nothing about him. It felt as if he were going down a steep set of stairs in the dark with no handrail to hold on to. He didn't want to fall. Didn't want to fail. Not when God had chosen him to bestow this incredible blessing on.

Blue Belle Wade. Wait until his family found out about her. They'd be as shocked as he'd been. Even more so, seeing as how they had no idea he'd ever been married. So many things he would have done differently if given the chance. But there was no going back in life, only forward. And with that in mind, he intended to make it up to Blue for being absent from her life for so long, even if that absence hadn't been his choice.

Taking a deep breath, Tucker headed inside, closing the front door quietly behind him as he made his way to the kitchen. The coffee mug Autumn had been using sat on the kitchen table, but she was nowhere in sight. Crossing the kitchen, he grabbed himself a mug and filled it with coffee. Then he busied himself with starting breakfast for his guests.

Tucker caught himself, mentally changing that to for

his daughter and her aunt. His daughter was not a guest. She was family. *His family.* That thought had him whistling a happy tune as he moved about the kitchen.

"Care to tell us what's going on with you today?"

Speaking of family. Tucker turned to find Jackson and Garrett standing just inside the kitchen entryway, worried frowns on their faces. They'd clearly come before finishing up that morning's tasks.

"Everything okay with the horses?" he asked, worried that something might have happened with one. His brothers looked so serious.

"They're fine," Jackson replied. "It's you we're concerned about. You never call off when there's work to be done."

He'd spent a long, restless night, caught up in thoughts of his little girl. He'd also spent a good bit of time praying for the Lord to give him the strength to find it in himself to forgive Summer as Autumn had, because at that moment the depth of her betrayal was still too fresh to get past the simmering resentment he felt inside.

"Judging by the happy little tune you were whistling when we came in," Garrett said, "I'm guessing you're not under the weather."

"No," Tucker replied, feeling guilty for causing his brothers unnecessary worry. He hadn't made mention of Blue when he'd called to let them know he wouldn't be meeting up with them at the main barn that morning, because that was the kind of news he preferred to give them in person. "I'm not under the weather."

His oldest brother's frown deepened. "That being the case, care to let us in on what's really going on with you, then?"

Where did he begin? Tucker sent a quick prayer heavenward for some guidance from the Lord in the best way to handle this situation. One that affected him as well as his family. "I—"

"You're really tall," a tiny voice stated, cutting into Tucker's response.

His gaze shot between his brothers to see Blue standing there in the living room, looking up at Garrett and Jackson with youthful curiosity. She was wearing a long flannel nightgown covered in bright pink butterflies. Matching pink kitten heads peeked out from under the ruffled hem of her nightgown. A stuffed rag doll that looked as though it had gotten most of the stuffing loved right out of it drooped from her tiny hand.

His brothers' eyes widened in unison at the unexpected interruption before they pivoted on booted heels to look down at Blue. For the first time since Tucker could remember, his big brothers were rendered utterly speechless.

"Come on into the kitchen, sweetheart," he told his daughter, whose gaze was still fixed on her suddenly mute uncles.

Jackson and Garrett parted to let her through, their attention doing a slingshot in his direction as she passed by with a sleepy smile.

"Morning, Daddy," she said in the sweetest little singsong voice he'd ever heard. Her words grabbed at his heart. He was somebody's daddy, something he'd never expected to be after Summer had run out on their marriage. Not only had he been too hurt to think about trusting in love again, but also his still being legally wed to Summer had been keeping him from giving another relationship a chance.

Tucker returned his baby girl's smile, an unfamiliar warmth seeping into his heart as he did so. Then he placed his hands on her tiny shoulders and slowly turned her to face his brothers. "Blue Belle Wade, these two hulking giants who don't seem to be able to pick their jaws up from the kitchen floor are your uncles. That's your uncle Jackson on the left and your uncle Garrett on the right." He glanced down at his daughter, recalling she was only four. "Do you know what left and right are?"

She held out her hand, making and L shape with her fingers. "This is my left because left starts with *L*."

"Very good," he praised. He didn't know enough about children to say for sure, but something told him Blue was an extremely bright child.

"Uncles?" Jackson muttered in confusion as he stared at Blue.

Tucker looked up at his brother with an answering nod.

Garrett attempted to process what he'd just heard. "Blue Belle Wade?" he repeated slowly, his gaze fixed on Blue with her bright smile and reddish-brown curls.

"My daughter," Tucker said, still trying to come to grips with it all himself.

Garrett's wide-eyed gaze snapped up to Tucker. "Your what?"

"His daughter," Blue announced proudly, her tiny chin lifting.

"Daughter?" Jackson repeated, understandably confused by Blue's announcement.

"Who's hungry?" Tucker said with forced calm. He didn't want his brothers' raised voices to startle his daughter. "We can talk more about this while we eat. I'm making bacon and eggs."

Blue's gleeful expression fell. "But Aunt Autumn always makes me pancakes."

"I'm making pancakes, too," Tucker promptly amended, causing his brother's gazes to swing sharply in his direction.

Jackson snorted. "Since when do you make pancakes?"

"He's not," another female voice chimed in. "I am."

His brothers stepped aside as Autumn made her way past them into the kitchen to stand beside him and Blue.

This wasn't how he'd envisioned this moment to go. He hadn't even had a chance to prepare his brothers for the shock of finding out they were uncles. "I don't have a pancake mix," Tucker admitted guiltily.

"The best pancakes are made from scratch anyways," Autumn said with a smile and then leaned over to speak to Blue. "Sweetie, I thought I told you to wait for me in the bathroom while I grabbed your hairbrush and ponytail holder from your suitcase and a change of clothes."

"I was hungry."

"Even so, you shouldn't be wandering around by yourself."

"I wasn't by myself," she said, looking up at Tucker who stood on her other side. "I was with my daddy."

A slight frown tugged at Autumn's lips as she straightened. "Yes, I suppose you were."

Tucker looked over to find Garrett and Jackson staring at Autumn, mouths agape. And he understood why. They'd known Summer from the rodeo, had known their little brother had been sweet on her that rodeo season. And with Blue calling him daddy he could just imagine what they were thinking. Only they had it all wrong.

Clearing his throat, he said, "Jackson and Garrett, I'd like you to meet Autumn Myers, Summer's twin sister."

"Her twin?" Jackson said as if having trouble accepting that this wasn't the Summer they had once known, standing there.

"Identical twin," Autumn supplied with a sad smile.

Tucker wanted to explain why his wife wasn't there and her sister was, but he didn't want to mention Summer's passing with his daughter standing there. Her mother's loss had been traumatic enough for her as it was.

"My mommy's in heaven," Blue said sadly.

Tucker's heart ached for his little girl. No child should ever have to speak those words.

An uncomfortable silence fell over the room.

Clearing the emotion from his throat, Tucker said, "Her aunt Autumn brought Blue here to meet her family."

"And maybe I'll get to live here if you want me," Blue reminded him.

"As I said before, wanting you isn't an issue," he replied tenderly. "I do without a doubt. You belong here."

"Tucker, please," Autumn warned in a hushed voice beside him. "Don't get her hopes up. It's too soon."

"*You* have a daughter," Garrett said disbelievingly.

Tucker nodded. "I do."

"All these years and you've never said anything?" Jackson grumbled, clearly hurt by what he thought had been Tucker's decision to keep Blue's existence from them.

"Why don't Blue and I give you men a few moments of privacy while she gets dressed for the day?" Autumn said, taking her niece by the hand. "Just give me a holler when you're ready for me to start on those pancakes."

His brothers parted to let them through.

"Are my uncles mad at my daddy?" Tucker heard Blue ask as Autumn led her away. Any answer her aunt might have given was lost as the two scurried toward the entryway.

Garrett waited a moment and then turned to face him. "I can't believe you kept this from us."

Tucker hated the censure he saw in his brother's eyes.

Jackson crossed the room to grab a couple of coffee cups from the cupboard. "I wouldn't have expected this from you," he muttered as he placed them onto the counter and then reached for the coffeepot. "Momma raised us better than that."

This was going to be even harder than he'd imagined it would be, not that he'd had much time to think about how everything was going to play out. Just one sleepless night in the barn. He took a seat at the table and dragged a hand down over his face, feeling the stubble of his unshaven jaw. "I didn't know about Blue," he said, the admission stoking the flames of his resentment toward Summer for keeping his daughter from him. "Not until last evening when Autumn showed up on my doorstep to tell me about Summer's…passing." The word caught in his throat.

"I'm sorry," Garrett said solemnly. "I know how much she meant to you at one time."

Enough to marry, Tucker thought, his jaw tightening.

Jackson walked over and handed Garrett a steaming mug and then both men settled themselves into the empty chairs across the table from Tucker, disapproval etched into their tanned faces.

"I know what you're both thinking," Tucker grumbled. "And you're wrong."

"You just told us that Blue is your daughter," their oldest brother said, pinning Tucker with his gaze.

"She is. Only I didn't know Summer was carrying my child when she walked away from our marriage."

Jackson nearly choked on the sip of coffee he'd just taken. "Marriage?"

"You both know I fell pretty hard for her when we met. By the time rodeo season came to an end, I couldn't imagine leaving her. She felt the same." At least, he'd thought she had. But if she had, she would have told him about the baby. Would have given him the chance to think about giving up the rodeo life, instead of making the decision herself to end something they had started together. "We both decided to put down roots in Cheyenne, the place where we'd first met. So I bought her a ring and got married at the courthouse."

"You have something against church weddings?" Garrett asked with a disapproving frown.

"We wanted a quick, small, private wedding."

"Can't get more private than a courthouse wedding," Jackson muttered angrily as he brought his coffee cup to his lips. "You might have at least included your immediate family in something as sacred as the exchanging of your wedding vows."

Garrett's downturned mouth pulled tighter. "And to think we all believed you had stayed behind when rodeo season ended to work a job until the next year's circuit began anew."

He had found filler work in Cheyenne to help pay the bills. That much was true.

"Did your rushed marriage have something to do with Summer having your baby?"

Tucker pinned his oldest brother with his gaze. "Blue came after the fact. I rushed into a hasty marriage with Summer because I was young and thought love was something it turned out not to be," he replied, feeling the need to clarify things.

"We all knew you were always one to jump feet-first into the fire," Garrett said crossly, "but marriage, Tucker? Never mind the not including us when the nuptials took place, because you and I both know I would have done my best to talk you out of it with you being only twenty-four at the time. But why not tell us about your marriage afterward?"

"Summer and I agreed to take a little time to settle into marriage before telling our families. My family actually," he amended, "as my wife led me to believe she had none. But things changed. My wife changed." He went on to tell his brothers everything he knew, but there were still so many unanswered questions he might never get answers to now that she was gone.

Empathy replaced the hurt and anger he'd seen in Garrett's eyes. His brother released a heavy sigh. "I'm sorry you had to go through that. It certainly explains why you've avoided any real relationship since that summer. I put it off to your not wanting the distraction while competitively riding. Then after we started up our rodeo stock company I thought it had something to do with your delving hard into that. Never in a million years would I have guessed the truth having anything to do with you being married."

Jackson sat back against the kitchen chair and shoved

a splayed hand back through his thick hair. "I still can't process the fact that my baby brother is a married man."

"Widowed," Tucker said flatly. Then, fighting back the emotion that had been roiling around in his gut all morning, he said, "And it was my forgiveness she should have been seeking at the end."

"There's no denying that Summer did you wrong," Jackson acknowledged with a frown. "But she did right by asking the Lord for forgiveness. If you were there, then maybe—"

"But I wasn't," Tucker ground out, cutting his brother off. "I didn't even know where *there* was. She left without so much as a goodbye and never made any attempt to contact me, or let me know where she was. At some point, she came back to Cheyenne, but I must have already moved back home."

"It's possible she tried to find you at some point, but you were already gone," Garrett said hopefully.

"Summer knew I was born and raised in Bent Creek. She could have found me easy enough. But my wife chose to keep my little girl from me." A myriad of emotions filled him at that moment, feelings he didn't know how to deal with.

His brothers exchanged worried glances and then Garrett said, "It's going to be okay."

"How?" Tucker demanded. "I've missed so much. My daughter's first smile. Her first steps. Her first birthday." Shoving away from the table, he crossed the room to stand at the sink, staring out the bay window that looked out over the back pasture. "I'm her father," he said, his voice breaking, "and I don't even know when my daughter's birthday is."

Chairs scooted back from the kitchen table and then

heavy-booted footsteps crossed the wood planks that made up the kitchen floor. A second later, he was book-ended by his older brothers.

Garrett clasped a hand over his shoulder. "I can't even begin to imagine what you're feeling right now, but I do know that the Lord has seen fit to bless our family with your little girl. And while we can't change the past, and the time we've lost with her, we can set our sights on the time we're going to have with Blue in the years to come."

Jackson nodded. "Garrett's right. What really matters is seeing to it that Blue is happy. We've got the rest of her life to celebrate her birthdays and holidays, and worship together."

If only it were that simple. "I pray that's how it goes," he replied. "First, I have to prove myself capable of caring for Blue to her aunt. Autumn has custody of my daughter, and, while she's here honoring her sister's wishes, she's made it perfectly clear she's not going to simply turn her niece over to me."

"Then you'll prove yourself capable," Jackson said determinedly. "All of us will."

Garrett looked to them both. "Good plan, but care to tell me how we do that when none of us have the slightest idea of how to care for a child, let alone a little girl?"

"Looks like I'm going to have to call Mom sooner than I'd planned," Tucker said with a sigh. "I'd hoped to wait a few days until I'd had a chance to come to terms with suddenly being somebody's daddy."

"Don't," Jackson said with a frown. "They've wanted to go on this trip for as long as I can remember. What's a few more weeks?"

Tucker shook his head. "It can't wait. I won't lose Blue." If it came down to it, he'd fight for her legally.

But a legal battle wasn't something he wanted to put his daughter through. So that left proving himself to Autumn.

"You won't," Jackson said with conviction. "We'll figure something out."

Garrett nodded in agreement.

Tucker glanced toward the doorway. "We'll talk more later. Right now, my little girl is eagerly awaiting pancakes."

"See there," Garrett said with a grin, "you're already stepping into daddy mode."

Jackson slapped Tucker on the back. "All I can say is better you than me. I'm nowhere ready to settle down to that kind of responsibility yet. However, I am looking forward to being Blue's favorite uncle."

"You're going to have to settle for second favorite," Garrett told him as they made their way out of the kitchen. "I have access to kittens."

"Using your job to win her over," Jackson grumbled. "That's low. Guess I'll have to break out the friendship card and take Blue to Sandy's Candy's." Sandy was a classmate of Jackson's who made the best homemade fudge in the county. But she also had counters filled with assorted sweets, including an entire section of penny candies.

Tucker felt some of the worry that had been pressing down on him since awakening that morning lift away. He would make this work and be the father Blue deserved, because he wasn't in this alone. He had his family there to support him, to help Blue settle into what would be her new life. And, most important, he had the Lord to turn to when things got tough.

Chapter Three

"Are my uncles coming for pancakes today?"

Tucker looked to Blue who was seated across the table from him next to her aunt Autumn. A large lace bow now held her curls in place as they trailed down her back in a neat ponytail. She'd changed out of her nightgown and into a fancy ruffled dress. "Not today, sweetheart."

"Don't they like pancakes?" she asked with a worried frown.

He could understand why she might think that. His brothers hadn't stuck around the morning before after discovering they had a niece partially because they felt they needed to give Tucker some time alone with his "guests." But he knew, having experienced the same shock of discovering Blue's existence, that Garrett and Jackson probably needed a little time to process everything. "Your uncles have to check on the horses and see to a few fence repairs."

"I don't like horses," Blue said with a frown, a sticky drop of pancake syrup clinging to her tiny chin.

Tucker's smile sagged with his daughter's announcement. How could a child conceived by two parents whose lives had once revolved solely around horses dislike them? More important, how was he supposed to see to it that his daughter was happy there at the ranch when she had an aversion to the very thing that put food on the table for his family? *Her* family.

Autumn picked up her napkin, dipped it into her water glass and then dabbed at the sticky syrup that had dribbled down Blue's chin. "Sweetie, we talked about this on the way here. You can't blame Alamo for what happened."

"Alamo?" he asked as he watched the ease with which Summer's sister cared for his daughter.

"Mommy's horse," Blue replied as she stabbed at another piece of syrup-laced pancake.

"The horse she was riding the day of the accident," Autumn explained as she set the damp paper napkin down next to her plate. "She hadn't owned Alamo all that long, so she had no way of knowing how he would react to being spooked. I have to imagine that most horses would be a little shaken up by a snake in their path."

He nodded. "Some horses tend to be afraid of snakes. Some aren't." His horse wasn't, but Hoss knew enough to give a snake a wide berth if they happened to cross paths. Same went with Little Joe, his more recently acquired saddle horse. "If only she'd been riding Cinnamon," he muttered with a frown. "He'd never been prone to spooking." One of the best quarter horses he'd come across in both manner and spirit.

"There have been far too many if onlys in our lives lately," Autumn responded with a sigh, her gaze shifting to Blue. Then she looked back to Tucker, a hint of something that could only be described as condemnation in her eyes. "She had to sell Cinnamon after Blue was born."

"Why?" he asked, unable to comprehend his wife ever parting with her beloved horse.

Autumn's pretty mouth twisted in a sign of irritation and one slender brow lifted.

"Babies take money, Mr. Wade," Autumn pointed out. "Medical bills, diapers, formula. Then there's childcare, because as a single parent, Summer had no choice but to work to keep a roof over their heads. So, as you see, my sister had no choice but to sell her horse."

Was she attempting to point blame in his direction for the difficulty Summer had gone through? Because it felt an awful lot like she was. "She had a choice," he said with forced calmness. He might not know much about raising children, but he knew enough to keep adult issues between adults. "I'd be more than happy to discuss it with you further at a more appropriate time," he said with a nod toward Blue, who seemed totally oblivious to the conversation going on around her. Her interest lay in swiping up every bit of the remaining syrup on her plate with her fingertip.

As if just realizing what she was doing, Autumn reached once more for her damp napkin. "Sweetie, it's not polite to lick the syrup off your finger." Taking his daughter's hand in hers, she proceeded to wipe it clean.

Blue's tiny mouth fell into a pout. "But I get to lick cotton candy off my fingers. And icing. And—"

"That's different," Autumn replied, a hint of frustration in her voice. She set the napkin down and stood, collecting both hers and Blue's plates and forks. "You're still sticky," she told her as she turned and started for the sink. "Why don't you run on into the bathroom and wash your hands with soap and water while I do up these dishes?"

"There's no need for you to do that," Tucker countered, his thoughts still dwelling on the fact that she blamed him for Summer's having to struggle financially.

Blue shifted in her chair, her gaze trailing after her aunt. "Can we go pick flowers afterward?"

Autumn shook her head. "It's October, sweetie. Not a very good time of year to be searching for flowers."

It was good to see his daughter had a fondness for the outdoors. After having spent the previous day stuck inside thanks to a sudden drop in temperature that preceded a brief thunderstorm that rolled in, Tucker looked forward to showing her around the ranch. Not that he had minded getting to know his baby girl while playing dozens of games of Go Fish and Old Maid. Autumn had spent some of that time making work calls, and the rest observing the two of them. Until he proved himself, he had no choice but to accept that everything he did was going to be under Autumn's close scrutiny.

"Actually," Tucker said, "I happen to know where we can find some yellow rabbitbrush in bloom."

Blue's face lit up. "I like yellow!"

"Don't you have to help your brothers with those repairs today?" Autumn asked.

He shook his head. "Jackson called this morning to tell me they were going to focus on the two worst sections of the fence line today and see to the rest tomorrow. Garrett has a few vet calls he needs to make today, which means I'm free to take Blue out to find those flowers after breakfast."

Blue straightened in her chair, beaming excitedly. "Yay! Can we go now?"

* * *

Autumn smiled. "I'll get you ready as soon as I finish cleaning up the kitchen."

Tucker nodded. "I'll give you a hand with these breakfast dishes. Then I'll go grab a quick shower before we go look for those blooms. That is, if it's all right with your aunt Autumn."

Blue swung her gaze around. "Can my daddy get a shower before we go for a ride?"

"Yes." Autumn wasted no time in responding, a grin parting her pink lips. "He may."

"That's not what I meant," he muttered, a flash of heat spreading through his whiskered cheeks.

A snort of laughter passed through Autumn's curved lips, drawing his attention in her direction. He couldn't help but notice how pretty she was when she wasn't scowling at him with condemnation. Her humor-filled gaze met his. "For future reference, children take almost everything that is said quite literally."

"I'll be sure to keep that in mind."

She looked to Blue. "What Tucker...that is, your daddy," she promptly corrected, "meant to say was that he needs to make sure your going for a ride with him would be all right with me."

"The invitation was for the both of you," Tucker clarified.

"Oh," Autumn said, as if surprised by his wanting to include her. "I thought—"

"You've thought a lot of things about me that I hope to have a chance to set to rights," he said determinedly.

"Can we go?" Blue pleaded, her face alight with excitement. "Please, Aunt Autumn!"

Autumn looked to Tucker. "I'd hate to—"

"Don't say *impose*," he told her as he stood to carry his own dishes over to the sink. "I want to show the two of you around. Give Blue an idea of what it will be like to live here at the Triple W Rodeo Ranch."

"*If* she lives here," Autumn immediately countered as if he'd forgotten her telling him he had to prove himself before she'd turn care of Blue over to him. Care he rightfully should have been a part of from the beginning.

"Rest assured my daughter will be with me." He'd lost too much precious time with Blue as it was thanks to Summer.

"Do yellow rabbits live in the flower bush?"

His gaze still locked with Autumn's, he said in confusion, "Yellow rabbits?"

A semblance of a smile returned once more to her pretty face. "I did warn you to prepare yourself for this. And now you have a perfect example of a four-year-old's never-ending and sometimes completely unexpected questions." She turned to Blue. "Sweetie, there is no such thing as a yellow rabbit."

"But I ate one at Easter."

Tucker's brow lifted.

"Real rabbits don't have bright yellow fur," Autumn went on to explain to his daughter. "Only candy bunnies do." She turned to him, explaining further, "She's referring to marshmallow Peeps."

How did she get all of that out of his daughter's question? Did the ability to decipher a child's way of thinking just come naturally for some, or was it something one learned over time? He prayed it was the latter, because it clearly wasn't instinctive for him. Autumn's clarification had made things clearer on his end, however.

He turned to Blue, who was watching them from

where she remained seated at the table. "They call it yellow rabbitbrush because the yellow flowers that grow on them are a favorite treat of jackrabbits."

"Oh," his daughter said with a sigh, sounding disappointed.

If he could have, he would have covered the bushes they were going to see in marshmallow bunnies. But those edible delights were somewhat scarce in October. However, he had something else up his sleeve that he was fairly sure his daughter would be just as excited over.

"We might even stop by your grandma and grandpa's place to collect some eggs from the chickens in their henhouse on the way home."

"I have a grandma and grandpa?" she squeaked excitedly.

"You sure do," he said with a grin. "They're not home right now because they're on a trip but you'll get to meet them very soon."

"Do their chickens live in a house like yours?"

"A much smaller version," he answered with a chuckle. "Now scoot and get those hands washed up, or you're going to end up with chicken feathers sticking to your fingers."

With a giggle, she hopped down and raced from the kitchen.

He looked to Autumn. "You might want to have her change into a pair of jeans."

"Blue loves her dresses," she said, slender brows drawing together in what appeared to be irritation at his request. "Most little girls do. And if you're trying to make her into something she's not—"

"We're going on a hike," he reminded her. "With plants and trees and rocky ground. Probably not the best conditions for that pretty little dress she's wearing. But since you are her legal guardian, it's your call."

"Oh, I'm sorry," she said with a sigh. "I thought you were trying to…" Her words trailed off as she searched for what Tucker assumed was a less accusatory explanation.

"Turn her into a cowgirl?" he supplied.

She lowered her gaze guiltily.

"Considering she's mine and Summer's," he continued, "that's bound to come naturally. But I won't force my daughter to be someone she doesn't want to be when she comes to live here."

Her averted gaze snapped up to lock with his. "That transition, should it come at all, will be done in a slow, well-thought-out manner to assure Blue suffers no long-term emotional trauma from being uprooted from the only life she's ever known."

What about the emotional trauma that had been done to him? But this wasn't about his issues. It was about what was best for his little girl. He understood Autumn's reluctance to turn over custody of her niece after being such an integral part of his daughter's life, but this was something he wasn't backing down from. "I agree we need to make the transition for Blue as smooth as possible, but you need to start preparing yourself, as well. My daughter *will* be in my life and I'm not referring to brief holiday visits."

"I could drag things out in court if it came down to it," she replied.

"But you won't."

She shook her head, and with a resigned sigh said, "No. I wouldn't put her through that. If you prove capable of taking care of my niece, I will put my trust in the Lord to watch over her when I'm not here to do so. However, my niece *will* be in my life," she said, repeating his earlier words. "And *I'm* not referring to brief holiday visits."

"I wouldn't have it any other way," he said honestly, admiring her fire when it came to protecting Blue. "My daughter is your family, too. Is that what you're worked up about? That possibility that I'll cut you out of her life?"

She turned away.

"Autumn, I wasn't the one who walked away from my marriage. Summer was." He frowned. "I'll be the first to admit that we were both too young to really know what we were getting into, but I would've done my best to make things work between us if she had only given me a chance. Baby and all."

Her shoulders shuddered, and he knew by her silence that she was fighting back tears.

"Autumn…" he said, reaching out to place a comforting hand on her shoulder. He understood her pain. She had already lost her sister. She feared losing Blue as well, something he would never do to her.

She held up a hand, but remained standing as she was. "I'm okay. A little worse for wear after a lot of sleepless nights, but I'll pull it together."

Her conviction was strong, and he imagined she would do just that. Autumn seemed to have an inner strength his wife had never quite mastered. Hers was carefully controlled. Her decisions well-thought-out, where her sister hadn't always taken the time to consider the effect her words or her actions might have had on those around her.

He forced himself to let his hand fall away, but he

remained where he was. "I can only imagine how hard this has been on you. Losing your sister that way. Suddenly having to take on the responsibility of raising her child. Not to mention the financial burden…"

She turned to face him. The thick tears looming in her light blue eyes made them appear as if they were liquid silver. "There wasn't anything sudden about it. I gave up the real estate business I had built up back home in Lone Tree to come to Wyoming and help my sister with her little girl, both emotionally and financially, long before the Lord called Summer home. I found part-time work as a Realtor, planning my appointments around Summer's waitressing job so one of us could be home with Blue at all times. Everything was perfect until…" A sob caught in her throat.

His heart ached for this woman who had dedicated so much of her life to caring for his daughter. "They were blessed to have you."

"No," she countered without hesitation. "*I* was blessed to have them. They filled an emptiness I had inside me that I never knew was there." Her teary gaze drifted toward the empty doorway. "That little girl is everything to me. I love her with all my heart and I will do right by her." Her teary gaze returned to him. "So, natural father or not, you're gonna have to climb a very high mountain to reach the point where I feel she'd be better off with you than with myself and the life she already has in Cheyenne."

She'd already made that point quite clear, but he wisely kept that thought to himself. She had a right to feel the way she did. He was a stranger. A man who she had believed for years had done her sister wrong. And while he was the one who had truly been ill-treated, he intended to put his all into winning Autumn over. She deserved that much, knowing now the selfless sacrifices she'd made in her own life to make Blue's better.

"Whatever it takes," he said softly, fighting the urge to brush away a stray tear from her cheek. At that moment, she looked weary and vulnerable. Not at all like the lioness protecting her cub that he'd seen her be.

"I should go check on Blue."

"Make sure you both wear comfortable shoes," he called out as she started from the kitchen. "We'll be hiking up a trail that has bits of stone scattered about it to get to the flowers I promised to show Blue."

"We will." She paused in the doorway and cast a glance back over her shoulder. "Thank you for including me." Before Tucker could reply, she was gone.

Autumn sat quietly, looking out the passenger-side window of Tucker's truck as he drove them across his property. Not that she would have had a chance to say much with her niece chattering away from her car seat behind them. Tucker's warm, husky laughter told her he didn't mind Blue's constant barrage of questions and comments one bit. In fact, and much to her dismay, he was doing and saying all the right things where his daughter was concerned, and Blue was eating her daddy's attention right up.

"I didn't think you had any nieces or nephews," Autumn muttered with a glance his way. That was the only thing that could explain his comfort level around Blue. Yet, Summer hadn't mentioned Blue having any cousins on Tucker's side.

He shook his head. "I don't. My brothers are as single as they come, with no plans to settle down anytime soon."

She frowned at his reply. That meant Tucker was just a natural with children. She should have known that by how quickly her niece had taken to him.

"I take it one of my brothers caught your interest this morning."

The question was so unexpected, Autumn found herself choking. "What?" She turned to find him attempting to smother a grin, that lone Wade dimple that Tucker and both of his brothers had inherited in the family gene pool etched deep into his tanned cheek.

He cast a quick glance in her direction. "You looked a little put out to hear that my brothers are committed bachelors," he explained, his gaze shifting back to the road, or, in their case, the pasture ahead.

Confusion must have lit her features, because he added, "You frowned when I made mention of their firm commitment to bachelorhood."

"What's interest?" Blue piped up from the back seat of the extended cab.

Autumn cast a disapproving glare his way. Leave it to her niece to lose interest in the scenery outside just when Tucker had made his offhanded comment. "Children miss nothing," she reminded him.

"I see that," he said, that devastatingly handsome grin still intact.

She had no doubt that his smile was what had first drawn her sister to this man. Rugged good looks aside, it was that playful curve of his lips with that lone-dimpled grin, one that exuded both humor and confidence and put others at ease, which was nearly irresistible. *Nearly.* But Tucker Wade was the enemy. At least as far as she was concerned, he was. The man was stealing Blue's affection away with his silly jokes and eagerness to go that extra mile to make his daughter happy.

"Will you look at that?" Tucker announced, pointing toward a sparsely wooded hillside a short distance ahead, one made up of a few scattered pines, dirt, rocks and splotches of dried-up grass.

"What?" Blue said excitedly, tipping sideways in an attempt to see out the front window of Tucker's truck, her view mostly blocked by the passenger seat Autumn was in.

Glancing up at Blue in the rearview mirror, Tucker smiled. "The rabbitbrush is just over the top of that hillside."

Autumn gasped, her head snapping around in his direction. "Are you telling me you intend to drive us up that mountain?"

Tucker chuckled. "It's a hill, not a mountain. And a poor excuse of a hill at that."

"When it involves my niece's safety, it might as well be a mountain," she said sharply.

"I would never do anything to risk her safety," he said with a frown. Tucker slowed the truck, coming to a stop along the foot of the hillside. "We'll leave the truck here and walk the rest of the way."

Her skeptical gaze shifted, taking in the rocky outcrop before them.

"It's easier than it looks," he assured her.

"I think it would be better if we made our way back to the house," she argued, feeling far less confident than Tucker was about the ease at which they'd be able to traverse the *hill*.

"But I wanna see the yellow rabbits," Blue whined.

"You won't see any yellow rabbits," Autumn reminded her niece. "Only yellow flowers."

"I'm hoping she'll get to see more than that," Tucker stated as he cut the engine. He turned in the seat, his green eyes meeting hers. "Trust me."

Trust him? She didn't even know him. But there was something about Tucker Wade that made her feel she could do just that. Trusting a man didn't come easy for her. The last time she'd placed her trust completely in a man, he'd trampled all over it. Her heart, as well.

"Please?" Blue joined in, drawing Autumn back from her thoughts of the past.

A soft sigh passed through Autumn's lips. "Okay, we'll give it a try. But if the trail gets to be too much for Blue—"

"I'll carry her," Tucker said matter-of-factly.

Her gaze slid down to his strong arms. He could probably carry the both of them up that rather large hill if he had a mind to.

"You, too, if need be," he added, causing her gaze to snap back up to his grinning face.

Had she voiced her thoughts aloud? She hoped not.

"I really want Blue to see this," he added determinedly.

Autumn cleared her throat and looked away. "I'm perfectly capable of hiking up a hill." Not that she could remember the last time she'd done so.

With a nod, he opened the driver's side door and stepped down. "The offer still stands should you have need of it," he said with that irresistible boyish grin of his before shutting the door behind him.

Much to her chagrin, Autumn found herself grinning, too. She immediately wiped it away. She couldn't let

Tucker Wade and his charming cowboy smile get under her skin. Not only for her niece's sake, but for her own. This man made her feel at ease in a way she hadn't allowed herself to be around a man for a very long time. Not since she was a naive eighteen-year-old who thought she'd met "the one."

Parker Booth, a Texas cowboy every bit as smooth talking as this Wyoming one, had known all the right things to say. Had made her feel like she was the most special girl in the world with his sugary words. They'd dated all summer, and Autumn was certain she had found "the one." A week before she was to leave for college, Parker let it slip that it was her fun-loving, barrel-racing twin he had really wanted. Only Summer hadn't reciprocated his feelings, so he figured Autumn was the next best thing. Tender heart broken, and refusing to be any man's second choice, Autumn had ended things with Parker, and sworn off cowboys altogether.

"This is supposed to be a fun outing," Tucker Wade's deep voice rumbled close to Autumn's ear.

She jumped, startled from her thoughts, and then looked up at Tucker. "I never said it wasn't."

"That expression you were wearing on your face a moment ago pretty much said it for you."

"This outing isn't about my enjoyment," she said, because admitting the real reason behind her frown wasn't something she intended to share with anyone. Even Summer hadn't known the truth about why Autumn only dated business professionals. She would have felt somehow responsible for the hurt Autumn had experienced. So while Summer dated ranch hands and rodeo cowboys, Autumn only went out with career-focused businessmen. Men who were not her type. Men she knew she'd never risk having her heart broken by. Men un-like Tucker Wade. It seemed she and her sister weren't so different after all.

"That's where you're wrong," Tucker said as they started walking again. "But I'll let you decide for your-self once we get there."

They continued working their way up and around the somewhat wooded, rocky hillside with Blue chat-tering away, her busy conversation directed to no one in particular. The trail was decently wide and free of the larger rocks and prickly shrubs and trees that littered the incline on either side of them. It was also a much easier hike than Autumn had first thought it would be. The air was brisk, but it felt good to be outside doing something physical, having spent most of her time in-doors with Blue or in her office at work.

"Owie," Blue yelped suddenly, her hurried steps halt-ing.

Autumn nearly tripped over her niece, Blue's stop had been so abrupt.

Tucker stepped around Autumn, concern etched in his tanned face. "Blue? What's wrong?"

"I got a rock in my shoe," her niece replied with a tiny pout. "A real big one."

He clicked his tongue as he knelt in front of his daughter. "Those pesky rocks. Always trying to sneak back up to the top of the hill in someone's shoe."

Autumn watched in silence as Tucker lifted his lit-tle girl with ease and settled her atop his bent leg. Her niece who was normally on the shy side around men, no doubt from having spent most of her life around her momma and Aunt Autumn, had taken so easily to

Tucker. She wanted a daddy. Just like all the other children she knew had.

Tucker smoothed back a tendril of reddish-brown, baby-fine hair from Blue's face. "What do you say we have your aunt Autumn take a look?" he suggested, his tone low and soothing. One she imagined he used when one of his horses needed to be gentled.

Blue gave a tiny nod and then stuck her leg out.

Autumn brushed a couple of stones from the path before settling onto her knees in front of them. "We'll just shake those troublesome little stones right on out of there," she said with a tender smile as she untied and then slipped Blue's tennis shoe from her foot. Turning it over, she gave it a small shake, sending two offending pebbles back to the ground below.

"All gone," she said as she slid the sparkly, cotton-candy-pink tennis shoe back onto Blue's foot. Then she promptly worked its rainbow-colored shoestrings back into a neat bow. When she looked up, she found Tucker's green eyes watching her with a mixture of curiosity and something she couldn't quite put words to. And then he smiled, that lone dimple cutting deep into his tanned cheek. The effect that single gesture had on her was unsettling.

It would be easy to blame the unexpected quickening of her heartbeat to be the result of their brief hike up the hill, but she had never been one for mistruths—even to herself. Springing to her feet, Autumn took a hurried step back, her boot skidding on the miniscule pieces of stone that covered the trail.

Tucker was on his feet in an instant, Blue firmly ensconced in one arm as he reached out to steady her.

"Careful there," he said in a low rumble. "Don't want you twisting an ankle."

She was normally very alert, but Tucker Wade was so… She struggled to find the right words, finally settling for *thoroughly distracting*. This man, no matter how charming or handsome, was her niece's daddy. Reason enough to fight this pull he seemed to have on her senses. But even more troubling was the fact that he had been her sister's husband. The last man on Earth she should ever find herself attracted to.

Keeping her gaze averted, Autumn managed a quick, "Thank you."

"No thanks necessary," Tucker replied as he bent to set his daughter back on her feet.

Blue clung to his neck, refusing to be put down. "I think you need to carry me."

"Blue," Autumn gently admonished.

"That so?" Tucker said with a chuckle, making no attempt to free himself of the adorable little burr clinging to him.

She nodded. "So no more rocks try to sneak up the hill in my shoe. Their family would miss them if I took them away," she added, a mix of worry and sadness in her tone.

Like Blue misses her momma, Autumn thought with a painful tug at her heart. She wanted to reach out and pull her niece into her arms in a comforting hug, but held back giving Tucker a chance to respond. To show he wasn't prepared to deal with the fragile emotions of the young daughter who had been thrust unexpectedly into his life.

"I would never take you away from your aunt Autumn," Tucker said as he started back along the trail,

Blue firmly attached to his side. "She's a very important part of your life, and when you come to live with me we'll be sure to visit her often. And, of course, she'll always be welcome here."

He thought Blue was referring to her? She considered correcting his misconception, informing him that it was the loss of her mother that had stirred her niece's concern for the rock's "family," but Blue's next comment as she and her daddy crested the hill had the words faltering at the tip of her tongue.

"Could Aunt Autumn come live here with us, too? So she wouldn't miss me."

Tucker's response was lost to Autumn as he and Blue disappeared over the other side of the hill. Not that she needed to hear the words being spoken to know he'd had to explain to his daughter that her aunt's joining them at the ranch wasn't a possibility. She only prayed he'd done so with soothing words, reassuring her niece that Autumn would still be a very active part of her life if Blue ended up living with him. And Autumn was determined to cling to that *if*, because she wasn't anywhere close to being emotionally prepared to let her niece go. There was still a chance Blue wouldn't want to come to live there with her daddy on his ranch filled with horses. If that were the case, Autumn would, without a moment's hesitation, do everything in her power to keep custody of her.

As she crested the hill behind them, Autumn discovered not a sloping descent, but a slight grassy grade that spilled out onto an expanse of land dotted with flowering bushes. Tucker stood a few feet away with Blue by his side, shrieking in delight as she watched a cloud of brightly colored butterflies hovering above the clusters of yellow flowers that were abloom atop the leafy green bushes.

Autumn gasped as she took in the sight before her. Never in her life had she seen so many butterflies gathered in one place. Breathtaking didn't even come close to describing the beauty God bestowed before her at that moment.

Tucker glanced back over his broad shoulder. "Worth the climb?"

She moved to stand beside them, her gaze fixed on the fluttering of colorful wings in front of her. "Worth the climb."

They stood in silence for a moment longer before Tucker looked her way. "Last evening when you said you weren't surprised Summer hadn't told me about you, why is that?"

Her lips pressed together for a moment before replying, "Summer and I were twins, but we were two very different people. I secretly envied my sister's ability not to take life so seriously. I always felt the need to shoulder everyone else's problems. But it seems my sister harbored some feelings of jealousy toward me as well, resenting the way people would turn to me when they needed something, especially our grandma, who Summer felt loved me more."

"Did she?" he asked, his tone casting no judgment.

"No," she answered. "Our grandma loved us both the same. I just happened to be the one who was good at caring for sick people, or handling situations that might arise." Eyes tearing up, she said, "Summer only opened up to me about the resentment she felt toward me when her condition worsened. She wanted me to know how grateful she was for the time we had spent together these past few years raising Blue. She was right. It allowed us to reconnect as sisters and friends."

"I'm glad the two of you were able to strengthen your relationship."

"Me, too." So very glad.

Tucker's gaze trailed after his daughter. "How long will you and Blue be staying in Bent Creek?"

She watched her niece, who was now standing amid the gathering of colorful butterflies, and felt an unexpected pang of loss. She hadn't lost Blue to Tucker. And maybe she never would if the Lord answered her prayers. "I've cleared a month from my work schedule to bring Blue out here to meet you and, if your schedule permitted, get to know you better," she told him. "If we end up staying that long, we might have to shop for some additional clothes to wear." It was important that she spend the time to really get a feel for the kind of man Tucker Wade was beyond the research and newspaper clippings her sister had on him. "But I'm not promising we'll be here for the full month. Too many factors come into play." Like his not being the man her sister thought him to be. She needed to know that Summer's faith in Tucker, a man she had chosen to walk out on, was well and truly deserved.

He gave a nod. "Understandable. Then we'll take it day by day. I'm just grateful for the opportunity to get to know my daughter while you and I sort things out."

She didn't want to be there "sorting" things out. If it were up to her, she'd be on her way back to Cheyenne that very moment. But her sister had wanted this, with her dying breath she had wanted this, and so far Tucker Wade was turning out to be a very likable man. One who appeared to be truly eager to spend some real heartfelt time with the daughter he'd never known existed.

"You don't have to worry about Blue and I imposing on you any more than we already have," Autumn said. "I've made a few calls and there are a couple of bed-and-breakfasts nearby that are able to accommodate us during our stay." She hadn't made any concrete reservations before setting out for Bent Creek, unsure of how things would go once they'd gotten there. Tucker could have easily rejected the idea of being a father, even argued that he wasn't Blue's daddy, but he hadn't. He'd taken one look at his baby girl and he'd known.

"Your being here isn't an imposition," he said, keeping his voice low.

She looked up at him, arching a skeptical brow. "You've slept in the barn for two nights now." Guilt gnawed at her for putting him out of his own house, even if she hadn't been the one to suggest it.

"Like I told you yesterday morning, it wasn't the first time."

She tilted her head. "So it's customary to move to the barn when guests arrive here in Wyoming?"

"Not exactly," he answered with a grin. "I'm just saying that when my brothers and I were boys we'd sleep in the barn some nights. There and in the pasture under the stars."

"But you're not a boy any longer," she pointed out. "You're a full-grown man."

"Can't argue that," he teased.

"Tucker," she said in exasperation.

He tempered his smile, his expression turning more serious. "If sleeping in the barn means I'll have my daughter close by, then I'm more than willing to do so.

I want you and Blue to feel comfortable. Say you'll stay on here at the ranch."

"Tucker…"

"Please."

She appreciated his giving up his own comfort for theirs, but if they stayed on she wouldn't spend her days feeling guilty for chasing him out of his own house. "I won't have you sleeping in the barn on our account," she said firmly. "If we decide to accept your hospitality for our stay here, you have to promise me you'll sleep in your own bed and not out in the barn."

"I promise."

"Then we'll stay."

He smiled down at her. "Just so you know, I would've agreed to sleep in a briar patch if that's what it took."

Before she could reply, Blue exclaimed excitedly, "Now I know why the rocks wanna come up here. They would get to live with butterflies!"

Autumn felt the confidence she'd had in Blue's wanting to remain with her in Cheyenne slipping just a notch. But her niece wouldn't be living up on a hill surrounded by butterflies. She'd be living on a ranch with strangers, relatives or not, surrounded by horses which she was now painfully leery of.

Blue giggled, drawing Autumn's attention her way. A blue-and-green butterfly had come to rest on her niece's tiny shoulder. Blue's gaze shot up to Tucker as it fluttered away. "He thought I was a flower," she exclaimed.

"Because you are," he replied. "Bluebells are among the prettiest of all flowers."

Her niece's face lit up at her daddy's compliment.

Autumn fought to suppress a groan. It was no wonder her sister had been so taken with this man and his sweet words. How was she supposed to compete with uncles and grandparents, blue skies filled with rainbow-colored butterflies and a daddy who was such a smooth-talking cowboy he always seemed to know just the right thing to say?

Chapter Four

Tucker pulled up to his house, relief sweeping over him when he saw Autumn Myers's sporty little car still parked in his drive. While he had set out early that morning to tend to ranching duties, just as he had for the past several days, it was the first time he'd felt a nagging sense of unease about leaving. His gut told him that Autumn, who seemed to have enjoyed their outing to see the butterflies three days earlier, had even agreed to stay on at the ranch for an undetermined amount of time, was having second thoughts about her decision to remain in Bent Creek.

It hadn't been anything she'd said. It was more in her actions. After their playful hike up the hill in search of some blooming rabbitbrush and the butterflies he knew would be hovering around it, Autumn had been less free with her smiles when it came to him. As if she had decided to put up some sort of emotional wall between them. He supposed he couldn't really blame her. In her eyes, he was the enemy. The person who could take away the very thing she loved most. And there was nothing he could say that would ease her worry, because Blue was his daughter. She belonged with him. That didn't mean he wanted to push her from Blue's life. Far from. Family was, and had always been, important to him and Autumn was all that remained of Blue's mother's side.

That morning, before he'd headed to the main barn, which sat on his parents' property a few miles down the road, Autumn had been unusually quiet. Not that his daughter's excited ramblings over the stray kitten that had shown up the day before, no doubt Garrett's doing, had left much room for anyone else to speak. More concerning, however, was Autumn's avoidance of any sort of eye contact with him during breakfast that morning.

So, as he'd gone about his ranch work that day, his thoughts had been centered largely on Autumn, wondering if she would just up and leave without a word like her sister had. It was that worry that had Tucker sending a fair share of prayers up to the Lord that day. Whether it had been divine intervention in answer to those prayers, or simply Autumn's decision to remain, his daughter and her aunt were still there.

Tucker didn't think he could bear having his daughter brought into his life only to have her taken away from him again. He didn't even know how to contact them if they had been gone. All he knew was that they lived in Cheyenne, a city with a population somewhere around sixty thousand.

Shutting off the engine, he stepped from the truck and started for the house. Three strides in, the front door opened, followed by the screen door as his daughter shot outside to greet him. "Daddy!"

Tucker's heart squeezed at the exuberant greeting. The sight of his baby girl awaiting him at the edge of the porch, a blanketed bundle in her arms, had a grin spreading across his face. He'd never given much thought to having children, not with his still being legally wed to Summer, and he'd be the first to admit that suddenly finding out he was somebody's father scared the day-lights out of him, but he couldn't thank the Lord enough for this precious gift He had bestowed upon him.

Tucker picked up his pace as he cut across the yard. "Did you grow taller since I left to check on the horses this morning?"

His daughter giggled and shook her head, causing the mass of chestnut curls pulled up into a ponytail at the back of her head to swing to and fro. "Nope."

"You sure?" he teased as he reached the porch where Blue stood waiting at the top of the steps. "You look taller."

"That's 'cause I'm standing up here and you're down there."

He couldn't help but feel a surge of pride at her re-sponse. His baby girl was a bright little thing. "Ah, that must be it," he replied with a chuckle as he started up the few stairs.

As soon as he stepped up onto the porch itself, Blue set the bundle in her arms down on the floor beside her and then turned to wrap her tiny arms around his legs in an affectionate hug. "I missed you."

There was no stopping the moisture that gathered in his eyes as he stood there, soaking up the love of his baby girl. A pure, trusting love that took time to grow be-tween adults, but seemed to come so easily for children.

"I missed you, too," Tucker managed past the knot in his throat. He glanced down past his daughter to the tiny head that had just popped out from beneath the cover-ing of the old lap blanket. "Well, look who's still here."

"Bitty was taking a nap," his daughter announced with a smile.

"Bitty, huh?" Tucker returned her smile, making a mental note to thank his brother for the tiny calico kitten he'd left on the front doorstep for Blue in a small wooden crate. Not that anyone had seen Garrett dropping the kitten off, but Tucker had seen that very same crate in his brother's office two weeks past.

The sleepy-eyed calico stepped free of its covering and gave a long, yawning stretch.

His daughter nodded. "I called her that 'cause she's itty-bitty."

"That she is," Tucker agreed, glancing down to watch as the kitten wound its way around his leg as if in greeting and then wandered off across the porch.

"Where's she going?" Blue said in a panic as she watched her kitten go.

"I'm sure Bitty's hungry after her nap," he told her. "She's probably off to hunt for some field mice. She'll be back."

The screen door creaked open behind them, drawing both of their gazes away from the departing kitten.

Autumn stepped out to join them on the porch, that smile he'd been wishing for taking him by surprise as it moved across her face. "Hello," she greeted.

"Hello," he replied, thinking that this was what his life could have been like if Summer hadn't taken it all away. A family there to welcome him home when his work was done each day—affectionate little kitten included. But that wasn't his life. And Autumn wasn't his wife. In fact, she was turning out to be nothing at all like her sister had been. He couldn't help but wonder what his marriage might have been like if Summer had been a little more like her steadfast, loving twin.

"You're early," she said a little anxiously.

Tucker nodded. He had cut his day a little short because of fears that now seemed to have been unfounded. Autumn hadn't run off like Summer had. But placing his trust in another woman didn't come easy for him. His wife had seen to that. "Ranchers don't keep the usual business hours."

"I should've known that," she said almost apologetically.

"I wouldn't expect you to." He noted that she hadn't taken the time to put on her jacket. Instead, she stood, arms folded as she braced against the gentle bite of the fall air. A dish towel dangled from one of the hands curled about the sleeves of her blouse.

Following the line of his gaze, she said, "I was doing up some dishes when I heard Blue go outside."

Blue looked up at her. "I saw Daddy's truck out the window."

Noting that his daughter wasn't wearing a jacket either, he mentally scolded himself for not noticing sooner. Scooping Blue up, he said, "Let's get the two of you back in the house. The air's a little brisk outside today."

Autumn nodded in agreement and then turned to hold the door open as Tucker carried his daughter inside.

Once there, he lowered Blue to her feet and turned to Autumn. "I wasn't so sure you'd be here when I got home today. And I want you to know that if I've done or said anything to make you feel even the least bit uncomfortable, I'm sorry."

She shook her head. "You haven't done anything. If I'm a little out of sorts, it's because of everything going on in my life right now. At times, it can be overwhelming."

"Understandable. Know that I appreciate your choosing to see this through."

"I'm doing this for Blue. She deserves to have the chance to get to know her daddy," she said, glancing down at her niece.

He looked to Blue and smiled. "Her daddy is so happy to have her here."

Blue returned his smile. "Aunt Autumn said we get to keep living with you!"

Autumn shook her head. "Not live with, sweetie. We're only visiting with your daddy for a spell." She looked up at Tucker, meeting his gaze. "I—" The sound of approaching vehicles outside drew her gaze toward the narrow windowpanes that lined the front door.

Tucker looked past her and then rolled his eyes with a groan. "I told them they're becoming pests."

"Told who?" Autumn asked.

"My brothers," he grumbled.

"My uncles!" Blue exclaimed as she raced over to one of the windows to peer out.

"I'll take care of this," Tucker said as he moved toward the door.

"Where are you going?" Autumn asked as she started after him.

"To send them on their way."

"Why do they gotta leave?" Blue whined.

He stopped, turning to his daughter. "Because they've dropped by nearly every day since you've been here. I told them both that they need to give the two of you some breathing room."

"I don't need room," Blue said. "See." She drew in a deep breath and then let it out.

"Tucker," Autumn said, reaching out to place a staying hand on his arm. "I'd like for you to invite them to stay for supper."

"Yay!" Blue exclaimed, clapping her hands excitedly.

Tucker searched her face. "You sure about that?" He didn't want her to feel more overwhelmed than she already was, which his brothers in their eagerness to interact with their niece might have a tendency to do.

She smiled. "I'm sure. Besides, it'll give me a chance to see how they are with Blue for a longer period of time than the brief visits they've made here this week."

That was precisely what he was afraid of. Dinner might not work out in his favor if that were the case. Jackson and Garrett, whose hearts were in the right place, were every bit as clueless as he was when it came to children. Put the three of them together and Autumn was bound to focus on all the reasons not to leave Blue in their care instead of the most important reason—they were family. And family stayed together. They loved each other unconditionally, had each other's back and held strong in their faith.

"I'll extend the invite," he said, praying they wouldn't send Autumn running for the hills with his daughter in tow. "Dinner won't take long to put together. I picked up a couple of boxes of spaghetti last time I was at the grocery store. Should be enough to feed all of us, and I can whip it up pretty quick."

"That won't be necessary," Autumn told him. "I've already prepared this evening's supper. I'll just go pre-heat the oven and stick it in to warm for a spell."

His brows shot up. "You did?"

"I helped her," Blue said with a bright smile. "It's a surprise. Are you surprised?"

Looking down into Autumn's pretty ice-blue eyes, he said, "Very."

"It's not spaghetti," she said, almost anxiously, "but there should be more than enough to feed two additional dinner guests."

Whatever it was, he appreciated her having gone to the trouble of making dinner. He'd been doing all the cooking that week. And what man didn't appreciate coming home to a home-cooked meal? "I'm sure whatever you came up with will be more than fine," he told her. "But you didn't have to make anything. You're my guest. I should be cooking for you."

"Blue and I thought it was time we made dinner for you."

His daughter nodded in agreement.

Autumn's gaze lifted and there was no missing the hint of concern in those thickly-lashed blue eyes of hers. "I hope you don't mind."

"Mind?" he said, shaking his head. "Not at all. It's nice coming home to find I've had a surprise dinner planned for me." It was a small taste of the kind of life he might have had. But warm welcomes home and special dinners had been denied him. First by Summer, and then by his own determination never to risk his heart again. He'd remained married when he could have tracked Summer down to end things legally. It guaranteed that he couldn't—wouldn't—make the same mistake twice. If only the past few days hadn't shown him what that decision had cost him.

Tucker cleared his throat and looked back toward the door. "I guess I'll go extend that invite." Not that his brothers wouldn't have made their way to the house without one. Stepping outside gave him the chance to sort through his rambling thoughts and, at the same time, distance himself from the woman responsible for them being that way.

"Thank you for inviting us to dinner," Garrett said to Autumn as he settled into the chair next to Tucker's. His warm, lone-dimpled grin was the carbon copy of not only his brothers', but his niece's, as well.

Jackson nodded. "Yes, thank you. We only meant to stop by for a visit." He looked to Tucker. "Against my brother's orders I might add."

She couldn't help but smile at the glower Tucker was shooting them both. "I heard. However, I'm glad you did. It'll give me a chance to see how you all interact as a family."

"Probably not the best month to look for us to be overly loving to each other," Jackson muttered as he stabbed a forkful of chicken from the oval-shaped dish in the center of the table and dropped it onto his plate.

Autumn looked his way. "Excuse me?"

"It's October," Garrett added, as if that explained everything.

"We're coming off the back end of rodeo season," Tucker explained. "That means after putting in thousands of miles together while taking our stock to the dozens of rodeos we were contracted for, we tend to feel a little less warm and fuzzy toward each other."

"Fuzzy?" Blue piped in. "Like my teddy bear?"

Garrett chuckled. "Not quite, little darlin'. What your daddy's saying is that we tend to need a little breathing room from each other right after rodeo season ends."

"To keep us from wanting to strangle each other," Jackson added.

Blue's eyes widened with worry.

"Wrangle," Tucker blurted out as he cast a chastising glance in his brother's direction. "Your uncle meant to say to keep us from wanting to wrangle each other."

"What's wrangle?" she asked.

"That means to argue over something," Autumn answered for them as the three men sat exchanging troubled glances, no doubt realizing the current flow of their dinnertime discussion wasn't in their best interest when it came to convincing Autumn her niece would be in good hands with them. Then she turned to Tucker, focusing on something else that had been said. "Thousands of miles?"

He winced, looking as if he wanted to kick himself. "It's not as bad as it sounds. Rodeo season is only a few months long and for smaller events usually only two of us go."

She nodded, her gaze dropping to Blue. "Sounds very time-consuming."

"It can be," he answered honestly. "But I'm willing to change up my schedule to accommodate my daughter's needs. And my parents will be more than willing to help out whenever necessary."

"I see," she said stiffly. "I guess that means they took the news of their having a granddaughter well, then?" Autumn could only imagine what a shock such a revelation must have been for them.

Anxious glances were exchanged among the three men.

Seeing the men's sudden unease, she looked to

Tucker, pinning him with her gaze. "Your parents still don't know?"

His frown returned. "Not yet. But not because I'm worried about how they'll react to hearing they have a granddaughter. I just wanted a few days to let all of this settle in before calling them."

"It's been a few days," she responded flatly, disappointed that he felt the need to keep news of his having a daughter from the very people who brought him into this world.

"What my little brother's not saying," Garrett cut in, "is that he knows Mom and Dad will pack up and rush back to Bent Creek the moment they find out about Blue."

"And that would be a bad thing why?" she asked.

"Because they've been talking about taking this trip to Jackson Hole for as long as any of us can remember," Jackson said. "When Mom was hospitalized with pneumonia this past spring, Dad told her she had to get better because he was buying an RV and taking her on that trip she'd been longing for."

So Tucker wasn't hiding the fact of Blue's existence out of any sort of shame or embarrassment—he was doing so out of consideration for his parents' long-awaited trip. She found herself warming up to this kind-hearted cowboy with each passing day.

Maybe if Tucker had known about the baby her sister had been carrying at the time, things might have turned out differently for them all. He might have chosen to settle down in one place. Made something of their hasty marriage. But he hadn't known. Her sister's decision had not only deprived the man of his daughter, it had deprived Blue of the chance to know her father and all the family that came with him.

"I'm hungry," Blue said, squirming restlessly in her chair.

"You and me both," Tucker said with a smile directed specifically at his little girl. "We should eat before this meal your aunt Autumn made us gets cold."

"Can I say the prayer?" her niece asked, casting a pleading glance in Autumn's direction.

"That would be nice," Autumn told her. "Now close your eyes and bow your head."

Blue did just that and began in her soft little voice, "Thank You, Lord, for this meal we're gonna eat. And for my new daddy. Amen."

Her niece's words had a happy smile stretching wide across Tucker's handsome face.

"Oh, and thank You for my uncles, too," Blue added, folding her hands together and squeezing her eyes shut once more. "They're really tall. And for Aunt Autumn. She sells houses. And for all the pretty butterflies that live over the hill. And—"

"Sweetie," Autumn said, gently cutting her off, "why don't we finish thanking the Lord for all of the blessings he's bestowed upon us when we go to bed tonight?" There was no telling how many more things Blue had yet to be grateful for. Autumn fought to suppress the pinch of hurt she felt while Blue was giving her thanks. She reckoned she should be grateful her niece had placed her above the butterflies, but there was a time not too long ago—six days ago to be exact—that she was at the top of Blue's prayer list. Now Tucker seemed to be the center of her niece's world and Autumn knew she'd be lying to herself if she didn't say that it hurt just a little.

"Your daddy and your uncles have to be very hungry after working on the ranch all day."

"But I didn't get to thank God for the chicken we picked up at the store 'cause you burned—"

"Amen," Autumn blurted out, cutting her niece off. "Everyone dig in." Cheeks warming, she leaned over to tuck a dinner napkin down into the front of Blue's shirt. When she turned back to reach for her own napkin to place it on her lap, she found three big, strong cowboys grinning at her. Her face warmed even more.

"Something you're not telling us?" Tucker asked, dark brows raised in question.

She groaned, knowing if she didn't fess up, Blue would do it for her. "I might have accidentally allowed the water to boil away while cooking that spaghetti you mentioned having just bought at the store."

The corner of Tucker's mouth twitched. "You burned spaghetti?"

Could this moment get any more embarrassing? The last thing she needed was for Tucker Wade to tally up reasons for her not to be the best choice when it came to raising Blue. Reason number one—her poor cooking skills. There was no getting around that fact. Showing houses and nursing the elderly was her specialty. Summer had been the one more at home with horses and in the kitchen.

Ignoring Tucker's teasing grin, Autumn said, "You told us to help ourselves to anything we wanted from the kitchen while you were away. Blue came across the spaghetti in the pantry while we were fixing our lunch. She asked if we could surprise you with it for dinner. I thought it was the least we could do, considering your opening your home to us during our stay here. And spaghetti isn't all that hard to make as long as you don't let the water boil away."

"'Cause the noodles can catch fire," Blue stated as she dipped her spoon into the small mound of mashed potatoes on her plate. "That's why we had to go to the store to shop for dinner."

The men's dimples disappeared as their mouths dropped open.

"Fire?" Tucker choked out.

"The smoke was stinky," Blue added, crinkling her nose.

"There were no actual flames," Autumn said in her own defense. "Just a little smoke."

"Not as much as that time we made brownies," her niece agreed. "And not as stinky as when you burned my hot chocolate." Blue's expression changed, her gaze dropping to the plate in front of her. "Momma made the best hot chocolate."

The humor faded from Tucker's eyes at the mention of Summer, not that Autumn could blame him. Because of her sister, Blue had no fond memories of her daddy as she was growing up.

"Your grandma Wade's hot chocolate is pretty good, too," Tucker told Blue. "She'll have to make you some when she gets home."

Blue gave a small nod, but the sadness still filled her face.

Autumn hated feeling as though she had failed her niece. If only Summer were still with them. Life could go back to the way it had been when they'd all been happy. Would her sister have ever told her the truth about Tucker? Or would she have gone on letting Autumn believe the worst about Blue's daddy?

She glanced over to find Tucker watching her and shrugged apologetically. "Except for baking an occasional berry pie, cooking has never been my forte." And she was only good at that because she used to bake a berry pie every year for the annual pie Bake-Off back home in Braxton.

"I can't even make a pie," Tucker admitted. "So you're one up on me."

Garrett nodded. "I'd take chicken over spaghetti any day, so I guess that makes me glad you let the water boil away."

"This meal looks a lot more appetizing than some of the meals Tucker has served us in the past," Jackson muttered. "Although I'll admit his cooking has improved greatly over the years."

She gave them a grateful smile, but all she could focus on was the fact that Tucker Wade could cook. Another point in his favor.

"Nothing wrong with store-bought chicken," Jackson said as he stuffed a forkful of the rotisserie-baked chicken into his mouth.

They were being so kind, despite the resentment they had to feel, having Blue kept from them for so long. Autumn felt the sting of tears and knew she was on the verge of an emotional breakdown. "Please excuse me," she said, pushing away from the table. As she stood, all three men did so, as well. Their mannerly gesture had her stifling a sob.

"Aunt Autumn?" The concern in Blue's voice held Autumn in place for a long moment, but her niece would be more worried if her aunt were to break down right in the middle of dinner.

"It's okay, sweetie," she said, her voice breaking slightly. She prayed the Lord would grant her the strength to hold it together until she could make her way out of the room. "There's something Aunt Autumn needs to do before I eat. But you can go ahead and start without me. I won't be long." That said, she turned and hurried from the kitchen.

"Autumn?" Tucker called after her.

She didn't stop. Couldn't stop. Not when it felt like the weight of the world was pressing down on her.

Booted footsteps followed her out onto the front porch and down the steps into the front yard.

"Autumn, please," Tucker said. "Tell me what's wrong."

She kept on walking, tears sliding down her cheeks. "I'm okay," she called back over her shoulder. "Please go back inside and enjoy your dinner."

Instead of doing as she asked, he lengthened his stride, easily catching up to her. "You're crying," he said in surprise. "If this is about the spaghetti…"

"It's not," she said, fighting to hold back the tears. "Well, maybe it is a little."

"If my teasing you about it upset you, I apologize," he said, sounding truly remorseful. "I suppose I'm used to having my brothers around. We're always trying to get each other's goat."

"Summer did most of the cooking," she said, her bottom lip quivering. "But it's not just about my below-par cooking skills. Or your finding humor in my burning the spaghetti. It's wanting so very badly for this to be just some awful nightmare I'm gonna wake up from. Not so much you or your brothers, but the losing my sister part. Very possibly my niece, as well," she added with a hiccupping sob. "Blue is the only family I have left and, while I'm trying to leave it in the Lord's hands, I'm terrified my prayers won't be answered." Just as they hadn't been when she'd prayed to the Lord not to take her sister from them.

"Autumn," he said with an empathetic sigh. Drawing her into his comforting embrace, he rested his chin atop her head as her silent sobs made her shoulders tremble. "I can't even begin to imagine what you've had to go through, but I thank the Lord Blue had you in her life when Summer passed."

For the first time since her sister died, Autumn was the one being comforted. All her efforts and emotional energy following Summer's accident had gone toward consoling Blue. She'd held back her grief, not wanting to cause her niece any more sadness than she was already feeling after losing her mother. Suddenly that grief was spilling out and she was helpless to stop it.

Tucker held her, soothing her with words of comfort and faith as the tears came full force, her sobs no longer silent. When the storm of emotions finally subsided, Autumn lifted her head from Tucker's tear-dampened shirtfront and pushed away. "I'm sorry. I don't know where that came from." She couldn't even bring herself to look him in the eye after such an emotional outburst.

"Grief has no time limit," he said softly, "stirring up when you least expect it. I know because I still have moments when the loss of my sister hits me."

Autumn lifted her gaze to his. "You lost a sister? Summer never said anything."

"That's because she didn't know about her," he said solemnly. "Mari's death is something I avoid talking about, even with my family."

Yet, he was sharing his loss with her? She couldn't

help but be touched by it. "How old was your sister when you lost her?"

"Six."

Dear Lord, she was practically a baby. "What happened?" As soon as the question was out, Autumn shook her head. "You don't have to answer that."

"Meningitis," he answered anyway. "She'd had a really bad ear infection that worked its way into her bloodstream. By the time the doctors figured out that it was something more serious and began treatment, Mari had taken a turn for the worse. The Lord called her home that same night."

She had come there with so many preconceived notions about Tucker Wade that were nowhere close to the man she was coming to know. And now they shared another bond, beyond that of her niece. They had both experienced the pain of losing a sibling. A sister.

She wiped at the dampness left behind on her cheeks by her tears. "Thank you for opening up to me about Mari." Especially after admitting that he never spoke of her with anyone, even Summer.

He shrugged as if what he'd just done hadn't been a huge emotional undertaking for him. "I didn't want you to think you were alone when it came to losing a sister. I've always had my brothers to lean on."

"That was very kind of you." She lifted her gaze to look up at him, tears once again filling her eyes. "More kindness than I deserve." Tucker opened his mouth, no doubt to contradict her statement, but Autumn didn't give him the chance to. She owed him the truth. "It wasn't my choice to bring Blue here."

He nodded. "And I appreciate your respecting your sister's last request."

"It was the right thing to do. But I came here already resenting you and the unwanted changes you might bring about in my life," she admitted. "I came here determined to uncover all of your faults and failings, so I could take Blue home for good. But you're nothing like the man in my imaginings. You're kind and compassionate. You seem to have a natural inclination to know all the right things to say and do when it comes to Blue. And you can cook," she added with a sniffle. "How am I supposed to compete against someone who has no flaws?"

"No flaws?" He snorted. "Sweetheart, I'm the furthest thing from perfect there is. I procrastinate when it comes to cleaning out the fridge, or going grocery shopping. I don't always take time to shave," he said, scrubbing a hand over his lightly stubbled chin. "And I always forget to put the lid back on the toothpaste. Should I go on?"

His words brought a smile to her face. "I'll be sure to make note of those particular flaws when making my final decision."

"You know this doesn't have to be a 'someone wins and someone loses' situation. We can work this out together."

"Tucker, it's not that simple," Autumn replied, her expression growing serious once more.

"Life never is," he said. "But you learn to work around it."

"Like it or not, someone is gonna lose in this situation." She just prayed that someone wouldn't end up being her niece.

He frowned. "I'll be the first to admit I don't have all the answers right now, but I do know one thing. I want my daughter to be happy. Placing her in the middle of a lengthy custody battle isn't going to make that happen, so I intend to do a lot of praying to the Lord for guidance as we work through this situation."

Tucker had been denied his only child. He could easily have turned his bitterness for what her sister had done to him on her and gone straight to his attorney to fight for custody of Blue, which he had every right to. But he had put his daughter's emotional well-being first and was taking the time to get to know her, allowing her time to get to know him, as well.

"Dragging my niece through a court battle is something I'd prefer to avoid as well, if at all possible."

"Then we will," Tucker said assuredly. He cast a quick glance over his shoulder and then back to Autumn. "Look, this probably isn't the best time for us to have this conversation. Blue's bound to start wondering where we've run off to. Why don't we head back inside and have some of that chicken dinner you put together for us?"

"Maybe you should go on in and make excuses for me. My eyes must look awful after crying the way I did."

"Your eyes are as pretty as ever," he said and then cleared his throat as if immediately regretting his words. "I mean they're not the least bit swollen. Come back in and join us. Later, we both can begin mulling over ways to make this situation work for all involved. That is," he added with a slight grin, "if my flaws don't prove to be far too numerous."

With a nod, she walked with him back to the house, a smile pulling at her lips. Tucker Wade thought her eyes were pretty. "Just see that they don't, Mr. Wade. I would hate to add any more flaws to the list I'm mentally compiling to the ones you've already given me."

He let out a husky chuckle. "Appears I'm my own worst enemy."

"Tell you what," she said as they made their way up onto the porch. "You forget about my burning the spaghetti and I'll cross all previously mentioned flaws off of my list."

He glanced her way as he reached for the screen door, and a wide smile spread across his tanned face, the sight of which made her heart skip a beat. "Spaghetti? What spaghetti?"

Chapter Five

Movement in the kitchen entryway had Tucker glancing up from the cup of coffee he was finishing off before heading out to the main barn. For a moment, it was Summer he saw standing there, the thought of which had Tucker's jaw clenching even though he knew that it couldn't be his wife.

Autumn's shoulder-length hair, at least where the cut fell in the front, was slightly mussed, as if she'd taken a walk outside where a slight breeze filled the cool, crisp morning air. Instead of the more polished, professional dress style he'd seen her wear since coming to the ranch, she was dressed in an oversized loose-fitting sweatshirt and a pair of black leggings, reminding him more of her sister in her casual attire.

But this wasn't Summer. Acknowledging that, he managed a smile. "Morning."

"Morning," Autumn replied as she moved into the room.

Pushing away from the table, Tucker stood. "I hope I didn't wake you."

She shook her head. "You didn't. I've been up for a

while, going through work emails. I heard you moving about the kitchen. Do you have a moment to talk? There's something I really needed to say to you."

Tucker's gut tightened. Was this the day she had made the decision to head back to Cheyenne with his daughter? Nine days was not nearly enough time to sway Autumn over. And the last thing he wanted to do was to hurt her any more than she was already hurting. He'd seen the emotional pain she tried so hard to hide.

"I'll make time," he said as he stepped around the table to slide a chair out for her. "Can I get you something? A cup of coffee? A glass of orange juice?"

"No, thank you," she replied as she took the offered seat with a grateful smile. "We really haven't had any time alone to speak," she began. "You've either been working the ranch, or others have been around. Your brothers. Blue."

He nodded in understanding. Though he'd cut back on the hours he spent working during her and Blue's stay there, Autumn was correct about their really having no time for any private conversation between the two of them. Blue rarely left his side when he returned home, except for when he went out to the barn. And Garrett and Jackson had been by several times that past week to visit. His brothers had even hung a wooden swing from one of the trees in the front yard for Blue to play on, which his daughter happily spent hours on.

"You should have said something," he told her as he returned to his seat. "I would've found time for us to talk in private."

"I was gonna last night, but you had plans," she replied.

"I'm sorry to have left you and Blue here to entertain

yourselves last night, but I had a prior obligation I didn't feel right backing out of."

"Of course not," she said. Yet, Tucker wondered if he shouldn't have called the nursing home to tell them he wouldn't be in while his daughter was visiting. But he'd needed to check in on Old Wylie, and see how he was recovering after his recent struggle with gout. The long-retired rodeo cowboy had no family to look in on him, so Tucker had taken it upon himself to watch out for him. Thankfully, his old friend had appeared to be hale and hearty. Like the Old Wylie who had taught Tucker so much of what he knew about being a professional rodeo rider. And for that Tucker was grateful.

"What was it you wanted to talk about?" Tucker asked, preparing himself for the worst, hoping for the best.

Autumn lowered her gaze to the table. "This has been weighing on my mind since last week, so I figured it was time to get it out in the open."

His heart sank. "Sounds serious."

"Not so much serious as it is embarrassing," she mumbled with a frown, her gaze still downcast.

"Embarrassing?"

Autumn looked up and he immediately noted the hint of color in her cheeks. "I'm referring to my teary out-burst last week. I think I owe you an apology for my behavior that evening, though it's a rather belated one at this point."

Relief swept through him for the umpteenth time since Autumn's arrival. She wasn't there to tell him she and Blue were leaving. The tension in his limbs imme-diately eased. That past week had been a series of emo-tional ups and downs for him. At times, tension rode him hard, knowing he had to prove himself not only to Autumn but to his little girl. He couldn't—no, he wouldn't let his daughter down. But there was also that niggling doubt at the back of his mind—what if he failed? Then there were those times when Blue would hug him so lovingly, so acceptingly, or when Autumn would grant him a heartfelt smile, making him feel less like her enemy and more like…well, more at ease, that his confidence in his ability to be Blue's father buoyed.

"You don't have anything to be embarrassed about," he told her. "Or apologize for." He curled his fingers around the ceramic mug on the table in front of him to keep from reaching out to cover her hand with his as he had the sudden urge to. Autumn touched a soft spot inside him. One he hadn't known still existed. His wife's leaving all those years before had hardened his heart where other women were concerned. Not that he couldn't be kind to them, or blame them for what Summer had done. He had just gotten used to being emotionally unavailable. But something had changed after Autumn and his little girl had come into his life.

"I never should have allowed my emotions to spill out the way they did," she said. "That was so unlike me. I'm normally the one responsible for holding things together. Not collapsing into a puddle of uncontrollable tears."

He lifted his gaze to hers. "I get what you're going through. Losing a sibling is probably one of the hardest things a person can go through in their life. At least, you're able to talk about your sister. It's more than I can say for myself, and far more time has gone by since Mari's passing."

"Only with you." Her softly spoken confession drew his attention once more. "You're the only person I've shared my true feelings with. I would never let Blue see me like that, and I don't really have any close friends in Cheyenne to talk to. I spent all of my free time with Summer and Blue."

"Surely you have other family besides Blue down in wherever it was you grew up in Texas that you can turn to when the grief gets overwhelming."

She looked perplexed for a moment before shaking her head. "Braxton. A town similar in size to Bent Creek." Her frown deepened. "Did you and my sister ever really talk before the two of you eloped?"

He sighed. "Probably not as much as we should have. At least, not about the things that one realizes are important as they grow wiser with age. At the time, we were all about competing in the rodeo and the excitement of falling in love. Or what I guess we both thought to be love at the time."

"In my sister's defense, she didn't grow up with parents who were shining examples of true love. Our daddy was never in the picture and Momma didn't like the picture she was in. She preferred travel and adventure to raising kids. We were cared for mostly by our maternal grandma."

Tucker listened intently, taking in all the information his wife had failed to share with him. Had she believed he would have judged her by her parents' past if she'd shared this information with him? Or was it because she longed to leave her past behind her? So many questions he would never have the answers to.

Autumn went on, drawing Tucker back to the conversation. "Summer and I longed for our momma to show us some sort of motherly love, but we learned pretty young that not everyone's cut out to be somebody's parent. So we shut her out of our hearts."

"I didn't know any of this," he admitted with a frown. "But then your sister always steered our conversations away from her life in Texas."

"I'm not surprised. She wanted to get away from the life we had growing up. And when college didn't turn out to be the answer for her, she went back to barrel racing, which allowed her to leave her past behind doing something she had always loved."

"You've made it clear that you aren't close to your mother, but does she know about Summer's passing?"

"I have to reckon she knows," Autumn replied with a sad smile. "She was killed in a whitewater rafting accident the summer before my sister and I started high school. Grandma Myers became our full-time caretaker, raising us alone through those troubling teen years and loving us until she passed away when we were seventeen. Thankfully we were able to avoid being placed into the system. We both had part-time jobs outside of school and were just shy of turning eighteen, so the judge granted us our emancipation."

He couldn't even fathom what it had been like to live the kind of life she and Summer had. Tucker found himself wanting to wrap Autumn in a comforting embrace, just as he had the evening before. Thankfully there was a table between them to hold him in place. But that didn't keep his heart from going out to her. Life hadn't been easy for Autumn or Summer. Not only because of the losses they had suffered, but because of the love they'd been denied by their parents. He sent up a silent prayer of thanks to the Lord for blessing him and his brothers with a tight-knit family whose foundation was built on love and faith.

"I'm sorry," he said, not knowing what else to say.

She met his gaze, her own glistening with unshed tears. "It was a long time ago." Reaching up, she fingered a small gold cross that hung from a delicate gold chain around her neck.

"Your mother's?" he asked, nodding toward the cross.

"My grandma's," she replied. "She used to tell us it was a reminder of her faith. That wearing it close to her heart helped her to stay strong when times were tough." She let her hand fall away. "Summer didn't care for jewelry, so Grandma Myers left it to me in her will."

He had to imagine Autumn had sought comfort from that precious family heirloom quite often since Summer's passing. Grief was a hard road to travel. Even more so when one tried to walk it alone. He knew that firsthand.

"Are you still in contact with friends back in Texas?" he pressed, needing to know she wasn't completely alone. That she still had someone she could turn to.

"Yes. My best friend lives in Braxton," she answered, and relief swept through him. "Hope moved back to town right before I left for Wyoming, but we stay in touch."

"It's good to know you at least have her to call and talk to when you're feeling down." It was long-distance comfort, but it was better than nothing at all.

"Oh, I wouldn't do that to her," Autumn said, shaking her head.

"Excuse me?"

"Hope went through a really rough time emotionally after leaving Braxton. Now that she's home and has finally found real joy in her life—" she paused, a smile returning to her pretty face as she thought about her friend "—having reunited with and finally married her high school sweetheart, the last thing I would wanna do is bring her down with my troubles. Not that Hope doesn't call to check up on me. I make sure to keep things light, and usually manage to redirect the conversation so we end up discussing her and Logan instead."

"Autumn, she's your best friend," he said with a disapproving frown. "I would think she'd want to know when you're feeling down."

"If things become too much to bear, I'll turn to Hope," she assured him. "But I tend to have pretty strong shoulders. Last week being the exception. And I have the Lord to turn to, even if he doesn't answer my every prayer."

He knew without her saying that Autumn was referring to Summer's dying. He and Autumn had more in common than Tucker thought. They both refused to burden others with their emotional hardships, instead suffering the hurt they harbored inside in silence. He had to admit that it had felt surprisingly good to open up to her about the loss of his own sister. Like a piece of his long-withheld grief over the loss of his sister was finally lifted. He could only pray their talk, brief as it may have been, had offered her the same bit of solace.

"Aunt Autumn?"

Her head snapped around at the sound of her name being called out. "I'm in the kitchen with your daddy."

Blue wandered in all sleepy eyed, her red-brown curls hanging limply over her tiny face. "Are we gonna go see the butterflies this morning?"

"Not this morning, sweetie," Autumn replied. "Your daddy has work to do."

His daughter's lower lip pushed outward. She would

go visit her butterflies every day if she had her way. They'd already been back to see them several times. Tucker made sure to take a different route across the ranch each time to get to the base of the hill, giving Blue closer glimpses of the broncs from behind the safety of his truck's window. Each time, he noticed her watching the galloping herd with more and more interest.

"While I can't drive you to see the butterflies this morning, I'd like to show you my barn," Tucker said with a smile.

Blue's expression grew uneasy. "Are there horses in there?"

Since they'd arrived, his daughter had steered clear of his barn and his two saddle horses. Other than giving her the opportunity to be close to horses while inside his truck, he hadn't pushed Blue for more. He had, however, done a fair amount of praying that the Lord would help her make peace with her fears, her nightmares included. And seeing as how his daughter hadn't had a single nightmare since coming to Bent Creek, he knew the Lord had been listening.

"I'm pretty sure my saddle horses are waiting outside in their pen for their morning grain. Would you like to help me feed them this morning?"

"Tucker…" Autumn said softly, no doubt trying to remind him of Blue's fear when it came to horses.

He hadn't forgotten, but he also knew that his daughter needed to face her fears or she would never overcome them. His gaze shifted back to Blue. "What do you say, sweetheart? Want to help Daddy feed his horses this morning?"

Blue took a step back, shaking her head. "I don't like horses."

His smile threatened to sag at his daughter's decla-
ration, but he forced it to remain intact. Tucker wanted
so badly to make her fears go away, but seeing the wary
look that filled Blue's eyes and pinched her features had
him second-guessing his efforts to help her.

"If you don't want to," he began, wondering why he'd
ever thought suggesting Blue help him feed his horses
that morning was a good idea, "then—"

"I have an idea," Autumn said, cutting him off with
a cheery smile aimed in his daughter's direction. "We
haven't gotten to see inside your daddy's barn yet and
I'd really like to. Why don't you and I walk out with him
and just watch while he feeds his horses?" Before Blue
could turn the suggestion down, or run from the room
in a panic, she added, "We can stand on the other side
of the fence and watch while his horses eat their breakfast. Just like we used to do with your momma. Then
maybe afterward, your daddy will have time to give us
a quick tour of his barn."

Just like she had done with her mother, Tucker
thought regretfully. If he had known that, he absolutely
wouldn't have suggested it. The last thing he wanted to
do was stir up painful memories for his daughter. But
how was he to avoid it? He had no idea what kind of
memories she had since he'd never been a part of them.

Tucker had just opened his mouth to tell his daughter
that she didn't have to go with him to the barn when she
surprised him by saying, "I like to feed them apples."

His heavy heart lightened at her words. Blue hadn't
written horses out of her life completely. There was,
much to his relief, a glimmer of hope that his daughter
might yet come around. "They love being fed apples,"
he told her, a smile stretching wide across his face. "In

fact, I think I have a small bucket of apples out in the barn. If you like, you can give them each a couple of slices before they eat their breakfast." His gaze shifted to Autumn. "And it would be a pleasure to show you ladies around the barn afterward. Not that there's much to see."

Blue giggled as she sidled up against her aunt who was still seated at the table. "I'm not a lady."

Tucker raised a brow, fighting to hide his amusement. "You're not?"

Her head of springy curls shook from side to side. "No."

He sat back in his chair and pretended to study her. "Well, I know you're not a cat. You don't have any whiskers."

She giggled harder and then swiveled her flannel-nightgown-covered backside around in demonstration. "No tail, either."

"True," Autumn joined in. "Not even the tiniest little bobtail that I can see."

"A peacock?" he teased.

"Nope," his daughter said with a determined shake of her head. "No feathers."

He sighed as if in exasperation. "Then I give up. What are you?"

She smiled up at him. "Your little girl."

She'd said it with such pride and happiness, Tucker felt an unexpected rush of what had to be love fill him. Clearing his throat to push away the knot of emotion that had gathered there, he said, "That you are."

"If we're gonna go out to the barn with your daddy, then you need to go get dressed," Autumn told Blue. "We can eat breakfast when we get back."

"Okay!" Skipping excitedly, his daughter bounced out of the room.

"You need to dress warm!" Autumn hollered after her as Blue scampered away. Then she looked to Tucker. "I will go offer my assistance, but Blue's taken a mind to dress herself these days." She stood to leave.

Tucker sprang to his feet, as well.

Autumn laughed softly. "You don't have to do that you know."

"Do what?"

"Stand every time I enter or leave a room."

"Can't help it," he said. "It's how my mother raised us. When a lady enters the room, you stand. Same goes when she takes her leave." He reached for his cowboy hat, placing it atop his head.

"If only all mommas could install such manners in their sons," she said with a smile as she walked away.

"I'll wait for you and Blue out on the porch," he called after her. He needed to call Jackson and let him know he was going to be a little late getting to the main barn that morning. And for a very good reason. Blue was going to give his horses a chance. If only he could get Autumn to let down her walls and give *him* a chance. And he wasn't so sure he meant that solely in regard to his daughter.

Autumn handed Blue her jacket and then grabbed her own from the chair by the guest bed. "We'll need these. Fall mornings can be quite chilly." Unlike the weather she'd grown up in down in Texas.

Her niece slipped her coat on and then waited while Autumn bent to zip her snuggly inside it. "Can Bitty go with us?"

Her gaze drifted over to the tiny ball of speckled

white fur perched atop the deep-set windowsill looking out. "I think she's content to sit on the windowsill, soaking up the warming rays of the morning sun. You two can play together after we get back and have had our breakfast."

Blue looked disappointed, but only for a moment before her attention was drawn elsewhere. "Can I take my doll?"

Autumn smiled. "If you want."

Blue ran over to grab the well-loved rag doll from the bed. Then she turned back to Autumn. "We're ready."

"Your daddy is waiting for us outside," Autumn told her as she opened the bedroom door and motioned for Blue to lead the way.

Tucker was standing in the front yard, talking on his phone when they stepped out onto the porch. He gave a wave as he hurried to finish his call. A second later, he shoved the cell phone into the front pocket of his jeans and started toward them. "All set?"

"All set," Autumn told him, taking Blue's hand in hers.

"I see you brought a friend," Tucker said to Blue as they headed for the barn. His normally long strides were noticeably shortened, Autumn had to assume, for their benefit. Always considerate.

Blue appeared pleased that her daddy had noticed her prized possession. "Miss Molly," she told him.

Tucker's step faltered at his daughter's pronouncement.

"She named her doll after something her momma used to say," Autumn explained, sensing he may have already known that by his reaction.

"Good golly, Miss Molly," Tucker muttered as if the

saying caused him discomfort. And maybe it did. Her sister had hurt him. He had to be sensitive to things that brought back memories of his runaway wife.

"Did Momma say it to you, too?" Blue asked, looking up at him as they crossed the yard.

"Not to me in particular," he answered. "It was something your mother would say when she was frustrated or surprised over something."

A nearby whinny had Blue's head snapping in that direction. As soon as she saw the two horses watching them from beyond the fence, she sidled closer to Autumn, clutching the floppy rag doll to her chest.

Tucker, whose green-eyed gaze was fixed on the pair of horses, was grinning from ear to ear. "Will you look at that?" he said. "They're excited to see you."

Blue eyed them cautiously. "They are?"

He looked down, no doubt seeing the fear on his daughter's face, and his smile deflated like a party balloon that hadn't been knotted well.

"Maybe Molly can help you feed apples to the horses," Autumn suggested, smiling reassuringly when Tucker's grateful gaze lifted to meet hers.

"Does she have to ride them?" Blue replied, biting at her bottom lip.

"Not if she doesn't want to," he said. "To be honest, I'm not sure I'd have a saddle small enough for her to sit on."

"Can she ride with you?" her niece asked as she released her hold on Autumn's hand to reach for Tucker's.

He was winning her niece over, Autumn thought sadly. And she was helping him to succeed. How foolish was she?

"With me?" Tucker replied, his brows lifting in unison as he looked down at his daughter.

Blue nodded. "In case she's scared."

"And that would make her feel safe?" Tucker queried as he studied his little girl.

Her niece whispered something in her baby doll's ear and then looked up at her daddy once more. "She says it would. 'Cause you're big and strong and wouldn't let her fall."

Was Blue still talking about her doll? Or was this conversation more about her niece's wants and fears? Autumn prayed it was the latter. Her niece used to beg her momma to take her for rides on her horse. It was said that time healed all wounds. Maybe, just maybe, this was the case for Blue.

"If it would make her feel safer," Tucker began, "then I would be more than happy to let Miss Molly ride with me anytime she wants to."

Blue brought the rag doll up to her face once more and then lowered her again. "She says she wants to feed them apples first."

He chuckled. "Miss Molly certainly knows her mind. Why don't you run on into the barn and grab a couple of big fat juicy apples from the bucket sitting just inside the door?"

She hesitated, her gaze fixed on the nearby barn where the wide red door stood partially open.

"There aren't any horses inside," Tucker hurried to assure her. Reaching out, he ran a hand down the nose of the horse closest to him. "I only keep these two here at my ranch. The rest of the horses live at the main ranch where the chickens live."

"Where we collected eggs that day," Autumn reminded her, not that it was necessary. Blue's memory was as sharp as a tack.

"Okay," her niece said, her anxiety about venturing into the barn apparently put to rest by her daddy's reassurance. Blue took off in a happy skip across the yard, her doll flopping around at her side as she went.

Autumn stepped up beside him, watching her niece make her way to the barn to fetch the apples. "I never thought I'd hear her asking to ride a horse again, or see her entering a barn for that matter."

Taking his gaze off Blue, he glanced down. "Blue didn't ask to ride."

Autumn looked up at him in confusion. That was certainly what she'd gotten from the conversation.

"Miss Molly did," he said with a warm chuckle.

Laughter escaped her lips. "I suppose she did. And what a visual that brings to mind. A big, strong cowboy riding around on his horse with a tiny, well-loved rag doll held securely in the saddle in front of him."

He shot her a playful grin. "You forgot handsome."

"I figure that goes without saying," she told him, her words promptly followed by a warmth spreading through her cheeks. She wasn't supposed to notice things like that, even if he had prompted it.

Thankfully, Tucker let the comment go, carrying on as if she hadn't just admitted she thought him handsome. "If it comes down to my having to give Miss Molly a ride, my brothers aren't to hear one word about my doing so."

She couldn't resist. "And if they happen to catch wind of it?"

"They'd never let me live it down. Not to mention the hit my rough and tough cowboy reputation would take."

She appreciated the way he turned things around, joking about his own embarrassment to save her from her own discomfort. "No need to worry," she said with a smile. "Your secrets are safe with me."

Those green eyes studied her for a long moment before Tucker replied, the teasing leaving his tone, "As are yours with me."

Blue came racing out from the barn with an apple in one hand and her doll in the other. She handed Tucker the apple. "This is for the brown horse."

"That's Hoss," he told her.

"What's the other horse's name?"

He glanced toward the pen. "That handsome fellow would be Little Joe."

"I'll be back." She took off for the barn again.

"Where are you going?" Autumn called after her.

"Molly and me gotta go get an apple for Little Joe, too," Blue hollered back over her shoulder as she raced away.

"Yes, we mustn't forget Little Joe," Autumn said, looking to Tucker with a grin. "You wouldn't happen to be a fan of old Westerns, would you?"

"You know *Bonanza*?" he said in surprise.

"You sound surprised."

"I might have expected Summer to have known where my horses' names came from, but not you."

She placed a hand on her hip. "And why ever not?"

He looked her over. "Well, because you aren't exactly the type I picture watching old cowboy shows."

"I'll have you know I've watched several seasons of *Bonanza*. All reruns, of course, but I'm very familiar with the Cartwrights," she told him, chin lifted high.

"I'm impressed."

"Summer had a thing for Little Joe," she admitted. "Myself, I was more partial to Daniel Boone."

"Daniel Boone?"

"Gotta love a man confident enough to walk around in a coonskin hat," she said, making him chuckle.

"I have to confess that out of all the tips my brothers gave me over the years on ways to stir a woman's interest, a coonskin hat was not among them."

"Here we go!" Blue exclaimed as she hurried back with the remaining apple, handing it to her daddy.

"Hoss and Little Joe will be so grateful to you for these apples," Autumn told her as she lifted her niece, placing her atop her hip.

"But God made them," Blue said as she held her doll to her.

"Yes, He did, and I am quite sure your daddy's horses are very grateful to the Lord as well for this sweet feast they are about to receive," Autumn told her as Tucker pulled out his pocketknife and cut into one of the apples. "But you're the one who's bringing these gifts from God to Hoss and Little Joe. I think they'll be mighty grateful to you, as well."

"Your aunt Autumn is right," Tucker said. "Feed them apples and they will love you forever."

"But I'm not gonna feed them," Blue said, her gaze shifting to the horses. "Molly is."

He seemed a bit taken back by the confusion, but recovered quickly. "I think Miss Molly might need a little help holding the apple slices," he told her. "They practically weigh more than she does."

Blue dropped her gaze to the ground, biting into her lower lip.

"Sweetie," Autumn said, "if you decide not to feed

your daddy's horses the apples, you and Molly can watch while I feed them." Blue had already taken a huge step by even considering just getting close to the awaiting quarter horses, let alone possibly hand-feeding them.

Her niece's green eyes lifted as she looked sheepishly to Tucker.

He gave her a reassuring smile. "It's okay, sweetheart. You can do it another time if you aren't feeling up to it today."

Blue seemed torn by indecision, looking from her daddy to the horses and back. Then she said something to her doll before saying to Autumn, "You and daddy can feed them. Molly and me will watch."

"I'm guessing your aunt would probably prefer to stand with you and Molly and watch while I feed Hoss and Little Joe some apple slices."

"Your guess would be wrong." She could tell Tucker was surprised by her words and decided to let him in on a little secret. "I might look the business professional type most of the time, but I did grow up in Texas with a sister who lived and breathed horses."

"Momma breathed horses?"

Autumn laughed. "No, sweetie. It's a saying that means she loved everything about them."

"Oh," she said.

She returned her attention to Tucker. "I sometimes helped Summer care for her horse when we were in high school, feeding, watering and grooming him, depending on our work schedules. You might even be shocked to learn that I have even ridden a horse before."

Tucker chuckled, shaking his head. "You are just chock-full of surprises, Miss Myers."

"Just goes to prove you can't always judge a book by

its cover," she said with a sly smile. "Shall we go feed those poor horses before they whinny themselves hoarse trying to get our attention?"

"Good idea," he said, walking alongside her to the pen. "I apologize for the assumption I made."

"Apology accepted," she said softly. "And it's understandable. While most identical twins tend to share the same likes and dislikes, my sister and I were two very different people."

"You say that like it's a bad thing," he commented. "God might have created the two of you as mirror images of one another, but He also chose to give you each your own special individuality." He glanced her way. "You are who you were meant to be."

She had spent so many years growing up dealing with comments that made her feel like she and Summer had somehow failed God by not being alike in every sense. Maybe the separate paths they had taken in life had been gently guided by the hand of God.

"Watch your step," Tucker warned, drawing Autumn from her thoughts. "The ground's a little uneven around here. Don't need you two taking a tumble."

Heeding his warning, Autumn trod carefully, Blue balanced securely on her hip. When they reached the fence, she lowered her niece to her feet just far enough away from the fence so that the horses couldn't reach her with their investigative sniffs unless Blue was ready for them to.

"Boys," Tucker said, "I've brought these pretty ladies…" He paused, his gaze sliding over to Autumn and Blue before amending his words. "Make that one pretty lady and my beautiful baby girl to see you. I'm expecting you both to be on your best behavior around them."

The horses nickered in response.

Tucker nodded. "Why, yes, they do have a special treat for you."

"We do!" Blue exclaimed, stepping closer. "We brought you apples!"

Tucker looked as pleased as punch with his daughter's sudden change of heart where his horses were concerned. He held up one of the apple slices. "You probably already know that it's best to feed horses smaller pieces of apple to avoid their choking on them. Hoss and Little Joe don't always mind their manners as best they should and would most likely try to swallow their apples whole if given the chance."

Autumn watched as Tucker held out his hand, offering the bit of apple to the larger of the two horses, a beautiful sorrel-colored gelding.

"Here you go, Hoss," he said in a soothing tone as the horse sniffed at the apple, finally helping himself to the crunchy slice.

Little Joe whinnied, attempting to nudge his way in past Hoss.

Tucker chuckled. "Okay, okay, you get one, too."

"Can I feed him?" Blue said unexpectedly, drawing everyone's attention her way.

Face beaming, Tucker said, "Sure you can. Step on over here beside me."

Blue edged her way over to him, her nervous gaze fixed on the two horses.

Autumn's heart was in her throat. This was the closest Blue had gotten to a horse since Summer's accident.

Tucker knelt beside her, placing an apple sliver in her hand. "Now hold your hand out slowly so Little Joe can scent what you are giving him. Keep your hand upturned and fingers laid flat so he can nibble the apple right off your hand."

She sidled up against Tucker as if he would protect her from all the bad in the world. And maybe that was how things would be if he kept proving himself worthy of his daughter. Autumn felt the sting of unshed tears at the backs of her eyes. She wasn't ready to give up her niece to Tucker or anyone. Why couldn't he have been different? Arrogant. Closed off. Caring only for his own happiness. Unwilling to be saddled down with a child. But Tucker was none of those things. He was, from what she had researched and now had had time to see for herself, a really good man.

"That's it," she heard Tucker say. "Just like that."

Pushing her troubled thoughts aside, Autumn watched as her niece fed Little Joe from her upturned palm. *Thank You, Lord.*

Blue giggled and began to squirm. "That tickles."

Tucker's husky chuckle resonated in the early morning air. "He's making sure he gets every single morsel of apple from your hand."

Satisfied he had, Little Joe pulled back, chewing on his special treat.

"I think you've definitely made a friend in Little Joe," she told Blue.

Her niece looked to her daddy, who was still kneeling beside her. "Can I be Hoss's friend, too?"

"You want to give him an apple slice?"

She nodded.

Smiling, he handed her another piece. "Have at it, sweetheart."

"Look at me, Aunt Autumn," Blue exclaimed with

another burst of giggles as Hoss nibbled at the apple chunk in her upturned hand.

"Look at you," Autumn said, her voice catching.

Tucker's gaze shifted to Autumn and his smile widened as he held an apple slice out to her. "Join us?"

It meant a lot that Tucker was trying to include her. Especially because it was such a special moment for Blue who was finally pushing past her fear when it came to horses. Coming forward, Autumn accepted the offered fruit.

"All done," Blue announced with a joyous grin as she stepped back from the fence. She hurried to wipe her damp, horse-kissed hand off on her jeans.

Autumn opened her mouth to tell her not to wipe her messy hands on her clean clothes, but then closed it. She wasn't about to do or say anything that would take away the joy Blue was feeling at that moment.

Tucker stood, scooping Blue up in one strong arm. "It's your aunt Autumn's turn now," he said, turning to face her.

Something told Autumn that he was testing her. Not quite believing that she was as comfortable as she claimed to be around horses.

Little Joe whinnied, urging her on.

"Patience is a virtue," she told the horse who had stretched his neck through the open slats of the fence to reach the treat in her hand. Autumn extended her arm, unfurling her fingers, allowing Little Joe access to what he wanted. "Like that, do you?" she cooed as she reached out with her other hand to stroke the horse's neck.

The gelding nickered softly.

"I think he likes you," Tucker said as he stood beside her, grinning.

She snorted. "Only because I'm feeding him."

"Oh, I don't know," he countered. "I think he'd find you likable with or without food."

Autumn glanced up at Tucker. When her gaze met his, her heart gave an odd little start. "I—" Her response was cut short by Blue's sudden shriek.

Arms flailing, her niece tried to grab for her doll as it was pulled into the pen. "Molly!" she cried out.

Tucker set Blue on her feet and then straightened. "Hoss!" he scolded as he climbed into the pen to retrieve the pilfered rag doll.

"He's eating her!" Blue said with a sob.

It certainly did appear that way, Autumn thought with a frown.

"I won't let him eat Molly," Tucker called back as he attempted to coax the horse to release its newly found treasure.

When it didn't appear that Hoss was in a mood to co-operate, Autumn thought it best to get Blue away from the situation. Reaching for Blue's hand, she said, "Let's go back to the house and see about fixing you some pancakes."

"What about Molly?" Blue whimpered, craning her neck to look behind her as Autumn led her away.

"Your daddy will get her back after Hoss is through playing with her," she replied, trying to sound as if she believed that to be true. "Then he has to get to work. Your uncles are expecting him. Molly will just have to go help with the chores and then your daddy will bring her home when they are all done."

"Okay," Blue said with a disappointed sigh. "Do you think Daddy will give Miss Molly a ride on his horse if he rides it to work today?"

Autumn managed a smile. "You can count on it." After what had just occurred, she had a feeling Tucker would take Miss Molly out for a fancy dinner if the doll requested it. She just prayed her niece's favorite toy hadn't become dinner herself.

Chapter Six

Tucker took a break from the loose fence post he'd been reinforcing to grab a bottle of water from the insulated cooler bag he kept in his truck. Bringing the bottle to his lips, he took several long swallows as he looked out over his handiwork. The repair was taking longer than usual, but then his focus wasn't fully on the task at hand. It was on Blue.

His gaze shifted to the dirty, mangled doll lying atop the passenger seat of his truck. Miss Molly. Tucker's stomach knotted. Twisting the lid back onto the bottle, he shoved it back into the cooler and then reached for the doll. Its yarn hair, or what remained of it after Hoss had chewed on it, was now matted and damp.

He stepped back and held it up, frowning as the sun spotlighted the extent of the damage that had been done to Miss Molly. Not only was this bound to make Blue dislike horses even more, he couldn't help but wonder if she'd blame him for it, as well. After all, Hoss was his horse. And he'd been the one holding Blue, making it easier for the hungry gelding to make a grab for her doll. Hand dropping to his side, he leaned back against his pickup, his gaze drifting toward the herd of broncs that were grazing and frolicking in the distance. At least, they were having fun. They'd earned it. After months of rodeo competition, these finely-honed, well-bred horses had done the Triple W proud, serving up countless award-winning and championship rides. They were not only his and his brothers' livelihood, they were, without a doubt, their pride and joy. The horses were as close to having children as any of the Wade brothers had ever gotten. Until Blue.

Now Tucker was a daddy, one whose baby girl feared these proud and majestic creatures before him. A fear she had bravely tried to get past that morning when she'd volunteered to hand-feed an apple to Little Joe. Then Hoss had to go and snatch Miss Molly right out of his daughter's hand.

Tucker bit back a groan of frustration. How was he supposed to convince Blue to come to live with him at the ranch, a horse ranch, when even her doll didn't appear to be safe from harm's way when it came to his horses?

Tires rumbled across the ground just beyond his truck. Tucker craned his neck to see who it was.

His brother Jackson pulled up next to Tucker's pickup and cut the engine. Then he stepped out and rounded the front of his truck, peeling off his thick leather work gloves as he went. "You planning on doing any work today, or are you just admiring the view?"

Tucker pushed away from his truck, muttering, "I've been working. Trying to, at least."

"Everything okay?" Jackson asked, his tone far less jesting. "I know it's been quite a shock, finding out about…" His words trailed off as his gaze dropped down to Tucker's clenched hand. "Is that a rag doll?"

"Used to be," he muttered, holding the remnants of Miss Molly up for his brother to see.

Jackson arched a brow. "What happened to it?"

He looked down at the limp, nearly headless doll and his gut twisted. "Hoss decided to floss his teeth with Miss Molly's hair."

"Miss Molly?"

"Blue's doll," he grumbled, as if he really needed to clarify that.

Jackson let out a low whistle. "Looks to me like he tried to floss with her entire head."

Tucker shot him a glare. "You're not helping matters." He already knew the doll was ruined. Blue's treasured little doll was now a stump in a dirty, horse-slobbered dress.

"Does Blue know?" his brother asked, concern knitting his brows.

"Not the extent of the damage my horse did," he said. "But she was there when Hoss made off with her doll. Autumn took Blue back to the house, pretty much in tears." He looked to Jackson. "How am I supposed to tell my little girl that her precious rag doll is done for? She's already lost her mother."

Jackson nodded. "That won't do." He stroked his chin in thought, his gaze fixed on the doll. Then his expression eased. "I've got a plan."

"I'm all ears."

"We'll take Miss Molly to Garrett."

Tucker stared at his brother in confusion. "Taking this doll to Garrett is supposed to fix everything?"

"He's a doctor, isn't he?"

"He's a vet," Tucker said in frustration. "Molly isn't a cow ready to calve, or a horse with digestive issues. She's a rag doll." Glancing down, he added disheartened, "Half a rag doll."

Jackson grabbed Miss Molly from Tucker and started back around his truck.

"Where are you going?" Tucker called after him.

"Get in," his brother said. "We're going into town to buy a mop before we go hunt Garrett down."

"A mop?" *Had his brother been out in the sun too long?*

"Miss Molly is going to need some new hair," Jackson told him as he whipped open the driver's-side door. "And Garrett is just the man to sew Miss Molly's new locks back onto her head. That would be *after* he stitches her head back fully onto her body."

For the first time since Autumn had rushed Blue off toward the house that morning, Tucker felt his heart lighten. Jackson's plan just might work. It had to. His little girl was counting on him to set things right.

An hour and a half later, all three Wade brothers were gathered around the examination table in Garrett's clinic, a small outbuilding that served as home base for his veterinary practice. Garrett, thank the good Lord, had been able to put Miss Molly back together again in an impressively neat and tidy manner. Most of the dirt had been scrubbed clean from her flimsy body and frilly dress. Her head had been firmly reattached. And while her neck was admittedly a little squattier as a result of the tussle she had been in with his horse, the slight imperfection was covered up by the brand-new much fuller head of hair their brother had so skillfully replaced.

"I can't believe I'm performing surgery on a doll,"

Garrett muttered with a shake of his head as he tied up the last stitch.

"Blue's doll," Jackson reminded him.

Tucker nodded.

His brother lifted his gaze to look at them. "You do realize that *she's* the only reason I'm doing this. Therefore, if word gets out and I start having little girls and their dolls lining up on my doorstep for repairs, the two of you are going to tend to them. Not me."

"Point made," Jackson said. "No one's going to find out about your baby doll doctoring skills from me. My lips are sealed."

"Same here." Tucker nodded in agreement.

"Good to know," Garrett said as he snipped off the piece of thread left dangling from the knot he'd just made. Then he took a step back to admire his handiwork. "There you go," he announced. "As good as new."

Tucker's throat clogged with emotion as he stood staring at the tiny rag doll. "Thank you," he muttered hoarsely. "Both of you." Things had seemed so hopeless when he'd finally gotten the doll back from Hoss. The frantic tug-of-war that had nearly separated Miss Molly's head from her body had left him fairly convinced that no amount of fervent prayer was going to be able to fix things. But his brothers hadn't given up hope and their faith had persevered.

"Well?" Garrett said.

Tucker looked up at his oldest brother.

"Are you just going to stand here admiring my handiwork, or are you going to take Miss Molly home where she belongs?"

He shifted uneasily. "We've still got work to do on the fence."

Jackson snorted. "A lot of help you'll be to us with your thoughts drawn back to those two pretty girls at the ranch."

"Jackson's right," Garrett told him, adding softly, "Go home."

Garrett cleaned up the snips of thread and strands of mop fibers from the examination table. "You need to be spending more time with Autumn, proving yourself worthy of her trust where her niece's happiness is concerned."

Tucker frowned. "Yeah, this morning was a good example of that. My horse ate her doll."

"Those things happen," his oldest brother replied. "I'm sure Autumn understands."

"What about Blue?" he demanded. "It might not be Autumn who throws up a roadblock when it comes to my getting custody of Blue. It might very well be my daughter. Especially after what happened this morning."

"She'll forget all about Hoss trying to eat Miss Molly after you return her baby doll to her," Jackson told him. "Besides, we're her family," he said as the three of them made their way out of the clinic. "Blue should be with us."

"Autumn is her family, too," Tucker reminded his brother with a sigh. "And Blue loves her aunt. How am I supposed to take my daughter away from the woman who helped raise her?"

Jackson pulled his car keys from his jeans pocket. "No way around it, Tucker. This is a rough situation. Someone's going to come out on the hurting end."

"That's what Autumn said," Tucker observed, his shoulders sagging under the weight of the situation.

"It's the truth," his brother continued. "But you're

Blue's father. You should've been the one helping to raise her all these years."

Garrett nodded in agreement as he walked them out to Jackson's truck. "Are you going to church Sunday?" Jackson asked.

"Can't say for sure," Tucker replied. "It depends on what Autumn and Blue are going to do. She didn't seem comfortable with it last week when I asked her and Blue to join me for Sunday services, which is why I went alone."

"Maybe now that they've been here for well over a week, Autumn will feel settled in enough to accept your invitation for her to join you for church."

"If they decline my offer to go to church this weekend, I'll probably stay home. I'd like to spend every moment I can with my daughter while she's here."

"It would be nice to have you all there."

He nodded. "I know, but I won't pressure Autumn into doing anything she's not completely comfortable with."

"You might find yourself rethinking that when the time comes for her to leave with your daughter," Jackson stated as he slid behind the steering wheel. "I suggest you take that gift you have with horses and use it to coax Autumn over to your way of thinking." That said, he closed the driver's-side door and started the truck.

Garrett accompanied his youngest brother the remainder of the way around to the passenger side. "Look, Tucker, I know this is a tough situation. Just know that whatever you need Jackson and I to do to help move matters along, all you have to do is ask."

Tucker opened the passenger door and then turned back to his brother. "I appreciate the support you and

Jackson have given me, despite my having disappointed the both of you by keeping my marriage to Summer from the family."

Garrett shrugged. "Can't change the past."

If only he could. "And I might take you up on your offer to help out. That is *if* I can convince Autumn to consent to spending some alone time with me after church on Sunday."

Garrett nodded. "Consider it done."

"Hopefully, it'll give her and me the time we need to iron some things out regarding custody of my daughter."

"There shouldn't even be any ironing required as far as I'm concerned," Jackson grumbled as he fastened his seat belt.

He glanced back over his shoulder at his brother. "I don't want this situation to become ugly. Autumn's got a lot to lose as well when all is said and done. So I'm hoping, with the good Lord's guidance, we'll be able to figure out a solution that works best for all involved in this tangle my wife created for us with her lies."

"Autumn should be thankful you're the kind of man you are," Jackson muttered. "Another man might not be so considerate of her feelings where Blue is concerned."

"She's not Summer," he said in Autumn's defense. "She's giving and selfless, and determined to do what's right when it comes to Blue. I won't hold her to blame for her sister's bad decisions."

"It's true. Autumn isn't Summer. You might want to keep that up front in your mind, little brother," Garrett warned with a studying glance.

"What exactly are you getting at?" Tucker asked as he hopped up into the truck.

"Autumn might not be Summer," his brother replied.

"But she is her identical twin. Don't let your heart confuse the two of them and risk losing what matters most when the time comes—Blue."

"Not a chance," Tucker replied, closing the door. His denial, however, didn't keep Autumn's sweet smile from drifting through his mind as they drove away.

"In here!" Autumn called out when she heard the front door open and close. She'd seen Tucker's truck coming up the drive from the living room window and had felt an unexpected stirring of excitement. It wasn't as if she'd been alone with nothing to do all day. She had been doing her best to keep Blue busy and her niece's thoughts away from the loss of her favorite doll. They'd watched a movie on Autumn's iPad, had colored for hours and were now entertaining Itty Bitty. So why then had she reacted to Tucker's coming home the way she had?

Before she could truly mull over that troubling thought, Tucker stepped into the room, his gaze searching until he found them seated on the floor in front of the fireplace where a flame burned low and warm. He immediately removed the cowboy hat from his head in a polite gesture, an action that came as no surprise at all to her. "Hello," she greeted with a tempered smile, not wanting him to know how ridiculously happy she was to see his grinning face.

"Daddy!" Blue exclaimed, jumping to her feet.

His daughter's warm welcome seemed to take Tucker off guard. Had he expected Blue to be upset with him for his horse's behavior that morning? Surely not. Hoss was a horse. He hadn't known better.

Tucker's gaze settled on the kitten purring loudly

in his daughter's arms. He blinked hard. And then he blinked again. "Is Bitty wearing a dress?"

His daughter offered up a toothy smile as she nodded her reply. "Isn't she pretty?"

"Uhm…yes, very pretty," he managed, his anxious gaze darting in Autumn's direction.

Autumn laughed softly. "Blue has decided to donate all of Miss Molly's dresses to Bitty after trying one on her for size and finding it a perfect fit."

"I see," he replied, his attention sliding back to the contented kitten. "Green seems to be her color." His gaze lifted once more to his daughter's face. "But I'm afraid Bitty might have to give one or two of her newly acquired dresses back to Miss Molly. We can't have your doll traipsing about the ranch in just one dress."

What did Tucker think he was doing? Autumn, who was no longer smiling, was tempted to lead him out into the hallway and ask him that very question. She had spent a good portion of that morning calming Blue down and helping her niece come to terms with the fact that her baby doll wasn't going to be riding back to Cheyenne with them when they left for home. And then Tucker comes home all smiles, acting as if nothing had ever happened. The fact that he had so quickly forgotten something that had been so emotionally devastating to his daughter was beyond disappointing.

"Tucker…" she began, trying to keep her voice unaffected by her irritation with his thoughtlessness. Only the remainder of her words caught in her throat as he reached into the hat that he had just removed and pulled out Blue's baby doll, which was, much to her shock, all in one piece!

"Miss Molly!" Blue cried out, immediately setting

the bedecked kitten down so she could go collect her precious doll.

Tucker handed the toy over to her, his grin widening as his daughter hugged it tight. "Miss Molly and I would've been home sooner, but we had a few fence posts that needed shoring up around the ranch first."

"She has white curls," Blue noted in confusion.

He exchanged a brief glance with Autumn before looking back down at his daughter. "She decided it was time for a change, so we got her hair done and came home to surprise you with it."

Blue lifted her gaze to his. "It's pretty. Can I get my hair done like hers?"

Tucker stammered, searching for a reply he clearly hadn't expected to give.

"Your hair is far too pretty to think about changing it," Autumn answered for him, feeling guilty for having immediately thought badly of him. It seemed there was a great deal of truth in the saying about old habits dying hard, her having spent the past several years thinking Tucker was the worst sort of man.

"Not to mention," Tucker joined in, "God chose that color especially for you so your hair can match your daddy's."

Blue's eyes narrowed as she studied Tucker's hair. "But you don't have any curls."

He ran a hand back through his thick, wavy hair. "If I let my hair grow out as long as yours is, you can bet there would be some curls."

She giggled at that. "Daddy, you can't have girl hair."

"A good thing," he told her. "It gets too hot when I'm out working the ranch to have anything but short hair under my cowboy hat."

"Will I have to wear a cowboy hat when I come to live here?"

"Only if you want to," he replied and then cast a worried glance in Autumn's direction.

She nodded, letting him know that it was okay. Blue had brought the subject up; Tucker hadn't. "You can worry about that later," Autumn told her.

"I have my uncles' hair, too," Blue said, shifting conversation gears once more.

"You do," Tucker said with a confirming nod. "We all get our hair color from your grandma Wade." Glancing past Blue, he nodded toward the assortment of coloring books lying open on the floor. "So what sort of mischief have you two girls been up to while I was away?"

"We were coloring with Bitty," Blue replied matter-of-factly.

Tucker's brow lifted, and Autumn had to suppress the urge to giggle at the bewildered expression on his face. "Your kitten can color?"

"Bitty can't hold a crayon," Autumn explained. "But she can help Blue pick out what color to use."

His gaze settled on the kitten that was playfully batting a lime-green crayon around on the floor in front of the fireplace where Autumn and Blue had been coloring. "She can, huh?"

Blue's head bobbed up and own. "I lay my crayons out on the floor and she sniffs the one I'm supposed to use next," she explained with adorable patience.

"Thus, the purple pumpkin in the princess's vegetable garden," Autumn said with a grin.

Tucker let out a husky chuckle, his own grin doing funny things to Autumn's heart. "I should have known

Itty Bitty was a very smart kitten when she chose my ranch house to be her new home."

"Box and all," Autumn agreed with a knowing grin.

"Do you wanna color with us?" Blue asked hopefully.

"It's been a while since I've colored," he admitted honestly. "Do you think Bitty might be willing to help me, too?" he asked as the dress-wearing kitten gave up its current source of entertainment to twine itself around Tucker's denim-clad leg.

"I'm thinking it might be time for Bitty to go outside for a spell," Autumn said. They had yet to pick up a litter box and she didn't want any accidents in the house. "I'll take her outside for a bit, but I'm quite sure Blue would be more than happy to help you pick colors."

"I could take her out," he offered, scooping the kitten up in his large sun-browned hand.

Autumn stepped over to ease Bitty from his gentle hold. Tucker deserved to spend some alone time with his little girl without her aunt continually hovering nearby. "I've got a few work calls I need to return," she told him. "That is, if you don't mind my leaving the two of you for a bit."

"Not at all," he said with a shake of his head. "Do what you need to do. Blue and I will make do until you can come back in and join us. Later, if you like, I could grill us up some burgers."

"With cheese?" Blue asked hopefully.

Autumn watched as that infamous Wade dimple cut into Tucker's tanned cheek with another one of his devastatingly handsome grins. "I think I can make that happen. Besides, what good is a burger without a big slab of cheese melted atop of it?"

He looked to the kitten in her arms. "Are you sure you don't want me to run her outside? It's a little chilly out."

"I'll throw on my jacket before I go out," she told him. "Besides, I think the two of you need a chance to spend some father-daughter bonding time together. But thank you for offering to include me in your coloring endeavors."

"I've told you before," he said, his green eyes locking with hers. "You're part of Blue's family. You're always going to be included in our lives."

She was beyond touched by his words, words she knew to be genuinely expressed. "Thank you for that, Tucker," she said softly. "It means a lot." She started for the door and then paused, glancing back over her shoulder at Tucker. "And burgers for dinner, ones oozing with cheese, sounds really good."

"You've got it," he said before turning away. She watched as he crossed the room to join Blue, who was already stretched out across the throw rug, surrounded by assorted coloring books and scattered crayons. Settling his large frame onto the floor across from his daughter, his back to Autumn, Tucker said, "All right, sweetheart, looks like it's just you and me."

"And Miss Molly," Autumn heard her niece say as she stepped from the room.

Looks like it's just you and me. Blue and her daddy. Just as Summer had wanted it to be. And judging by the effort Tucker was putting in to prove himself to be a good man and, more important, a good daddy, it seemed to be a part of the Lord's plan, as well.

Having enjoyed the cheeseburgers Tucker had promised to grill for them, he, Autumn and Blue had returned to the living room to spend a little quiet time before turning in for the night. His gaze drifted over to where Autumn sat in the matching rocker/recliner, flipping through the coloring book Blue had chosen for him to do his coloring in. She was smiling, looking completely relaxed. As if she belonged there, in his chair, his house, his life.

She's not Summer. Garrett had warned him to keep that first and foremost in his mind. And he had. At least, he thought he had. Why then did it feel so natural spending time with Autumn? Was it because she reminded him of his late wife? That same pretty, heart-shaped face. Same ice-blue eyes. Same slender build. But that was where the similarities ended. Summer had been harder around the edges. Autumn was softer, more open, more—

"Another trait my niece inherited from her father, I see," Autumn said with a smile, her head turning in his direction.

"Excuse me?"

She held up the open coloring book, pointing to a page where two little princesses were picking wildflowers in a field. "Blue's ability to stay within the line when coloring seems to have been inherited from her daddy's side, too. Just look at these cute little princesses you colored," she said, flashing him a playful grin.

"I had a good instructor." He glanced toward the sofa where Blue had fallen asleep shortly after they'd finished eating the cheeseburgers he'd grilled for them. His daughter looked so small as she lay curled up on her side beneath one of the blankets his mother had crocheted for him over the years. Her tiny mouth was lifted into a slight smile as she slept, as if dreaming of something that made her happy.

"I should probably put her to bed," Autumn said quietly. "But she looks so peaceful lying there."

"I was just thinking the same thing myself."

"I didn't have a chance to thank you earlier for saving Miss Molly."

He looked away, a frown tugging at his mouth. "Don't. It was my fault Miss Molly ended up being a chew toy for my horse. I should've known Hoss would be drawn to the doll."

"From experience?" she asked.

Tucker's head snapped back around. "What?"

"I'm not sure how you can take the blame for something you couldn't have known for certain would happen. That is, unless you make it a habit of carrying dolls out to the barn with you when you're seeing to your horses."

His smile eased its way back into place once more. "Can't say that I do."

"Then that settles it," she said. "You had no way of knowing Hoss has a thing for floppy old rag dolls."

"Well, I know now," he replied, keeping his voice low. "And you can rest assured that it'll never happen again."

"No doubt."

"You should have seen the tug-of-war Hoss and I had when I was trying to get Blue's doll back. He nearly tore poor Miss Molly's head off."

She glanced toward the doll, now all in one piece thanks to his brother's stitching skills, lying atop the blanket next to Blue. "She looks better than new." Glancing back at Tucker, she said, "Is there anything you can't do when you set your mind to it?"

He snorted. "A lot, I'm afraid. And I can't take credit

for the repairs that were done to Miss Molly. That honor would go to my brothers. Jackson came up with the idea to use a mop head to replace the doll's mangled hair. And Garrett did all the stitching."

"I'll be sure to thank them the next time I see them."

"You can thank them tomorrow," he told her. "That is, if you and Blue will consider joining us for church in the morning. We can swing by and grab lunch in town after Sunday service lets out."

She looked as if she were about to refuse his invitation.

"It would give you a chance to see a little bit of Bent Creek beyond the ranch," he added hopefully.

"You're forgetting that Blue and I made that emergency run into town to buy dinner the afternoon that I…um…"

"Burned the spaghetti?" he supplied with a grin.

She rolled her eyes, a faint blush filling her cheeks. "I'm never gonna live that down, am I?"

He chuckled softly. "Sooner or later, I suppose. Seriously, though, I'd like to show you around Bent Creek after church. Something beyond a quick trip to our local grocery store."

"I think that would be nice," she said and then sobered slightly. "I'm ashamed to admit that it's been far too long since I've attended church. Not since I was at Summer's memorial service."

Was her last memory of church too painful to bring herself to step into the Lord's house again? Or did she blame God for Summer's dying? Was that why she hadn't gone to church since her sister's passing? Whatever her reasons, Tucker didn't want to pressure her into anything she wasn't ready for. "If you'd rather not go, I understand."

"No," she said with a shake of her head, her gaze drifting over to her sleeping niece. "It's time. Not only for my sake, but for Blue's, as well."

He was glad to hear that. He wanted his daughter to be raised with the Lord being a very significant part of her life, just as He had been for Tucker and his brothers. "You'll have all of us there for support should you find yourself in need of it."

She gave an appreciative nod and then said with a halfhearted smile, "I can only pray that I will be strong enough not to need that support. Especially since I've already drenched one of your shirtfronts with my tears."

"Tears are a part of the healing process," he said softly. "And I have plenty of shirts to go around. You feel the urge, cry away." He didn't mean at that very moment, but it suddenly looked as if she were going to take him up on his offer.

"It's getting late," Autumn said, pushing out of the overstuffed recliner she'd been sitting in. "I should get Blue settled into bed if we're gonna make it to church in the morning."

Tucker stood, as well. "I need to go out and check on the horses before turning in for the night."

She started for the sofa, drawing his gaze to his sleepy little girl. "Here," he said, stepping up beside her. "Let me get her for you." He eased his hands under Blue's sleeping form, lifting her into his arms. Miss Molly tumbled from his daughter's limp hand.

"I've got her," Autumn said quietly as she bent to reach for the fallen doll baby.

They walked together until they reached the hallway,

which was too narrow for them to walk comfortably side by side while Tucker was carrying Blue. He inclined his head with a smile. "After you."

Returning his smile, Autumn moved ahead of them. When she reached the guest room, she and Blue had been staying in, she opened the door and held it while Tucker carried his little girl inside. Then she hurried around him to draw the covers down.

Tucker lowered his daughter onto the mattress. Blue stirred, her eyes remaining closed as she murmured sleepily, "I love you, Daddy."

Tucker's heart slammed against his chest at those softly spoken words. Leaning in, he placed a tender kiss on his daughter's baby-soft cheek. "I love you, too, sweetheart." Then he straightened and turned to find Autumn watching him, moisture filling her eyes.

He felt like he needed to say something, but wasn't sure what that something should be. He settled for offering her a tender smile. "'Night, Autumn."

"'Night, Tucker," she said, looking as if she were about to say more. Instead, she turned away, fixing her watery gaze on Blue.

With one last glance at his daughter, Tucker strode from the room. But his little girl wasn't the only female filling his thoughts as he stepped out into the night to go check on his horses.

Chapter Seven

Sunday morning arrived, bringing with it a cloudless sky and the cheerful chirping of birds outside the bedroom window. The sound was soothing. Or had been before a loud rumbling along the drive outside put an end to the birds' sweet melodies.

Autumn stepped over to the bedroom window. Lifting the curtains aside, she watched as a large motor home bounced up and down and to and fro as it made its way up Tucker's somewhat uneven drive, leaving a trail of rising dust in its wake.

"Is it a train?" Blue asked from where she sat on the bed awaiting help with her tennis shoes.

"No, sweetie, it's not a train," she said as she stood peering outside.

"It sounds like one," her niece noted.

The oversize vehicle came to an abrupt stop in front of Tucker's house. "A train has to have tracks to travel on," Autumn explained somewhat distractedly, her gaze fixed on the goings-on outside. A man who looked to be in his mid- to late fifties leaped from the driver's side of the RV and raced around to open the passenger door, helping a slender auburn-haired woman down.

The woman, who looked to be slightly younger than the man assisting her, reached up to fuss with her short auburn curls as she looked anxiously toward the house. Then she slid her purse onto her arm, shoving the strap up over her shoulder, never missing a step as she hurried toward the house. The man kept pace beside her, looking every bit as anxious as she did.

He leaned in to say something to her and the woman nodded, slipping her arm through his as if for support.

Behind Autumn, Blue inquired with more persistence, "Was it thunder?"

She shook her head, her stomach twisting in a knot. Not thunder, but it could end up becoming an emotional thunderstorm. From the urgency in which the motor home had pulled in, and the anxious looks on the couples' faces, she had to assume Tucker had finally made that call to his parents.

No sooner had that thought crossed her mind than the barn door flew open and Tucker came striding out, his urgent, lengthy strides quickly eating up the distance between himself and his parents.

"No, sweetie," Autumn answered as she let the ruffled curtains fall back into place. Turning from the window, she crossed the room and hurried to buckle Blue's shiny black patent leather shoes. Thankfully, they were both dressed and ready for that morning's church service. It appeared her niece was about to make a very important first impression. "I believe we're about to have some very special company."

"Who is it?" Blue said, scooting off the foot of the bed where she'd been perched.

"I think I'll let your daddy introduce you." It was only right. With one last glance in the mirror to make certain she looked properly presentable to be meeting Tucker's parents, Autumn held out her hand to her niece. "Ready?"

Blue nodded. "Ready."

They made their way out of the guest room and down the hall just as the front door swung open and Tucker's momma stepped inside.

The older woman gasped. Her trembling hand flew to her mouth as she stood staring at her only grandchild, tears shimmering in her eyes.

Tucker's daddy stood a step behind her, his green eyes—eyes the same shade as Tucker's—widening and then welling up with unshed tears as he looked down upon his newfound granddaughter.

Tucker squeezed past their immobile forms and moved to stand beside Autumn and Blue. "Mom, Dad, I'd like you to meet your granddaughter, Blue Belle Wade." Then he knelt beside his daughter, saying in a voice filled with emotion, "Sweetheart, this is your grandma and grandpa Wade."

"The ones that have chickens?" Blue asked as she stood looking up at them.

Tucker chuckled, his gaze shifting to his parents. "We took a ride by your place to see your chickens."

"I got to put eggs in a basket," she told them excitedly and then held up a tiny hand with all five fingers extended. "Five of them. But one broke, so only four got to come home with us."

"She's precious," his momma sighed, clearly smitten already.

"And smart as a whip," his daddy boasted.

"She's a fast learner," Tucker agreed.

"She's got my smile," Mr. Wade added with a wide grin that displayed that infamous Wade dimple.

Tucker's momma moved to kneel in front of her granddaughter, tears in her eyes. "Hello, Blue."

"Why are you sad?" she asked worriedly as she looked up at her grandma.

"Oh, I'm not, honey," the older woman answered with a tender smile. "Not sad at all."

"But you're crying," Autumn's niece pointed out.

She laughed softly. "I suppose I am at that. But these are happy tears," she explained. "Very, very happy tears, because I finally get to meet my precious granddaughter. Do you think your grandma Wade might have a hug from you?"

Blue looked to Autumn.

"It's okay, sweetie," she told her niece with a reassuring smile. "Give your grandma a great big squeeze."

Tucker's momma held out her arms, and Blue stepped into them, wrapping her tiny arms around her grandma. More tears slid down the older woman's cheeks as the two embraced for the first time ever. "My sweet, sweet baby," she said.

"But I'm not a baby," Blue said somewhat defensively.

Tucker's momma loosened her hold and leaned back to look at Blue. "Of course, you're not. You're a big girl. One I am so very happy to finally have a chance to meet. You look so pretty all dressed up in your Sunday best."

"Thank you," Blue said almost shyly.

"If you have a spare hug to give," Tucker's daddy said, kneeling next to his wife and Blue, "your grandpa wouldn't mind having one, too."

This time Blue didn't look to Autumn. Instead, she released her hold on Tucker's momma to hug her grandpa."

When the embrace ended, Tucker's daddy stood, helping his wife to her feet. Then he cleared his throat and looked away.

"Dad?" Tucker said worriedly. "Everything okay?"

"Never been better. Just got a speck of something in my eye," he muttered as he swiped a hand over the tear-dampened lashes Autumn had glimpsed before the man had turned away.

Autumn felt her own tears building as she looked on. The older couple's joy was palpable. There was no denying their welcoming acceptance of Blue as their grandchild, despite the lengthy delay in their finding out about her. Precious years Summer had taken away from them they could never get back. Autumn had to wonder if they would harbor resentment toward her for the actions her sister had taken since Summer was no longer able to be held accountable for what she'd done.

"Mom, Dad," Tucker said, drawing everyone's attention as he motioned toward Autumn, "I'd like for you to meet Blue's aunt. Miss Myers is Summer's twin sister."

Was, Autumn thought sadly, but now wasn't the time or place to point that out. She greeted his parents with a warm smile. "It's a pleasure to finally meet you, Mr. and Mrs. Wade."

"Emma, please," his momma insisted. Then she cast a chastising glance her son's direction, muttering, "And *finally* is right. You've known about my grandbaby for twelve days and last night was the first time you saw fit to call us?"

"Now, honey," his daddy said soothingly, not that Tucker's momma sounded angry with her son as much as hurt. "Tucker explained his reasons for not calling us right away. Our son's heart was in the right place, even if we would have preferred to hear about our granddaughter the second her existence was made known to him." He turned to Autumn, and then, taking a step forward, surprised her completely by giving her a big, warm, welcoming bear hug. "God bless you, Miss Myers," he said, his voice choked with emotion.

As soon as he released her, Emma Wade gathered Autumn into what could only be described as a motherly hug, not that she'd ever been on the receiving end of one of those from her own mother. "Our family will forever be grateful to you for what you've done for our son. For all of us," she said, looking to Blue.

She hadn't done anything yet, Autumn wanted to tell them. No decision had been made with regard to Blue. She'd brought her niece there because it was the right thing to do. Not only to follow through with Summer's last request, but because Blue deserved to know that part of her family. But she wasn't anywhere near mentally prepared to turn her niece over to someone else's care.

"Do you have any kitties?" Blue asked, looking up at her grandparents.

Tucker's momma released Autumn and smiled adoringly down at her granddaughter. "Lots of them as a matter of fact. They like to stay near the barn, chasing field mice."

"Where the horses are?" her niece asked uneasily.

Tucker's parents exchanged glances at Blue's wide-eyed response to her grandma's reply.

"Blue's a little wary of horses," he explained as gently as he could, seeing as how a full explanation wasn't possible with Blue standing right there.

"Do your kitties have a house like the chickens get to sleep in?" her niece went on, thankfully far too distracted by thoughts of kittens to let memories of her momma's accident invade the special moment.

Emma Wade's smile widened. "I suppose they do, if you count the barn. That's where they spend most of their time."

"Do you make cookies?"

"I have three boys," his momma answered. "Making cookies comes with being their mother."

Blue's face lit up. "What kind of cookies?"

"All kinds," her niece's newly discovered grandmother answered. "Chocolate chip, iced sugar cookies, kiss cookies and oatmeal raisin to name a few. Do you like cookies?"

Autumn watched her niece's head bob up and down quite enthusiastically. "I like peanut butter cookies," she told her grandma.

"Then we'll just have to see about making you some."

"Maybe you can help Grandma Wade make a batch after we get home from church," Blue's grandpa suggested and then looked to Autumn. "That is, if it's okay with your aunt."

"You're going to church?" Tucker said in surprise.

His momma looked his way. "When have you known your father and I not to attend Sunday services? We would've gone to one we found in Jackson, but after your call last night all we could think about was getting home to see our grandbaby. We packed up our campsite last evening and started for home before daybreak this morning." Her attention shifted back to Blue and her expression softened even more. "I have every intention of sitting in church today with my family and thanking the good Lord for blessing us with this beautiful little girl. Even if my clothes do look a little travel weary, I'm sure the good Lord will forgive me."

"If we don't get a move on, there won't be any forgiveness needed," Tucker's daddy said with a grin.

Tucker nodded, his gaze shifting to Autumn. His expression grew serious. "You and Blue ready?"

She wasn't certain whether he was referring to their being ready for that morning's church services or for the addition of more family to Blue's life, but she knew there was no turning back either way. If Blue were to end up living in Bent Creek, she wanted to get to know the people her niece would be surrounded by, the church she would build her faith in, the town she would become a part of. That didn't make any of this any easier. Each step toward a new life for Blue made Autumn feel the impending loss of her own happiness even greater. *Dear Lord, continue to give me the strength to do the right thing.*

With a slow nod, she said, "I'll just go grab our coats." Then Autumn set off back down the hall to the guest room she'd been sharing with Blue, thankful for a few moments alone to collect her emotions and prepare for the changes that were yet to come in her and Blue's lives.

Tucker watched as his parents whisked Blue away from the restaurant they had gone to eat lunch at after church, the three of them piling into his parents' RV to go back to their house and help her grandma bake cookies. His brothers were already on their way there and would, no doubt, hang around until the baking was done. They never missed out on a freshly made batch of his mother's cookies.

Beside him, Autumn stood watching as well, almost longingly as she tucked her coat tighter about herself.

"We could go with them," he suggested, not wanting her to feel ill at ease by Blue's going off without her. "I know it's gotten colder." A front had moved in while they were attending services, causing the temperatures to drop. Billowy gray clouds filled the afternoon sky, effectively blocking the sun's warming rays.

"I don't mind a little cold," she said, turning to face him.

"If you're sure."

"I'm sure," she said with another glance in the direction Blue had gone with his parents.

"Maybe about braving the weather," he said, "but I'm not so certain you're comfortable with your decision to allow Blue to go home with my family."

She looked up at him, managing a smile. "I wouldn't have agreed if I was at all uncomfortable. It's just hard seeing my niece ride away without me, but Blue needs to spend some time with her grandparents and her uncles without my intrusion. Besides, I'm looking forward to seeing more of Bent Creek with you. Thank you again for offering to give me a tour."

"First of all," he said, "you are *not* an intrusion. And secondly, I should be thanking you, not the other way around. Or, at the very least, apologizing."

Confusion filled those thickly-lashed silver-blue eyes of hers. "Apologizing for what?"

His mind went blank as he took in her pretty upturned face. The sunlight made the blue of her eyes look more like liquid crystals, while the brisk fall air added a touch of color to her cheeks.

"Tucker?"

Her sweet voice had him shaking off the unexpected reverie and focusing on what she'd asked him. "I'm sorry about my parents' surprise visit this morning," he answered. "If I had known they were coming, I would have given you a heads-up to prepare for…well, their excitement."

"They were that," she said, laughing softly.

"No kidding," he added, his own laughter joining hers. "I thought a herd of elephants was stampeding their way up the drive when I was in the barn this morning."

"Your daughter thought it was a train," she said. "I don't think I've ever seen a motorhome move at that rate of speed before. At least, not down a dirt-and-gravel road." Her smile changed suddenly, giving way to a fretful frown.

"Autumn?"

She looked up with a worried expression. "Tucker, please tell me your daddy doesn't normally drive as fast as he did this morning."

"He wasn't going as fast as you might have thought he was," he told her, wanting to set her mind at ease. "Even a slight increase in speed in an RV as it's traveling over an uneven road like the one coming up to the house is bound to make the vehicle's approach appear more reckless than it actually is. I promise you, Blue is in good hands with my family."

Her pretty features eased with his reassurance.

"Truth is, my parents thought they might never have grandchildren."

"They have three sons," she said. "Why would they think that?"

"Because I had no inclination to marry, for reasons they didn't know at the time. Garrett was head over heels for a girl he dated all through high school, but she got sick their junior year and ended up dying the following year of leukemia. He's never dated anyone seriously since then."

"That's so heartbreaking."

He nodded. "I don't think Garrett ever really got over losing her."

"And Jackson?"

"He was a real ladies' man until several years ago when the nearly two-thousand-pound bull he was riding threw him to the ground and then trampled him, crushing his hip and his leg in the process," he said with a frown. "He hasn't dated since."

"That's why he limps," she said in understanding.

"Yes. There was a time the doctors didn't know if he would ever be able to walk on that leg again."

"Your poor brothers."

"Enough about my brothers," he said. "Let's get on with that walk I promised you."

They started down the sidewalk, Autumn's curious gaze taking in the town around her as they went. She noted that, like the town she had grown up in, all but a few of the storefronts were occupied. A sign that Bent Creek was thriving economically.

In the center of town, a monument surrounded by neatly trimmed shrubs stretched up toward the sky. "Eighteen twenty-eight," Autumn said, reading the raised date that ran down the stone pillar.

"The year Bent Creek was first founded," Tucker explained. "The town is small with our population here being just under five thousand, but we've got a lot of the modern conveniences you'd find in a bigger town. A feed store, a leather and boot store, a full-service auto parts store, a local rodeo, not to mention the best fishing around."

Humor lit her eyes. "I see. All the things a nearly five-year-old girl would wanna have in her life."

His smile sagged. How had he not given more thought to what he was saying when trying to sell Autumn on all the positive things his town offered? Of course, a young girl didn't care about a boot store or how reasonably priced an oil change was.

Autumn reached out, placing a gentle hand on his arm. "Tucker, I'm only teasing. Looking around, I can see Bent Creek has a lot to offer Blue. A library, a local art gallery and even a YMCA. Do they have a pool?"

He nodded. "They do."

"That's good to know. Blue loves to swim."

Tucker made a quick mental note of that. "Does she like donuts?"

"She does. All things sweet, in fact," she said and then added reflectively, "Just like her momma used to."

He remembered that about his wife and wondered if having a sweet tooth could be genetic. "Well, we've got a donut shop at the far end of town that serves up some of the best coffee in the county." He paused and then muttered with a knowing frown, "Not that Blue would care one iota about the quality of their coffee." Was he ever going to get this parenting thing right?

"Probably not," Autumn agreed with an empathetic smile, making him wonder if he'd spoken that last thought aloud. "But I'll bet they serve hot chocolate there, as well," she continued, confirming that his fear of failure as a parent wasn't what she'd been referring to.

He nodded. "They do."

"Good hot chocolate?" she asked almost longingly,

making Tucker wonder if Autumn Myers had a sweet tooth herself.

Truth was Tucker found himself wondering a lot of things about his daughter's aunt. Like her favorite color, where she'd liked to travel to if given the chance and if she missed living in Texas. He already knew she was loving and giving, and possessed a strength of character that ran deeper than most. She had overcome an emotionally painful upbringing, yet still strove hard to focus on the positive things in her life. He couldn't help but admire Autumn for that. It was something he wished he were better at doing.

Tucker smiled, feeling more at ease with Autumn than he had with any woman since he'd left Cheyenne. "Why don't we get a couple of cups of it to go before we head back to the ranch for your tour there and you can judge for yourself?"

"I would love to get some hot chocolate," she said with a sigh. "It's always been a weakness of mine. Just ask my best friend, Hope. We used to drink it at every sleepover we had. With mini marshmallows if some were available."

More bits and pieces of her life Autumn was choosing to share with him. Her willingness to open up to him in that way meant a lot to Tucker. "Then we definitely need to get you some."

They worked their way along the sidewalk lining one side of town while Tucker told her a little bit more about Bent Creek's history.

"You know so much about this place."

"I should," he told her. "I grew up here."

"No," she said. "It's more than that. It's clear just listening to you talk that you have a deep-rooted love of this tiny town."

He nodded. "I suppose I do. But I have to admit it took my going away, riding the circuit and living elsewhere to make me realize what I had left behind."

"They do say that home is where the heart is," she said, looking away.

"I take it yours is still back in Texas."

She shrugged. "At one time. But then I discovered that my heart is wherever my niece is. So it appears that old saying might not always ring true, because my home might not be where my *heart* is one day soon."

His heart went out to her, but they both knew the outcome of their situation was going to leave someone hurting. And it seemed it would be her. Apparently, he was succeeding in winning her over, which was what he'd set out to do. So why then did it feel as if he were losing at that same time? "When Blue comes to live here—"

"If," she corrected, shoring up her shoulders.

So, she wasn't completely sold yet. He could accept that. Yet, the possibility of Autumn deciding Blue was not better off in his care, forcing him to seek legal means to gain custody of his daughter, had Tucker frowning. The last thing he wanted to do was go to battle against Autumn over his daughter, but he would if it came down to a choice between a life with or without her in it.

Autumn sighed. "I suppose while I'm putting myself out there, I might as well admit that you're doing a surprisingly good job of convincing me that Blue might just be better off here with her daddy and his large, loving family. Might," she reiterated.

Her words lifted a huge weight from his shoulders. "I wouldn't expect you to make your decision just yet. Not until you've had a chance to see more of who I am and what I do. Today—" he glanced up at the ever-darkening sky "—if the weather holds, you'll get to see more of the ranch, including the broncs and their weanlings."

"Weanlings?"

He looked back at her with a smile. "Little ones. They'll be out stretching their legs. We'll just have to find them. And if you have any questions about what I do, feel free to ask as we go."

"You can count on it," she said. "Because that all comes into play as well in my decision. I intend to take everything I've seen and learned while staying here into consideration. I just hope…" Her words trailed off.

"What do you hope?" he asked.

"That you're truly in this for the long haul," she told him. "Because raising a child is a lifetime commitment."

"I have every intention of loving and cherishing, and seeing to the raising of my daughter until my last breath," he told her, meaning it with all his heart. "How could I consider doing anything less? Blue is a blessing from God. One whose very existence in this world has made me what I never even knew I longed to be until she came into my life—a father."

"You'd be surprised how many men there are who don't share your sentiments," she said, her words catching slightly.

Regret filled him. How could he have been so insensitive in his choice of words? Not when she'd told him about her own father's abandonment after learning about the double blessing God had bestowed upon him. "Autumn…"

She held up a hand to cut off his apology. "Please don't. You and I know there's no changing the past, as much as we'd long to be able to. But we can make certain Blue never feels like she was set aside by either of us, no matter what the outcome may be."

"Agreed," he said with a determined nod.

They walked in silence for several long moments before Autumn said, "I enjoyed the Sunday service today."

"I'm glad. It was nice having you and Blue accompany me," Tucker replied, grateful that Autumn had redirected their conversation. Her past made him angry on her behalf, made his heart hurt for her, made him wish there were something he could do to right the wrongs done to her in her life. But she was correct. There was no changing the past. Not for any of them.

"It was nice being there," she admitted with a soft smile. "And Reverend Walker's sermon was really uplifting. I can see why the place was so packed."

The church had been filled to capacity that morning, but that was pretty much the norm. "Being introduced to so many people had to be a little overwhelming for you. Maybe even awkward," he added, "considering the curious glances that kept coming our way."

"I didn't mind," she said, setting his mind at ease. "Not really. I wanna know the people my niece might be surrounded by if she were to come live here with you. Their curiosity is completely understandable, seeing as how you introduced Blue to them as your daughter with no time to really explain how that came about."

"I suppose I should prepare myself for the whole truth to come out," he said with a sigh.

"Tucker, it's not your fault the marriage failed," she said, surprising him with her words of support.

"Sometimes I wonder," he said solemnly.

"I know my sister…knew," she corrected sadly, "and

aside from the fact that she had a tendency to be impulsive with some very important decisions in her life, I think fear drove her away from you."

"Fear?" he repeated. "You think Summer was afraid of me?"

"Not at all," she didn't hesitate to respond. "I think she was afraid the past would repeat itself, and, like our folks had done, you would abandon her just like our daddy did our momma once you'd learned about the baby."

"I never gave Summer any reason to believe——"

"You didn't have to," she told him. "It was already rooted deep inside of her. Our daddy wanted nothing to do with our momma once he'd learned she was carrying his child…children, actually. Maybe the thought of having two babies at once, when he wasn't prepared for even one, was enough to send him running. Then Momma did pretty much the same thing. Maybe she was overwhelmed. Maybe she resented us for our daddy's leaving. Whatever the case, I think Summer pulled away from you before she could be the one left hurting again."

He hadn't considered that, but then it was hard to get past the bitterness he'd felt toward Summer for so long. Autumn had a way of putting things into perspective when it came to her life. To Summer's life. "How is it you are so different from your sister? And I don't mean that in a bad way. Just honest."

"The Lord gives us the choice to either focus on the bad in our lives, or on the blessings we've been given," she explained. "I try to focus on the good, no matter how bad things get. Even if it's not always possible to do so. But Summer was never able to push away the bad."

He glanced her way. "You're a very special woman, Autumn Myers. I hope you know that."

She glanced away, as if she'd been made uncomfortable by his compliment. But he didn't regret giving it. She was special. However, he decided to direct their conversation to something far less personal.

They crossed a side street to the corner Abby's Donuts sat on. Tucker's gaze was drawn to the donut shop's large storefront windows that lined that side of the building. "The good news about coming here after church," he said, "is that it's nowhere near as busy as it is before church when people are stopping in to get their morning coffee and a quick bite to eat." He reached for the door, but it opened before his hand could come to rest on the handle, forcing him to take a step back.

Justin Dawson, Bent Creek's sheriff and his brother Jackson's best friend, offered a nod of greeting. "Tucker." Then he stopped dead in his tracks as his gaze landed on Autumn, who stood next to Tucker on the sidewalk.

"Justin," Tucker said, returning the nod. "Missed you at church this morning."

"I'm on duty," he replied distractedly. "Just stopped in for a quick cup of coffee." Curiosity lit his eyes as he tipped his hat to Autumn. "Ma'am."

Realizing he'd neglected to make introductions, Tucker said, "Autumn Myers, this is Sheriff Dawson."

"Justin," he countered as he extended a hand in greeting. "An old family friend of the Wades."

She accepted the offered hand with a warm smile. "It's a pleasure to meet you, Justin."

Tucker gritted his teeth, suddenly feeling the need to list all the reasons why it shouldn't be a pleasure for her to meet Justin. But the man really had no faults big enough to lay out there that would make a difference. And why did it matter? Autumn was free to smile at any man she pleased. Even if it suddenly didn't please Tucker.

"Pardon my surprise," Justin said as he released her hand, "but I can't say that I've ever seen Tucker parading a female around town, let alone one as pretty as you."

She blushed at the compliment. Then again, the color in her cheeks might have been from the damp chill filling the air. Tucker decided to go with the latter. Autumn was, as she put it herself, a reasonable woman. One who clearly knew not to be drawn in by his friend's flirtatious words. At least, he hoped that were the case.

"You haven't seen me 'parading' anyone around, because I believe in holding to the vows I made when I got married," Tucker countered with a frown.

Justin's head snapped around so fast it was a wonder he didn't suffer whiplash. "Excuse me?"

Tucker sighed. This wasn't how he'd planned on letting the truth out to close friends, but there it was. "The reason you haven't seen me with another female is because I got married when I was riding the rodeo circuit several years back."

"You're married?"

"Not any longer," he replied.

"Why don't I go on in and get the hot chocolate?" Autumn suggested, clearly uncomfortable by the turn their conversation had taken. "Give you two a chance to speak in private."

"You sure?" Tucker asked worriedly, searching her gaze.

"I think I can manage to pick a few donuts out all by myself," she told him with a reassuring smile.

"This talk can wait until a better time," Justin insisted. "You two go ahead and enjoy your afternoon."

"You've already said you're a close friend of the family," Autumn told him. "I don't mind Tucker taking a moment to explain to you what's going on in his life." She turned back to Tucker. "What kind of donut would you like?"

He pulled his wallet from the back pocket of his jeans and withdrew a twenty-dollar bill, holding it out to her. "I don't have a preference. Just grab me whatever catches your fancy. I won't be long."

She nodded, her attention shifting back to Justin. "If you'll excuse me."

He gave a polite nod, not that Autumn would have seen it. She had already turned away, disappearing into the donut shop, the door drifting shut behind her.

Tucker watched her go, knowing that he could have handled things better when it came to telling Justin he was, or at least had been, married. But seeing his friend smiling at Autumn the way he had been, well, it mattered. Even when it shouldn't.

"I'm sorry if I stepped into something I shouldn't have," his friend said. "Jackson never made mention of your being married. Neither did Garrett for that matter."

He turned to look at his friend. "It's not your fault. No one knew. Not even my family."

"You eloped?"

"We did," he confirmed. "But things didn't work out the way my wife hoped they would and she chose to walk away. Only she failed to tell me that she was carrying my child at the time."

Justin's jaw dropped. "*You* have a child?"

Tucker nodded. "A daughter. One I only just found out about. Blue's four, almost five."

"Close to Lucas's age," he noted, referring to his nephew. "He'll be seven in December. So how did you find out about…Blue, wasn't it?"

"Blue Belle Wade," he acknowledged with a father's deep-felt pride. "Autumn brought her here to meet me after my wife, her sister, confessed what she had done, something she only did to set things right with the Lord before dying."

"Your wife died?"

"Six months ago." He went on to explain the events that had transpired and how he was doing everything he could to prove to Autumn that his daughter belonged with him.

"You're a good man, Tucker," his friend said. "Everyone in Bent Creek knows that. And if it comes down to a court battle I'm willing to testify on your behalf. Just say the word."

"I appreciate that, Justin. However, I'm hoping Autumn and I can work things out without having to go the route of a messy court battle."

"I hope she feels the same way," he said, taking a drink of coffee from the cup he'd carried out with him.

"I know she doesn't want to put Blue through any more undue stress. She loves my daughter like she was her own," he told Justin. "Not surprising since Autumn helped to raise Blue. I believe in my heart she'll do what's best for her, whatever that may end up being."

"I can understand her not wanting to put your daughter under any more stress," his friend said with a heavy sigh. "Lainie and her son are still struggling to come to terms with Will's death and it's been nearly eight months."

Lainie was Justin's little sister. A widow at the ripe young age of twenty-eight. Her husband, Will, had died after their car was struck by a drunk driver. "I take it you still haven't been able to convince her to move back to Bent Creek yet?"

He shook his head. "Mom and Dad and I have all tried. Lainie's determined to stay in Sacramento, wanting to keep Lucas's life as close to normal as possible given the circumstances." He met Tucker's gaze. "But I'm still worried about her."

"Understandable. But your sister's a grown woman. All you can do right now is continue to let her know there's a place for them back here if she decides Sacramento isn't where they need to be."

"I intend to," he said with a troubled frown. "I just wish my sister was here where I could lend her a hand, even offer her a shoulder to cry on if she needs it."

Tucker glanced toward the front window where inside he could see Abby, the owner of Abby's Donuts, filling a pastry box with Autumn's selections. "I'm sure Lainie knows her family is only a phone call away."

"I suppose so," he said. "Speaking of family, is yours planning on attending this year's fall barbecue?"

"They never miss it." The town's annual barbecue was a big event. Most of Bent Creek attended the festivities. Grills were set up just outside the enclosed pavilion at the town's park and ribs were brought in, along with Abe Johnson's specialty barbecue sauce. Everyone brought covered dishes and their own tableware. And there was always some sort of musical entertainment planned for that afternoon's events.

"What about you? Will you be there?"

Tucker shrugged. "I'm not sure what my plans are yet. It all depends on how long Autumn and Blue will be staying here."

"If they're still here, then bring them along," Justin suggested. "Kids love picnics. Even if they're inside. Especially when there's a table set up specifically for desserts."

"I'll be sure to use that as my selling point," he said with a chuckle.

"Seriously though," the sheriff said, "I hope to have a chance to meet this little girl of yours before she goes back to Cheyenne."

"I'd like that, too," Tucker had no sooner said when the skies above let loose a mixture of both rain and snow. He reached for the door. "And, Justin…"

"Yes?"

"If you don't mind, could you keep Blue and I in your prayers?"

"You don't even have to ask," his friend said with a farewell nod before striding away.

Tucker stepped into the donut shop and removed his cowboy hat, shaking off the slushy drops that had accumulated atop it before moving farther inside. Hat in hand, he made his way up to the counter where Autumn was paying for the donuts and hot chocolate she had purchased.

"There's one of my favorite customers," Abby said with her usual playful greeting.

Autumn glanced back over her shoulder, her gaze coming to rest on Tucker. A slender brow lifted. "Favorite, huh?"

He chuckled as he moved to stand beside her. "Okay, so I confess. I might have a bit of a sweet tooth myself."

"And here I was thinking you came by so often just to see me," Abby said, feigning disappointment as she handed Tucker the box of donuts Autumn had selected.

Abby was at least ten years older than his mother, so Tucker knew she was only teasing him. That and the fact that she was already happily married to her husband of forty-plus years. A part of him wished he had managed to find the kind of long-lasting love Abby and his own parents had. The other part of him, the part in charge of sound reasoning, said a forever-kind-of-love hadn't been part of God's plan for him.

Autumn's gaze moved past him to the window. "Oh, no," she gasped. "It's raining."

"Sleeting, actually," he told her as he tucked the box under the crook of his arm. "Looks like our tour of the ranch will have to wait until tomorrow."

He'd be lying to himself if he didn't admit that it pleased him to see the disappointment that registered on her face with his announcement. It meant that Autumn had been looking forward to their outing and learning more about the business he and his brothers ran.

She glanced once more toward the sleet-splattered windowpanes and then turned back to him, a sweet smile moving across her pretty face. "Until tomorrow, then."

Tucker found himself wishing their tour didn't have to wait. Surprisingly, he was eager to share that part of his life with Autumn. For Blue's sake, of course. At least, that was what he was trying very hard to convince himself of.

Chapter Eight

Tucker pulled up to his house, his mouth caught up in a wide grin. The cold front from the day before had long since passed. The afternoon sun shone brightly in the cloudless sky above. Even the temperature had risen, making it feel more like a September afternoon than a mid-October one. He couldn't have asked for a more perfect day to tour his and his family's ranches.

He was about to go fetch Autumn and Blue when they stepped out onto the porch, offering waves of greeting. His daughter was dressed in blue jeans and her fall coat. She was wearing the pale pink cowgirl boots Tucker had bought for her. The ones with the tiny silver, glittery stars on the outer sides of the boots' shafts. Autumn was in jeans as well, but instead of cowgirl boots she wore hikers that were both stylish and low-heeled enough to be practical for the outing they had planned. Not that his daughter's aunt wasn't quite skilled when it came to moving about in heels of any height.

It took a moment for it to dawn on him that Autumn was lugging Blue's car seat with her. He mentally kicked himself for being so distracted by Autumn's choice of footwear that he hadn't even thought to jump out and retrieve it from her. He was out of the truck and moving toward her in long, hurried strides.

Blue skipped ahead of her aunt. "Hi, Daddy!"

"Hi, sweetheart," he replied, his heart swelling as it did every time his daughter called him Daddy. His gaze lifted to Autumn's pretty face and he gave a slight nod. "Afternoon. Here," he said, reaching for the seat, "let me get that for you."

"Thank you," she said, relinquishing her hold on it.

They walked to his vehicle where Tucker placed the seat inside the back of the roomy cab and then attempted to secure it properly. Only he couldn't figure out exactly how to do so. If only he had paid more attention when Autumn had done this before.

For a moment, Tucker considered winging it and then decided it was better to admit his inability to perform the task at hand than to take even the slightest risk with his daughter's safety. Glancing back at Autumn with a frustrated frown, he said, "I can saddle a horse, but I can't figure out how to buckle in a car seat."

She smiled in response as she stepped up beside him to demonstrate. "I was the same way at first. You'll learn."

He would learn. Her words gave him more hope that his daughter would soon be living with him. Bending, he scooped Blue up and placed her into the car seat Autumn had managed to secure.

"Do you need help?" Autumn asked from behind him.

"Thanks, but I can at least handle this part." He gave the shoulder harness belt a tug to make certain it was firmly latched in. "Are you ready to go see Daddy's other horses?" he asked Blue, unable to deny his own excitement. He'd been wanting to do this for a while, but had waited until he felt Blue was ready. Her growing interest in Hoss and Little Joe and her willingness to be near them convinced him it was time to see how she did around the rest of the horses.

His daughter's head gave a slow bob up and down. "Can we go see the butterflies, too?"

"We'll have to do that another day when you're both wearing your tennis shoes. We wouldn't want those pesky little stones scratching up your and your aunt Autumn's pretty shoes."

"Then can we go to my grandma and grandpa's after we see the horses?"

Tucker's smile softened even more. Blue had taken to her grandparents like a honeybee to a brightly blooming flower. "I think we can make that happen if it's all right with your aunt."

Blue tipped forward to see past his large frame. "Can we, Aunt Autumn?"

"If time allows. We wouldn't wanna interrupt their dinner."

"Okay," his daughter said, settling back against her car seat, seemingly satisfied by her aunt's response.

Tucker stepped back and closed the passenger door. Then he looked to Autumn. "I think we're ready." Reaching past her, he opened her door and then helped her up into the truck's cab before making his way around to the driver's side.

"Don't forget what I said about asking questions if there's something you'd like to know," Tucker said as he settled behind the steering wheel. Putting the truck in gear, he pulled away from the house.

A short distance down the road that ran past all of

his family's ranches, Blue exclaimed, "Look at all the big brown chickens!"

Tucker glanced out Autumn's window, chuckling as he spied the flock of wild turkeys his daughter had caught sight of. "Those are turkeys. They run wild in these parts."

"Do they lay brown eggs?"

"More of a beige," he answered. "They're bigger than the eggs a chicken lays, and are usually speckled."

They came over a rise, and Blue's attention shifted elsewhere. "Tiny horses!"

Autumn gasped as she watched the young horses race across the range. "They're adorable." She looked to Tucker. "I take it those are the weanlings."

He nodded.

"That's the main barn up ahead," he said, indicating the large building that sat off to one side in the distance.

"I remember seeing it when we stopped by your momma and daddy's to collect eggs that day."

"It's the largest of all our barns and was already set up with fencing to hold a lot more horses. We use it to store grain, equipment for training green horses, rodeo equipment, those kinds of things. The horses themselves are free range."

"Meaning?" Autumn asked.

"Meaning they spend their days and nights out on the range."

"Don't they get cold?" Blue asked.

Tucker met his daughter's questioning gaze in the rearview mirror. "No, sweetheart, they don't. Broncs are strong and adaptable, and made to survive in this kind of country whatever the weather."

"It's back," Blue said.

"What's back?" Autumn asked.

"The bee," his daughter replied. "I hear it buzzing again."

Again? It was too cold for bees. How could… Tucker suddenly recalled having left his cell phone in the pocket of the coat he'd been wearing when he went out to work that morning. As the day had warmed up, he'd switched to a lightweight jacket he kept in the back seat of his truck.

"That would be my phone." He pulled over, placing the truck in Park. Then he jumped out and opened the passenger door. Reaching into the coat's pocket, he pulled out his cell phone which, at this point, had stopped ringing.

Tucker pulled up the missed call list to find that he hadn't answered several calls from the nursing home. Concern filled him. "Excuse me a moment," he said apologetically to Autumn and his daughter. "I need to make a call."

Closing the truck's door, he returned the call.

"Sunny Days Nursing Home," a woman answered. "Susan speaking. How may I help you?"

"Susan," he said, "Tucker Wade calling. Someone there has been trying to reach me."

"That was me," she said, sounding relieved.

"Is it Wylie?" he asked worriedly, praying complications from his recent surgery hadn't set in.

"I'm afraid so," she replied. "He woke up from a nap disoriented and has been out of sorts ever since. We were wondering if you might be available to come by and see if you can settle him down before we have to call the doctor in."

He glanced toward the truck where Autumn and Blue

waited for him. Once again, their tour was going to have to wait. Maybe the good Lord was trying to tell him something. Like giving Autumn a glimpse of who he was might not be in his best interest. But he couldn't figure out why that would be. "I'll be there in about twenty minutes." As soon as he swung by and dropped Autumn and Blue off at the house.

Guilt stabbed at Tucker as he settled in behind the truck's wheel and started the engine.

"Tucker," Autumn said worriedly. "Is everything okay?"

"A friend needs me. It's nothing to worry yourself over," he said as he turned the truck around. Glancing her way, he added with a sigh, "But I'm afraid we're going to have to put off our tour until I get back."

"You're leaving?"

"There's something I need to see to that can't wait. I'll drop you and Blue off at the ranch on my way. I'm not sure how long I'll be gone, but I'm hoping it won't be too long." He didn't see any need to get into the details. Telling Autumn about Old Wylie would only bring back sad memories of her own grandma's failing health before she'd passed.

"No grandma's?" Blue said with a pout.

He hated disappointing his daughter, but this couldn't be helped. "We'll head back out when I get home and finish our tour. Afterward we'll stop by and visit with Grandma and Grandpa Wade."

Autumn tried not to show her displeasure with Tucker's abrupt change of their plans. One he didn't care to offer an explanation for, other than a friend needed him. Well, his daughter needed him, too. Blue had been so excited to go on a tour of her daddy's ranch and see the weanlings. It was still hard to believe how much she had overcome since arriving there, most notably her intense fear of horses. Not that her niece's uneasiness when it came to the four-legged, doll-swiping creatures was completely diminished. But with Tucker's help, Blue had made great strides in reconnecting with her love of horses again.

"We'll just play it by ear," Autumn said stiffly.

"Thank you for understanding," Tuckered muttered distractedly, his fingers tapping the steering wheel in a nervous rhythm.

Her understanding? If he only knew how wrong he was. Despite Tucker's reassurance otherwise, something, no make that someone, had gotten him all out of sorts. She doubted it was one of his brothers. She felt confident Tucker would have told her so. The sheriff? She didn't think so. This was someone he preferred not to make mention of by name. Her troubled thoughts began to stir. Could his caller have been a woman? Tucker had never said anything about being in a relationship with anyone, but it stood to reason that a man as handsome and as personable as Tucker Wade would have plenty of women vying for his attention.

If Tucker were seeing someone, then it only made sense that whomever she was would feel understandably neglected. Tucker had spent all his free time with Autumn and his daughter since their arrival there. More troublesome was the possibility that if there was a woman in Tucker's life, one who had the ability to make him drop everything, plans with his daughter included, to run to her in all haste, Autumn was going to have to reevaluate Tucker's commitment to his daughter.

Tucker made no further attempt to explain his being called away. In fact, he drove in silence the rest of the trip back to his place. If not for Blue singing silly little made-up songs about horses and chickens and kitties, the drive would have been beyond uncomfortable.

When Tucker pulled up in front of his ranch house, Autumn was more than ready to get out of his truck. "Stay there," she told him. "You're in a hurry. I'll see to Blue." She didn't wait for his assistance before jumping down from the truck's cab and getting her niece out of the car seat.

"We'll talk when I get back," he called after her.

"If you can spare the time," she cast back over her shoulder as she led Blue away toward the house, unable to look back as Tucker drove away.

"Are you mad at Daddy?" Blue asked as they made their way inside the cedar-sided ranch house.

Autumn forced a smile. "No, honey. Just a little disappointed that we couldn't finish our tour." And a lot disappointed in your daddy, she struggled not to add. Blue had to come first to whomever she ended up with. If Tucker weren't willing to do so, then Autumn most certainly would.

"I'm hungry."

"Let's go see what we can throw together for dinner," she told her niece.

"Can I have a grilled cheese?" Blue asked.

Autumn smiled. "I think I can manage that."

They made their way into the kitchen where her niece settled herself onto one of the kitchen chairs. "Daddy likes grilled cheese."

As far as she was concerned, Tucker could fend for himself. "It would be cold before your daddy gets home."

Whenever that would be. And what would Tucker have done if she hadn't been there to leave Blue with? Drop her off with one of his brothers? His parents? That was not what she considered taking on responsibility.

A short while later, a knock sounded at the front door. Before Autumn could go answer it, the door cracked open. "Tucker?"

"Jackson?" she called out as she stepped from the kitchen.

"Did the nursing home get ahold of my brother?" he asked as he moved toward her with that slightly off-kilter gait of his. He looked every bit as troubled as Tucker had been after he'd made his phone call.

"Nursing home?"

"Apparently, Old Wylie is having a bad spell. They've been trying to reach my brother for over an hour with no luck. I told them I would see if I could find him."

"Uncle Jackson!" Blue exclaimed from the kitchen doorway, a half-eaten grilled cheese sandwich pinched between her fingers.

A wide grin spread across his face at the sight of her. "Hey there, kiddo."

"Did you come for a grilled cheese sandwich?"

"Not today," he told her. "I have an errand to run."

"Sweetie," Autumn said, "go back to the table to finish your sandwich. I'll be in as soon as I'm done talking to your uncle Jackson."

"Okay," she said, taking a bite of her sandwich and then added around a mouthful of cheese and bread, "Bye, Uncle Jackson."

"Bye, cutie-pie."

She smiled at the affectionate nickname her uncle had given her and then disappeared back into the kitchen.

All of the anger that had been building up inside Autumn toward Tucker after he'd left without any real explanation was immediately replaced by guilt as she turned back to his brother. "I take it Old Wylie is a relative of yours?"

Tucker's brother shook his head. "No. He's an old rodeo rider who took Tucker under his wing when my brother was first starting out, teaching him the ins and outs of bronc riding. Unfortunately, Old Wylie has been having bouts of dementia and sometimes he has these panic attacks. Tucker's the only one who seems to be able to calm him down."

Autumn put a hand to her mouth. She felt ill. She'd judged Tucker so badly. So wrongly.

"Autumn?" Jackson said, his worried frown deepening. "You okay?"

"Yes," she said with a nod. "I just know how frightening it can be for an older person when they are feeling panicked or confused. My grandmother..." She didn't finish her explanation. Instead, she said, "Tucker is already on his way to the nursing home."

That announcement didn't appear to relieve Jackson at all. "I'd best get going. He'll need Hank." No doubt seeing the confusion on her face, he added, "His guitar. He left it in the back of my truck."

Tucker played guitar, she thought in surprise. Confused, she asked, "What does his guitar have to do with your brother being called to the nursing home?"

"A great deal," he replied. "My brother goes to the home a couple of times a month—that is when we're not on the road with the rodeo—to sing and play for Old Wylie and the other residents there."

"Your brother sings?" Summer had never made mention of it. And since arriving at Bent Creek she'd never even heard Tucker so much as hum a tune.

Jackson nodded. "He does. But most people don't know about his musical ability. He never played or sang around anyone other than family until he started doing it at Sunny Days. Old Wylie is a fan of old-time camp-fire songs, so Tucker took his guitar in one time to indulge the old man. His playing and singing there ended up becoming a regular thing for all of the residents."

"That's so sweet of him," Autumn said, Tucker's kindness touching her deeply.

"Don't tell him that," Jackson said with a grin. "We cowboys don't like to be thought of as sweet. Makes us sound soft."

Autumn laughed. "You are soft. All of you Wade brothers. I've seen you around my niece. Marshmallows have nothing on you three."

He chuckled in response. "You might be right. At least when it comes to Blue. I should get going. I need to get Hank to Tucker. Hopefully, my brother will be able to calm Old Wylie down." He started back out the door.

"Jackson…"

He paused to look back at her.

"Would you mind if I took Hank to Tucker?"

He shrugged. "I suppose I could stay here and keep an eye on Blue while you run Tucker's guitar to him."

"No need," she said with a grateful smile. "I'll take her with me."

His brows creased. "Are you sure? Some of the residents there are not in the best shape. It might be upsetting for her."

"I'm sure," she told him with a smile, grateful that her niece's well-being was foremost in his mind. "Blue and I occasionally pay visits to nursing homes back in Cheyenne. Your niece loves to hand out pages she's colored to the residents. Not as much as she loves sitting with them and spinning all sorts of tales that keep her aging audience quite entertained." Her smile softened. "I suppose she's a lot like her daddy in that way."

"I suppose it's true what they say then. The apple doesn't fall far from the tree," he agreed.

She hoped not. The last thing she wanted to be was anything at all like her own parents had been. Autumn turned, calling out to Blue. "Blue, sweetie, go get your boots and coat on. We're going for a ride." Then she looked back to Jackson. "You can give me directions to Sunny Days while I walk out with you to get Hank."

With a nod, he followed her outside.

When they arrived at the nursing home less than ten minutes later, Autumn reached for Blue's hand, Tucker's guitar held securely in her other hand. The sound of masculine singing filtered through the hallway, growing louder as they neared the recreation room.

"I can hear him," Blue said in an excited whisper, having learned that quiet voices were best for places like this.

Autumn could, as well. Tucker had a beautiful voice, not that she would ever word it that way to him. She was learning that men of his breed liked to think themselves manly men. The thought made her smile. Those three hulking, ex-rodeo riding brothers couldn't get any manlier if they tried. She gave Blue's hand a gentle squeeze. "I'm not so sure he even needs Hank." They slowed, turning to step through the open doorway.

The oversized, window-lined room was filled with what were clearly Tucker Wade's adoring fans. Seated on settees and chairs, and a few scattered wheelchairs, the residents were undeniably enthralled by Tucker's melodic voice. Despite not having his trusty guitar to accompany him, he was singing his heart out, his grin aimed at one particular resident seated in the front row. The older man, despite his frail appearance, was clapping his hands and tapping a foot to Tucker's deep baritone voice singing "Back in the Saddle Again."

Standing there, watching Tucker bring joy to so many faces with his singing made Autumn's heart melt. There had been no singing cowboy during her grandma's final days, which had been spent in a nursing home very similar to the one she was standing in now. Her grandma would have enjoyed it so very much. Tucker Wade was turning out to be the most giving man she had ever known. She sniffed softly, her eyes misting over.

"Aunt Autumn, why are you crying?" Blue asked, forgetting to use her quiet voice, causing several heads to turn in their direction.

The shifting commotion at the back of the room drew Tucker's gaze in her and Blue's direction. The second he saw them standing there, his green eyes widened in surprise, the song he'd been singing coming to a jarring halt.

The abrupt end to the song had the home's residents stirring anxiously. Pleas for him to finish his song filled the room. Tucker shifted uneasily, a hint of color deepening his tanned cheeks.

Autumn hadn't meant to embarrass him. Truth was she wasn't even sure why she had volunteered to bring his guitar to him instead of letting his brother see to the task. But she'd judged him so unfairly. She'd wanted to make it up to him. Leaning down, she said to Blue, "We know the song your daddy was singing. How about we sing along with him?" Having seen her fair share of old Westerns, she knew plenty of cowboy campfire songs, many of which she had taught Blue to sing.

Blue nodded eagerly at the suggestion.

Lifting her gaze to Tucker, who stood watching her from across the room, Autumn began to sing. Blue quickly joined in and the two of them made their way through the gathered residents, their smiles returning once more. As they drew closer to Tucker, she held Hank out to him with a warm smile. "We thought you might be needing this," she whispered as Blue continued singing at the top of her precious little lungs.

With a nod of appreciation, he took the guitar and eased its strap over his head. Feeding his muscular arm through the loop, he let the weight of the instrument fall against his jean-clad hip as he began to play. Then his deep, baritone voice joined hers and Blue's, blending perfectly, as together they finished the remainder of the song.

After playing several more well-known songs, his singing accompanied by that of his daughter and her beautiful aunt, the home's staff began to escort the residents from the room for their evening meal. But Old Wylie was far too smitten with Autumn to concern himself with nourishment. Once introductions had been made, the older man had been more than content to chatter on, all cow eyed, with Autumn.

Tucker's gaze was drawn to Autumn's smiling face. She didn't appear to mind the older man's determination to chew her ear off. Instead, she sat grinning, laughing at Wylie's stories even if they verged on being what Tucker would consider very tall tales.

He turned his attention to Blue, who was seated at a table by the window, putting a puzzle together with one of the home's good-hearted volunteers. She never ceased to amaze him. At times, even humble him. When he'd first seen her standing just inside the recreation room's open doorway with Autumn, he'd pretty much been stunned speechless. Or songless as was the case.

When Autumn's pale blue gaze had met his, he'd not missed the sheen of unshed tears in her eyes. His first thought had been to sweep Blue out of the room, away from what was sure to upset her or at the very least, make his daughter uneasy. But Blue hadn't balked one bit at being surrounded by a roomful of elderly patients, some of whom were hooked up to oxygen, some in wheelchairs, even those like Old Wylie, who suffered from various levels of dementia. She had fallen into song, right alongside her beautiful aunt, making Tucker forget all about wanting to sweep her from the room. Instead, he'd waited where he'd been standing for them to reach him, moved by their sweet voices.

As if sensing his gaze upon her, Blue glanced up from the puzzle she was working on, and a happy smile stretched across her tiny heart-shaped face. A face he prayed he would spend the rest of his life being able to look upon.

Wylie's attendant returned to take him to supper, having allowed the older man extra time with Tucker and his guests. With a word of thanks to Tucker, she escorted her now much-calmer patient from the room.

When they had gone, Autumn turned to him. "Why didn't you tell us you were coming here?"

A slight frown pinched at his lips. "I didn't want to

bring up sad memories for you, your having had to care for your ailing grandmother and all."

Her expression softened. "I wish you would have. Seeing you here…" Emotion had the words catching in her throat. "Well, it was just so kindhearted of you. If I had known—"

He cut her off, saying, "I don't do this for the praise. God gave me the ability to play, so why not use it to make others happy?"

"You might not seek praise, but you most certainly deserve it. And I agree, the good Lord definitely blessed you with the ability to play *and* sing. You have a wonderful voice."

"If we're talking being blessed with the ability to sing, I'd have to say that *He* gifted you, as well."

Her cheeks pinkened. "Thank you."

He gave a slight nod. Truth was, Autumn had truly surprised him with her genuine ease around the home's residents. But his daughter had surprised him even more. "I can't get over how easily Blue adapted to things here."

She glanced toward his daughter, her smile softening even more. "Blue is a very bighearted little girl. And this isn't the first nursing home she's been to."

His brows drew together in confusion. "But I thought your grandmother passed away years ago."

"She did," she said, a hint of sadness lacing her voice. "But there are so many other elderly people spending their final days in homes like this who have no family to look in on them." Autumn went on to explain how she and Blue paid visits to different nursing homes back in Cheyenne with the hopes of brightening the residents' days, just as Autumn had once done for her grandmother before her passing.

"Thank you for teaching my daughter to treat others with patience and kindness."

"Tucker…"

"Yes?"

"Do you think it would be all right if Blue and I come back with you next time you play for the patients? If we're still here, I mean," she added. "Just to watch."

"I'd like that," he said. "In fact, you and Blue can join me in entertaining the residents."

She shook her head. "Oh, we couldn't do that. It's your special time with them."

"You and Blue made it even more special. And I know the residents really enjoyed having the two of you here." He reached out, placing his hand atop hers. "So did I."

"I'm glad we came," she said softly. "It gave me a chance to see yet another side of the man you are. Beyond the strong, loyal, loving brother, son and father you have shown yourself to be. You're compassionate to others and a truly devoted friend. A very likable man. I can see why my sister was drawn to you."

And you? he wanted to ask, but kept those words to himself. Withdrawing his hand, despite the urge to leave it exactly where it was, he said, "Well, you're pretty likable, too."

"Thank you." She glanced in his daughter's direction. "We should be going."

"I won't be long behind you. I just want to stop by the cafeteria and make sure Wylie is still doing okay."

She stood and looked down at him with a tender smile. "Do what you need to do. Blue and I will see you when you get home."

He watched as she crossed the room to collect Blue, his heart giving odd little lurches. Could he really let

Autumn go back to Cheyenne without telling her how he felt? Feelings he was still trying to work out. Because he'd opened his heart to a woman once before and had ended up being left to pick up the pieces after Summer had trampled over it. Did he dare risk it a second time?

Chapter Nine

"For years, I've been surrounded by men," Emma Wade said as she and Autumn peeled potatoes for that night's family dinner. "It's so nice to finally have another female around." Her gaze slid over to Blue whose job was to place the peeled potatoes, once they had been rinsed, into a bowl that sat on the table in front of her and then hand them to her grandma to cut into pieces. A tender smile moved over Emma's face as she corrected her previous statement. "Two females, counting Blue."

"It was kind of you to include me in tonight's dinner," Autumn told her as she walked over to the sink to rinse off another colander full of potatoes.

"You're family, honey," the older woman replied as she sliced into a wedge of potato. "Of course, you're invited to join us."

There it was again, being told that she was part of a family that had no real familial connection with her. At least, not directly. It would have been nice to truly be a part of this family. They were everything Autumn had wished for growing up, but had never had. Loving, giving, warmhearted and unfailingly loyal.

"Aunt Autumn's gonna come live with us."

The colander Autumn was holding under the water's stream clattered into the kitchen sink as it slipped from her grasp. She cast a glance back over her shoulder to find Tucker's momma staring at her wide-eyed.

"You are?"

Autumn gave an embarrassed laugh as she retrieved the potato-laden colander, which had thankfully remained upright when it slipped from her hands. "I think Blue would like that to be true. However, I do have an open invitation to come visit anytime I like if Blue comes to live here in Bent Creek with her daddy."

"Of course, you do," the older woman replied as she went back to dicing another potato. "I'm just sorry you've been put in such an emotionally draining situation. I hope Tucker's been sensitive of the position you're in."

Tucker, she thought with an odd ache in her heart. He was everything she wanted in a man. But he was not the man for her. Because if she gave in to her feelings and Tucker reciprocated she would spend the rest of her life knowing she was once again another man's second choice.

"It hasn't been easy for him, either," Autumn replied, "but we're working our way through it. Tucker has been incredibly understanding about my need to make certain I do what I feel is in Blue's best interest."

"Glad to hear it," his momma said. "I'd expect no less from any of my boys."

"Your son…all of your sons," she corrected, "are fine men who could give the gentlemen of Texas a run for their money in the manners department."

Pride lit the older woman's face. "Well, you be sure

to tell me if any of them have a lapse of manners and I'll set them straight."

Autumn laughed softly. "I'll do that." Not that she truly believed that would ever happen. Their manners were too deeply ingrained. And although Blue was too young to fully appreciate what she had gained by this trip, Autumn knew. Her niece now had a complete family on her daddy's side, all of whom wanted to make her a part of their lives. Family who would love and cherish her as she so deserved to be.

While she was so incredibly happy for Blue, to have been so easily accepted and loved without reservation, she had to admit, at least to herself, that a part of her envied her young niece. She immediately pushed the thought away, because envy had no place in her life, and busied herself with rinsing off the next batch of potatoes while Emma and Blue chatted away behind her.

The kitchen door swung open, and Garrett poked his head inside. "Afternoon," he greeted, immediately sweeping the black cowboy hat from his head.

"You're early," his momma said in surprise.

"My last appointment canceled," he answered as he stepped inside. "Figured I'd come over as soon as I had washed up." His gaze swept the kitchen. "Where's Tucker?"

"Jackson called to say an old tree uprooted between your place and his and was lying halfway across the road. Your father and Tucker went out to help him clear it away."

"Well, I had a surprise I wanted to show Blue, but I suppose it can wait. I'd best go lend them a hand."

Blue looked to Autumn in silent pleading. "But I like surprises."

"Honey," his mother said, clicking her tongue. "You can't dangle a carrot in front of a rabbit and then take it away like that."

Confusion lit Garrett's face.

Autumn fought to keep her smile from widening. The Wade brothers were mostly clueless when it came to children, but adorably so.

"You have a rabbit?" Blue asked excitedly.

"I...um..."

"No, sweetie," Autumn answered for Garrett, who appeared to be momentarily tongue-tied. "It's just a saying."

Relief swept over Garrett's features. "Maybe so, but in this case I really do have a rabbit."

Blue gasped. "You do?"

His smile widened. "I do. Its mother belongs to a customer of mine's little boy. Her baby needed a little extra care after he was born, so I've been watching over him and seeing to it that he gets the care he needs until he's ready to go back to his family."

Blue looked worried. "Will he be okay?"

"Better than okay," Tucker's brother assured her. "In fact, I'm taking him back to his mother after dinner this evening, but I thought you might like to have a peek at him. Maybe even pet him if you'd like to."

"I'd like to!" Blue said excitedly. "Are we gonna go to your pet store to see him?"

Garrett's husky chuckle sounded a lot like Tucker's, maybe slightly deeper. "I don't mean to disappoint you, honey, but I don't have a pet store. Just a small building that sits next to my house that I sometimes use to care for animals. However, we don't have to go anywhere." He thumbed back over his shoulder toward the door he'd just come through. "I have Mr. Cottontail out on the back porch in a special cage that will keep him safe from other animals and warm."

"Can I go see him?" Blue asked, turning pleading green eyes to Autumn.

"Maybe after we finish helping your grandma with the potatoes," she told her.

"Oh, I think you and I can handle the rest of these without Blue's help," Tucker's momma said. "Don't you?"

If she didn't mind, Autumn didn't, either. Blue had been happier these past couple of weeks than she had been in months. "I reckon we can manage," she agreed with a tender smile aimed in her niece's direction.

Blue jumped down from the table and started toward the door where her uncle waited.

"Hold on, sweetie," Autumn said. "You need your jacket."

"I've got it," Garrett said, lifting the tiny coat from the hook that held it on the rack beside where he stood at the door. Then he knelt to help her into it. "All set," he said, rising to his feet.

Autumn hurried over to zip her niece's weighted jacket. "It's a little chilly out," she told her with a loving smile.

"Okay," Garrett said, "let's go see that bunny."

With a squeal, Blue was out the door in a flash. He glanced back at Autumn with a grin. "A girl right after her uncle's heart." Shoving his hat back onto his head, he followed Blue out onto the porch, swinging the door shut behind him.

As soon as the door closed, Emma Wade shook her head. "That boy of mine, always going over and above to help those with animals in need. He's a large animal vet. How on God's green earth does a rabbit fit into that category?"

That made Autumn smile. "He has a good heart."

"One he should be using to find someone special," she muttered as she began cleaning up the peelings they'd left behind on the table. She looked up at Autumn. "How is he ever going to meet the right woman when he spends all of his time caring for animals? How are any of my boys going to find their other half for that matter? All they think about is horses and rodeos."

Autumn understood the root of Emma's frustration. She wanted her sons to be happy, and to her that meant finding someone to love. It was clear, just being around Tucker's parents for even a short time that they were very happy in their marriage. "How did you and Grady meet?" she asked as she gathered up their dirty paring knives.

Emma's expression softened. "We met at the Spring County Fair Rodeo. He had just gotten bucked off a bronc right in front of the bleacher seats my family and I were seated in. When he stood, our eyes met." The older woman's wistful smile widened. "It was as if his boots had taken root right there in that very spot, because he just stood there grinning up at me. They practically had to drag him from the arena. When the rodeo let out, Grady was waiting for us at the exit. He asked my father right then and there for permission to take me out."

"He didn't even ask if you had anyone special in your life first?"

Emma laughed. "Oh, no. Grady said the good Lord had him tossed onto his backside in that very spot for a reason—to meet his future wife."

"I take it your daddy said yes," Autumn said, thoroughly caught up in Emma's love story.

"My father said that Grady was welcome to join us for early church service the next morning. I think my father expected Grady not to show. But he did, greeting me that morning in his Sunday best, with that deep-dimpled smile. I nearly melted."

"Love at first sight," Autumn said with a sigh.

"We were definitely taken with each other," Tucker's momma said. "But the love came later, growing day by day as we got to know each other. And you know the rest."

"So you married a man whose life once centered around the rodeo and ended up happily married with three wonderful sons," Autumn replied. "Sons who hold the same passion for the rodeo as their father. I think you need to have faith. When love is meant to happen for your boys, for anyone, it will." She had to believe that. Because, unlike her own momma, Autumn truly did long to have a family of her very own. One she could share stories with, laugh with, go to church with, even have family dinners with. All the things she'd never gotten the chance to experience growing up.

Emma set the dish towel she'd been wiping the table with down and turned to Autumn. "How can someone so young be so wise?"

Warmth crept into Autumn's cheeks. "I don't know about being wise. I'm just a hopeless romantic." *Hopeless* being the key word in her case when it came to finding love. She had to wonder if she would even know what true love was if it ever did come her way. A love like Emma had found with Grady.

Booted footsteps sounded in the hallway. A moment

later, Tucker came to a stop in the kitchen doorway, a dimpled grin stretched wide across his handsome face. When his gaze met hers, Autumn's heart gave an unexpected kick.

"You're back sooner than I expected," his momma said.

"It was a small tree," he answered with a shrug of his broad shoulders as he stepped farther into the room. "Barely more than a twig."

"In other words," Autumn said, trying to suppress a smile as she moved past him to dry off the table Tucker's momma had just wiped down, "you left us here to do the hard work of peeling all of those potatoes while you and your daddy went off to push a few twigs off the road…"

Tucker's brow lifted in an exaggerated affront. "Are you calling me a shirker?"

Autumn laughed. "If the shoe fits…"

"If you two will excuse me," Tucker's momma said with a barely suppressed smile. "I think I'll go outside and have a peek at that baby bunny Garrett brought to show Blue." Without waiting for their response, his momma slipped out the back door, closing it quickly behind her.

Tucker groaned, drawing Autumn's gaze his way. "Is something wrong?"

"Tell me we're not taking the bunny home to live with us. I'm not so sure Itty Bitty would appreciate having to share her new home with a pet rabbit."

Autumn shook her head. "You're off the hook. The bunny isn't for Blue. Your brother has been tending to it and wanted Blue to see it before he takes it back to its owner tonight."

He exhaled a huge sigh. "Well, that's a relief. I had visions of my brother gifting Blue with a fluffy little lamb next."

"He'd better not," Autumn said, cringing at the thought. "I don't know anything about taking care of farm animals. I'm almost in over my head with a kitten."

"Oh, I don't know. I'd say you've adapted pretty well," he told her with that devastating Wade grin she'd become so fond of. "A good thing since I doubt my daughter is going to want to leave Bitty behind when the two of you go back to Cheyenne."

Autumn's smile sagged, despite the effort she made to hide her emotions. Tucker had no way of knowing she'd made her decision, the hardest she'd ever had to make. Blue belonged with her daddy. Only now she wouldn't just be leaving her niece in Bent Creek, she feared she'd be leaving a piece of her heart, as well. She prayed Summer would forgive her for falling for Tucker, something she'd never expected to happen. Not in a million years. But having seen him with Blue, with his family, with Old Wylie, how could she not?

"Autumn?"

She met Tucker's searching gaze.

"You okay?" he asked, concern etched in his features.

She mentally shoved her woes aside. There would be time enough later, when she was alone, to dwell on such things. "It's just that I've been so caught up in getting to know you and your family that sometimes I forget my time here is coming to an end."

"Speaking of time," Tucker said as he moved to stand in front of her. Taking the dish towel from Autumn's hand, he placed it on the table. "We've got some to spare before dinner is ready. What do you say we pick up our ranch tour where we left off the other day?"

She looked around, making sure the mess they had made while preparing the potatoes was all cleaned up. "Your momma has the roast in the oven and the potatoes are ready to boil. I suppose my job here is done." Her gaze shifted back to Tucker. "I'll go fetch Blue."

"Good luck getting her away from the bunny," he told her.

"Probably true," she agreed. And it would give her a chance to talk to Tucker about turning custody of Blue over to him. Just the thought of it had a lump of emotion forming in her throat. "But your momma is busy with dinner preparations. I don't feel right asking her to keep an eye on Blue, too."

His dimpled grin returned. "Blue is her granddaughter. I'm pretty sure my mom, my whole family in fact, would be more than happy to watch over her anytime we need them to."

"We'll ask them just to be sure," Autumn said as she reached for her coat.

"I'm good with that. Here, let me," Tucker said, reaching past her to lift the coat from its hook.

"Always the gentleman," she teased as she slid her arm into the sleeve he was holding up for her.

"I try my best," he replied with a grin as he held up the other sleeve.

"I don't think there's much trying involved," she said, glancing back over her shoulder at him. "Your momma taught her sons well."

"She did her best," he said as he settled the coat onto her shoulders. "I'm sure we didn't make it easy for her."

Autumn turned with a smile. "Real handfuls, were you?"

"You could say that," he said as he reached out to pull the front of her coat together. "Unfortunately for Mom," he continued, surprising her as he latched the zipper together and eased it carefully upward, "my brothers and I inherited a good portion of Dad's wild streak. But there's no denying that it came in handy during our rodeo days."

"How so?" she asked, trying to recall the last time someone had done something so thoughtful for her.

"A man has to have a little bit of wildness in him to climb onto a two-thousand-pound bull, or to mount a horse whose natural inclination is to buck and buck hard," he replied, giving her coat's zipper one final, gentle tug before releasing it.

"W-was it the same for barrel racers?" Autumn asked, trying not to focus on the small act of kindness that Tucker had just shown her. "Because Summer…" her words trailed off, her regretful gaze lifting to meet Tucker's. "I'm sorry. I shouldn't have brought my sister up after everything that's happened."

"She did me wrong," he said. "No doubt about it. But she was still your sister and Blue's mother. I don't want either of you to feel like you can't talk about her. And, to answer your question, yes, Summer definitely had a wild streak of her own. Her not being afraid to take risks helped make her one of the best barrel racers in the business when she competed."

Autumn turned back to where her purse hung from another hook on the coatrack and reached inside it to retrieve her cell phone. Sliding it into the front pocket of her coat, she said, "I should've taken time to go watch her compete in rodeos, but I was so busy trying to get my real estate business off the ground."

His smile softened as he reached for the door. "I'm sure your sister understood. You were both just trying to follow your hearts." Opening the door, he said, "And speaking of hearts, let's go see if my family minds watching over the little girl who has completely captured mine."

His wasn't the only heart that Blue had captured, Autumn thought with a sad smile as they stepped out onto the porch. Because she had finally accepted that Blue belonged there with Tucker and his warm, loving family. It wasn't what she wanted, but it was what her niece deserved, and Autumn would never deny her that. It was time to prepare herself for letting Blue go.

Tucker walked Autumn out to his truck. Then he settled himself behind the steering wheel. "My mother really likes having you around."

"I enjoy being around her," Autumn replied. "Around your whole family, for that matter."

They pulled away from the ranch house and then turned onto the road that cut across his family's land. "I don't think they could like you any more if they tried," Tucker told her. Himself included. Especially after she'd brought his guitar to him at the nursing home. That day he'd seen more than just her beautiful, smiling face and deep-rooted love for his daughter. He'd seen her put herself out there to sing for the home's residents, quite beautifully at that. He'd watched her kindhearted interaction with those around her, making each and every one of their elderly audience feel special. But it was her tender compassion and patience when it came to Old

Wylie that had managed to whittle away the last protective layer he'd kept around his heart since Summer
had walked out on him. Lord help him but he was falling for Autumn and falling hard.

"Are those yours?"

Drawn from his thoughts, Tucker followed the line
of Autumn's gaze to the herd of broncs moving across
the distant pasture. Their lean muscular forms moved
together in a majestic grace that seemed so at odds with
the wild, bucking creatures they became the second they
left the chute and entered the rodeo arena.

Tucker smiled. "Mine and my brothers'. Would you
like to have a closer look at them?"

She glanced his way, excitement lighting her eyes.
"Very much so."

"There's a gate just up the road," he told her. "We'll
go in there."

Autumn couldn't seem to take her eyes off the horses.
A good thing, Tucker thought. Because he couldn't seem
to keep his eyes off her.

"You've mentioned selling your real estate business
in Texas to move up here to Wyoming to help Summer
out," Tucker said, needing to redirect his thoughts.

She gave a slight nod. "I did."

"Do you ever regret it?"

Autumn took a long moment to mull the question
over. "I can't say that I do. I thought about it long and
hard before making the change. Summer would never
have asked me to. She would have continued to try to
handle things on her own. But my sister's pride wouldn't
have guaranteed a roof over their heads, or food on the
table. So I made the decision for them."

"I'm grateful you did."

"No, I'm the one who's grateful. It allowed me to spend precious time with my sister that I might not have had if I had chosen my business over helping Summer out during her time of need."

Autumn had to be the most selfless person he'd ever known. Blue was blessed to have such a loving aunt in her life. "I'm thankful you were there for them. I'm just sorry you had to give up something that meant so much to you."

"I'm still able to do what I love," she added with a soft smile. "I just work for someone else now."

He had to admire her outlook on things. He wasn't so certain he'd be as accepting of them if he were in her position. It had to be hard going from running your own business to answering to someone else.

"So how does this rodeo contracting thing work?" Autumn asked as they drove down the road.

Pleased by her interest in something he was passionate about, Tucker went on to explain the most important aspects of his business from contracting with rodeos to transporting the horses to the events. Then he gave her a quick rundown on how things worked once the rodeos began.

"That's quite a demanding schedule," Autumn remarked.

He shrugged. "It's not so bad. Our working hours depend on a multitude of things, the season, changing weather conditions, foaling time and whether or not we are in the midst of rodeo commitments. You and Blue couldn't have come at a better time," he told her. "It's October, which means rodeo season has ended and our bucking horses are enjoying some free time to do their own thing. Same goes for my brothers and I for the most part."

When they reached the gate that he'd told Autumn about, Tucker turned off the road and put the truck in Park. "I'll be right back." Jumping out, he hurried around to open the heavy metal gate. Then he slid back in behind the wheel and pulled through the opening. "Give me a sec to close the gate and then we'll get going."

"There are so many horses," Autumn said as she watched them through the window.

"The Triple W has one of the largest selections of broncs, which includes some of the most sought-after rodeo broncs around."

"They're magnificent."

Tucker's chest puffed with pride. "We tend to think so. Even of the retired ones."

She looked at him questioningly.

"When our broncs have done their time in the rodeo, we put them in an area we've fenced off especially for retirement stock. They can roam at leisure and enjoy their final years."

Autumn looked back out over the expanse of land before them and the herd that was now traversing one of the rocky hillsides. "They're very blessed to have found a home here."

"I hope you'll feel the same way about Blue coming to live here," he said. "Everything you see is a part of her heritage, her future. She'll be able to travel with me during rodeo season and learn the ins and outs of the family business from a young age."

"Travel with you to rodeos?" Autumn repeated, her expression changing.

"Only if she chooses to," he hurried to add. "If she's not comfortable with it, she can stay here."

"Stay here with who?" she asked, her words sounding more clipped.

"Her grandparents," he said, questioning his own reply even as it left his mouth.

Autumn sat back, her expression pained. "This isn't gonna work."

Tucker's brows drew together in confusion. "What isn't going to work?"

"Blue's staying here," she said, taking him by surprise. "I was prepared to let her go, to leave her here with you when I went back to Cheyenne. But, after this talk, I realize it wouldn't be in Blue's best interest."

Tucker struggled to form a response to her announcement. "I don't understand. What did I do to make you feel Blue shouldn't be with me?"

"Let me verify something. Will you be gone for months with your rodeo business? Or will someone be going in your place for even part of that time?"

"We've had this discussion before. I'll be away for at least a month of that time. Maybe longer. It depends on our schedule. But my parents are more than willing to keep Blue for me while I'm away."

"Blue's emotional security is more important than any schedule. And while you have so many wonderful qualities to offer a child, the truth is your life isn't conducive to raising one. Not with all the traveling you have to do when rodeo season rolls around. That being the case, I don't feel comfortable leaving Blue here to be, at times, shuffled around and left feeling as if she'd been abandoned by her daddy."

All Tucker could focus on was Autumn's sudden

change of heart where custody of Blue was concerned. Or was it all that sudden? Had this been her plan all along? To make him think she was giving him a chance when she really had no intention of turning Blue over to him. Maybe she wasn't so different from her sister after all. Just as his wife had done, Autumn was going to take his daughter away from him. And to think he'd nearly made a fool of himself by telling Autumn how he truly felt about her.

"I've done everything you've asked of me to convince you my daughter belongs here with me, but it's not enough. Would it ever have been enough?" he demanded. "Because you knew what I did for a living before you showed up on my doorstep that day. Yet, here you are using my rodeo business against me."

Tears filled her eyes. "Yes, I knew what you did. But I thought things might change once you realized you had responsibilities toward Blue. And while I adore your momma, your leaving Blue for days, even weeks on end to be cared for by her is not much different than what my momma did to us, leaving care of Summer and I to our grandma."

"I'm not your mother or your father," he growled in frustration. "And I'd appreciate your not comparing me to them." Swiping his cowboy hat from his head, Tucker dragged a hand back through his hair. What frustrated him the most was her not being able to see that unlike her parents he would do everything in his power to see to his daughter's happiness. Even if he had to be away for short periods of time. That meant he loved Blue no less. Taking stock to the rodeos was his livelihood.

"I think we should head back now," Autumn said with a sniffle.

He looked at her and even now, after her telling him she would be taking his daughter away from him, he still felt the urge to brush the trail of hot, salty tears from her cheeks. Fool he was.

"Agreed," Tucker replied. "I've got more meaningful things I could be doing right now, like spending time with my daughter before you take her away. Speaking of which, do you intend to let me tell Blue goodbye when the time comes, or will you just slip away with her like Summer did all those years ago?"

She gasped at his harsh words, and Tucker knew immediate regret at having spoken them. "Unlike my sister," she said, her words choked with emotion, "I would never do that to you. But I suggest you say your goodbyes to Blue tonight, because we'll be leaving for Cheyenne first thing tomorrow morning."

"Tucker," Garrett called after him as Tucker crossed his parents' yard to his truck.

Stopping, he turned to find not only Garrett, but Jackson striding his way, concern written all over their faces.

"The barn," his oldest brother said as he moved right on past him. "Now."

He looked to Jackson who only shook his head as he followed Garrett.

Tucker wasn't up for this. Whatever "this" was going to be. Sitting there at dinner, knowing what Autumn planned to do, had filled him with hurt and anger, and a whole lot of frustration. But he fell into step behind his brothers.

Garrett closed the barn door behind them, guaranteeing privacy. Then he turned back to Tucker. "Let's talk."

Tucker's frown deepened as his brothers stood pinning him with their stares, arms folded unbudgingly across their flannel-covered chests. Dinner at his parents' place that evening had been strained. At least, where he and Autumn were concerned. Not that she'd made any mention of their disagreement to his family. She'd been polite to everyone, smiling when the conversation required it and acting as if she hadn't just trampled all over his trust. More tellingly, he supposed, was the fact that Autumn had avoided meeting his gaze as they sat across the table from each other, directing her conversation to everyone but him.

Exhaling deeply, Tucker muttered, "Autumn and I had words."

Jackson snorted. "I don't think either of us would have to be professional investigators to have figured that one out."

Tucker shot him a warning glance. "This is no joke. It's my daughter Autumn intends to take away from me."

Jackson threw up a hand. "Wait a minute. What?"

"She's taking Blue home," he said, his voice breaking. "She's going to fight me for custody."

Surprise registered on Garrett's face. "Why?"

"I thought the two of you were working everything out," Jackson said.

He nodded. "We were. Unfortunately, Autumn has had a change of heart where my rodeo travel time as part-owner of the Triple W comes into play."

"Unless I missed something," Garrett said, "Autumn knew what you did for a living when she came here to see what kind of father you would be to Blue. Why is she having issues with it now?"

"There's so much more to it than my being away at times," he said, turning to face them as he filled his brothers in on a bit more of Autumn's background and how she had essentially lumped him right in with her parents when he'd mentioned that his mom and dad would watch over Blue on occasion when he had to travel for work.

"That explains the weird tension between you and Autumn at dinner tonight," Jackson said.

"I didn't do anything wrong," Tucker said in his own defense.

"We know that," Garrett said. "And I'm pretty sure Autumn does, too. But her past feeds into her protective instincts where Blue's concerned."

"I'm not Autumn's parents," Tucker ground out. "My leaving Blue with Mom and Dad isn't abandoning my daughter."

"Maybe not," Jackson acknowledged. "But think about it, Tucker. How would you feel if the proverbial shoe was on the other foot? What if you gave up custody to Autumn and she left Blue in someone else's care while she went out of town for her job for extended periods of time?"

He'd been so hurt by Autumn's unfair condemnation of him that he hadn't allowed himself to appreciate the true depth of her concern. Shame for the way he had handled his end of their conversation filled him. How would he feel if the roles were reversed and he was going to place his daughter in the hands of someone who wouldn't personally be around to see to Blue's care for days, even weeks on end?

Tucker yanked off his hat and dragged a hand back through his hair. Then he looked up at his brothers. "I would've done the same thing."

"There you have it," Garrett said. "So what are you willing to do to keep you daughter in your life?"

Hadn't he already done everything in his power to prove to Autumn that Blue belonged with him? Everything, apparently, except give up his part of a business he'd built from the ground up alongside his brothers. A business he took immense pride in. But that pride had never been felt as deep as the love he had for his little girl. A business didn't greet you with open arms when you came home at the end of the day. It didn't make you see flowers and butterflies, even family dinners in a whole new light. It didn't love you unconditionally.

Slapping his hat back onto his head, Tucker stepped past his brothers and pushed open the barn door.

"Where are you going?" he heard Garrett say.

"To set things right," Tucker replied. He was man enough to admit he'd made a mistake. He just prayed Autumn could find it in her heart to forgive him.

Tucker paused in his front yard, having caught sight of Autumn through the living room window. She was seated on the sofa, book in hand as she read her nightly bedtime story to Blue, who was snuggled up against her aunt's side. Dragging in a deep breath, he gathered up his courage and made his way inside.

Autumn looked up when he entered the room and then stiffened, closing the book she'd been reading to Blue. "That's enough for tonight," she told Blue. "You need to get to bed. We've got a long drive ahead of us tomorrow."

Blue's sleepy eyes lifted. "But I don't wanna leave."

His daughter's words touched his heart. He didn't want her to leave, either. If Autumn would give him a chance to make amends and set things right, maybe things would work out after all.

"I know you don't, sweetie," Autumn replied with a sad smile. "But we've got to get back to Cheyenne."

"Daddy!" Blue said, her tired eyes lighting up the second she saw him standing there in the doorway.

"Hello, sweetheart."

Autumn stood and reached for Blue's hand. "We were just getting ready to go to bed. Come on, sweetie. Give your daddy a good-night hug before we go to bed."

They crossed the room to where he stood waiting. "'Night, Daddy," Blue said, looking up at him with a hint of a pout to her lips.

"'Night, sweetheart," he said, bending to kiss the top of her head. "I'll see you in the morning." If he couldn't convince Autumn to stay, he'd at least be there to see his daughter off until he could get her back through legal means.

As they started past him, Tucker said, "Autumn..."

She paused in the hallway to glance back at him.

"I was hoping you might be able to spare a few minutes to talk after you settle Blue into bed."

"I was under the impression you'd said everything you needed to say already."

A frown tugged at his mouth. "I owe you an apology for the way I reacted earlier."

She studied him for a long moment, as if judging his sincerity. Then her gaze dropped down to his sleepy-eyed daughter. "I'll meet you out on the porch in ten minutes." That said, she led Blue away down the hall.

Less than ten minutes later, Autumn sat waiting for Tucker as he returned from the barn where he'd settled the horses for the night. She was seated on the porch swing, moving back and forth in a slow glide. "That didn't take long," he said.

"Blue was out the second her head hit the pillow."

"May I?" he asked, inclining his head toward the empty space beside her on the swing.

With a sigh, she stopped swinging, allowing him to settle his much larger frame next to hers.

"I'm sorry," he said again as he extended his long legs to set the swing into motion once more.

"No," she said softly. "I'm sorry."

Her apology took him by surprise. "You have nothing to apologize for," he told her, his hand covering hers. "I can't tell you how much I regret comparing your decision to leave tomorrow to Summer's actions," he went on as he settled back against the cool, wooden slats of the porch swing. "You're nothing like your sister. I know that you would never have walked out and taken my daughter away without letting me know of your intention to do so."

"No," she said softly. "I could never have done that to you. No matter what was said between us."

"Speaking of what was said earlier. I talked to my brothers after dinner," he began.

Autumn sighed, nodding knowingly. "When the three of you stepped outside for a spell."

"Yes."

"I reckon they think me an awful person for changing my mind about turning custody of Blue over to you."

He gave a chuckle. "Hardly. My brothers took your side if anything."

Her eyes widened in surprise. "They did?"

"Let's just say they convinced me to put the proverbial shoe on the other foot. And that's when I realized

I would've done the same thing if I were in your position. So I asked them if they'd consider buying me out if that's what it took to keep Blue in our lives."

She looked up at him, wide blue eyes reflecting the gentle glow of the porch light. "You would walk away from your part of the business?"

"I told you from the start that I'm willing to do whatever it takes to have my daughter in my life. If selling my share of the business can make that happen, then I'll do it."

Tears sprang to her eyes, a few glistening drops escaping to slide down her cheeks.

"You would do that for Blue?" she said as if his willingness to actually do this was beyond her ability to comprehend. Then again, for Autumn, it might be. Her father hadn't given up anything for his daughters.

"You did," he reminded her with a tender smile. "Selling your real estate business to help support your sister and her little girl—my little girl. Which means you know better than anyone the sacrifices some people are willing to make for those they love."

She nodded, looking off toward the moonlight-shrouded barn. "Yes, I do."

"I want my daughter here with me, Autumn," he said in a gentle plea. "I can't lose her again."

She looked his way. "If you're willing to make that kind of sacrifice for Blue, then you deserve the chance to raise her. It's what Summer wanted."

"But not you," he stated.

"No," she said sadly. "For purely selfish reasons," she added. "But it's Blue's needs that matter most to me. If you're prepared to begin seeing to your daughter's needs, and if it's okay with Blue, she can stay here with you when I go back to Cheyenne tomorrow."

He blinked hard, unsure if he'd heard her right or not. "You'd leave her here?"

"It's not like you're a stranger," she replied. "You're her father."

He was that.

"Look, Tucker, I'd keep Blue with me forever if I could. But she belongs here. Shuffling her back and forth while custody legalities are being seen to would be too hard on her. I love her enough not to put her through that." She looked up, searching his gaze before adding, "Unless, you'd rather wait."

"No," he said, shaking his head determinedly. "I've waited long enough."

"Yes," she said with a tender smile. "You have." She folded her arms in front of her as if warding off the night's chill.

Slipping his arm around her shoulders, Tucker drew Autumn closer to his side. An act that felt as natural as breathing. He looked down at her, searching her face. "Will you be okay? I know how big a part of your life Blue has been."

She teared up again. "God has a plan for us all. *His* bringing you into Blue's life means He has other plans for me. Maybe returning to the life I once had back in Texas is the path He's guiding me toward."

"Texas?" he repeated. "Why would you think that?"

"Hope called when you were out in the barn, to tell me that she'd heard my real estate business was back up for sale. The woman who bought it from me has decided to retire and move back to Virginia. I think I might put in an offer."

"And leave Blue?" he said in disbelief.

"She won't be with me," she reminded him. "She'll be here with you. And I would visit her often. Just as I used to do before I moved in with her and her momma."

"But Texas is so far away," he complained, his mouth tightening with a frown.

She closed her eyes, her expression pained. "I don't think I can stay in Cheyenne without Blue. Or Summer," she said, her voice catching. "At least in Texas I won't feel quite so alone."

He didn't want her to feel alone. Ever. But the thought of her being more than a thousand miles away… Tucker tried to suppress the unexpected feelings that brought about. He'd never thought he'd ever allow another woman close to his heart, but Autumn hadn't just gotten close, she'd latched on to it. "Don't go."

"What?"

"Stay here," he told her. "Take time to really think this out." He searched her beautiful face, wanting to burn it into his memory as he felt what could have been slipping away. "Do it for Blue. Do it for *us*."

Opening her eyes, Autumn looked up at him with a frown. "I'm not, but taking my time isn't gonna change the way I'll feel when I leave here."

Tucker dragged a hand down his lightly whiskered jaw. "I hate this. I don't want to be the cause of your sadness."

"You're not responsible for this situation we find ourselves in. My sister is," she told him, forcing a soft smile. "And as much as I have loved helping to care for Blue, it never should have been my place to do so. It should have been yours. And now you're gonna have the chance to be the father Blue has always needed in her life."

"I will do right by her," he said, his words tight with emotion.

"I know you will," Autumn said, looking out over the ranch. "She'll be happy here. I know it in my heart."

Tucker found himself wishing for things he had no right to. Because Autumn was Summer's sister. He shouldn't feel anything for her. But he wasn't ready to see her go, not yet. "Are you dead set on leaving tomorrow?"

Worry creased her slender brows. "Are you having second thoughts?"

"Not at all," he replied. "I was just hoping you might consider joining us for the town's annual fall barbecue. It's only a few days away. You'd get to meet more of the people Blue will be growing up around. And, while it's not an actual outdoor barbecue, there is an abundance of picnic dishes to choose from. Did I mention there's an entire table devoted to desserts?"

"An entire table, huh?" she teased.

"Two if that's what it takes to sway you," he said with a grin.

She smiled up at him. "It's working."

If he had his way, desserts wouldn't be the only thing he'd be swaying her over to his way of thinking on. Because the feelings he had developed for Autumn ran too deep for him to just sit back and watch her walk away.

Chapter Ten

Autumn knew that delaying her departure, even a few days, was dangerous to her heart—but she'd agreed to stay anyway. Not that Tucker would ever know how foolish she had been in allowing herself to fall for him. A man she had no right to feel anything for. She'd agreed because she was nowhere near ready to leave Blue, or Tucker for that matter, and her attending the barbecue with them gave her the reason she needed to stay on just a little while longer.

Her gaze shifted to Blue, who was doing pirouettes around the bedroom to make the floral chiffon dress she wore flare out around her. She was so excited to be going to the barbecue and had insisted on dressing up even though the event, according to Tucker, was casual dress.

Her heart pinched as she watched her niece. Tomorrow they would be separated for the first time since Autumn had gone to live with Summer. She and Tucker had sat down with Blue and explained things to her as best they could. Blue had accepted the news that she would be living with her daddy from there on out exceedingly well, which, for Autumn, might have hurt her feelings if not for the fact that her niece had told him that she wanted Autumn to stay, too. *In a perfect world*, Autumn thought with a touch of melancholy.

A horn honked outside. Stopping midspin, Blue ran over to look out the window, waving excitedly at her daddy. Tucker had run into town to help his brothers and several others set up tables and chairs for that evening's festivities.

Autumn crossed the room to the closet to grab their jackets. "Time to go, sweetie. Our carriage has arrived."

"That's not a carriage," her niece countered as she turned from the window and raced for the doorway. "It's Daddy's truck!"

"I take it your daddy isn't really a prince, either?" Autumn called out as Blue disappeared from sight.

She stepped out into the hallway to find Tucker standing just inside the front door, grinning from ear to ear.

"I might not be a prince, but I am charming," he said, that dimple of his deepening. "Or so I've been told."

Autumn laughed softly. "You are that." Looking to Blue, she said, "Here's your coat."

As her niece slipped into hers, Tucker took Autumn's from her hand and helped her into it. "Thank you," she said.

"My pleasure." Opening the door, Tucker made a sweeping motion with his hand. "Your carriage awaits."

Blue gave an exasperated groan. "Daddy, it's not a carriage," she said as she stepped outside. "It's a truck."

"That's too bad," he told her. "Because you look just like a princess this evening. Speaking of which…" he said as he turned back to Autumn.

"I know what you're gonna say," she said, cutting him

off. "But casual dress is not in your daughter's vocabulary when it comes to parties of any kind."

"It's a good thing you chose a career in real estate, because mind reading doesn't appear to be your forte."

She looked up at him questioningly.

Serious green eyes met hers. "I was just going to say that you look really pretty today."

His compliment gave her butterflies. She had chosen to wear jeans and a deep cobalt sweater that brought out the blue in her eyes, and, of course, her favorite pair of high-heeled riding boots. "Thank you."

"You're welcome." Placing an arm at the small of her back, Tucker escorted her and Blue out to his truck.

She wanted to lean into his strength. To keep him by her side forever. But he wasn't hers to keep. Neither was Blue. All she could do was relish the time she had left with him. With them. She glanced down at Blue whose tiny, perfect hand was wrapped snuggly around her own, and wondered how her heart would ever be able to function with her leaving so much of it behind in Bent Creek.

The mouthwatering aroma of barbecued ribs greeted them the moment they pulled up in front of the enclosed park pavilion where that afternoon's festivities were being held. "Mmm…" Autumn groaned. "Will you just smell those ribs."

"Wait until you taste them," Tucker told her as he pulled into an empty parking space.

"I wanna swing!" Blue exclaimed, having spied one of the park's two playgrounds.

"After we say hello and eat," Autumn told her.

They were greeted at the door by Tucker's family who led them back to the seats they had saved for them. Paper divider plates and plastic silverware lined the tables atop the red-and-white-checked plastic tablecloths. Mason jars filled with baby's breath and white carnations made for very cheery centerpieces. It was so very picnicish that it almost made one forget that winter was just around the corner.

"I hope you brought your appetite," Grady Wade said to Autumn. "There's enough food here to feed the entire county."

Autumn glanced around, finding that Tucker's daddy hadn't been exaggerating. "Starving, actually," she told him with a smile.

"Me, too!" Blue chimed in.

"Why don't we go check out the dessert table," Jackson said in a rather loud, conspiratorial whisper to Blue.

"Honey, she hasn't even eaten yet," his momma scolded, though her words weren't truly reprimanding.

"Desserts are the first to go," he told his momma. "I've learned to grab mine before sitting down to eat or risk getting stuck with something that doesn't quite satisfy my sweet tooth."

"Makes sense to me," Tucker's daddy said.

"Come on, Blue," Garrett said, sweeping her up in his arms. "There's a slice of peach cobbler calling out my name."

"Food can't talk," Autumn heard her niece say as her uncles and grandpa led her away.

"You can't pull anything over on my daughter," Tucker said, sounding like the proud daddy he was.

Tucker's momma stood clicking her tongue. "I'd best go make sure they don't go heaping sweets on Blue's plate like they tend to do on their own. You two go fix yourselves a plate of some real food."

"Don't be fooled," Tucker muttered to Autumn as his

momma walked away. "She's going to take her pick of desserts right along with Dad and my brothers."

Autumn muffled a giggle. Then, noting the way Tucker stood watching his family as they hovered around the dessert table, said, "Real food's greatly overrated. Don't you think?"

He looked her way with a grin. "A girl after my own heart." He nodded toward the table of sweets. "Shall we?"

Autumn gave a conspiratorial nod. "Let's."

After being delayed by several people stopping them to exchange idle chatter, Tucker was finally able to work their way across the room to the dessert table.

A familiar voice spoke up from behind them as Tucker and Autumn filled their plates with sweets. "I see you made it."

Tucker turned just as Justin stepped up to join them. "We did," he said with a nod and then looked to Autumn. "You remember my daughter's aunt."

"Not a face many men could easily forget," he replied with a widening grin. He gave a polite incline of his head. "Autumn."

"Justin."

Not a face many men could easily forget? While the compliment was undeniably true, Tucker hoped Autumn could see through Justin's flirtatious words. His friend could be a real smooth talker when it came to females, but he was not the settling-down kind.

"Who knew this town had so many charmers in it?" she said, looking to Tucker with a teasing grin.

Well, he for one didn't care for Justin trying to charm his girl. *His girl?* Talk about getting ahead of himself where Autumn was concerned. But if the night went the way he hoped, that was exactly what she would be. *His* girl. "We were just heading over to the dessert table. Care to join us?"

"Already been there. Got to be quick on the draw to get the best desserts at these things." He glanced around. "I was hoping you'd have brought your little girl."

"We did," Tucker replied. "Blue's at the dessert table as we speak, filling her plate with sweets along with the rest of my family."

Justin looked toward the dessert table, his eyes widening the moment he caught site of Blue. "She looks just like you. Only a whole lot prettier."

"Come on," Tucker said. "I'll introduce you to Blue."

"Let her eat first," Justin replied. "But I'll be expecting introductions before you head home."

He nodded. "You've got it." Looking to Autumn, he said, "Let's go grab ourselves some dessert while there are still choices left to make."

Once everyone had eaten, Tucker turned to Autumn who was seated next to him at the table. "Let's take a walk."

She looked to Blue, no doubt intending to include her in the invite, but his mother jumped in, bless her quick thinking, because she knew what Tucker had in mind. He'd talked to his mom and dad earlier that morning. "You two go on ahead. I told Blue I'd take her over to see Maggie Reynold's new baby. She caught sight of her when we were over at the dessert table."

"If you're sure," Autumn said.

"Go," his mother ordered with a bright smile.

They stood, Tucker placing his hand at Autumn's back

as they worked their way outside, their walk somewhat delayed by people wanting to exchange pleasantries.

"I thought we'd never make it out here," Tucker said as they headed for one of several walking paths that ran through the town's park.

"In need of some fresh air?" she teased.

He paused beneath the shade of a large oak and turned to her. "In need of some privacy."

"Privacy?" she said somewhat worriedly. "This sounds serious."

He nodded. "You could say that. I wanted you to know there's been a change of plans about selling my share of the business."

A mixture of hurt and disappointment moved across her pretty face before she looked away. "How am I supposed to tell Blue she won't be staying here with her daddy?"

"Blue will be staying here," he assured her.

"Tucker…"

"Hear me out, Autumn. Please," he said tenderly. "When I went out to my parents' place earlier, my father approached me with an alternative plan. I'll remain in the partnership I have with my brothers, but when rodeo season rolls around my father will accompany Garrett and Jackson instead. I'll stay back and oversee things here with the help of a few part-time ranch hands, just as Dad usually does when my brothers and I are on the road."

"But your momma…"

"Is all for it," he assured her with a smile. "After going to Jackson Hole, Mom's hooked on camping in their new trailer. Traveling to rodeos would give them that opportunity."

She gave him an apologetic smile. "I thought—"

"You have to learn to trust me," he said with a smile.

Her eyes glistened as she stood looking up at him. "I'm sorry, Tucker. Past hurts sometimes have me expecting the worst when it doesn't exist." She reached out, curling her fingers around his hand and giving it a gentle squeeze. "But deep down I really do trust you, Tucker. And I'm so glad you were able to work things out so you didn't have to give up your share of the business. You deserve to be happy."

He caressed the hand curled around his with his thumb. "You deserve to be happy, too."

Silver-blue eyes searched his own, softening. "I never thought I'd be saying this at the end of my time here, but I'm really gonna miss your cowboy charm, Tucker Wade."

"Not Justin's?" he teased.

"Only yours," she said, her pale blue eyes softening.

"Daddy! Aunt Autumn!"

They both turned to look in the direction from which they'd come.

"Over here!" Autumn replied, slipping her hand from Tucker's.

A second later, Blue came running toward them, his mother doing her best to keep up behind her. His mother gave him an apologetic smile. "The music started. Blue was afraid she wouldn't get to dance with the two of you."

Autumn bent to scoop his daughter up. "Not a chance of that happening."

Before Tucker could protest, before he could tell Autumn that there was so much more he needed to say to her, she was walking away, his daughter curled happily around her.

Chapter Eleven

The next morning, Tucker stood watching as Autumn bent to kiss his sleeping daughter farewell. She turned from the bed, thick tears looming in her beautiful eyes. The sight of which tugged hard at Tucker's heart.

With one last glance back at Blue, Autumn hurried from the room.

He fell in step behind her. "You don't have to leave."

She turned to him as she stepped out onto the porch. "Another day or two isn't gonna make this any easier for Blue or for me."

"What if I want you to stay?"

She looked up at him with a tender smile. "Tucker, you don't have to worry about Blue. She's gonna be happy here. I feel it in my heart. Otherwise, I'd never be leaving without her. And you're gonna be the best daddy ever."

"I wasn't asking you to stay for my daughter's sake."

She searched his face, clearly not understanding.

Unable to piece together the right words, Tucker lowered his mouth to hers hoping to show Autumn without words how he felt about her.

His heart lurched when she leaned into him, hands flattening against his chest as she returned the tender kiss. Any doubts he might have had about her feelings toward him were quickly forgotten.

"Autumn…" he said with a sigh when the kiss ended.

She pulled away with a gasp. "I can't do this. Not again."

"Do what again?" he asked, confused by her words.

"I vowed not to be any man's second choice ever again," she told him, tears in her eyes. "I've already been down that road with a cowboy I thought truly cared about me only to find out I wasn't the sister he would have chosen if he'd been given the choice. I'm sorry, Tucker," she said with a sob. "But I'll never be the woman you want." Turning, she practically ran to her car as Tucker stood watching in stunned silence, his heart sinking.

Autumn couldn't be more wrong. She was the only woman he wanted. The woman he loved. And as she drove away, he knew, without a doubt, that she'd taken his heart with her.

In the three days that followed Autumn's leaving, Tucker tried to stay busy, focusing on his daughter's wants and needs, but Autumn's sweet smile lingered painfully in his every waking thought. Regret like he'd never known before filled him. If only he had told Autumn how he felt sooner. Maybe then they would have had time to work through her reservations.

She'd spoken to Blue on the phone every single evening before his daughter went to bed, but she'd carefully avoided any real conversation with him. He hadn't pushed, wanting to give her time to think things over. Just as he had done himself after she'd gone. Her parting words had him reexamining his feelings, wondering if Autumn might have been right. That what he felt toward her was somehow related to what he had once felt for his wife. But it hadn't taken him long to put that possibility to rest. While it was true he'd met and married Summer first, that, in no way, made Autumn his second choice.

Any feelings he once had for Summer were nothing more than a distant memory at this point in his life. The feelings he had for Autumn were well beyond the youthful infatuation he once felt for her sister. Their relationship was built on trust and respect and a shared love for his daughter, but there was so much more. He found himself wanting to know everything about Autumn, wanting to comfort her when she was down and laugh with her over even the silliest of things. All those things he could no longer do with her living on the other side of the state, or Texas if the offer she'd talked about making on her old business went through.

"I miss Aunt Autumn," Blue said as she fed Hoss another chunk of apple.

"Me, too, sweetheart," Tucker said with a nod. And he'd wasted enough time letting Autumn think otherwise. Instead of giving her time, which, in hindsight, might have made her think she was right about his feelings for her, he should have done whatever it took to convince her otherwise. She didn't belong in Cheyenne, or even Texas. She belonged here with him and Blue, and it was past time to put that cowboy charm of his to real use and win over Autumn's heart once and for all.

* * *

Would he ever stop filling her thoughts? Autumn wondered with a sigh as images of Tucker's face the moment before he'd kissed her drifted through her mind. So tender. So determined. So Tucker. Oh, how she missed him and his beautiful little baby girl.

The doorbell chimed in the hallway, startling Autumn. She rarely had any visitors out here, and her place was a bit out of the way for salespeople to come calling. Maybe it was someone from work, stopping by to check on her. They knew she had returned to Cheyenne, but had extended her leave another week due to the emotional fallout from having given Blue up. She knew that it had been the right thing to do, but that hadn't made it any easier. Since leaving Bent Creek, she hadn't been able to focus on anything but how much she missed Blue and Tucker.

The doorbell rang again, more persistently this time.

With a sigh, Autumn pushed away from her desk and went to answer it. When she opened the door, a loud gasp left her lips. "Tucker," she said, her hand pressed to her chest in a failed attempt to still her racing heart. Seeing the anxious expression on his face, her gaze immediately went in search of her niece. Then she looked up at Tucker, dread filling her. "Where's Blue?"

"Back in Bent Creek, baking cookies with her grandma," he replied. "Or, at least, she was when I called to let them know I was almost here a few minutes ago."

"Why are you here then if Blue is okay?" Not that she wasn't drinking in the sight of him, noting as she did so that he looked tired. His dark, whiskered chin told her he hadn't shaved for what looked to be days. Was taking care of a child more than he'd been prepared for?

Was that why he was here? To work out some other sort of arrangement?

"I came to tell you that you're wrong."

She blinked hard. "Pardon me?"

"I'm fully aware that you're not Summer, just as you know I'm not whoever the man was who broke your trust. There is only one woman who holds my heart. The beautiful, selfless, loving woman the Lord brought into my life, along with my precious little girl. A woman who's steadfast and responsible. A woman willing to sacrifice her own happiness for a little girl who happens to be very special to her daddy."

Tears in her eyes, Autumn took a moment to let Tucker's heartfelt words sink in. He loved her and only her.

He reached out, laying a hand against her cheek. "I've missed you."

"I've missed you, too," she admitted, leaning into his tender touch.

"My whole life changed the day you came into it," he told her. "Not only did you bring me the most precious gift ever, you gave me a taste of what I'd been living without for so very long—true happiness." His smile widened as he added, "And love."

A soft sob escaped her lips. "Tucker."

"I love you, Autumn Myers," he went on. "And I can't bear the thought of you being as far away as Cheyenne, let alone Texas. Blue and I need you. Come back to Bent Creek and start your own real estate business there. There are office fronts available and I promise to be there for you, doing whatever you need to help you take back the dream you so selflessly gave up to help raise my daughter."

Tears spilled down her cheeks. "I love you, too. And I can't think of anything I'd like more than to be living closer to you and Blue."

"With us if I have my way," he said, sinking down onto one knee.

Autumn's hand flew to her mouth as Tucker pulled a blue satin ring box from his shirt pocket. He raised its lid to reveal a vintage filigree-styled engagement ring perched inside.

"You can set the date," he told her. "I'd never want to rush you into something you're not ready for. But I want you to know that I am in this for the long haul. Say you'll marry me, Autumn. Help me to raise my daughter. Let my family be yours. Share my friends. Even my horses if you have a mind to."

"Oh, Tucker." She felt cherished and loved, and so very wanted. Glancing down at the ring he held so hopefully in his hand, she said with a teary sigh, "It's so beautiful." Everything he'd said had been beautiful.

"I'm glad you like it."

She looked up to see the love reflected in his eyes, and her heart swelled with love for this adorably charming cowboy standing before her, a man willing to risk so much for her. Lifting her tear-filled gaze, she said with a tender smile, "If it's true what they say about *home* being where the heart is, then there is no other place I would rather be than in Bent Creek with the two people who mean the very most to me. So, yes, Tucker Wade, I'll marry you."

A wide grin stretched across his face, putting his whisker-covered dimple on full display. Oh, how she adored that dimple.

"I didn't think I could ever be as happy as I was the day I found out Blue was mine. But I was wrong."

"Oh, Tucker," she said, pressing a hand to her heart.

He eased the antique ring from its nest of blue. "This was my grandma Wade's. I know it's old, and maybe not the style you would have chosen, but I wanted to have something to give you when I asked you to marry me."

"It's perfect," she breathed as he slid the ring onto her extended finger. It was as if the ring had been made just for her. Looking up into his smiling face, she said, "I love it. Even more so because it was your grandma's. And I love you."

"Now about setting that wedding date…" he said with a grin.

Epilogue

"It's time," Emma Wade said quietly as she handed Autumn her bridal bouquet.

"Yay!" Blue exclaimed with a twirl, the knee-length light blue tulle dress she wore lifting as if floating around her.

Autumn didn't have the heart to shush her, despite knowing everyone in the church on the other side of the closed doors had to have heard. This was a day of happiness for so many. Her gaze moved to the ribbon-wrapped bouquet of bluebells and baby's breath she held in her hands. Tucker had special ordered the flowers for their wedding in memory of her sister. It had been such a thoughtful thing for him to do, considering his past with Summer. But then Tucker was that kind of man.

"My sentiments exactly," Tucker's momma said with a smile as she handed Blue the basket of silk rose petals she was to carry with her down the aisle. Ones the same shade as Autumn's bouquet. "Remember what you're supposed to do?"

Her niece nodded. "Put them on the floor so Aunt Autumn's dress can scoop them up."

Emma laughed softly. "Such a smart girl. Now Grandma's going to go take her seat in the pew. When the music starts, Mrs. Pratt will open these doors and then you start down the aisle to your daddy. Your aunt Autumn will be right behind you."

She was so grateful to have Emma there. Tucker's momma had welcomed Autumn into her home for the three months she and Tucker had decided to wait to be married. Tonight, she would be sleeping in her own home, Tucker's home, where they would start their life together raising Blue and any other children the good Lord saw fit to bless them with.

Emma stepped over to give Autumn an affectionate kiss on the cheek. "You look beautiful, honey."

"Thank you, Emma. I feel beautiful today."

"Grady and I are going to miss having you with us, but I'm getting something I've wanted for a very long time," she said with a tender smile. "A daughter."

"And I'm getting something I've only ever dreamed of having. A mother," Autumn said, giving Emma a loving hug.

Tears filled the older woman's eyes as she slipped into the church, closing the door behind her.

Moments later, the organ began to play and the large, ornate church door swung open. And there, at the end of the aisle, stood the man who held her heart, his two brothers by his side.

His gaze locked with hers and a wide smile slid across his tanned face.

Blue gave a quick wave to her daddy, who waved right back, before setting off down the white runner tossing flower petals to and fro with youthful exuberance. As soon as she reached the altar, her niece took her place next to Hope, who had flown from Texas with Logan to be Autumn's matron of honor.

The "Wedding March" began to play and it was all Autumn could do not to run to Tucker in her eagerness to be at his side now and forevermore. Instead, she forced herself to move toward him in slow, mindful steps, taking it all in as she made her way past the rows of friends and family who had come to witness their becoming man and wife in the eyes of God.

As if reading her mind, or perhaps feeling the same need to be by her side, Tucker stepped toward her, meeting her halfway where he crooked his arm. "If it's all right with you, I'd like to start our marriage the way we're going to live our lives together—meeting each other halfway and traveling down the road of life as one."

"I'd love nothing more," she told him as she slipped her arm through his. She would gain so much that day. A husband who loved her, the opportunity to take part in the raising of her precious niece, a family to call her own and a place to finally call home. She was truly blessed.

* * * * *

"Isaac, we have a visitor. This is Leah Porte. She's an *Englischer* friend of ours, staying with us a few months. Leah, this is Isaac Sommer."

For a moment Isaac was struck dumb by the newcomer. With her dark hair tamed back under a *kapp*, and her chocolate eyes, he barely noticed the ugly red scar bisecting her right cheek.

Leah stepped forward. "How do you do?"

"Fine, *danke*. Where do you come from?"

"California."

"Please, sit. Both of you." Edith Byler gestured toward the table.

Isaac found himself opposite Leah and gazed at her as the family gathered around the table. When all heads bowed in silence, he found himself praying he could get to know the visitor better.

At once, chatter broke out as the family reached for food.

"We hope you'll have a pleasant stay with us." Ivan Byler scooped corn onto his plate .

"I...I'm not familiar with your day-to-day life." The woman toyed with her fork. "I don't want to be seen as a freeloader."

"What is it you did before you came here?" Ivan asked.

"I was a television journalist," she replied. Isaac saw her touch her wounded cheek and glance toward him. "But after my...my car accident, I couldn't do my job anymore."

Journalist! What kind of God-sent coincidence was that? He smiled. "Maybe I should have you write some articles for my magazine."

"Magazine?"

Edith explained, "Isaac started a magazine for Plain people. He uses a computer to create it. The bishop gave him permission."

"An Amish man using a computer?"

"Many *Englischers* have misconceptions of how much technology the *Leit* allows," Ivan intervened. "You won't find computers in our homes, or cell phones. But while we try to live not *of* the world, we still live *in* the world, and sometimes technology is needed to keep our businesses running. So, some bishops have decided a little technology is allowed."

"What's the magazine about?" Leah asked.

"Whatever appeals to Plain people. Farming. Businesses. Land management."

"And you want *me* to write for it?" she asked. "I don't know anything about those topics."

"But that's what a journalist does, ain't so? Learn about new topics," Isaac replied. Her opposition made him more determined. "Besides, you're about to get a crash course while you stay here. Maybe you'll learn something."

"I already said I had no intention of being a freeloader."

He nodded. "*Gut.* Then prove it. You can write me an article about what you learn."

"Sure," she snapped. "How hard could it be?"

He grinned. "You'll find out soon enough."

Don't miss
The Amish Newcomer *by Patrice Lewis,*
available September 2020 wherever
Love Inspired books and ebooks are sold.

LoveInspired.com

SPECIAL EXCERPT FROM

✦ HARLEQUIN
SPECIAL EDITION

*An explosion ended Jake Kelly's military career.
Now his days are spent alone on his ranch, and his
nights are spent keeping his PTSD at bay. But the
ex-marine's efforts to keep the beautiful Skylar Gilmore
at a distance are thwarted by his canine companion.
Every time he turns around, Molly is racing off to the
Circle G looking for Sky. Maybe the dog knows that two
hearts are better than one?*

*Read on for a sneak peek at
The Marine's Road Home,
the latest book in Brenda Harlen's
Match Made in Haven miniseries!*

"Actually, I think I'll try a pint of Wild Horse tonight."

She moved the mug to the appropriate tap and tilted it under the spout. "Eleven whole words," she remarked. "I think that's a new record, John."

He lifted his gaze to hers, saw the teasing light in her eye and felt that uncomfortable tug again. "My name's not John."

"But as you haven't told me what it is, I can only guess," she said.

"So you decided on John…as in John Doe?" he surmised.

She nodded. "And because it rolls off the tongue more easily than the-sullen-stranger-who-drinks-Sam-Adams, or, after tonight, the-sullen-stranger-who-usually-drinks-Sam-Adams-but-one-time-ordered-a-Wild-Horse." She set the mug on a paper coaster in front of him. "And I think that's a smile tugging at the lips of the sullen stranger."

"I was just thinking that next time I'll order a Ruby Mountain Angel Creek Amber Ale," he said.

"Careful," she cautioned with a playful wink. "This exchange of words is starting to resemble an actual conversation."

He lifted the mug to his mouth, and Sky moved down the bar to serve a couple of newcomers, leaving Jake alone with his beer.

Which was what he wanted, and yet, when she came back again, he heard himself say, "My name's Jake."

The sweet curve of her lips warmed something deep inside him.

Don't miss
The Marine's Road Home *by Brenda Harlen,*
available August 2020 wherever
Harlequin Special Edition books and ebooks are sold.

Harlequin.com

HARLEQUIN

Heartfelt or suspenseful, inspiring or passionate, Harlequin has your happily-ever-after.

With new books published every month, you are sure to find the satisfying escape you know you deserve.

SIGN UP FOR THE HARLEQUIN NEWSLETTER

Be the first to hear about great new reads and exciting offers!

Harlequin.com/newsletters